DRAGON AGE™

THE CALLING

DAVID GAIDER

DRAGON AGE™

THE CALLING

TITAN BOOKS

BioWare

Dragon Age: The Calling
ISBN: 9781848567542

Published by
Titan Books
A division of
Titan Publishing Group Ltd
144 Southwark St
London
SE1 0UP

First edition March 2010
10 9 8 7 6 5

Copyright © 2009 by Electronic Arts, Inc.
Cover art by Ramil Sunga.

Visit our website: www.titanbooks.com

Did you enjoy this book? We love to hear from our readers. Please email us at readerfeedback@titanemail.com or write to us at Reader Feedback at the above address.

To receive advance information, news, competitions, and exclusive Titan offers online, please register as a member by clicking the "sign up" button on our website: www.titanbooks.com

A CIP catalogue record for this title is available from the British Library.

Printed and bound by CPI Group (UK) Ltd, Croydon, CR0 4YY.

To Lee, my biggest fan

ACKNOWLEDGMENTS

Recognition has to be given to my good friends who provide me with much-needed feedback, and who willingly leap on me in order to stop me from tearing up my own work whenever I'm overcome with idiotic self-loathing. Their patience and indulgence are a source of strength and will always be appreciated. In particular, a thank-you to Jordan for being my co-conspirator and for making me a better writer in every way. I hope I can do the same for her one day.

Big thanks also go out to Danielle and Jay for permitting me to mercilessly plunder their personas for my own purposes. The pain has been brought, and it is awesome. You guys made it easy for me, as always.

Lastly, a huge shout-out to BioWare and the online community for their support and constant enthusiasm. On those days when I'm not pulling out my hair in frustration, I am grateful to have what feels like the best job in the world.

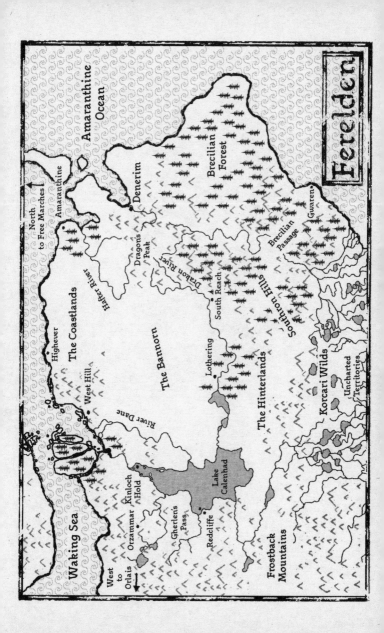

1

In the absence of light, shadows thrive.

—Canticle of Threnodies 8:21

Less than a year earlier, the only way Duncan would have seen the inside of a palace would have been at the sword-point of a prison guard. Perhaps not even then. In Orlais, lowly street thieves didn't receive the benefit of a judgment handed down personally by the local lord. There, the best one could hope for was a bored magistrate in a dingy courtroom as far away from the glittering estates of the aristocracy as they could manage.

But this wasn't Orlais, and he wasn't just a street thief any longer. He was inside the royal palace in Denerim, the capital city of Ferelden . . . and he was not particularly impressed.

The city was gripped in the winter winds that blew in from the south, and Duncan had never been so cold in his entire life. Everyone in Ferelden wrapped themselves up in thick leathers and furs, trudging heedlessly through the snowy streets, and yet no matter how much clothing he wore he could still feel the chill right down to his bones.

The palace was little better. He had hoped for some warmth here, at least. Perhaps a few mighty hearths with fires blazing, enough to keep the place toasty warm. But no, instead he was left sitting alone on a bench in a hall with frosty stone walls that loomed high overhead. There were probably pigeons nesting in the wooden rafters, judging by the filthy floors, and he saw little in the way of ornamentation. These Fereldans liked their doors large, solid, and made of oak. They liked their wooden sculptures of dogs and their smelly beer and they even seemed to like their snow. Or at least that was what he had been able to tell in the day or so since he'd arrived.

What they didn't like were Orlesians. There had been only a handful of palace servants and functionaries that passed through the hall while he waited, and all of them had shot him glances that ranged from suspicion to outright hostility. Even the two elven maids that came through with shy eyes and nervous twitters had stared at Duncan as if he were surely about to run off with the silverware.

Still, it was possible that all the looks might have had nothing to do with the fact that he was from Orlais. He didn't look the part, after all. His swarthy skin and mop of dark hair marked him as Rivaini, for one. The black leather armor he wore was covered in straps and buckles, running all the way up his arms and legs in a manner far removed from the more practical local style. Not to mention the twin daggers on his belt that he didn't bother to hide. None of those things marked him as a reputable person, not by Fereldan standards.

Really, if anyone was staring at him it should have been for the grey tunic he wore, adorned with the symbol of a rearing griffon. In any other nation in Thedas that griffon alone would have drawn raised eyebrows and nervous glances . . . but not in Ferelden. Here it was all but unknown.

Duncan sighed listlessly. How much longer was he going to have to wait?

Eventually the great wooden door at the end of the hall swung open and admitted a female elf. She was petite even for her kind, almost waiflike, with short mousy brown hair and large expressive eyes. She looked annoyed, as well, which didn't surprise Duncan in the least. As a mage, she would have drawn more stares even than he. Not that she dressed much like a mage, eschewing their traditional robes for a hauberk of finely meshed chain and a long blue linen skirt, but she did carry her staff with her. It was polished white, with a silvery ball clasped in a claw at its end that gave off a constant and diffuse flow of magical power. She brought it everywhere.

The elf strode across the hall toward him, her boots clicking on the stone floor loud enough to echo. Her annoyed expression gave way to amusement as she reached him.

"Still here, I see," she chuckled.

"Genevieve would cut off my feet if I went anywhere."

"Ah, poor Duncan."

"Shut up, Fiona," he snorted. His rejoinder lacked heat, however. He knew the elf probably did have some sympathy for him . . . well, a little, perhaps. Maybe a smidgen. There simply wasn't anything she could do to help him. He sighed and glanced up at her. "Did you see the Commander?"

Fiona nodded soberly toward the door behind her. "She's still negotiating with the captain of the city watch, thanks to you."

"Negotiating? She does that?"

"Well, *he's* negotiating. She's staring him down and not budging an inch, of course." Fiona regarded him with a raised eyebrow. "You're rather lucky, all things considered, you know."

"Yes, lucky," he sighed, sinking dejectedly back down onto his bench.

They waited for several minutes, the mage leaning on her white staff next to him, until finally the sound of voices approached from beyond the doors. They slammed open and two people entered. The first was a white-haired woman, a warrior wearing a white cloak and formidable-looking plate armor that covered her entire body. Her face was sharp and worn with many years of command, and she strode with the powerful confidence of one who expected no impertinence and usually found none.

The second was a dark-haired man in the resplendent yellow robes marking him as First Enchanter Remille of the Circle of Magi, the ranking mage in Ferelden. It was perhaps odd, then, that his pointed beard and the waxed curls of his mustache marked him as an Orlesian. The sort of man, Duncan assumed, who believed he could fare far better away from the Empire, even if it meant assuming a position of authority in a backwater nation that had thrown off Orlesian rule only eleven years ago. At least in this case, his belief seemed to be correct.

The mage simpered after the warrior, and she did her best to ignore him. "Lady Genevieve"—he wrung his hands nervously— "are you certain—"

She paused, spinning about to glare at him. "You may call me Genevieve," she snapped. "Or Commander. Nothing else."

"My apologies, Commander," he quickly assured her. "Are you certain that was necessary? Your order does not wish to antagonize King Maric, after all. . . ."

"We have already antagonized King Maric." Genevieve shot a withering glance in Duncan's direction, and he did his best to shrivel up out of sight behind Fiona. "And our order will bow to no authority, especially not some foolish watch captain who believes he possesses more power than he does." She cut off further protest by marching over to where Duncan sat.

He avoided her glower. "I trust you are satisfied?" she demanded.

"Maybe if I'd gotten away with it."

"Don't be a child." Genevieve gestured sharply for him to rise and he reluctantly did so. "We did not come to Ferelden to engage in nonsense, as you are well aware. You are no longer the boy I found in Val Royeaux. Remember that." She took his chin in her gauntleted hand and raised his head until she was looking him in the eye. He saw little more in her expression than checked rage layered in disappointment, and his face burned in embarrassment.

"I hear you," he said glumly.

"Good." She let him go and turned back to the hovering First Enchanter. "I trust the King is ready to see us, then? We won't have to come back?"

"No, he'll see you. Come."

The mage led the three of them down a long and dark hallway. If anything, it was even colder here than elsewhere, wind whistling through cracks in the walls. Duncan was certain he could spot frost, and his breath came out in white plumes. *Just brilliant,* he groused to himself. *We came here to freeze to death, apparently.*

They reached a large antechamber, a place filled with a scattering of dusty chairs that he imagined might at other times hold whatever nobles awaited their audience. Four others rose and stood at attention as they entered: three men and a dwarven woman, all wearing black cloaks and the same grey tunics as Duncan. Two of the men were tall warriors dressed in the same bulky plate armor as Genevieve, while the third was a hooded archer dressed in leathers. The dwarf wore a simple robe underneath her tunic, though naturally she was no mage.

The First Enchanter barely paused, sweeping past them and throwing open the enormous double doors that led into the throne room. Genevieve went after him and waved impatiently at the others to follow.

The throne room was slightly more impressive than the rest of the palace. Duncan did his best not to gape and stare as they walked in. The vaulted ceilings in the chamber rose at least thirty or forty feet, and the room was large enough to hold hundreds of men at once. There were galleries on each side of the room where he could imagine dignitaries shouting angrily at each other while the crowd below shouted and jeered. Or did Ferelden not work like that? Perhaps their gatherings here were dignified and quiet? Perhaps the court danced a great deal and this was a place where they held fantastic balls as they did in Orlais?

It seemed doubtful. The throne room had a dour look to it, and felt so empty he rather doubted there were many gatherings here at all, never mind balls. Tapestries hung on the walls, most in dull colors depicting scenes of battle from the days of some long-forgotten barbarian king. Dominating one of the walls was a massive wooden carving, a scene in bas-relief depicting a barely clothed warrior slaying what looked like werewolves. An odd choice, he thought.

The throne at the very end of the hall was little more than a massive chair with a high back, topped with what looked like a carved dog's head. It looked small up there on the large dais, raised above the floor by a small number of steps and flanked by bright torches. But one certainly couldn't miss it.

There was a man sitting casually on the throne, and Duncan wondered faintly if that was supposed to be the King. If so, he looked like a man who hadn't slept in a long time. His blond hair was unkempt and his clothing was hardly what Duncan would call regal, consisting of a rumpled white shirt and riding boots still covered in dirt.

The dark-haired man standing next to him, in a suit of grey armor, looked much more like a king. That one had eyes like a hawk, and he followed their entry with an angry intensity.

"Your Majesty, it is good to see you in such excellent health," First Enchanter Remille said when he finally reached the dais, bowing low with a great flourish. Behind him, Genevieve dropped to one knee, as did the others. Duncan reluctantly followed suit. He had been told that their order owed fealty to no nation and no king, but apparently they still bent knee when they felt like putting on a good show.

"Thank you, First Enchanter," the blond man on the throne responded. That meant he was the King after all, Duncan assumed. "So these are the Grey Wardens you were so keen on me meeting," he said, studying those present with intense interest.

"They are, Your Majesty. If I may?"

The King gestured his assent. Pleased, the mage turned toward those behind him, making a wide arc with his arm as if presenting something large and grand. "May I introduce to you Genevieve, Commander of the Grey in Orlais? It is she who told me of the order's need, and thus I bring her here to you."

The man bowed again and withdrew slightly as Genevieve stood. Her stark white hair all but glowed in the torchlight. Taking a moment to adjust her breastplate, she stepped forward, her expression grim. "I apologize for the delay in our arrival, King Maric. It was not our intention to anger you."

The stern man in the grey armor snorted derisively. "You Grey Wardens seem to get into a great deal of trouble in Ferelden, despite your best intentions."

Genevieve's expression did not change in the slightest, though Duncan noticed her back stiffen. She took a great deal of pride in the honor of the order, and could be prickly at the best of times. The King's friend would be wise to watch his words a little more carefully.

The King seemed mildly embarrassed. He waved a hand toward the man beside him, chuckling lightly. "This is Teyrn Loghain of Gwaren, though I don't know if you would have heard of him in Orlais."

She nodded curtly. "The Hero of River Dane. Yes, we have all heard."

"You hear that?" King Maric teased his friend. "It appears you have a reputation in the Empire. That should make you happy."

"I am thrilled," Loghain said dryly.

"If the Teyrn is referring to our order's exile from Ferelden two centuries ago," Genevieve began, "I can offer an explanation."

Loghain gave her a direct stare. "Of course you can."

She clenched her jaw, tightly enough for Duncan to see the tendons standing out on her neck, and for a long moment an uncomfortable silence ensued. All that could be heard was the crackling of the torches behind the throne.

The First Enchanter interjected himself between them, making conciliatory noises. "Surely there is no need for us to discuss something that took place so long ago, yes? What the leader of the Grey Wardens did then need not have any bearing on today!" He looked to King Maric pleadingly.

The King nodded, though he didn't seem very pleased. Whether it was because of the Teyrn's anger or Genevieve's response, Duncan couldn't tell. "This is true," he murmured.

"I have something much more recent I would like to discuss," Loghain growled. "Why did you keep us waiting for so long? If I had gone to such great lengths to gain a private audience with Maric, I would go out of my way to avoid angering him. Particularly if I was about to ask for a favor, no?"

The King shrugged. "They haven't asked for anything yet, Loghain."

"They will. Why else the formal introduction? Why else the display?"

"Good point."

Genevieve appeared pained as she searched for the right response. "One of my people committed a crime in your city, King Maric," she finally stated. "I needed to deal with the matter before things got out of hand."

Duncan grew cold with dread. *Here it comes*, he thought.

Loghain appeared ready to launch an angry retort, but the King cut him off, sitting forward in his throne with a great deal of interest. "A crime? What sort of crime?"

Genevieve sighed heavily. She turned around and gestured for Duncan to step forward. Her eyes bored into him, however. *Step out of line now*, they said, *and I will make every second of your life that follows a nightmare that you will never forget.* He gulped and scuttled quickly forward to stand beside her.

"This young man is Duncan," she explained, "recruited into our order a few months ago from the streets of Val Royeaux. I'm afraid he attempted to ply his former trade in your marketplace, and when chased by your guardsmen he got into a fight with one of them. The man was injured, but lives."

"I could have killed him," Duncan interjected defensively. Noticing Genevieve's outrage, he quickly bobbed a nervous bow toward the King. "But I didn't! I could have, but I didn't! That's what I meant, err . . . Your Highness. My lord."

"Your *Majesty*," Loghain corrected him.

"My guards can be a little overzealous at times," the King explained amiably. It took Duncan a moment to realize that the man was actually speaking to him and not to Genevieve. "Loghain is determined to turn Denerim into the most orderly city in the south. Truly I think all it's done is drive the criminals underground."

"I'd have been tempted to go there, myself," Duncan joked, and then quickly quieted as Genevieve clenched her gauntleted fists tightly enough for him to hear the faint grinding of metal. He did his best to look meek.

"He is quite skilled, King Maric," Genevieve offered tersely. "I believe, however, that the young man thinks if he misbehaves we will release him from his duty. He is wrong."

The King seemed intrigued by this. "You do not enjoy being a Grey Warden?" he asked Duncan.

Duncan was unsure how to respond. He was surprised that the King was speaking directly to him again. Even the lowliest baron in Orlais would have sooner been covered in oil and set on fire than be caught noticing a peasant. It made them much easier to pickpocket. Maybe this man couldn't tell he was a commoner, on account of them all being Grey Wardens? He assumed he should feel flattered, though he wasn't certain all this attention was necessarily a good thing.

Genevieve kept her eyes focused on the King, her expression pointedly neutral. So Duncan shifted from foot to foot and said nothing, while the King stared at him curiously and waited for an answer. Couldn't he interrogate someone else? Anyone? Finally Teyrn Loghain cleared his throat.

"Perhaps we should move on to why they're here, Maric."

"Unless the King wishes to have the boy arrested," Genevieve offered, completely serious. "We are in your land, and it is your law we must abide by. The Grey Wardens will comply with your wishes."

Duncan's heart leaped into his throat, but he needn't have worried. The King dismissed the idea with a wave of his hand. "No, I think not. The cells in Fort Drakon are full enough as it is." Loghain was clearly biting his tongue, but said nothing. Duncan bowed a few times as he retreated to the back to stand once again with the other Grey Wardens, sweat beading on his forehead.

Genevieve nodded graciously. "Thank you, King Maric."

"I am more interested in why you're here. If you will?"

She paused for a moment, clutching her hands together in a thoughtful gesture that Duncan recognized. *She's trying to decide how much she should tell him.* He also knew what her answer would be. The Grey Wardens had many secrets, and never said more than they absolutely needed to. He had learned that much very quickly.

"One of our own has been captured by the darkspawn," Genevieve said slowly. "Here in Ferelden. Within the Deep Roads."

"And?" Loghain frowned. "How does this concern us?"

She appeared reluctant to continue. "This Grey Warden . . . has the knowledge of the location of the Old Gods."

Both the King and Teyrn Loghain stared at her, stunned. The air in the hall became thick with tension as nobody immediately spoke. The First Enchanter stepped forward, tugging at his curled mustache anxiously. "As you can see, my lords, this was why I thought the matter of utmost delicacy. If these darkspawn prove able to learn the location of an Old God—"

"Then a Blight begins," Genevieve finished.

King Maric nodded gravely, but Loghain shook his head angrily. "Do not believe it." He scowled. "There has not been a Blight for centuries. We barely see the darkspawn on the surface at all, never mind a full-scale invasion. They are trying to scare us, nothing more. This order has been waning in importance since the last Blight and would do anything to frighten the world into believing they still have relevance."

"I assure you, it is true!" Genevieve shouted. She strode forward to the throne, dropping to one knee before the King. "There are only a few Grey Wardens who possess this knowledge, Your Majesty. If these darkspawn somehow know that he is one and wrest this information from him, they will rise to the surface in a new Blight. And they will do so here, in Ferelden."

"Are you certain?" the King breathed.

She looked up at him, her eyes intense. "You have seen the darkspawn with your own eyes, my lord, have you not? You know that they are no legend. *Neither are we.*"

Her words hung there, and King Maric paled visibly. Duncan could tell by the man's horrified expression that Genevieve was correct. He had seen the darkspawn for himself. Only someone who had would look like that. The King rubbed his chin thoughtfully. "I assume you are asking after permission to enter Ferelden to search for this missing Grey Warden?"

"No."

The King and Loghain looked at each other, nonplussed. "Then what is it you need?" Loghain asked her.

Genevieve got to her feet, retreating a step from the throne. "If all we needed to do was search, we could have entered the Deep Roads at Orzammar and you would have been none the wiser. Your domain, King Maric, encompasses only the surface, as I'm certain you well know."

Loghain looked as if he were about to object, but Maric held up a hand. "Fair enough," he said, his tone even.

"We have a good idea where to search for our missing comrade. What we don't know is how to get there. We believe that the two of you are the only ones alive who do."

"Are you suggesting what I think you are?" Loghain asked incredulously.

"Fourteen years ago, both of you traveled in the Deep Roads," Genevieve explained. "You encountered a unit of the Legion of the Dead, led by Nalthur of House Kanarek, and they assisted you in your revolt against Orlais. We know you did this, because you told King Endrin during your visit to Orzammar three years ago, and it was entered into the Memories by the dwarven Shaperate."

"Everything you say is true." The King nodded.

"You journeyed through the Deep Roads under eastern Ferelden, a place no dwarf has traveled in well over a century and lived to tell the tale." Genevieve sighed, her expression grim. "You two are the only ones alive who have been to Ortan thaig. That is where we need to go."

For several long minutes the throne room was quiet again. Duncan could hear the shuffling of the other Grey Wardens as they remained on their knees behind him. He glanced back at Fiona, but the elven mage refused to look his way. No doubt she was pleased simply to remain in the background. He wished he could have done the same.

The First Enchanter clenched and unclenched his hands, sweat beading on his forehead despite the chill in the air. Genevieve waited patiently as the two men on the dais digested what she had told them.

"Surely the dwarves must have maps . . . ," King Maric began.

"Insufficient." She shook her head. "The Deep Roads have changed, and we may need to travel beyond Ortan thaig. We need a guide, someone who has been there." She turned toward Teyrn Loghain. "We were hoping to ask for your assistance, Your Grace. You are well known as a fine warrior and in no—"

"Absolutely not," Loghain stated flatly.

"Can you not understand how vital this is?"

"I understand how vital *you* think it is, or at least how vital you would like us to think it is." He waved a hand dismissively. "Who knows what you are really up to? Wouldn't it be wonderful for the Hero of River Dane to find himself surrounded by Orlesians in a place where his death could be ascribed to anything at all?"

"Don't be a fool!" Genevieve stormed up the steps toward him. Duncan tensed and waited for the guards to jump out of hiding and attack before she reached the Teyrn, but none did. He had to wonder just how many rulers would agree so readily to a private audience alone with a group of armed Grey Wardens. Not many, probably. Even so, neither man on the dais seemed alarmed, so much as angered, by Genevieve's sudden advance. "We do not ask these things lightly! Have you no concept of what a Blight would mean to this land if it began here?"

He remained where he was, staring her down with his pale blue eyes. "We can offer you directions, if you like. You'll find the thaig the same way we did, no doubt still infested by a horde of giant spiders. I suggest bringing fire."

"We need more than directions! This is a matter of urgency!"

"Maric and I were there briefly, years ago." The contempt was obvious in his voice. "What is it you expect us to remember, fool woman?"

"Something!" she insisted. "Anything!"

"I'll go," the King quietly announced behind them.

It took a moment for the others to hear him. Loghain was just about to launch another retort at the furious Genevieve when he paused. He turned around slowly, staring at King Maric in confusion. "What did you say?"

"I said I'll go." The King seemed equally surprised by his statement, as if the words had come unbidden from his mouth. "I'll do it. I'll lead them."

A pin dropping in the throne room would have made more noise. Duncan coughed nervously and glanced at Fiona kneeling next to him. She looked as bewildered as he felt, and shrugged at his unspoken question. She had no idea why the King would suddenly agree, either. The entire situation was too bizarre. The First Enchanter appeared as if he were rooted to the spot, his face twisted in discomfort.

"You'll do no such thing!" Loghain lost his composure completely. Duncan almost thought the man might draw his sword. On his own king? Things worked very differently in Ferelden, after all.

Genevieve stepped forward, horrified. "We could not put you at such a risk! You are the King of Ferelden, and this is a dangerous task to request."

"I quite agree." Loghain added his voice to hers. "No one should be risked on such a foolish plan . . . No, it is not even a 'plan'! It is a faint hope based on . . . what? How can you even be certain this Grey Warden of yours is still alive?"

She gritted her teeth, studiously fixing her gaze on the King. "We are *certain*."

"How? What is it that you aren't telling us?"

King Maric stood from his throne, cutting them both off. "I am going," he said firmly. "I will take them down to Ortan thaig. I believe I remember the way."

Teyrn Loghain stared at the King accusingly, clearly full of heated objections but unwilling to continue voicing them in front of an audience. From the way the King looked back at him, almost resentfully, Duncan could tell there was a fight waiting to happen. He could tell that this Loghain was more than an advisor. He seemed almost like a brother, perhaps. Or the King's keeper.

Genevieve seemed at a loss, but bowed low and backed off. Duncan could understand her confusion. He had thought the idea of asking the Hero of River Dane to come was desperate enough, but this bordered on the ludicrous.

Surely the King would soon change his mind, and the Grey Wardens would be asked to fend for themselves. Perhaps they would even be kicked out of Ferelden again; he really couldn't say. Duncan wasn't sure that would be a bad thing, either. Abandoning the entire idea of heading into the Deep Roads and facing horrible creatures like the darkspawn had its appeal.

First Enchanter Remille crept forward toward the throne, his hands out in supplication. "Is His Majesty certain that this is wise? Wouldn't the Teyrn be a better choice to—"

"No," the King cut him off. "I have made my decision." He sat back down in his throne, keeping his eyes locked on Genevieve and refusing to look in Loghain's direction. "I will contact you shortly, Commander, to make arrangements. Until then, I'd like it if you all left me alone with the Teyrn."

The First Enchanter looked as though he wanted to speak again, but Genevieve shook her head at him. She bowed gracefully to the throne and turned to leave. Duncan and the others went with her. The two men on the dais barely noticed them go.

Once the hall was cleared out, Maric sat back in his throne and waited for the inevitable recriminations from Loghain. He wore that suit of heavy grey armor every time Maric saw him now. He had taken it from the commander of the chevaliers at the Battle of River Dane, a war souvenir that he had worn to the victory parade in Denerim years later. The people had loved him for it, and Maric had been amused.

The amusement had lessened over the intervening years. At first, Loghain and Maric and Rowan had worked tirelessly to restore Ferelden after the war. There had been so much to do, so many issues left behind by the Orlesian withdrawal that it seemed like there was never enough time for anything.

It had been a breathless time, exhilarating in its way. Harsh decisions had needed to be made, and Maric had made them. Each one had taken a small piece of his soul, but he had made them. Ferelden had grown strong again, just as they had always wanted. Loghain was a hero, and both Rowan and Maric were legends. When Rowan finally gave him a son, Maric had thought that perhaps a bit of happiness was finally possible.

And then she had died, and everything had changed.

Loghain stared at him as if he had no idea who Maric was. Suddenly, he drew his sword and pointed it at Maric's chest.

"Here," he offered curtly.

"I have my own sword, thank you."

"It's not for you to take. It's for you to throw yourself on, since you seem so eager."

Maric pinched the bridge of his nose and sighed. He had known Loghain to dislike dramatics, once. It seemed that the years had given him an appreciation for it. "Perhaps you'd prefer to throw yourself on it instead?"

"I'm not trying to kill myself." Loghain's expression was dark, almost hurt. "This will make it quicker, easier. At least this way we'll have a body to burn. I won't need to explain to your son why his father went off on a mad mission and never returned."

"The darkspawn are real, Loghain. What if the Grey Wardens are telling us the truth?"

"And what if they aren't?" Loghain walked over to the throne, putting his hands on the armrests and leaning down to look Maric directly in the face. "Even if you think the fact that they have come from Orlais meaningless," he pleaded, "you must know that the Grey Wardens have *always* had their own agenda. They serve no nation, and no king. They will do what they think is best to deal with this threat, and won't care about you, or Ferelden, or anything else!"

He had a point. Two centuries ago, the Grey Wardens had taken part in a plot to overthrow the Fereldan king. It had failed, and the order was exiled, but what few people knew was that it had taken the entire Fereldan army to drive them out. Thousands of men pitted against less than a hundred, and the Wardens had very nearly won. They were a force to be reckoned with, no matter their numbers.

"It's not just that," Maric muttered.

"Then what? Because Rowan is dead?" Loghain stood up, pacing a short distance away as he shook his head. "You've been like this ever since I returned. You barely see your son; you barely lift a finger to rule the nation that you restored from ruins. At first I allowed it as part of your grief, but it has been two years now. It's as if you wish to disappear." He turned to look at Maric, his eyes full of so much concern that Maric couldn't meet them. "Is that really what you want? Does the madness of this plan mean nothing to you?"

Maric steepled his hands together and considered. He hadn't wanted to tell Loghain, but it seemed like he had no other choice. "Do you remember the witch we met in the Korcari Wilds?" he began. "Back during the rebellion, when we were fleeing the Orlesians?"

Loghain appeared taken aback, as if he hadn't expected a rational explanation. He hesitated only a moment. "Yes. The madwoman who nearly killed us both. What of her?"

"She told me something."

Loghain looked at him expectantly. "And? She babbled many things, Maric."

"She told me that a Blight was coming to Ferelden."

He nodded slowly. "I see. Did she say when?"

"Only that I wouldn't live to see it."

Loghain rolled his eyes and walked a step away, running a hand through his black hair. It was a gesture of exasperation with which Maric was well familiar. "That is a prediction that almost anyone could safely make. She was trying to scare you, no doubt."

"She succeeded."

He turned and glared at Maric scornfully. "Did she not also tell you I was not to be trusted? Do you believe that now, too?"

There was a tension in that look, and Maric knew why. The witch had said of Loghain, "*Keep him close, and he will betray you. Each time worse than the last.*" It was the only one of her pronouncements to which Loghain had been privy, and obviously he remembered it well. Perhaps he thought that if Maric believed one, he believed the other. Loghain had never betrayed him, not to his knowledge. It was something to keep in mind.

"You think it's a coincidence?" Maric asked, suddenly uncertain.

"I believe this witch was serving her own purposes, and would lie about whatever she thought convenient. Magic is not to be trusted, Maric." Loghain closed his eyes and then sighed. He shook his head slightly, as if what he was about to say was madness, but he opened his eyes anyhow and spoke with conviction. "But if you truly believe that the witch's warning has merit, let me be the one to go into the Deep Roads, not you. Cailan needs his father."

"Cailan needs his mother." His voice sounded hollow, even to himself. "And he needs a father who isn't . . . I'm not doing him any good, Loghain. I'm not doing anyone any good here. It will be better if I'm out there, helping the kingdom."

"You are an idiot."

"What you need to do," Maric ignored him, "is to stay. Look after Cailan. If something happens to me, you'll need to be his regent and keep the kingdom together."

Loghain shook his head in frustration. "I can't do that. Even if I believed this cryptic warning, I would not agree that it was worth placing you in the hands of these Orlesians. Not without an entire army to surround you."

Maric sighed and sat back in the throne. He knew that tone. When Loghain believed he was in the right, there was no dissuading him. He would sooner call the guards in here and attempt to have Maric locked up in the dungeon than see him do this.

In Loghain's mind, the Grey Wardens were Orlesian. The First Enchanter was Orlesian. This had to be some manner of plot—not that it would be the first. There had been several assassins over the years, as well as more than a few attempts by disaffected banns to overthrow him, and while Loghain could never prove that the Empire was behind them all, Maric did not disbelieve his theories. Perhaps he was even right about this.

But what if he wasn't? The witch had been crazy, almost certainly, but Maric still found it impossible to discount her words entirely. She had saved their lives, put them on the path out of the Korcari Wilds when otherwise they would have died. He had almost forgotten her warning about the Blight, but the very instant First Enchanter Remille had told him of the Wardens' request for an audience, he had remembered.

The thought of a Blight here in Ferelden was almost too much to bear. The old tales spoke of vast swarms of darkspawn spilling out onto the surface, blackening the skies and tainting the earth around them. They spread a plague by their very presence, and those the disease didn't kill, their armies did. Each Blight had come close to destroying all of Thedas, something the Grey Wardens knew better than anyone.

Surely such a disaster was worth risking almost anything to avert. Loghain could dismiss the idea, but Maric was less convinced. What if the witch was correct? What if the whole point of receiving such a prophecy was that it gave you a chance to try to prevent it?

"You're right," he admitted with a heavy sigh. "Of course you're right."

Loghain stepped back, folding his arms and looking at Maric skeptically. "This is new."

Maric shrugged. "They're desperate and asking too much. We can give them advice, maybe even draw out a map with as much information as we can remember. But going into the Deep Roads again? No, you're right."

"You give them advice." Loghain frowned. "I have had my fill of Orlesians for one evening. Especially that lickspittle Remille. You know he cannot be trusted, I assume?"

"He's Orlesian, isn't he?"

"Fine. Joke about it if you wish." He turned and began walking toward the small door off to the side of the dais. "I will send someone to tell the Grey Wardens to come back, but do not take too long with them. There is much that needs to be done in the morning, Maric. The ambassador from Kirkwall wishes to discuss the raider situation off the coast, and I trust that if you can stir yourself for an audience such as this, you can manage it for actual business?"

"I'll do that," Maric answered. As he watched his old friend storm off, he found himself left with a weary hollowness. Perhaps he even felt a bit of pity, and then guilt for pitying a man who had done so much for him. For all of Loghain's protests about how he remained in Denerim to help run things, Maric knew why he really didn't return to Gwaren. A perfectly lovely young wife was there, raising their perfectly lovely young daughter.

They were all running away from something.

The Grey Wardens and the First Enchanter returned to the hall tentatively, looking around and obviously confused by the fact that Loghain was now missing from the dais. Maric felt about ten years older, hunched over on his throne and nowhere near ready to lead anyone anywhere.

Genevieve strode forward, the picture of a mature yet confident warrior. It made him think of what Rowan might have been like had she lived to that age. She would never have been so crisp and businesslike, however, he was sure. Rowan had been all heart, always showing concern for her kingdom and doting on their son every chance she got. She had enjoyed being a queen just as she had enjoyed being a mother, far more than she had ever enjoyed being a warrior.

In fact, he found instead that the white-haired Commander reminded him of Loghain.

"Have you changed your mind, King Maric?" Genevieve asked, with the tone of one who expected that this was the only reasonable course of action.

"No," Maric answered with a grim smile, though from her tense frown she obviously found this of no reassurance. "Provided that no one else knows I am traveling with you and we move secretly, I will go with you. Loghain will remain here. Unless *you've* changed *your* mind?"

She shook her head, dispensing with any hesitation. "Not at all. We need to move quickly, and I am certain nothing I could say would make you more aware of the risk than you already are."

"Good." He stood and strode down the dais toward her. She looked distinctly uncomfortable as he shook her hand. "Then let's dispense with the 'king' business, shall we? I'm as tired of it as you are, believe me."

"As you wish . . . Maric." There was the slightest hint of a smile as she inclined her head. Perhaps she wasn't as like Loghain as he had thought. "But if you'll allow me one indulgence, perhaps I might assign one of my people to you? Someone to watch over your safety and see to your needs?"

"If you feel that is best, by all means."

Genevieve beckoned to the young man she had introduced earlier, the one who had committed the crime. The lad was darker-skinned than the rest: Rivaini blood, perhaps? The boy grimaced, reluctant to approach, though a warning look brought him quickly enough. Once he stood at the Commander's side, he sighed as if the entire effort was an imposition of severe magnitude.

No subtlety there, Maric thought to himself. Wherever the Grey Wardens had found him, he was clearly accustomed to expressing his every thought and feeling. After so many years spent in the court, Maric might even find such company a refreshing change.

"Duncan, seeing to the King's needs will be your responsibility," Genevieve said, her tone making it clear there was to be no argument on the matter.

"You mean, like fetching him chamber pots and cooking his meals?"

"If he wishes, yes." As the lad scowled, she smirked with no small amount of amusement. "Think of it as your punishment. If you fail to acquit yourself in the King's service, he can always elect to have you thrown in prison when we return."

Duncan looked helplessly at Maric, his sullen expression saying, *Please don't make me fetch your chamber pot.* Maric was tempted to laugh, but kept himself under control. There weren't likely to be many chamber pots in the Deep Roads, after all. This would be no pleasure trip.

"Allow me to introduce you to the others," Genevieve continued. "This is Kell, my lieutenant. He has a sensitivity to the darkspawn taint, and will be our tracker once we're in the Deep Roads."

The hooded man who stepped forward had the most strikingly pale eyes Maric had ever seen. He bore a grim expression, and moved with a deliberate caution that spoke of an acute self-awareness. From the thick leathers and the longbow strapped to his back, Maric would have taken him for some kind of hunter. Kell inclined his head politely but said nothing.

"And this is Utha, recruited from among the ranks of the Silent Sisters. She will not be able to speak to you, but most of us understand the signs she uses."

The dwarven woman who stepped forward wore a simple brown robe covered by her Grey Warden tunic. Her coppery hair was twisted into a long, proud braid that went down almost to the middle of her back, and she carried no weapons that Maric could see. He seemed to recall that the Silent Sisters fought with their bare hands—was that true? Despite her small size, she looked solid and muscular enough that he wouldn't want to tangle with her, weapons or no.

"These other two gentlemen are Julien and Nicolas. They have been with the order almost as long as I have."

Two tall men stepped forward, each dressed in the same kind of heavy plate armor that Genevieve wore. Both of them had burly mustaches in the typical Orlesian fashion, though otherwise they couldn't have been more different. The first, Julien, had dark brown hair cropped close to the skull and a short beard. He had a reserved air to him, his eyes shadowed but expressive, and he gave Maric a curt nod. The other, Nicolas, had blond hair almost to his shoulders and no beard to speak of. He clasped Maric's hand and gave it a vigorous shake, grinning boisterously.

Julien had a greatsword strapped to his back that was almost as large as he was. Nicolas, meanwhile, had a spiked mace strapped at his waist and an enormous shield on his back adorned with the griffon symbol. They both walked with the quiet confidence of warriors who had used those weapons often.

"And this is Fiona, recruited from the Circle of Magi in Montsimmard just over a year ago."

The elven woman who stepped forward was dressed in a chain hauberk and a blue skirt, clutching a white staff at her side. He wouldn't have picked her out as a mage if he'd seen her elsewhere without her staff, and it had nothing to do with her being elven. Most of the mages he'd ever encountered had been more like First Enchanter Remille: men, and the sort used to getting their own way. She was pretty, too, even if she had a chilly expression as she looked at him, and her bow was so slight it could barely have been called one at all.

First Enchanter Remille approached, distinctly discomfited.

He clutched at his yellow robes nervously as he bowed several times to Maric. "Begging your pardon, Your Majesty, but time is of the essence. We should be under way to Kinloch Hold as soon as possible."

Genevieve nodded. "The Circle has offered us some magical assistance prior to heading into the Deep Roads. We have very little time, but I believe this will be useful."

"Why so little time?" Maric asked.

"We have never heard of a Grey Warden who wasn't killed by the darkspawn on sight." The thought made her grow silent, and her eyes became distant for a moment. Then she brusquely turned to walk to the great doors at the end of the hall. Maric followed her, the others falling in line behind them. "The fact that he is still alive is remarkable enough, and speaks of something unusual. We need to reach him before they take him farther into the Deep Roads, and before any information they might get from him spreads."

"And if it does? What then?"

"Then we kill every one of them that knows," she said somberly. He believed she meant it. The idea that this small band could be a threat to the darkspawn, rather than the other way around, seemed surprising to him, but perhaps it shouldn't be. The Grey Wardens only recruited from among the very best, so the story went. Even though there hadn't been a Blight for centuries, their legend had lived on. They were held in high regard by the people, and had a presence in every nation outside of Ferelden.

That regard came with wariness in some circles, however. In other nations the Grey Wardens were often treated as an order that had outlived its purpose, the traditional tithes given only reluctantly. Even so, they were never openly disrespected. For all their small numbers in current times, their ability was unquestioned.

"I do have one question for you, if I may," he asked.

"By all means."

"Who is it that we're looking for, exactly?"

Genevieve stopped before the doors, turning to face Maric directly. He saw her hesitate once again, considering exactly how much she should tell him. If he was going to travel with them into the most dangerous part of all Thedas, one would hope that eventually the Grey Wardens would trust him enough to let him in on their secrets. Loghain certainly wasn't wrong about the order having its own agenda, at least.

"His name is Bregan," she said, her tone curt. "He is my brother."

2

And so is the Golden City blackened
With each step you take in my Hall.
Marvel at perfection, for it is fleeting.
You have brought Sin to Heaven,
And doom upon all the world.

—Canticle of Threnodies 8:13

The powerful stench in the air reminded Bregan of rancid meat.
There was a strange humming off in the distance, a sound he could
just barely hear but which filled him with dread. He felt around
blindly and found he was lying on stone. It felt oddly grimy, however, as if covered in a layer of soot and grease.

He was still in the Deep Roads. The sense of the miles of rock
above him was strong, as if there were an invisible weight pressing
down on his body. He took a deep, ragged breath and immediately
gagged as the smell of decay overpowered him. He rolled over and
retched uncontrollably, his empty guts roiling, but nothing came
out but ugly gasps. Sharp pain stabbed through him, reminding
him of the injuries he had suffered.

As Bregan brought his agonized heaving under control, shaking and sweating, he considered what had been done to him. His
armor was gone, as were his sword and shield, but they had left him
his robe and his tunic, encrusted with blood and filth as those
were. His injuries, meanwhile, had been dressed. In the utter dark-

ness he couldn't quite tell what they had been dressed with. Some sort of poultice, it seemed, bound with a rough cloth that felt similar to burlap.

But who had brought him here? Who had tended to his injuries? He remembered reaching a ruined thaig. He remembered being swarmed by darkspawn in the Deep Roads, overwhelmed by their numbers from all sides, and then . . . ? Nothing. He recalled the feeling of their black blades slicing into his flesh, remembered their talons puncturing his armor and digging into his shoulders and legs. By all rights he should be dead. Darkspawn showed no mercy; they didn't take prisoners.

Bregan closed his eyes and carefully reached out with his senses. There were darkspawn all around him. Not in the same room, perhaps, but nearby. He could feel them tickling at the edge of his mind. As always, the sensation came with a feeling of foulness, as if a poison had seeped under his skin.

He closed his eyes and attempted to force the awareness of their presence back out. How he had always despised it. Every Grey Warden gained the ability to touch the darkspawn from afar, and most considered it a gift. He had always thought it a curse.

The humming continued. Behind that sound, however, he could hear other things. There was movement, things slithering against rock. The sound of sloshing water. All of these things were muted and faint, but they were there. From time to time the quality of the smell would change, as well; it would become something burnt and charred. He would feel a strange pressure against his mental senses, as if something were . . . pushing against his mind. And then it would pass.

Apprehension tugged at him, and his heart began to beat more rapidly. Moving awkwardly, Bregan got up off the ground and onto his hands and knees. He attempted to discern the limits of his environment. He felt some kind of fur pelt, dirty enough that he was glad his captors hadn't decided to toss him onto that instead of the bare floor. He felt smooth walls, definitely a place that was built and not a natural cave.

His hands came across something soft and sticky, like a putrescent growth that spiderwebbed its way across the rock. The darkspawn corruption. He forced down his revulsion. Best not to think too hard about it.

Then a new sound began. Footsteps, boots on stone and not far away. Bregan turned to face the source, the first hint of direction he'd had since he awoke, and sensed a darkspawn approaching. He crawled away from it, his alarm giving way to terror. Was there a door there? Would he even see whatever was approaching him? His inability to adjust to the utter blackness around him was maddening.

The steps grew louder, echoing until they were ringing in his head. And then came the grinding sound of a metal door being opened, and suddenly there was light so bright it seared his eyes. He shouted in pain and recoiled, covering his face as he did so.

"My apologies," came a male voice. It was soft and oddly resonant, with an unearthly timbre, yet not unpleasant. The words seemed clipped, as if the speaker was unaccustomed to using them.

Bregan sat back up, blinking hard and holding up a hand to block out the worst of the light. It was difficult to make out anything, and his eyes watered from the painful effort. He could make out a vague shadow within the light, carrying what appeared to be some manner of glowing rock. The shadow moved into the room but maintained a respectful distance.

"The light is necessary," the cultured voice continued. "I suspect my arriving in the dark would have been unpleasant for you. I am correct in assuming that you cannot see in the darkness, yes?"

Was this a darkspawn? The emissaries were capable of speech, but he didn't recall any record of a Grey Warden having actually *spoken* to one. They were the spellcasters of the darkspawn, and he had heard one on occasion taunting the front lines, or crying out in anger as the Grey Wardens pressed the attack. He had even heard of them delivering ultimatums from across the battlefield, but never anything like this. He felt with his mental senses, and yes, this was indeed a darkspawn before him. The very same sense of foulness touched his mind.

"I shall wait," the voice said. "Your sight shall return in time."

It took only a few moments of rubbing for Bregan's vision to finally begin to clear. What he saw in the light of the creature's glowstone did nothing to assuage his confusion. It was an emissary, a darkspawn who might have been mistaken for a human were it not for its corrupted flesh and wide, fishlike eyes. It had no hair, and its lips were peeled back from its sharp fangs to reveal a permanent, hideous grin. Instead of the usual assortment of decayed leathers and pieces of armor that the darkspawn wore, however, this one had a simple, soot-covered brown robe. It carried a gnarled black staff in one hand and the glowstone in the other.

It also seemed quite calm, studying Bregan with its eerie eyes. He shuddered, not sure how to react at first. His instinct was to rush it, to snap its neck and get away. An emissary had command over magic, but like any mage it needed time to summon its power. If he moved quickly enough, even its staff would do it no good.

"Have your injuries healed?" it asked quite suddenly. "I understand humans have the power to heal magically, but alas, that is not something I am capable of. Even our knowledge of your medicines is . . . limited."

"I don't understand," Bregan stammered.

The creature nodded, seemingly sympathetic to his plight. Bregan was having difficulty resolving the fact that civilized behavior was coming from such a monstrous being. All the lore of the Grey Wardens, centuries upon centuries of knowledge painstakingly gained throughout the Blights . . . nothing suggested that the darkspawn ever did anything but mindlessly attack and infect any living creature they came across.

"What is it you do not understand?" it asked patiently.

"Are you . . . a darkspawn?"

It did not seem surprised in the slightest by his question. "Are you a human?" The strange timbre of its voice seemed to roll around the word *human* as if it were a foreign word. Bregan supposed that, to a darkspawn, it probably was. "I think you are not," it continued. "I think you are a Grey Warden."

"I . . . I am both of those things."

It blinked at him, but Bregan couldn't tell if that indicated surprise or disbelief or something else entirely. Were darkspawn capable of emotions? They were capable of coordinated action. They were known to make repairs to their armor, even build crude weapons and structures from the remnants of dwarven supplies they found in the Deep Roads. There had just never been any evidence of actual *motivation* behind what they did, beyond the dark forces that drove them. Perhaps the Grey Wardens were wrong. Or perhaps they had known all along, and it was yet another of the secrets they kept, even from someone as high-ranking as himself.

It wouldn't be the first time, he thought bitterly. Slowly Bregan sat back, keeping a wary eye on the emissary—assuming that was what it was. If it had meant to kill him, it would already have done so. What Bregan couldn't be sure of was whether that boded something far worse for him.

The darkspawn shifted in its dirty robes, leaning on its staff in a manner that Bregan found disturbingly human. "Our kind can sense a Grey Warden, just as a Grey Warden can sense us. And you know why this is." It looked pointedly at him, but he declined to say anything.

"There is a taint that is within the darkspawn," it supplied its own answer. "A darkness that pervades us, compels us, drives us to rail against the light. It is in our blood and corrupts the very world around us." The creature gestured toward Bregan with a withered, taloned hand. "It is also within your blood. It is what makes you what you are, what you sense in us and we in you."

Bregan felt a sinking feeling in his stomach. He said nothing, and avoided meeting the darkspawn's alien gaze.

"You take that darkness into you," it continued. "You use it to fight against us. Your immunity to its effects is not complete, however. When the corruption takes its inevitable toll, you come into the Deep Roads. Alone. To fight against us one last time. This is why you came, is it not?"

The question hung in the air. Bregan still didn't look up at the creature, a powerful foreboding making him wary. The idea that the darkspawn could communicate in this fashion was one thing. That they were capable of knowing such things . . . that was quite something else.

He waited, considering if he shouldn't try to get out while he still could. Did it matter if they killed him? He had come into the Deep Roads to die, after all. What was the worst they could do, other than knock him out again and put him back in this cell?

The idea weighed down on him, made him hang his head low. The strange humming seemed to be everywhere. He could feel the greasy slickness of the taint inside him now; it permeated every membrane and filled every orifice. He wanted to scratch at his face, peel off the flesh from his bones. He wanted it out of him.

"Yes," he slowly admitted. "The Calling. That's what we call it when it's our time to come, to make an end to it."

"The Calling," it repeated, nodding as if in approval. "You wish a glorious end rather than succumbing to the taint? Is that what happens?"

"I don't know!" Bregan snapped. He looked up at the creature and was taken aback to find that it was staring at him with a strange clinical curiosity.

"No? Has it never happened before?"

Bregan lurched to his feet, ignoring the dull jabs of pain from his wounds and the nauseated rumbling of his stomach. The humming got even louder, and for a moment he swayed on his feet as light-headedness overtook him. "What are you?" he cried. He stormed toward the creature, got close enough that he could smell its carrion flesh, see its pale pupils watching his every movement. It didn't retreat. "Why have you brought me here? Maker's breath! I should be dead!"

"Is that truly why you came? To die?"

"Yes!" Bregan screamed. He grabbed the emissary by its robes, pulling it toward him as he reared his fist to strike. It didn't fight him. Bregan's fist shook as he gritted his teeth and stared the darkspawn in the face. He should hit it. He should kill it. He had no reason not to; why was he hesitating?

"I think," it whispered, "that you came because you felt you had no other choice."

Bregan let it go, shoving it away from him. The darkspawn stumbled back, almost falling to the ground, but righted itself with its staff. It seemed unconcerned. He turned away from it, shaking with fury. "I'm not going to give you whatever it is you want," he growled. "So you may as well go ahead and kill me."

For a long minute he heard simple rustling, the darkspawn smoothing its robes and regaining its composure. The humming thrummed in the distance, and behind it he could sense the other darkspawn. He could faintly make out the sounds they made, the unnatural rattling and the dry hiss that had haunted his dreams ever since the Joining, when he had taken their dark essence inside himself. He could feel them pressing in on the wall of his mind. Relentless. He broke out in a sweat and closed his eyes, trying to focus on the mad rhythm of his heart.

He had known. When the ceremonies for the Calling were done and the dwarves had all finished paying their solemn respects, they had opened the great seal on the outskirts of Orzammar. He had looked out into the Deep Roads and known it couldn't possibly be this easy. Better to fall on one's sword, end it quickly and cleanly no matter what the Maker might think of it. Better that than to walk slowly out into a sea of darkness and be drowned in it.

Yet he had gone. It didn't matter what he wanted. His entire life it hadn't mattered what he wanted; why should it be different now?

"The answer to your first question," the emissary intoned, "is that I am the Architect."

"Is that your name?"

"We do not have names. That is simply what I am. The others of my kind do not have even that much. They are simply darkspawn, and nothing more."

He turned slowly back, puzzled. "But you are? Something more?"

The darkspawn held up a finger. "What if I told you that there could be peace between our kind and yours? That such a thing is possible?"

Bregan wasn't sure what to think of the question. "Is that something that we would even want? I mean, peace with the darkspawn? It's . . . hard to imagine."

"The Grey Wardens have never been successful in wiping out our kind. Four times we have found one of the ancient dragons slumbering in their prisons beneath the earth, the beings you call the Old Gods." The Architect looked off into the distance, its demeanor melancholy. "They call to us, a siren song we cannot resist. We seek them out, and when they rise up to the surface, we follow. We must obey. And when your kind drive us back down, the cycle begins anew."

Bregan frowned. "Then the only way there can be peace is if the darkspawn are destroyed."

The Architect stared at him with sudden intensity in its pale eyes. "That isn't the only way," it said, the resonance in its unearthly voice making him shiver.

And then Bregan realized what the darkspawn sought from him. In a flash he ran forward, shoving the startled creature out of his way as he snatched the glowstone from its hand. The Architect stumbled against the wall of the cell, its staff clattering loudly to the ground. Not waiting for it to start casting a spell, Bregan darted out into the hall. He slammed the metal door behind him and it closed with a resounding *thoom*.

The hall was worse than the cell, overgrown with what looked like organic tendrils and sacs of black mucus. There were other doors, some rusted shut or all but covered in strange, barnacle-like growths. He ignored them and started running, holding the glowstone before him.

Already he heard the hue and cry beginning around him, angry hissing and the sound of creatures running in all directions. The darkspawn were connected to each other by the same dark force that the Grey Wardens used to sense them—the Architect had been completely correct about that much, though Bregan didn't want to know how it knew.

His attention was focused on expanding his senses, trying to discern where the darkspawn were moving. It was difficult. Their taint was all around him here, and every time he tried to push outward with his mind, the infernal humming noise just became stronger. Homing in on individuals when he was surrounded by such filth, it was as if every breath of it flooded him.

As he rounded a corner, he almost ran into a small group of darkspawn—real warriors, tall hurlocks with mismatched heavy armor and wicked-looking blades. They bared their fangs, hissing as they reared back in surprise.

Bregan didn't give them a chance to act. He charged the nearest, grabbing hold of its curved sword and kicking it in the chest. The creature was startled enough to let go, issuing a shout of dismay. He then spun around, slashing the blade across the neck of a second darkspawn. It fell, clutching at the black ichor that fountained from the wound.

The third darkspawn let out an ululating cry, bringing its blade swinging down on him hard. Bregan dodged to the side at the last moment, letting the creature overbalance, and then knocked it on the head with his sword's pommel. Tossing the sword up, he reversed his grip on the hilt and then stabbed down into its back. It let out a gurgle as he wrenched the blade about in the wound.

The darkspawn he had kicked was already recovering. It barreled into him with a roar, knocking him away from his sword, and bit hard into his arm. The fangs sank deep into his flesh, and he could feel the dark corruption oozing into his blood. If he were anything other than a Grey Warden, that would be the end of him right there. He would contract a wasting illness, bringing madness and delirium and eventually an agonizing death.

But Grey Wardens paid a heavy price to become what they were. And for good reason.

Bregan fought hard against the hurlock, gritting his teeth as it emitted a rattling screech right over his face. He could smell its fetid breath, see the glistening black tongue rolling behind its long fangs. Already the cries of other darkspawn were drawing near. They struggled on the stone, and then he got a hand free and jutted it hard under the creature's chin. It squealed in rage as he pushed its head away from him, harder and harder until it was stretched back, struggling to maintain its leverage.

Finally, when it let go of him, he shoved. It hit its head against the passage wall, hard enough for there to be a muted cracking sound. Before it could reorient itself, he snatched up the sword and jumped to his feet in one smooth motion. As the darkspawn attempted to rise, he hacked down. Once. Twice. And it was done.

He paused, gasping for breath, and leaned against the wall. A wave of weakness came over him, and he let the sword drop to the ground. The smell of the flowing ichor was pungent, overwhelming even the stink that surrounded him. The humming grew more strident, more insistent. It threatened to block off all other sounds. For just a moment he pressed his forehead against cool stone and closed his eyes.

He heard a reverberating hiss nearby, and as Bregan opened his eyes and turned, he saw another heavily armored darkspawn running at him with a spear. Barely pausing to consider, he grabbed the shaft of the spear behind the tip and pulled it hard into the wall. The darkspawn stumbled toward him, and he lifted his elbow to connect with its face. There was a sickening crunch of teeth and bone, and as the creature recoiled, he snatched the spear away. He spun the weapon around and thrust the point through its abdomen.

Not waiting for the creature to fall, he let go of the shaft and turned to leave. He had to get out. Quickly. Scooping up the fallen sword, he ran into a large open chamber. It was filled with many pillars, some half crumbled, others reaching to a distant ceiling. All of them were covered in black fungus and corruption. The glowstone sent shadows dancing everywhere.

As he raced through the room, he saw more darkspawn run in ahead of him. Some of them were short genlocks, with their pointed ears and toothy grins. When they spotted him, they raised their bows and began firing arrows. Two whistled by him. One struck his shoulder, but he ignored it and began charging toward them. With a loud cry, Bregan raised the sword and slashed it down hard as he mowed through the darkspawn line. He wasn't even paying attention to individual targets, just slashing hard and then spinning and slashing again as he ran past them. Ichor sprayed across his face, and for a moment the dizziness threatened to overwhelm him, but he bit down hard and fought it back.

The genlocks tried to rally their numbers, but there was nothing they could do. Some of them were falling back, trying to reorganize, but he was already through. He turned a corner into another passage, and as a larger hurlock roared and raced toward him, he cut it down without another thought and kept running.

There had to be a way out. There had to be. This was some kind of fortress, long abandoned by the dwarves when their ancient kingdoms were overrun by these creatures. If he could just find a way out, get back into the Deep Roads . . .

He stopped midway down a flight of cracked stairs. He could hear the darkspawn not far behind him, as well as more ahead of him. It was like an anthill stirring to life. His shoulders sagged and he dropped his head low, breathing heavy. He tried to ignore the sweat pouring into his eyes.

Even if he got out of here, where was he supposed to go? He was supposed to be dead. Rightfully, he should let the darkspawn kill him, if they even would.

He stared at the sword in his hands. The blade was tinged with soot, irregularly shaped, with a sharp and curved point at its end, not unlike a large saber. The hilt was crude, wrapped in a leather that Bregan didn't really want to know the origin of. Poorly made, to be sure, but effective. That point could tear his throat out easily; just put it up to his neck and with one swift jerk it would be done.

There would be no way they could get the location of the Old Gods from him then. No way that he would be responsible for the beginning of another Blight, another invasion of the surface lands by these monsters. He had to assume they couldn't just read his mind somehow, or they would have already done so, but who knew what tricks the Architect had? Best that the knowledge died with him here.

Gritting his teeth, he raised the sword, the curve of the point covering his throat almost perfectly. Heading out into the Deep Roads to die fighting hadn't been his idea. It was centuries of Grey Warden tradition that had been forced on him, and he had reluctantly agreed, as he had agreed to everything in his life. It was better this way.

The blade wavered. A despairing wail escaped him and he began to shake. He let the blade drop to his side, closing his eyes as the sobs racked his body.

Darkspawn began to pour toward him from both ends of the passage, but he barely noticed. He stood numbly on the stairs and waited, the blackness closing in on his mind. The humming sound reached a crescendo, an urgency that tugged on the edges of his consciousness and stretched it thin.

It was inside him.

All at once, the darkspawn swarmed over Bregan and pulled him to the ground. They bit into his flesh, and several sharp objects poked him painfully. He didn't cry out and didn't resist. The glow-stone was borne away, and as the darkness became total something struck him on the back of the head.

It was better this way.

3

Those who had been cast down,
The demons who would be gods,
Began to whisper to men from their tombs within the earth.
And the men of Tevinter heard, and raised altars
To the pretender-gods once more,
And in return were given, in hushed whispers,
The secrets of darkest magic.

—Canticle of Threnodies 5:11

Duncan sat in the small boat, quite miserable and certain that it would tip over at any second and spill everyone on board into Lake Calenhad. The journey west from Denerim had taken them several days, and he wasn't even sure why they were bothering. If First Enchanter Remille had wanted to give them something, why hadn't he brought it with him to the capital? It seemed pointless to drag the Grey Wardens all this way, even if the entrance into the Deep Roads was supposedly not far from here. If time was as tight as Genevieve kept claiming, it seemed like it would make more sense to go after her brother now.

But no. Instead he was forced to squeeze into a boat that had room only for the King and the burly fellow with the oar, freezing as they navigated their way across the lake. The wind howled fiercely, and with each gust Duncan shivered. Really, he couldn't *stop* shivering, even with the fur cloak the King had given him to wrap up in. Was everywhere in this country cold?

Chunks of floating ice thumped against the boat with alarming strength and regularity. The oarsman was forced to concentrate on his task, sweating with the effort. Sometimes he would do little more than push the ice away from the boat with his oar. Other times he would start paddling furiously, only to reverse their course a moment later. What happened if the lake froze over completely? Did people just walk to the tower, then?

Only the King seemed unperturbed by the entire experience. He had been quiet since they left the city, mostly keeping to himself and asking very little of his appointed keeper . . . something Duncan heartily approved of. Once or twice the King had asked some probing questions about the Grey Wardens, questions Duncan had warily answered. Genevieve had warned him that the King might do so, and in the same breath had said that Duncan should tell the man as little as possible. The King had merely shrugged at the responses. He didn't appear to expect more.

It did make for several days of quiet, however. They had left Denerim by the North Road, traveling quickly along the Coastlands. It wasn't very busy at this time of year, according to Genevieve, and that meant less chance of them being either followed or recognized. Once the snows came, most traffic resorted to the sturdy ships that sailed the Waking Sea. They'd seen only a handful of others, merchants bundled up in woolens pulling their carts, and pilgrims forced to wait until almost too late in the season to travel. None of them had so much as glanced their way.

Dwarves didn't ride very well, but Utha did her best to suffer the indignity quietly. Really, Duncan thought she rode far more gracefully than the few other dwarves he had seen do it. Usually her people preferred to ride in carriages or carts, and not on the animals themselves, though he'd heard that in Orzammar the dwarves sometimes rode oxen. He'd asked Utha about it once, and from her grin he could tell she found the question amusing. Maybe it wasn't true? He didn't know; he'd never been to Orzammar.

Kell retrieved his warhound, Hafter, as soon as they'd left the palace. He was a giant of a dog, all muscle and teeth and shaggy grey hair. Duncan had no idea what breed of dog Hafter was supposed to be, only that he could tear out a man's throat in defense of his master. In fact, Duncan had seen him do so. Hafter bounded merrily along beside the hunter's horse, long tongue hanging out of his mouth. One would never guess the happy hound could transform into a killer at the slightest command.

Julien and Nicolas kept mostly to themselves, as they often did. Duncan supposed they had fought back to back for so long they were simply more accustomed to each other's company. Sometimes Genevieve rode with them, but usually she rode up front with Kell. There she kept her gaze intently fixed on the horizon, as if by sheer will she could somehow bring it closer.

Normally Duncan would have ridden with Fiona, and they would have chatted amiably during the trip as the quieter Grey Wardens shot them dark looks. He had come to know the elven mage fairly well in the months since he'd joined the order. Now, however, she mostly stayed away. On the few chances he did get to speak to her, she seemed agitated, and as soon as King Maric returned to Duncan's side, Fiona would scowl and move her horse away. She didn't trade a single word with the man, and brusquely ignored any of his attempts to make conversation.

The King had glanced at him quizzically, and he'd shrugged in response. Who could tell why the elf did anything? Not him.

The first night they spent in a village had been uncomfortable, to say the least. Genevieve hadn't liked the idea of being exposed, but they had left the city too hurriedly to properly equip themselves. A tense night had been spent in an inn, the King hooded and kept far from prying eyes. Duncan had rested on the wooden floor next to the King's cot, shivering and swearing at the icy Fereldan weather that seeped through his threadbare blankets and made for an unbearably sleepless night.

After that they'd avoided most of the small hamlets that dotted the road, skirting the edge of the central Bannorn as they headed westward. Only once had the King insisted they stop at a particular farmhold on the outskirts. It seemed unremarkable to Duncan, just a holding made of cracked and worn whitestone and fenced pastures given over mostly to goats and sheep.

Who was within was anyone's guess, and the Grey Wardens waited outside for the King to finish his business. Fiona had bristled at the brief delay even more than Genevieve, and her scowl at King Maric once he returned left little to imagine as to what she thought of the entire business. He ignored her, and she spent the next hour whispering an angry complaint to the Commander loudly enough for the rest of them to hear. Duncan assumed that they were meant to.

Afterwards Genevieve had driven them double time, stopping to camp only when it was absolutely too dark to ride and mercilessly stirring them all as soon as the first sliver of sun was sighted on the horizon. Duncan was happy to do the majority of the complaining, not that anyone listened to him. They were all exhausted and tense. The more time that passed, the more agitated Genevieve became. Finally reaching the shores of Lake Calenhad had been a relief.

Now King Maric sat not a foot away from Duncan in the small boat, staring out across the lake with his eyes half closed as the wind washed across his face and ruffled his blond hair. He seemed to take pleasure in it, Duncan observed, and even after giving up his fur cloak didn't seem the least bothered by the cold.

The King apparently noticed that he was being watched, and regarded Duncan in return. Duncan should probably have felt self-conscious at being caught, but didn't. For a king, this fellow was a very odd man. Who had ever heard of a king just up and leaving his palace, heading off into possible danger without so much as a send-off? The group of them had snuck out of Denerim like criminals, and not even Teyrn Loghain showed up to give them a proper scowl. It was very likely nobody even knew the King had left. The man deserved to be stared at.

"Are you curious about something?" he asked Duncan, slightly bemused. His breath came out in a plume of fine mist.

"Is that silverite?" Duncan asked, pointing at the King's armor, as valuable a suit of plate as he'd ever seen. It seemed light as well as comfortable, and reflected the dim sunlight with a brilliance that he couldn't help noticing. The amount that such a suit of armor would fetch on the black market boggled his mind.

"It is. I haven't worn it since the war, however. I'm surprised it still fits. Have you seen silverite before?"

Duncan pulled out one of his daggers and showed it to the King, who raised his eyebrows in surprise. It was made of silverite, as well. "I have two of these," Duncan explained.

"You're full of surprises. Should I ask where you got them?"

"You can if you want, but I won't tell you."

The King smirked. "Aren't you supposed to do what I ask? I seem to recall that being mentioned at some point."

"Fine. I bought them with the vast fortune that was left to me by my parents. They were once the ruling Prince and Princess of Antiva until they were unfairly deposed, and one day I will return to claim my throne."

King Maric chuckled gamely, and for a moment Duncan thought that maybe this King wasn't such a bad fellow after all. Then, as another chill gust of wind blew across the boat and set Duncan's teeth to chattering, the life drained out of the King's smile. A shadow passed behind the man's eyes, and he turned to stare out grimly over the water once again.

"I wouldn't recommend it," he muttered.

It was proving difficult to reconcile Maric the Savior—the man who, according to everyone, had single-handedly wrested his nation back from the Orlesians and then set about rebuilding it into a force to be reckoned with—with the sad fellow that sat across from him. Perhaps he shouldn't have mentioned anything about a throne? Maybe thrones were bad.

"My chances are pretty bad anyhow, I'm told." Duncan smiled apologetically. "And Antiva is a terrible place. All full of assassins and . . . Antivans. So maybe I'm better off."

The oarsman glanced back, huffing and puffing from the exertion as he rowed, but made no comment on their exchange. Duncan wasn't certain the man knew he was ferrying the King of Ferelden across the lake, to be honest. Genevieve had made all the arrangements and had already gone across with the First Enchanter.

The King was silent for several minutes, simply staring out at the lake. Just when Duncan thought that he should probably go back to shivering in his furs, however, the man abruptly turned and asked a question. "What are the darkspawn, exactly?"

"Don't you know?"

"I've seen them," he admitted, "and I was told a little about them back then, but you people are Grey Wardens. Your order has been dealing with them for centuries. You must know more about them than anyone."

Duncan chuckled. "They're monsters."

"And?"

"And what? I've been a Grey Warden for six months, maybe."

"So that's it? That's all you know? That they're monsters?"

Duncan rubbed his forehead, trying to think. It was hard when it was this cold. It snowed in Val Royeaux from time to time, but when it did everyone stayed indoors and the market district all but shut down. Those were difficult days to be a cutpurse. "Well, let's see. You know about the magisters, I assume?"

"I know what the Chant of Light says about them. It says that the mages of Tevinter grew bold enough to open a portal into heaven so they could usurp the Maker's throne, but instead corrupted it with their sin."

DRAGON AGE: THE CALLING   57

He nodded. "And were corrupted in turn, right. The first dark-spawn. What's wrong with that story? Not enough for you?"

The King peered at him curiously. "Doesn't it seem, I don't know . . . a bit pat?"

"Don't let the priests hear you say that!" Duncan laughed.

"But there must be more to it. Why are there so many? How do they live?"

Duncan spread his hands helplessly. "You're talking to the wrong Grey Warden. All I know is that the darkspawn spend all their time searching for the Old Gods."

"That's it? Nothing else? They must be boring at parties."

"That's pretty much it. They don't *think*, exactly."

King Maric gave him a significant look. "But they take prisoners."

He shrugged, avoiding the man's gaze. "Apparently."

For another hour they sat in silence, Duncan watching Kinloch Hold loom larger and larger before them. The thin spire appeared to rise out of the middle of the lake, and he wondered faintly how the mages had built it out there. Had they used magic to pull it up out of the rock? This tower looked elegant, at least from afar. Up close it was weathered and stained, the wider structure at the base standing on a rocky island almost completely covered in snow.

The only sounds were the low whistling of the wind and the rhythmic sloshing caused by the rowing. They passed directly under what had once been a giant causeway that led from the shore all the way out to the tower. Now it was just a crumbling arch, one of several. The fact that it was even partially standing after so many centuries was probably a tribute to the skill of those who had built it, Duncan supposed. He couldn't begin to guess why they didn't re-pair the bridge so that these long ferry rides weren't necessary. Maybe they didn't know how any longer? Maybe they forgot why they built a giant tower out in the middle of a lake, as well. That thought brought him no small amount of amusement.

"Have you ever been here before?" he asked the King.

"Once during the war. Then again for the last First Enchanter's funeral, though we didn't go inside. Otherwise the Chantry objects to me coming here, just in case."

"Just in case of what?"

"Just in case there are mages within who have learned a spell or two that they shouldn't have. Wouldn't do to have the King of Ferelden having his mind controlled, would it?"

Duncan's eyes went a bit wide. "They can do that?"

"I think it's more important that the Chantry believes they can."

Duncan had heard of blood magic. That was how the ancient magisters bent all of Thedas to their will, using the blood of their sacrifices to fuel their magic and open up portals into heaven. They were responsible for the Blights, according to the Chantry.

Andraste had thrown down the magisters with that accusation, claiming that magic was meant to serve rather than rule. It was a rallying cry that had spread across all of Thedas. It was the reason such towers as the one to which they were now rowing existed. In such places mages could be trained, and, more important, watched closely. If blood magic meant the mages could actually control someone's mind, maybe the priests had good reason to be so suspicious.

"I've been to one of the Circle's towers once," Duncan explained. "It was the one outside of Montsimmard, but it was nothing like this one. More of a fortress. That's where Fiona was recruited."

The King looked at him quizzically. "Fiona. That's the elven woman?"

"That's the one."

Duncan stared up at the tower again, which now loomed large and blotted out most of the sky. They had rowed into its shadow, and Duncan could make out the cave they were headed for amid the sharp rocks. Supposedly the base of the tower was in there, as well as a place to park the boat. If not, they would no doubt crash on the rocks and drown. Seemed simple enough.

"They were a gift," Duncan finally said, breaking the silence.

The King seemed honestly surprised. "A gift?"

"My daggers. Genevieve gave them to me."

"That's quite the gift."

"Maybe. They were an apology. Or at least I think they were."

Now the King was truly interested. "An apology? Your commander doesn't strike me as the sort of woman who does that often."

"She's not," Duncan said flatly. He turned his attention to the water rippling along the side of the boat, and the King let him be. The boat sailed serenely past a jagged rock that jutted out of the water, slimy algae pooled around it and clinging to its sides. A dirty gull sat on the rock and looked at him curiously, tilting its head to one side. Duncan ignored it and huddled miserably in his fur as another cold wind sliced across the lake and seeped into his skin.

"It's a mistake to bring him with us," Fiona told Genevieve as they waited in the docks underneath the tower. The cavern walls slick with moisture loomed high overhead, bathed in the orange glow of magical lanterns. In Orlais there were entire streets lit by such devices, the wealthiest districts in the entire Empire. There the Circle of Magi was paid handsomely to keep the lanterns lit, and once a month in the early morning a herd of young apprentices would make their rounds under the watchful eyes of a guardian templar. Every lantern would be checked to see if the chunk of specially enchanted chalk within had lost its dweomer, and replaced if it had. It was a painstaking process, and the Empire's elite took great pride in the fact that they could afford such a wild extravagance.

That such lanterns existed within the walls of the mage tower, however, was hardly indicative of its wealth. Here it was simply expedient. Fiona suspected that, unlike in Orlais, the tower was the only place she would see such devices in Ferelden. The idea that the practical locals would willingly spend coin for such a luxury, even had they any to spare, seemed laughable.

Genevieve unsurprisingly ignored Fiona's comment, keeping her arms crossed as she watched the opening that led into the cavern. She awaited the arrival of the King with the same unwavering intensity that she did almost everything. Fiona had explained her objection to the King's presence three times now since they had left Denerim, and each time the Grey Warden commander had responded with little more than indifference. No doubt she was well aware of all the reasons why taking royalty on their excursion might be considered unwise, and was proceeding anyhow.

Fiona scowled and turned away from the Commander before she said something to the woman that she would regret. It would not have been the first time she'd spoken her mind without thinking. Best not to give herself the chance to do it again.

The dock's platform was a solid block of stone, wooden posts spaced evenly along the water's edge to offer something to tie a boat to. As if there was a need for more than one, considering that only a single ferry operated out of the tiny hamlet at the edge of the lake. The few dour folk at the inn there had paid the Grey Wardens little heed, evidently accustomed to strange people coming and going. They'd been forced to cross the icy waters two at a time. What would happen if there was ever a pressing need to bring more people to the tower at once, or perhaps away from it, she really couldn't imagine.

Perhaps that was the way they preferred it? Where Fiona had been trained, they relied on tall stone walls to keep the suspicious outside world at bay. No doubt an entire lake worked equally well.

The platform was littered with old crates and wheelbarrows, as well as various other tools that might be used to cart arriving goods up into the tower. Did they bring all the needed supplies across the lake one boat ride at a time, too? She imagined that ships could always come from Redcliffe in the south, but that would be a long way to sail. That oarsman must be very busy indeed. A large dumbwaiter was closed off behind a warped and grey wooden gate, while a set of wide stairs curved up and out of sight into the shadows.

Even with the mystical lights, this was a dim and forbidding place. The staccato rhythm of droplets hitting the lake's surface was constant and almost maddening. The water was littered with bits of flotsam that pooled at the edges, lapping wetly against the stone with a whispery echo that made her skin crawl. The smell of damp and fetid oil was almost overwhelming.

Fiona had sworn she wouldn't step foot in another Circle after becoming a Grey Warden, not ever, and yet here she was. She had voiced her objections on that subject to Genevieve as well, but the response had been little better. Their mission was vital. Time was vital. Genevieve might as well have had those words carved into her flesh, she repeated them so often.

The possibility that there might be any truth to them made Fiona shiver.

She had seen a darkspawn only once in her entire life, on the very eve that she'd joined the order. She had not been a Grey Warden long enough to repeat the experience, and for that she considered herself fortunate. The few tales she had heard of the creatures had all said the same thing: The darkspawn had been defeated by the order for the final time long, long ago, never to arise again. Now she was told otherwise. The Grey Wardens had impressed upon her the fact that an entire army waited for the chance to spread over the surface lands again like a swarm of locusts. If that was indeed true, then they needed to be stopped, without question.

But why did they require the company of a human king in order to do it?

She left Genevieve standing at the edge and strode angrily back to Kell, who leaned casually against a far wall, his arms crossed and his head low. The hunter's hood was drawn, and he might very well have been sleeping. Fiona had seen the man sleep on his feet before;

it was almost impossible to tell. Even at rest there was a tension to his stance, as if he might spring into action at any moment.

Kell's grey warhound curled up at his feet. Hafter, at least, was openly snoring, his back paws twitching slightly as he dreamed. Every time she saw the beast she marveled at how huge it was. She would never have thought a hound could be a credible threat to an armed warrior, but the first time she saw Hafter racing toward an opponent with his fangs bared, she quickly revised that opinion.

Where she came from, they didn't allow dogs. She'd known a street cat once, a skinny thing she'd slipped nibbles of her evening meal. The cat always knew she would come, and every night without fail it would be sitting there in the moonlight waiting. It would perk up at the sight of her, and when she got near it would undulate ecstatically between her legs. To Fiona, the cat was a secret treasure in a world of ugliness.

And then one night it hadn't been there at all. Somehow she knew that it was gone forever, yet she continued to go out night after night in hopeless desperation. The last night she'd even forgone her evening meal entirely, saving the few scraps of fatty pork with the idea that perhaps a larger offering would attract the cat back to her side.

Finding only darkness outside, she'd wept bitter tears and prayed to the Maker. Perhaps in His infinite wisdom He might see fit to watch over a lone alley cat, wherever it was. Her fervent whispers drew the attention of a nearby vagrant, an elf who had lost one of his limbs and thus could no longer even work in one of the menial jobs allowed their people. No doubt he smelled the pork she carried, for he pushed her down and stole it. She'd fled screaming back to her father's hovel.

She never saw the cat again. When she was a child, her mind had shied away from the truth, preferring to believe that the cat had found a way past the tall walls that surrounded the alienage. Surely it had voyaged bravely into the human part of the city with all its fine food and fat mice. There a cat could live like a queen on the leavings of ignorant humans, feasting on scraps that would make any elf drool with envy. Her adult mind now knew better, that the poor creature had likely been snared by the very vagrant who had attacked her. Most of the elves she had known were too proud to prey on vermin and street animals, but not all. That her father had managed to shield her from that desperation as long as he had, surprised her still. After his death, all that changed.

Fiona knelt down and slowly rubbed her hand along the hound's coarse fur. His twitching slowed, and in his slumber he whined softly. When she reached the back of one ear, he half woke and curled his head inward in pleasure. She grinned and gave it a good scratch.

"You'll spoil him," came Kell's soft voice.

She glanced up at the hunter. He had not moved, but now she could see his pale eyes watching her with a wry smile. Kell was a man of few words, she'd found, but he always managed to make his point known.

"He deserves to be spoiled a little," she chuckled. "He fights beside us in battle. One day he will get a mouthful of darkspawn blood and that will be the end of him." As she scratched, the hound lazily rolled over onto his back. His muscled legs stuck up in the air and he made a cute, sleepy groan. She gamely rubbed his belly.

"Hafter is as much Grey Warden as the rest of us."

Fiona was surprised by that. "You mean he's . . . ?"

He nodded. "I doubt it will be his tainted blood that takes him in the end, even so." With a leather boot Kell reached out and affectionately nudged the hound along the ribs. Hafter opened his eyes and swiveled his head back in order to gaze with happy adoration at his master. She found it a peculiar expression for such a powerful beast, one so obviously bred for combat.

"No more than the rest of us, surely. Aren't all Grey Wardens destined to die in battle against the darkspawn?"

"Not all," he murmured, nodding toward where the white-haired Genevieve still stood. "There has been no Blight for the order to combat in centuries. Many of us live long enough to grow old, no matter how hard we might try otherwise."

"And then what? We take the Calling?"

He cocked an eyebrow. "Wouldn't you?"

She wasn't sure how to respond to that. Having only become a Grey Warden recently, the idea that she might one day live long enough for the dark taint to force her into such a choice seemed impossible. Yet if it did happen, if the immunity should one day wear off . . . the thought made her shudder. She had seen what happened to most when they became infected by the darkspawn corruption. Knowing that such vileness now swam in her blood made her shudder.

Still, she couldn't bring herself to be bitter about it. She was thankful to be a Grey Warden. More thankful than most.

Fiona patted Hafter on his belly to indicate she was done, and he sighed contentedly and rolled back over. His big brown eyes looked to Kell in a silent plea for more scratches. In response, the hunter reached into a belt pouch and produced a length of jerky. The massive dog leaped to life immediately, ears perked up as it eagerly awaited the treat. Fiona was very nearly bowled over.

"My apologies," Kell offered, tossing the jerky down. The dog snapped it up before it even touched the floor. It hardly seemed like it would take more than a moment for him to gobble it up, but his canine dignity demanded he trot off to chew in private around the corner.

Fiona smiled and picked herself off the stone, rubbing some of the dust and dirt off her hands. She turned to Kell, unsure if she should speak, and he regarded her expectantly.

"What do you think of this king being with us?" she asked.

"I think you should speak to Genevieve about it, and not I."

"Don't you think it would go poorly for the Grey Wardens if

the King of Ferelden died in our care? Is that what we really want?"

"Is that truly your objection?"

She scowled. Kell looked at her without any hint of mockery, and finally she sighed and turned to glance in the Commander's direction. "I don't think she would care even if it was." Her voice carried less bitterness than she felt.

If Genevieve heard, she made no indication. She remained where she was, staring resolutely out into the dim cavern. It would be hard for her not to have heard, however. Irrationally, Fiona wished she could pierce the woman's iron demeanor just once. The quiet rage she saw behind those eyes terrified her, but it would almost be better than the waiting. One day the Commander would break, all that anger she'd smothered behind a veneer of cold competence bubbling up to the surface like a volcano, and they would all pay the price for it.

"She's going to get us killed, you know," she muttered, just loudly enough that there was no way Genevieve could avoid overhearing. "The King, too. Just you wait and see." Fiona watched her closely, but the woman didn't even blink.

Kell's smirk told Fiona what he thought of her brave words, but he declined to add his own comment. As Hafter trotted back in their direction, nose sniffing madly in the hope that another piece of jerky might manifest itself, Kell nodded toward the cavern. Fiona had already heard the rhythmic splashes of the boat approaching. It seemed the King had finally arrived.

"Oh, joy," she griped under her breath.

Genevieve stirred, glancing back toward them with a steely gaze. "Kell, inform the First Enchanter that we will be coming up shortly. I do not wish to stay longer than we absolutely must."

The hunter quietly vanished up the stairwell, the warhound padding after him. Fiona and Genevieve locked gazes only for a second, and still that was enough time for Fiona to shiver at what she saw there. Had she likened the woman to a volcano? More like a shelf of ice, chill fog wrapped around it like a blanket, advancing inevitably across the water's surface in search of a helpless boat to crush under its immense weight.

The ferry slowly came into sight, blotting out the cave entrance for a moment as the oarsman swiftly paddled over the dark water. Poor Duncan huddled within a fur cloak, while King Maric sat next to him seemingly unaffected by the weather. Fiona kept her face deliberately neutral. Her father had always scolded her that anyone and everyone could read her every opinion on her face like an open book. Normally Fiona considered that to be a strength rather than a failing, but perhaps a touch of Kell's inscrutability would be advisable, considering the King was a man who could make all their lives a living nightmare if he so chose.

It took only a few moments for the boat to bump up hard against the platform. A rope was tied to a post, and both occupants disembarked with Genevieve's assistance. Duncan took off the fur coat and reluctantly handed it back to the King, who was looking around at the cavern with admiration.

"The last time I came here it was winter, too," he remarked. "But I think they've made it larger since then. Can they do that? They can probably do that."

Genevieve ignored his question. "Maric, we should proceed. I have no desire to stay the night, if we can at all avoid it."

"You mean we'll be rowing back right away?" Duncan cried in dismay. "Why didn't you just leave me at the inn?"

She leveled a direct gaze at him. "To do what? Guard the chickens?"

He didn't argue, just crumpled in his own misery in a way that almost made Fiona laugh. Duncan was only a handful of years younger than her, but there were times he seemed more like a boy than a man. She knew there was much more to him than that. The place where he grew up . . . that was the sort of place that forced one to mature quickly. Whatever Duncan suffered from, it was not naïveté.

"It might be kinder to knock him out for the trip back," Maric suggested with a mischievous grin.

"I think he will survive." Genevieve turned and marched up the stairs without waiting to see if she was being followed. Duncan trotted after her, and as the two of them disappeared Fiona belatedly realized the King had not moved. She had been left alone with him.

The man made no indication of a desire to go, instead standing there by the water's edge and watching her with a strange look she couldn't decipher. Was it anger? Concern? She had to admit he possessed a certain charm, something unexpected in a king. No doubt it was also deceptive. She'd learned a long time ago never to take such men at face value.

Shrugging indifferently, she turned to leave. The King could stand in the cavern until he froze, for all she cared. She certainly didn't feel the need to wait on him.

"Wait," he suddenly called out. "It's Fiona, isn't it?"

Fiona paused, her stomach sinking. Silently she cursed her too-expressive face. *You couldn't just blink and smile prettily like some vapid whore, could you? Would that be too difficult to master?* Taking a ragged breath, she slowly turned back around. "Is there something you wished of me?" she asked, keeping her tone as cheerful as she dared.

"Something I wished?" He seemed startled by her question. "I was actually hoping we could speak. I understand you have an issue with my presence."

"A man of your stature need not concern himself with my thoughts."

"Nice try." Maric wagged a finger and walked toward her. She stood her ground, refusing to retreat. She would be damned if she would retreat from anyone, even some fool of a king. "You might think I'm deaf, but I managed to overhear your objections to your commander on several occasions."

"So? Is it so unreasonable to believe that bringing the King of Ferelden into the Deep Roads is not a good idea?"

"Not if that's all it is."

Fiona snorted indignantly. It was an unladylike thing to do, she knew, but her patience was rapidly running thin. The Enchanter who had trained her had been an elegant woman with perfect manners and porcelain skin, and she had sighed laboriously every time Fiona had so much as twitched an eyebrow. It had only served to compel Fiona to do it all the more often, thus increasing the woman's suffering.

The oarsman sat forgotten in his boat nearby, trying his best to be unnoticeable. He fished a piece of sweetmeat out of his coat and furtively began nibbling on it, eyes flicking to Fiona and Maric as if he hoped they might go away and leave him to his meal. Or perhaps he enjoyed the spectacle. She couldn't rightly say.

"I apologize then, my lord, if I have offended you," she gritted out through a clenched smile. "It won't happen again."

He folded his arms stubbornly. "I'm not offended. If you have something to say, however, then say it."

She looked longingly toward the staircase. Escape was an option, but then King Maric would assume that she was fleeing. Simply telling the man off was tempting.

Genevieve had specified with severity that the man was not to be bothered, however, and that gave her pause. Being censored was something she would normally not abide, but she had seen what defying the Commander had brought Duncan. Genevieve was one of the few people she respected.

"Look," she began. "This is ridiculous. Why should you care what I think? Or what anyone thinks, for that matter?"

"Are you avoiding the question? Did your commander tell you to do that?"

Perceptive twit. She was not about to be outmaneuvered, however. "Is this what you do in your palace? Run around to all the servants and the groundskeepers and worry about whether or not they like you enough? That must keep you very busy."

"I think if one of the servants glared at me the same way you do, I would at least stop and ask why." He paused, the wry grin returning. "Or is it your opinion that I shouldn't care? That this would be unkingly of me, perhaps?"

"I've yet to see a single thing remotely kingly about you. No reason for you to start now."

"Oh-ho!" He seemed inordinately pleased to have dragged something out of her. She tried to rein in her rising temper, even though she could feel her control slipping. She had really never been very good at this sort of thing. "Have we stumbled on the problem? Your estimation of my kingliness?"

Fiona rolled her eyes. "That," she snapped tartly, "is a problem for your subjects. Of which I am not one. I do feel for them, however. How grand it must be to have a king that would so readily abandon them to play the hero."

Maric paused. "You think I've abandoned them? I'm here to help the Grey Wardens protect them."

"Of course you are," she chuckled incredulously. "And it's none of my business anyhow, is it? My business is killing darkspawn." She gestured toward the staircase. "And we should get on with it, no?"

"There are no darkspawn up there."

"There are none down here, either. Just a human with a large ego who insists that everyone like him."

"I never insisted you do any such thing."

"Then you shouldn't be worried that I don't." With that, Fiona walked away from Maric and marched up the stairs. She imagined he continued to stand there by the water's edge, staring after her in confusion as the oarsman shifted uncomfortably in his boat. She would leave it up to the King to decide if he should complain to Genevieve about being overly bothered. If anyone asked her about it, her opinion would be that she thought the man needed a little bothering.

Maric didn't follow her up, at least not immediately. It was a relief, really, and she breathed a little easier as she ascended into the dark heart of the tower.

Duncan was doing his best not to yawn.

It was the one thing that Julien had advised him against as the mages led the King and the Grey Wardens into the massive assembly hall at the top of the tower, whispering that at such official functions the worst thing one could do was yawn. At first, Duncan didn't think the advice was necessary. In fact, it was all he could do to keep from openly gawking.

The hall was domed, with a great window at the very top that allowed the sunlight to filter through. Marble pillars lined the hall, behind which rows of benches allowed for an audience of well over a hundred—and they were packed with people, robed mages ranging from young apprentices to elderly enchanters. A higher gallery at the end of the hall contained the templars and priests, all of whom watched with severe and disapproving expressions. How appropriate, Duncan thought, for them to look down on the proceeding from on high.

In the center of the chamber, standing in the beam of sunlight that shined down from the window, were the First Enchanter and an impatient-looking Genevieve. The mages around the room were straining their necks to gawk at the group of them, and a buzz of conversation rose. Duncan couldn't be sure if they were more amazed by the presence of the King or by the Grey Wardens. Grey Wardens were a rare sight here, after all. It was a slightly different reception than the order normally received elsewhere.

What followed, however, was a ceremony long enough to bring

him from awestruck amazement to utter boredom. The First Enchanter insisted on giving a lengthy speech, mostly extolling the honor of the Grey Wardens and lavishing praise on the King. Duncan had to wonder how this was okay, considering Maric was supposedly traveling with them secretly, but neither Genevieve nor the King appeared to object.

Each of the Grey Wardens was called up by the First Enchanter in turn and given black brooches that had been specially crafted for them. Duncan took a close look at his and found it unremarkable: polished onyx, without even a fancy setting or any particular embellishment. Completely functional.

Considering that they were intended to hide the Grey Wardens from being sensed by the darkspawn, however, they were extremely useful. Clearly this was why Genevieve was willing to delay their entrance into the Deep Roads and put up with the entire ceremony business. Though even she was slowly losing her patience, he could see.

King Maric was given a leather satchel full of potions, each of them contained in a delicate glass vial. According to the First Enchanter, this was a precious mixture of herbs that would enable Maric to resist the disease spread by the darkspawn. He was, after all, the only one in the group without the Grey Wardens' immunity. One full vial was to be swallowed each morning; according to Duncan's count, that meant the King had a two-week supply.

Rather optimistic of the First Enchanter, really.

Duncan mostly ignored the droning that followed, his attention wandering. At this point the Grey Wardens were mostly relegated to the sidelines anyhow, and Genevieve was clearly itching for an opening simply to excuse themselves and leave—not that First Enchanter Remille was providing one, of course.

So Duncan looked around, staring at the individual mages in the crowd. There was one in particular to whom his attention kept returning: a rather pretty young apprentice with tousled brown hair and intense doe eyes. And she was staring back at him, too. He looked away initially, but his eyes kept being drawn back to her. No, she was definitely looking at him and only him.

Then she discreetly waved at him and beamed. He reluctantly waved back, trying not to smile too encouragingly. Then he kept looking around. Maybe there was an exit nearby? He didn't know if he could stand much more of this.

It turned out he was in luck. There was a small door not ten feet from where he stood, guarded by two solemn templars more engrossed in the First Enchanter's speech than they were in their duty. Which amazed him, frankly, but to each their own.

Before anyone knew it, he was gone.

Duncan smirked with delight as he crept through the shadows deep within the tower. The thing about mages, he noticed, was that they liked to keep their passages nice and dim. Perhaps it leant an austere air to their studies, or perhaps they could only make so many of those strange lamps they dotted around the tower to provide light. Either way, it made sneaking around rather easy.

Those templars who weren't in the assembly hall didn't seem all that interested in looking out for people like him, either. They were far more interested in glowering at any younger mages who passed by. He'd seen two, one not much younger than himself, and another a girl who couldn't have been more than ten years old. They had nervously walked by one of the heavily armored templars and the man had all but spit on them. Both of them had squealed in fear, clutching their leather tomes to their chests as they ran off. The templar had chortled with amusement.

What would it be like, Duncan wondered, to be brought to a place like this? He'd heard that people with magical talent were sought out while they were young, taken from their families and

DRAGON AGE: THE CALLING   73

brought to the Circle. There they were trained to control their power or die trying.

Sounded a great deal like the Grey Wardens, now that he thought about it.

Passing quietly through the hall, he boldly crept behind one of the templar guards standing at attention. The man was practically asleep on his feet, Duncan noticed, though he had to wonder what it was that needed to be guarded so badly. Templars were almost everywhere, as were the female priests in their red robes. They numbered more than the mages, at least in this part of the tower. Did they fear magic that much?

He'd known someone once who could do magic. A friend who lived on the street as he did, named Luc. Duncan had always admired his knack with picking pockets, and then Duncan saw the trick. Luc would put his hand above the pocket, and whatever was inside would simply leap into his palm. Duncan had confronted him one night and Luc had confessed: He had always been able to do bits of magic.

Luc's father had been a mage who had come to see his mother at the whorehouse until she found herself pregnant. Then there was no mage, and his mother had worried constantly that Luc would develop magic of his own. So he'd hidden it from her, and hidden it from others as well. It was a curse to him, despite its uses.

Duncan hadn't told anyone, but somehow the rumor still got around. Before long, some of the other thieves grew suspicious. If Luc could make things jump into his hand, what else was he capable of? Could he be stealing from them? Perhaps he cast spells to make them forget, or perhaps he was dangerous.

Luc had been furious with Duncan, certain that he was responsible for all the attention. It didn't matter in the end. The templars came, and when Luc tried to run, they'd struck him down. Killed him in cold blood, right in front of Duncan. Nobody had said anything, of course. Just one more thief rotting in the gutter, and this one an apostate to boot.

Duncan knew where Luc kept his stash, hidden away in the attic of an abandoned chantry. He'd gone to collect it, considering that Luc wasn't going to need it anymore, and he'd been pleased by the amount of coin there. It was enough to get him through some hard winters and even put a roof over his head, at least for a little while. He'd felt badly about it, even so. Far better for Luc to still be alive, even if that meant being locked up in a tower like this one. One didn't acquire friends very often where Duncan came from.

He stuck his head into a dim chamber and saw that it was a library of some kind. Rows and rows of dusty books, and tables covered in even more books with candles burned nearly down to nothing. Duncan wasn't sure what a mage needed to read in order to learn his spells, but apparently it was a lot. There were two mages in there now, older men in their full enchanter robes, poking through various tomes as a templar glared at them next to a roaring fireplace.

Good thing books weren't worth stealing, so there was no need to go in.

He continued forward, avoiding the large chambers in the central part of the tower as that was where most of the people seemed to accumulate. He probably needn't have worried. Most everyone was down on the main floor with the King and the Grey Wardens, watching whatever formalities the First Enchanter had cooked up to honor them. It had made it a simple matter to slip away. With any luck, the long-winded Orlesian would still be talking long after Duncan found his way back . . . preferably with his pockets full of whatever trinkets he could find up here.

It occurred to him that it was very possible he could get into trouble again. The last time that had happened, he had ended up the serving boy of the King, after all. *Well*, he thought, *I'll just have to make sure I don't get caught this time, won't I?*

He ducked into an alcove and hid behind the statue there as the sound of footsteps approached. An elven man in grey robes passed by, this one with the same serene expression that he had seen on others similarly dressed. Fiona had called them "the Tranquil" with a fair amount of distaste. He had asked what that meant, but she refused to say. He knew that they seemed to act as the keepers of the tower, seeing to the day-to-day running of things and acting as the Circle's merchants to the outside world. Beyond that, he had no idea why Fiona would shudder whenever she saw them. Their emotionless manner was unnerving; perhaps that was it?

As the man glided past, Duncan reached out and snatched a ring of keys that he spotted on the man's belt. It was a simple matter to slip them free of their hook with nary a jingle. Duncan smiled to himself as the fellow kept on going, completely oblivious to his loss.

The keys were large and iron, the sort that you used in padlocks and gates. Or chests. That thought ran enticingly around Duncan's mind as he crept out from behind the statue. Where would these keys fit? Would the Tranquil get to wherever he was going and suddenly discover them gone? Would he assume he lost them and retrace his steps, or raise the alarm? Duncan needed to work quickly.

It took some time to move through the next several levels of the tower. He needed to scamper back into the shadows every time some templar roamed his way, and while he poked his head into just about every room he came across, there was always either someone inside or it was just another boring storage room or something filled with even more books. Everyone was so quiet, as well, moving around with a hush that seemed completely unnatural. It served to make Duncan nervous. Not that sneaking around the home of magic-wielders wasn't call for a bit of sweat as it was.

There were small side stairs that led up, allowing him to avoid the central staircase, and he noticed that as he moved up in the tower it became quieter and more cramped. The halls were narrow now, and he couldn't even hear the distant thumps of armored templars walking the halls. Good. That would make things easier.

The rooms up here appeared to be mostly dormitories, each with a set of beds and large chests. They ranged from the chaotic to the neat and orderly. Was this where the apprentices slept? That made him a bit dubious about his chances of success. It was unlikely that apprentices would own anything of interest, surely.

But then he reached a darker part of the halls, where the doors were all locked. The quarters of the senior mages, then? That held more promise.

Quietly he tried the keys on several of the doors. Nothing. The keys were too large, and while he was tempted to use the lockpick he kept hidden in his belt, he knew too little about the sorts of protections these mages might be using to guard their privacy. He had heard about traps that exploded in fire or electricity. He had once known a girl, in fact, who had been killed trying to open a chest belonging to a mage. Nothing left of her but some scorched bones and a pile of ashes. The guards had been able to do little else but gawk as the mage responsible rode off in his carriage, leaving the girl's remains to blow in the windy streets.

So, no. He wasn't going to force his way anywhere. As angry as Genevieve might be if he got himself stupidly caught sneaking around the mage tower, she would be utterly livid if he got himself killed.

He was just about to give up and look for a way to get even higher into the tower when he noticed the large door at the very end of the hall. It was at least eight feet tall, and made of a dark wood. It had an ornate brass handle that was completely unlike any of the others he had seen. More important, it had a very large keyhole. The sort that an iron key would fit into.

Smirking, Duncan approached the door and attempted to insert one of the keys on the ring. It slid in easily, but didn't turn. He waited for the bolt of lightning to strike him . . . and nothing happened.

Silently he exhaled.

He tried two more keys before he found one that slid in and turned. With a loud clacking sound, the door unlocked and opened inward. He tensed, almost expecting a magical beast of some kind to leap out at him, perhaps a demon. Demons were supposed to follow mages around like flies, weren't they? The whole tower could be full of them!

But nothing happened. There was just a shadow-filled room awaiting him, and his foolishness was the only thing keeping him from it. Shaking the nerves out of his hands, he walked inside.

There was a tall, arched window that let in faint light, and through it Duncan could just barely make out the lake below and the hint of land on the horizon. The shutters were open, and a crisp breeze caused them to clatter against the wall with a disjointed rhythm. He shivered, squinting to see everything else in the room. There was a fancy bed, with the sort of gilded posts he'd seen in Orlais from time to time. A desk made of a reddish wood he didn't recognize, covered with an assortment of parchments and leathery tomes. The silver inkwell might fetch a price, he thought, but not enough to make it worth stealing.

A massive wardrobe stood open, filled mostly with—no surprise there—cloaks and woolens and more mage robes, but as Duncan drew close he realized something. Several of those robes were ornamented in exactly the same manner as the First Enchanter's. Were these his quarters? The idea excited as well as terrified him.

It made sense. There were a number of small statues about the room, all elegant women carved from ivory. Exactly the sort of thing that was all the rage right now among the Orlesian nobility, or so he'd been told by a fence. The shield on the wall looked big, and expensive. The giant set of golden scales against the wall also seemed elaborate, if far too large to carry out. All these things struck him as the type of possessions an important mage might have carried with him to his new home.

If only he could find something actually small enough to take. He froze as he heard what he thought were footsteps out in the hall, but it was just the shutters banging against the wall once again, slowly at first and then once very loudly. The breeze that followed cut through him like a knife.

Duncan was about to start searching the desk more carefully when something tucked away at the bottom of the wardrobe caught his eye. Something glittering amid a pile of rolled-up linens. Hidden. A slow smile crept across his face as he knelt down and moved some of the rolls aside. This revealed a red lacquered box, longer than it was wide and with a small golden lock. Very fancy, the sort of thing one might keep jewelry in, he thought.

Ignoring any warning thoughts about magical protection, he examined the lock closely and then reached into his belt to retrieve two fine pieces of wire. The lockpick was small enough to do the job, he figured, and as he quietly plucked away at the lock mechanism he was pleased to see he was right. It resisted him with clicking sounds until finally it gave way and released. Cautiously he pulled it out and opened the lid of the box, half expecting it to explode.

It didn't. Duncan gasped as he looked in the box to see an ebony-black dagger lying upon red silk. The entire dagger seemed to have been carved from a single piece of glossy stone, looking almost as if it was made of glass. Was it obsidian? He had heard of such a material, but never actually seen it before. The hilt was beautiful, delicate ridges leading up to a pommel carved into a roaring dragon's head. As he lifted it out gingerly, he saw what looked like red veins within the black blade, tiny cracks along its surface. He would have thought it was blood, but running his finger along the side told him it was perfectly smooth. Not a stain or blemish.

Now this was worth stealing. This was something special, something that the First Enchanter prized enough to hide within his own chambers. Not hide well, of course, but how much could the man expect anyone to steal from him within his own tower?

Chuckling with amusement, Duncan slid the blade into his shirt. Where the smooth metal touched his skin he felt a tingle. Not unpleasant, and almost warm. It made him like the weapon all the more.

He closed the box, relocked it, and quickly rearranged the linens. No need for the First Enchanter to ever know he was even missing anything. With any luck, the fellow never checked his precious box and wouldn't be aware anything was amiss until Duncan and the Grey Wardens were long gone. *He did bring us here to help us out*, he thought. *Well, he's simply helping us out more than he guessed.*

Glancing around to make sure he hadn't accidentally moved anything else, he retreated out of the room and very gently closed the door. The lock gave a loud snap as it shut, which made him jump. He paused, listening intently for the sound of a reaction, but again there was nothing. It seemed he was alone up on this floor, after all. *Perhaps you should just stop jumping at every little thing, you idiot.*

As Duncan turned around, he had taken only two steps from the door before he realized that there was someone standing at the end of the hall, staring at him. He ground to a halt, his heart leaping up into his throat. It was the apprentice from the assembly hall, the one who had waved at him.

She must have seen him come out of the First Enchanter's quarters. But why was she just standing there? Did she think that he was going to attack her?

He wasn't, of course. If only there was somewhere to run! But he was standing at the end of a hallway; the only way out was to go through her. He remained completely still, a single bead of sweat running down his forehead as he waited for the mage to act.

Curiously, she smiled with delight and ran toward him. "I saw you leave, and I just had to follow!" She stopped short a few feet away from him. Her cheeks were flushed, and she nervously smoothed down her hair. "I had hoped that maybe your wave was an invitation, that maybe you . . ." Her voice trailed off suggestively.

Duncan narrowed his eyes at her, slowly catching on. "Oh. Yes, that."

"My name is Vivian. I cannot believe I am meeting an actual Grey Warden!"

Think fast, fool. "I . . . am Duncan. I was . . . looking for you. I thought—"

"You thought I might be up here?" The young woman's big eyes lit up and she stepped closer toward him, assuming a seductive stance as she ran a finger down his arm. "They say you Grey Wardens are clever. They also say you have a great deal of . . . prowess."

"Err . . . yes. Yes, we do, in fact."

She beamed with pleasure. "I hope I am not being too forward. My bed is in the dormitory, but most everyone else is in the assembly hall. We will be alone, at least for a little while."

Duncan glanced askance at her to see if she was actually being serious. She was. The expectant look she gave him left no question as to what she intended. He'd heard that mages largely dispensed with social customs among themselves, but he hadn't imagined it to go quite this far. Most Orlesian girls he'd known, even the rough-and-tumble ones in the streets, would have guffawed at this sort of display.

Not that he didn't like it, necessarily. For a mage, she was rather attractive in her way. And clean, too. That alone would be a step up from the few experiences he'd had, furtively groping girls in filthy back rooms at the flophouse, the act all sweat and desperation and over almost as soon as it'd begun. If this mage was looking for some kind of virtuoso performance on that front from a Grey Warden . . . well, he'd just have to give it his best shot, wouldn't he?

Flashing his most charming smile at her, Duncan leaned casually against the wall. It was the sort of pose he'd seen Kell perform, and from the mage's excited blush it seemed to have exactly the effect he was hoping for. "Vivian," he crooned, "you have just made this trip more worthwhile than you could possibly imagine."

Letting out something between a squeal and a giggle, she grabbed his leather and yanked him in for a kiss. He was taken by surprise and almost stumbled, but kept enough presence of mind to keep the dagger hidden in his shirt from showing itself. And then he was quickly lost in the moment.

She tasted like strawberries. Was that a mage thing? Duncan's mind flashed to Fiona and he thought that, no, it probably wasn't.

Evidently the sneaking-away bit didn't always end in disaster.

4

There in the depths of the earth they dwelled,
Spreading their taint as a plague, growing in number
Until they were a multitude.
And together they searched ever deeper
Until they found their prize,
Their god, their betrayer.

—Canticle of Threnodies 8:27

Maric shivered as the wind blew a flurry of snow across the rocky hills. They had been traveling most of the day, making their way on foot into the hills northeast of the tower. They did not ride horses this time, not for where they were heading. As the evening had approached, it truly seemed as if the heavens opened up above them. A blizzard had been unleashed, the wind howling amid the crags as they slowly plodded through icy paths.

He remembered these hills. If they pressed far enough north to reach the coast, they would find themselves near the fortress of West Hill. There he had suffered the worst defeat of the war, one that had very nearly cost him the rebellion entirely. Hundreds of men who had followed him lost their lives there, all because he had been a trusting fool. It had been a sobering lesson to learn.

None of them had spoken a word for hours, now. Genevieve wanted to make up for lost time, and so each of them buried their faces into their cloaks and endured the weather as silently as they could. The roads and peaceful farming hamlets now covered by a blanket of snow slowly gave way to a skyline dotted with tall trees and sharp cliffs that were all but uninhabited.

Poor Duncan walked beside him, more miserable than ever. Maric wasn't certain what the lad's exact heritage was, but perhaps a lack of resistance to the cold was simply in his blood. Clearly he would have gladly stayed behind at Kinloch Hold if that were an option, which was saying a lot considering how most people felt about mages.

Genevieve had been quite eager to get him out of there, however. Something had passed between her and Duncan, and Maric wasn't certain what. The Grey Wardens' commander had finally grown impatient after enduring the First Enchanter's ceremony for much of the afternoon, cutting the man off in midsentence as she spun about to go in search of her missing young thief.

To tell the truth, Maric hadn't been aware up to that point that Duncan was even absent. Eventually, Genevieve had returned with him in tow. Rather than being furious, however, the woman's expression had been more awkward mortification. She refused to comment on what the lad had been up to when Maric asked her, clamping her jaw shut and actually blushing. Duncan stood behind her, ashen-faced and looking like he wanted to do nothing more than crawl under a rock somewhere and die.

So the lad's misery was due to far more than the weather. Since they'd left the tower, the white-haired Commander had barely spoken to him. Whenever she did, she stared at him incredulously with those hard eyes of hers, and Duncan withered under the disapproval. Maric would have stood up for him, but for all he knew the lad had done something completely reprehensible.

For his own part, Maric didn't feel truly cold even in the blizzard, not until they spotted the doorway, a great slab of dark granite easily twice a man's height set into the side of a ridge and almost covered in a drift of snow. It would have been simple to miss, had he not known exactly where it was. It came into sight slowly amid the wind and the snow, and they approached cautiously. The closer they got, the larger it loomed and the more the chill seeped into Maric's heart.

This was the entrance into the Deep Roads that he had used years earlier, a desperate gamble to reach Gwaren without encountering the Orlesian usurper's army on the surface. It had only been through sheer luck that he had survived. In fact, he survived by luck on a number of occasions back then. The people of Ferelden who worshipped him now wouldn't believe the truth even if he told them, that their heroic king had managed to free them more through fortune than through skill or good decisions.

They would simply tell him that the Maker had watched over him, that through the Maker's grace Ferelden had been freed. And perhaps that was so. Still, his mind inevitably was drawn to the two women who had accompanied him into those dark depths. One had become his wife and the mother of his son, while the other . . .

He grimaced. He didn't want to think of Katriel.

It was she who had led them to this remote location the first time, calling on her mastery of history and lore. Once upon a time this doorway had been a way for the dwarves to ascend to the surface, no doubt to collect the resources that they needed, but since the darkspawn had overtaken the dwarven kingdoms it had become little more than an open sore long forgotten. Forgotten by anyone but people like Katriel, he amended silently.

Back then, they had found the entrance lying open, its great doors ravaged by time. When he visited Orzammar years later, he had asked the dwarves to repair the entrance and seal it. Loghain had worried that the darkspawn might use it to raid the surface, even though they clearly had not done so in centuries. Still, one could never be too careful.

It had never occurred to Maric that he would one day be returning here.

Another powerful gust picked up a pile of snow from the rocks and blew it in their faces. Genevieve shrugged it off and marched ahead to the entrance. Her thick white cape fluttered madly as she reached out with a hand to touch the dark stone, running her fingers along its surface. It seemed like she was feeling around for something.

"What is she doing?" Maric asked Duncan quietly.

The lad shrugged, not even willing to raise his face from the furs.

Finally Genevieve turned back and walked directly toward Maric. "You are able to open it, yes?"

"The dwarves gave me a key."

She nodded. "Then we camp here until morning."

"What?" Duncan spluttered with indignation. "Can't we go in now? Where it's warmer?"

The Commander turned a level gaze toward him, and he immediately shrank back from her. "We have no way of knowing whether there are darkspawn behind that door," she said tersely. "Just because the King did not find any here fourteen years ago does not mean the situation will have remained the same."

"Can't you detect them?" Maric asked. "Isn't that what Grey Wardens do?"

"I tried. I felt . . . a strange presence, very faint. I cannot tell if it is because the darkspawn are far below or because the doorway is simply too thick." Without waiting for a response, she turned and snapped to one of the large warriors standing nearby, "Julien, tell the others to spread out and find someplace close with shelter. I want to keep an eye on this doorway tonight."

It wasn't long before the Grey Wardens had efficiently set up a camp just over the next rise. Snow was piled high on top of it, but at least it offered relief from the sharp winds, and that was better than they'd had all day. Maric felt a bit useless as the others bustled around, setting up tents.

Kell gathered a small pile of frozen wood, and before Maric could ask how he planned on turning that into a fire the hunter produced a small flask from his pack. He poured out a bit of the contents, a bright yellow liquid that began to sizzle as soon as it touched the wood, and within moments a healthy blaze materialized.

"Impressive," Maric commented.

Kell grinned. "It works on darkspawn, as well. Sadly, we only have a little."

Before long, dusk gave way to night. Darkness pressed in around them, driven back only by the flames of the campfire. Above the hills, a black sky filled with clouds seemed to go on forever, lit by a moon that never quite seemed to show itself. The blizzard thankfully ended, though the wind continued to lash across the landscape, scouring the fields of snow smooth.

Within the camp, tension filled the air. Maric could see from the grim faces of the Grey Wardens that they didn't look forward to the morning any more than he did. At least they knew what they were likely to encounter in the Deep Roads. When he first came here, he hadn't a clue.

Once the tents were set up, Kell headed off with Duncan and his warhound to hunt. Genevieve strode to the top of the bluff, as from there she could keep an eye on the doorway. The warrior stood up there, one leg propped on the rocks and her cloak billowing behind her in the wind as she kept her watch. It was an intimidating pose, Maric thought. She seemed even more intense than before, if that were possible, as if she expected the doors to burst open at any moment.

He turned to the dwarven woman with the coppery braid, Utha, who shared the frozen log they had dragged next to the campfire. Her face was pretty, he thought. Most of the dwarves he had ever seen looked as if they were hewn from stone, all hardness and rough edges. This one, however, seemed almost soft. She stared into the blaze with an unsettling serenity, and was so very . . . still.

He couldn't imagine ever being like that. Even now his head

was filled with worry—what was Loghain doing, for instance? He had left a note explaining his plan, but the man might assume it was fake. He might believe that Maric had been kidnapped, and probably had the army searching for him even now. Loghain rarely desisted when he was determined to have his way.

And then there was Cailan, his young son, now no doubt wondering where his father had gone. His mind immediately shied away from such thoughts. No, he wasn't still at all.

Maric nudged the dwarf and pointed toward where Genevieve kept her vigil. "Is she always like that?" he asked. "Do you know?"

She regarded him with an impenetrable look, her brown eyes glittering in the firelight. She made several strange signals with her hands, and belatedly he remembered that she didn't speak.

The two warriors sat on the other side of the fire from them, and stopped their quiet whispering to each other as they noticed Maric's confusion. Nicolas, the blond and more talkative of the two by far, leaned toward him. "Utha tells you that it is love that drives our commander." The man's Orlesian accent was cultured and warm.

"Love? You mean love for her brother?"

He nodded. "They were very close."

"Can you tell me about him? I barely know anything about him. How was he captured? How can you even be certain he's still alive?"

The brown-haired man, Julien, picked up a long stick he had been using to tend the fire and began shifting several of the logs. Sparks flew, and when Nicolas glanced at his companion they shared a guarded and wary look. Maric had heard perhaps three words in total from Julien since they had left Denerim, and all of them had been directed at Nicolas. Still, the man's dark eyes said plenty. They said right now that Nicolas shouldn't be telling Maric any more than was necessary. More Grey Warden secrecy.

Utha frowned, raising a hand and agitatedly gesturing at the men. The fluttering of her fingers seemed to punctuate her words firmly. Nicolas scowled in response and reluctantly nodded. Julien said nothing, his eyes only darkening with concern.

"What did she say?"

"She says we have no right not to tell you more," Nicolas muttered.

The dwarven woman continued to sign at Maric, and then waited patiently as Nicolas translated. "His name is Bregan, and until one year ago he was Commander of the Grey in Orlais, leader of the order within the Empire. He held that position for a very long time."

"Did he quit?"

"He did not. He left the order for his Calling. It is a rite where a Grey Warden enters the Deep Roads alone."

"Alone!" Maric exclaimed. "Why would someone do that?"

"To die," Utha signed. "A far better fate than to allow the darkspawn taint to overtake our rapidly aging bodies. Every Grey Warden knows when their time for the Calling comes, and every one of them who has entered the Deep Roads for their Calling has died, until now."

Maric pondered this for a moment. Duncan had already explained to him how the Grey Wardens drank darkspawn blood in a ritual they called the Joining, taking the taint into their own bodies in order to effectively combat the creatures. They were more than simply skilled at fighting darkspawn; they knew them intimately. They sensed their presence, sometimes even gleaned their intent. This information was not something many people knew, and Genevieve had only grudgingly allowed the lad to impart it to him.

He wondered if it was the same taint that he had encountered in the Deep Roads years ago. He remembered it well, covering everything in the underground passages like a vile, black fungus. Maric had been fortunate not to contract the darkspawn's plague during his time there, and had always wondered if Rowan had. No one had ever been able to determine the nature of her illness, and though Maric had tried everything to help her, he had been forced to watch her wither away before his eyes.

It had been painful. Rowan had been a vital woman, and the slow sapping of her strength had galled her. Toward the end she had become a shadow, wanting nothing more than for the pain to simply stop. Maric had held her skeletal hand and felt his heart break as she had begged him in a cracked and hollow voice for release.

No, perhaps it wasn't so difficult to imagine why the Grey Wardens might prefer to go on this Calling of theirs.

The idea that anyone would make such a sacrifice, however . . . that they would subject themselves to a corruption that would slowly eat away at their bodies solely to combat a menace that hadn't threatened Thedas since the last Blight centuries ago?

But that was why they were here, wasn't it? If the darkspawn were able to use the captured Grey Warden to find their Old God, then a new Blight would begin. Their threat would suddenly become very real. Provided Genevieve and the others were telling him the truth.

The warning of the witch came to mind again, but along with it came Loghain's words as well. It would be easy to believe that the witch meant this event, that she was warning him this would lead to the Blight. But what if she hadn't meant that? What if she had been lying? He had nothing but doubts now, and that made him feel uneasy.

"How do you know her brother is even alive?" he asked. "If he went out into the Deep Roads, there's no way you can tell what's happened to him. Or can Grey Wardens sense that, too?"

Julien remained fixed on the flames, clenching his jaw in disapproval. Nicolas, meanwhile, wrung his hands and glanced nervously to where Genevieve stood on the ridge. She ignored them utterly, watching the cave entrance with her arms crossed and a fiery will shining out of her eyes. Yes, Maric could see why the others might be hesitant to anger their white-haired commander. There was no way to know whether she could actually hear them from where she stood, but he wouldn't put it past her. Obviously neither would they.

"The Commander and her brother were very close," Nicolas whispered. Utha nodded solemnly as if to confirm his words. "During all the time that I have known them, they were seldom far apart. They joined the order together, trained together, practically spent every waking moment together. I think she would have followed him into the Deep Roads, had it also been her time. In fact, I think she might have followed him anyhow, had her duties not held her here."

"So is she chasing false hope, then?"

"She is certain. She has had dreams."

Maric paused, not quite certain he'd heard the man say what he did. "Dreams," he repeated, keeping his voice deliberately neutral. Nicolas nodded, as did the dwarf. Julien shook his head in dismay, frowning. "You're aware of how mad that sounds, surely?"

"We're not mad." Fiona materialized out of the blowing snow, the elf's blue skirts whipping wildly about as she approached the fire carrying a large pack. She put it down next to the log, frowning at Maric coolly. "And neither is Genevieve. Dreams are not always merely dreams."

"And what are they when they're not dreams, then?"

She tapped her chin thoughtfully, perhaps pondering just how she might explain it to him. Or perhaps considering whether she should. That smoldering anger still burned within her dark eyes, just as it had when Maric had spoken to her last. "You've heard of the Fade, I hope?"

He nodded, though not with any confidence. The Fade was the realm of dreams, that place where men were said to go when they slept. It was where spirits and demons roamed, separated from the waking world by something the mages called the Veil. Maric couldn't say that he believed much in the entire concept. He dreamed, like any man, and if those dreams were really his memories of time spent in that realm, as the mages claimed, then he would have to take their word for it.

"There is no geography in the Fade," Fiona continued. "Place and time are far less important than are concepts and symbols. The spirits shape their realm to resemble the things they see in the minds of dreamers because that is what they believe our world is like, and they want desperately to be part of it. So they emulate a landscape that is based more on our perceptions and our feelings than on reality, drawing us in."

"And?" He spread his hands helplessly. "That means nothing to me."

"You dream of those you love because there is a bond between you. The spirits recognize this. That bond has power in the Fade."

"I once dreamed Loghain brought me a barrel of cheese. I opened it up, and there were mice inside. Made of cheese. Which we ate while singing sea chanteys. Are you saying this held some deeper meaning?" He grinned, suddenly amused by the indignant flare of the elf's nostrils. "Perhaps my bond with Loghain told me that he actually harbors a deep love of cheese? I should have realized it sooner."

"And every dream you have is such frivolous nonsense?"

"I have no idea. I forget most of them. Isn't that what happens?"

She tightened the furs around her as if she could somehow squeeze out her anger. The dwarven woman put a calming hand on the mage's leg, but her silent pleas were ignored. "The dreams that are not dreams are visions," Fiona snapped. "Because the Fade is a reflection of our reality as the spirits see it, it may be used to interpret that reality. We mages seek out visions. We look for patterns, and attempt to see the truth beyond our awareness. But a potent-enough vision can come to anyone. When it does, you should pay attention to it."

"Visions," Maric repeated incredulously. "And your commander has had these visions? This is why you're here? No other reason?"

The mage held up a slender hand, and a small orb of fire winked into being above it. It spun slowly, radiating a brilliant energy that lit up the entire camp. He felt a wave of heat across his face. "Visions are surely not so remarkable, King Maric, compared to some of the wonders this world holds." With a twist of her hand, the orb disappeared. The campfire seemed not quite as bright and warm as it had before.

She had a point. The witch had been a mage, as well, but was he to trust everything to magic, then? And visions? He wasn't so sure.

Fiona sat down on her pack, continuing to stare at him with open disapproval. So he busied himself by rubbing his hands and keeping his eyes fixed on the fire. There was a moment of quiet awkwardness among the others that none of them seemed willing to break. Utha looked at the mage with a clear expression of sympathy, though Maric wasn't certain why. The two warriors, meanwhile, struck up another whispered private discussion. Julien's eyes darted between Maric and Fiona, clearly the topic of their conversation, but whatever Nicolas was saying to the man couldn't be made out.

"We believe her," Fiona suddenly announced. It was enough to startle both of the warriors, who stared at her in surprise. Maric didn't look up, though he could feel those big brown elven eyes boring a hole into him. "That is why we are here. What I would be interested in knowing is why *you* are here."

The question hung in the air.

"Don't you want me here?" Maric responded, getting annoyed. "Didn't you come to my court specifically to ask for help? It might have been nice if you'd added that this was all based on a vision one of you had. I'll have to remember to ask more questions next time."

"*She* asked for your help." The elf pointed to Genevieve. "I know why she asked you. I know what she thinks you can do for us. Perhaps you even believed what she said. What I don't know is why you chose to come."

"Isn't defending the kingdom enough reason?"

"To come yourself? To voyage into danger so readily?"

"It was either me or Loghain, wasn't it?"

She thinned her lips, her expression skeptical. "You could have ordered him to accompany us."

"I'm not sure he would have complied."

"I would be willing to wager that he offered to come in your stead, no matter his feelings."

"Clever you."

Fiona paused, her eyes narrowing at him. Maric could feel the tension around the fire, the pair of warriors stiff and uncomfortable as they witnessed the exchange, while the dwarven woman calmly gazed into the campfire. For a moment he thought the elf might abandon her line of questioning, but he was wrong.

"Don't you have a young son?" she asked.

"Cailan. He is nine years old, yes."

"Isn't he without a mother? Perhaps we hear it wrong in Orlais, but my understanding is that the Queen of Ferelden is dead."

He was silent for a long minute, and noticed none of the others offered to change the subject or intervene. Perhaps they wondered the same thing. The thought of Cailan touched a painful place inside him. Like a coward, he'd left Loghain to tell the boy that his father was gone. Cailan would never have understood. His mother had disappeared, and now his father, too? If Maric had gone to tell him, however, he would never have come at all.

"She is," he admitted quietly. "Two years, now."

Fiona's lips pressed together in outrage. "And you feel no shame at depriving him of a father, as well?"

Maric felt the wash of grief tug at him, but he clamped down hard on the feeling. He would rather stick a fork in his eye than give this elven woman with her dark, angry eyes the satisfaction of seeing the pain she was dredging up inside him. "He hasn't had a father for some time now," he answered. His voice sounded flat and hollow, even to himself. "My staying in Denerim wouldn't have changed that."

"So you give up? This is Maric the Savior, the great King of Ferelden?"

Anger flooded through him. He'd thought to halt the witch's prophecy, to act rather than to sit back and wait for it to come true. He thought that perhaps her warning had meant he was supposed to be here, but he hadn't expected this. To be harassed and judged by this brash mage was simply too much. He shot up from the log, wheeling on her. She glared at him defiantly, as if she had every right to ask what she did, and that only served to intensify his rage.

"Maric the Savior," he repeated, spitting the words with contempt. "You know what people call me, so you think you know everything about me? You know how I should feel? You want to tell me what kind of king I should be, and what a terrible father I am?"

Her demeanor softened, but only for a moment. "Why don't you tell me what kind of father you are, then, King Maric?" she asked.

He turned from the fire and stormed several steps away. A blast of icy wind stopped him in his tracks. He let it wash over his skin, closing his eyes. The pounding of his heart slowly subsided, replaced by a familiar silence. It reminded him of those nights when the bustle of the court receded and he retreated to his quarters in the palace, only to be surrounded by a melancholy emptiness

that threatened to swallow him whole. So many days spent surrounded by finery and servants and all the things befitting a king,
but none of it touched him anymore.

How was he supposed to explain that to anyone?

"The truth," he mumbled into the wind, not even caring if those
behind him could hear, "is that I haven't been a father to my son
since his mother died. Every time I look at him, I'm reminded of
her, of all the might-haves and the should-have-beens. He deserves
better than that. He deserves a father who can look him in the
eyes."

Another gust of wind lashed across Maric's face, making him
numb. Numbness was good. He felt a tentative hand touch his elbow, a gesture that startled him a little. He opened his eyes and
turned, and saw the dwarven woman standing there gazing up at
him. Her eyes were full of sympathy, and she silently patted his arm.

"Maric the Savior is just a name, something they call me because they say I saved the kingdom," he told the mage. She remained seated by the fire behind him, not looking his way. "But
the truth is, I've never been able to save anyone."

With that he turned and walked off into the snow, leaving
them behind. The dwarven woman let him go, and if the others
stared after him they said nothing. He no longer cared if the elven
mage was satisfied by his answers. Let her despise him. It wasn't as
if what she accused him of was untrue.

It was dark away from the camp, and Maric found himself
trudging through shadowed drifts. The moon finally came out
from behind the clouds, its silvery radiance against the starkness
of the snow more than enough to light his way. When he crested
a rocky hill, he found his breath taken away by the sight—the entire valley seemed to stretch in front of him, a field of soft white
crowned by a sky full of glittering stars.

It was magnificent. He wasn't sure how long he stood there, his
breath misting as he watched the expanse. It seemed to go on

forever, broken only by the occasional group of pine trees. Why was it he couldn't remember the last time he had looked out over something so beautiful?

This is my kingdom, he thought sadly. *And I don't even know her any longer.*

The sound of quietly crunching snow signaled someone approaching Maric from behind, and he stiffened. "Leave me alone," he muttered without turning around. "Haven't you people questioned me enough already?"

"I apologize if my Wardens have been rude, Maric." It was Genevieve. He shivered in the chill and realized that she must have left her perch to follow him. Perhaps she intended to finish what the others started? "That is no way to address a king. I will remind them of their manners."

"Don't bother," he sighed. He wrapped his fur cloak around him as he turned away from the view. The Commander stood not far away, her white hair fluttering in the wind. He found the hard edge of her appraising gaze unnerving. "I told you all to treat me like a regular person, so I shouldn't be surprised when that's what you do."

Genevieve said nothing, though from her look he knew that she had more on her mind than his discomfort. She gave a curt nod, as if she had come to a decision. "Perhaps it would be better if you returned to your palace, Maric. We would not be able to escort you, I'm afraid, but I suspect you would be safer than if you accompanied us into the Deep Roads."

"You've changed your mind?"

She arched a pale eyebrow. "Have you not changed yours?"

He wasn't sure what to say to that, and for a moment the silence stretched into awkwardness. "I do not blame you if you do not believe in my visions," she finally said, gently enough that Maric was tempted to believe her. "Not even all of the Grey Wardens do. I was told by some that my brother is dead, and that there was nothing that could be done even if that was not the case."

She shrugged and slowly walked toward Maric, standing beside him and looking out over the same valley he had been admiring moments before. Her eyes softened as she scanned the horizon. "It was difficult to let my brother go, when the time came for his Calling. I think, for so many years, we assumed that when it came it would come for us both. I journeyed with him to Orzammar, toasted to his honor with the dwarves, and in the end I stood at the seal and watched him walk out into the shadows." Her voice took on an edge of bitterness. "My brother has always been as much a part of me as my arms. To have him wrenched away from me . . . it was unbearable." She glanced at Maric then, her eyes bright and cold. "But I was the one who counseled him to accept his fate. I stayed. When the first vision came, it felt as if he had reached back across those shadows and touched my heart. I felt him as surely as I feel my arms. I know that it was real."

Maric frowned. A new gust of wind rushed between them. Far off in the distance wolves howled, a lonely sound that only seemed to punctuate the emptiness of the land. "So why didn't you say anything about this?"

Genevieve laughed mirthlessly. "And what would you have said?" She stared at him, her tone completely serious. "I am intent on reaching my brother to prevent the darkspawn from learning what they must not. If it must be, I will kill him myself to prevent that from happening. This is not a rescue mission, Maric. I am not running to my brother's side; I am attempting to prevent a calamity."

She shrugged and looked back over the valley with a sigh. "And if there are those who do not believe as I do, then I will be forced to act without their aid. I do need your help, desperately so. But if you cannot lead us in the Deep Roads, then go . . . return to your son, Maric. No one will blame you for doing so, least of all I."

With that, the Grey Warden commander spun about and marched off. There was no appeal, no farewell. She was gone into the haze of snow within moments, and Maric knew that there would be no further question if he simply picked up his gear and returned to Kinloch Hold. He could be back in Denerim within a couple of days, calling off whatever alarm Loghain was undoubtedly already sounding and seeing his son again as Genevieve had advised.

The thought of Cailan made him pause. Everyone said that the lad looked just like his father, and he supposed that was probably true. The same blond hair, the same nose, and the same smile. But he had his mother's eyes. What would he say, looking into those eyes that would be full of so many questions, asking why he'd left in the first place?

He could imagine what Loghain would say. He would be relieved, and cover it up with irritation at all the trouble Maric had put everyone through.

It was far more difficult to imagine what Rowan would have said. He remembered her best as a warrior, a woman who had helped lead the rebellion to take back the kingdom from the Orlesians. She'd had an indomitable spirit until the sickness had taken her, and in many ways he had always considered her far stronger than him. They'd restored the kingdom together, but it had always been she who knew immediately when something was worth doing or needed abandoning.

He tried to imagine that Rowan would have urged him to return to their son. As a mother, surely she would have considered Cailan more important than any other consideration. Trouble was, he just couldn't believe it. He could picture her sitting in her favorite chair by the window in their chambers, brown curls cascading around her pale skin. She would have put down her book and looked at him, puzzled.

"You're back?" she'd have asked him, more accepting than surprised.

"Yes, I'm back."

"Didn't you think going was important?"

"Our son is more important than saving the kingdom, Rowan."

And then she'd have smiled at him with amusement, tilting her head in that way that told him she expected him to know better. "I wasn't talking about saving the kingdom, you silly little man." Her tone was full of affection, something that had grown over the years of their marriage and yet which he had never felt particularly worthy of. She held out her hand from her chair and he walked to take it . . .

. . . and then the image fled, and Maric was left with nothing but moonlight and blowing snow once again. His heart ached. It seemed to him like it had been forever since he had been able to remember what Rowan looked like. His memories had become maddeningly fleeting over the last two years, replaced by impressions and smells and snippets of conversation. Just then, however, she had seemed so *real*.

Much like a vision.

He smirked at the irony of the thought, especially considering the fact that he wasn't even asleep. Unless, of course, he *was* asleep, having fallen into some deep snowbank after wandering away from the camp, and was currently freezing to death while blissfully dreaming away. The Grey Wardens would maybe search for him come morning, and then look at each other and shrug, assuming that he'd decided to return to Denerim without a good-bye. They'd enter the Deep Roads, and come spring some travelers would perhaps find his remains half hidden in the mud. Probably steal his boots, too.

It was an intriguing thought. But what were the odds?

With a deep sigh, he began to walk back to the Grey Warden camp.

5

And down they fled into darkness and despair.
—Canticle of Threnodies 8:28

With the first light of dawn, a bloom of pink and orange, barely peeking over the horizon, the Grey Wardens arrayed themselves in front of the Deep Roads entrance with weapons drawn. Duncan tensed as King Maric approached the door. Without fanfare, he produced a stone medallion shaped like an octagon and inserted it into a similarly shaped depression in the center of the door. A loud crack shattered the quiet, startling a small flock of ravens nearby into sudden flight.

He watched as a line formed in the middle of the door. It became a crack, and then widened as the door split. The King stepped back cautiously. Slowly, with the sound of stone grinding heavily against stone, it opened up to reveal the gaping maw of the tunnel beyond it. A faint stench of decay belched forth from the shadows.

They waited. Duncan almost expected a horde of monsters to come rushing out at them, but none materialized. There was only silence.

The group began to step into the cave, but paused as Julien spoke. "Wait," he said softly. The dark-haired warrior crossed his hands in front of his chest and bowed his head, and several of the other Wardens followed suit. Duncan lowered his head and coughed. Prayer always made him nervous.

"*Though all before me is shadow,*" Julien intoned, "*yet shall the Maker be my guide. I shall not be left to wander the drifting roads of the Beyond, for there is no darkness in the Maker's Light and nothing He has wrought shall be lost.*"

"Amen," Maric whispered, and the others nodded.

Then they entered the Deep Roads.

There was a wide stairway that began not far within, and Duncan suppressed a shudder as they descended. It was warmer inside, he was thankful for that much, but the cold had been replaced by an unease that he just couldn't shake. It was like slowly walking into a pool of filth, the stink of it filling your nostrils and turning your stomach so that you had to will yourself to take another step.

The other Grey Wardens could feel it, too. He could see it in their grave expressions and in the way their hands tightened on their weapons. All of them possessed the ability to sense the dark-spawn, yet it seemed impossible that the creatures would stand out amid all the background corruption he sensed here. Genevieve re-assured them quietly that it was still so, but Duncan remained un-convinced. Probably she was just trying to ensure they didn't lose their nerve.

Only Maric couldn't sense anything, yet he seemed more af-fected by their descent than anyone else. He became withdrawn, his eyes darting to every dark corner and his skin ashen in the flick-ering torchlight. Duncan was tempted to ask the man what had happened to him in the Deep Roads so long ago ut decided against it. Clearly it was nothing pleasant.

They followed the stairway for what seemed like hours when the first signs of corruption became visible along the stone walls of the passage: spidery tendrils of black rot, along with a shiny film that covered everything like oil. Duncan touched it, curious, and found that the film wasn't actually wet. It was dry, with a tex-ture like snakeskin.

Genevieve snatched his hand away with a harsh look and warned him not to touch anything again. That confused him a little. Were they not immune to the darkspawn taint? Was that not one of the few benefits they received for being Grey Wardens?

"We didn't see it this early," Maric said, examining the walls more closely. "Last time we were down here, I don't think we saw anything like this until after Ortan thaig."

"Then it has spread," Genevieve pronounced.

Kell glanced around the passage with his unnaturally pale eyes. Duncan knew he was even more sensitive to the darkspawn than the rest of them. To him this must be like drinking sewage, and yet he gave no indication that it bothered him. "Almost to the surface?" he asked. "What does that mean?"

"It means we should be careful." With that, she drew her sword and continued down the stairs. The others shared uncomfortable looks but followed after.

It seemed to take forever before they hit the bottom, or at least what Duncan assumed to be the bottom. The feel of the weight pressing down from above and the oppressive darkness pressing in from all sides made him want to gasp for air. He felt trapped under fetid water, desperately clawing for the surface.

Fiona, walking next to him, regarded him with a concerned look. "Are you going to be all right? You look a bit sickly," she whispered.

He gulped a few times and forced himself to breathe. It wasn't exactly pleasant. "I feel like I'm going to vomit."

"Well, there's a cheerful thought."

"I'm serious! Can't you feel that?"

"We can all feel it. Well, most of us can." Her tone hinted at annoyance, and Duncan realized that she was talking about Maric. The man was walking up ahead next to Utha, oblivious to the scathing glare he was receiving from behind.

He smirked. "I heard you had it out with the King last night at the camp."

"I asked him a simple question."

"It didn't sound simple from what Genevieve said," he chuckled. "I'm just glad she was mad at somebody other than me for once."

Fiona sighed irritably. Raising her staff, she closed her eyes and murmured something under her breath. Duncan could feel the prickle of power surging through the air, and immediately the small globe on top of the staff began to glow. The light was strong and warm, stretching throughout the corridor and driving back the shadows just a little.

The others turned and looked at the mage curiously. "Don't waste your power," Genevieve said, but her words lacked her usual crispness. Even she was probably relieved to have the shadows driven back a little farther, he imagined.

"There." Fiona smiled at Duncan, pleased with herself. "Better?"

"Sure, except for the blinding light in my eyes."

"Now you're just being a child."

With the added light from Fiona's staff, Duncan could make out impressions in the wall behind the rot and decay. Runes, he suspected. Dwarven runes, though to what purpose he couldn't really guess. He'd been told once that the dwarves held a reverence for stone. Perhaps the words they carved into the walls of the Deep Roads were prayers? Prayers now tainted by filth; it had a certain symmetry, didn't it?

He could feel the darkspawn out there now. Genevieve was right. It just took some time to become acclimated. They were at the edge of his consciousness, lurking in the shadows far out of sight. It was that same feeling when someone was standing behind you, and you didn't hear them or sense them in any way; you just *knew*.

Could they feel the Grey Wardens in return? According to the First Enchanter, the onyx brooches they'd been given would render them invisible to the darkspawn senses, but Duncan wasn't so certain. His was pinned to his leather jerkin, and he turned it about to examine it more closely in the light. There were iridescent colors that slowly flowed just beneath the surface like a liquid. It was also cold, like touching a frosty lamppost in the dead of winter. He let it go, rubbing warmth back into his fingers absently.

"So did Genevieve make you apologize?" he asked Fiona.

The mage looked at him, puzzled. Her mind had clearly been elsewhere, but when she realized he was referring to King Maric, she rolled her eyes in annoyance. She had pretty eyes for an elf, he thought. Most elves Duncan had known always possessed such eerie eyes—light greens and purples, impossible hues that somehow made them seem alien. Fiona's eyes were dark and expressive. Soulful, his mother might have said. She'd always had a way with words.

"No, she didn't," the mage said curtly. "And I've no need to."

"He's not so bad, you know."

"You can't know that. You hardly know him any better than I do."

"Is it an elven thing? I knew a lot of elves back in Val Royeaux, and every one of them had a chip on their shoulders. Even the ones that didn't come from the alienage."

She shot him an incredulous look. "It's not as if we don't have a good reason to be bitter, you know."

"Yes, yes, I know. We terrible humans destroyed the Dales. One of the elves I knew fancied himself a Dalish elf, even painted up his face to look like them. I thought he'd finally gone off to the forests to search for one of their clans, but it turned out he'd gotten himself arrested. Anyway, he used to talk about the Dales all the time."

She stopped, stamping her staff down onto the stone so that the globe flashed brightly for a moment. Her exasperation with him was obvious. "There's more to it than that. Far more! Don't you even know?"

"Know what? That your people were enslaved? Everyone knows that."

"There was a time"—her eyes flashed crossly—"when elves lived forever. Did you know that, as well? We spoke our own language, built magnificent wonders across all of Thedas, had our own homeland—and this was long before the Dales ever existed."

"And then you were enslaved."

"By the magisters of the Tevinter Imperium, yes. Just one of their crimes, and probably not even their greatest." Fiona turned away from Duncan and ran a slender hand across the corruption covering a nearby wall. "They took everything from us that was beautiful. They even made us forget what we once were. It wasn't until the prophet Andraste released us that we even realized what we had lost."

"And she was human, wasn't she? We're not all so bad."

"Her own people burned her at the stake."

"I meant the rest of us."

She looked back at him, smiling gamely even though her eyes were tinged with sadness. "Andraste gave us the Dales, a new homeland to replace the old. But your people took that away from us, too, in the end. Now we either live in your cities as vermin or wander as outlaws, but either way we're unwanted."

Duncan smirked mockingly at her. "Aww. Poor elves."

The mage swung her still-glowing staff at his head, but he danced aside, laughing merrily. The sound seemed odd in the gloom. "Not sympathetic enough, I suppose?" He grinned. "I grew up on the streets, so if you were looking for reassurance on how good us humans really have it, you aren't going to get it from me."

"You did ask," she reminded him.

"About the King I did." He pointed at the others, who now had gotten ahead of them. Fiona noticed it, too, and began hurrying to catch up. He kept pace. "Those things you talked about . . . they happened so long ago hardly anybody who doesn't keep their nose stuck in a book would even know half of them. Elves aren't just slaves anymore."

"You think so?" Her look was dark, her tone suddenly brittle.

"Do you think slavery just up and disappeared that day for every one of us?"

"Even so, I'm pretty sure King Maric had nothing to do with any of it."

She nodded, her eyes fixed on the blond king where he walked far up ahead. As if sensing the scrutiny, the man stopped and glanced back in puzzlement. She didn't avert her gaze, and he sheepishly decided it was best to turn his attention elsewhere. "I know that." She nodded. "Do you think I don't know that?"

"You're smart, so I'm guessing you know that?"

She sighed wearily. "He thinks his life is difficult."

"Maybe it is. I sure wouldn't want to be a king."

"Why not?" Fiona frowned at Duncan, her anger rekindled. "Think of what you could do as king. You could do so much. You could change *everything*."

He laughed derisively. "I was raised on the streets, and even I know that kings can't do everything." He began to walk ahead, and Fiona stayed where she was, watching him go. "I don't know what it is you think he should be doing, but maybe you should tell him about it instead of me. Now I'm going to go and see if he needs anything. He'll probably send me to fetch a chamber pot."

"Has he sent you for a single one yet?" she laughed.

"He could start. If you keep glaring at him all the time, he'll probably need one."

More hours passed as they pressed farther into the Deep Roads. The signs of darkspawn corruption gradually became worse. Pools of brackish water filled portions of the halls, and Kell warned them not to touch any of it. A quick command to Hafter and the hound backed off, wisely deciding against slaking his thirst. Duncan was inclined to agree. There were bones of . . . things . . . floating in those pools. Something moved in the water that might have been worms, but he didn't want to think about it too closely.

The funguslike growths on the walls got thicker, as well. There were mounds of it, some looking like great misshapen beehives with dark tendrils radiating outward. The growths were covered in that same slick substance, like a putrid oil. Sometimes the stench of it got so thick it clouded the air and all but choked the torches. They gagged on it, and only at Maric's urging did they continue on.

He seemed to think they were headed in the right direction. Several times they had passed branches, and only at the first had the king hesitated. It was not, Duncan noticed, to figure out where they were supposed to go. His eyes were far away, lost in some memory he didn't speak of. When he finally spoke and pointed the way, he seemed quite certain.

Duncan wondered what lay in those other directions. One way looked much like the others here, and he wasn't all that sure just how the king was telling them apart. Those memories of his must be quite clear. If so, then maybe Genevieve was right to insist he come. If they'd accidentally gone down one of those other passages, who knows where they might have ended up?

They had reached the remains of a dwarven way station when Genevieve called for a halt. There was little left of the building aside from a hint of mortar walls and some crumbling tools, but the rest of them knew the Commander hadn't stopped them to admire the area.

They were getting closer to the darkspawn. The fact that they were also nearing Ortan thaig, according to Maric, wasn't lost on them, either. Duncan could feel the teeming masses of them ahead, like they were slowly approaching a black pit full of eyes all trained on him. The very idea filled him with a fear that twisted up his insides into a knot. His experience with the darkspawn was minimal, and now he was willingly venturing into a place where he would encounter more of them than he ever wanted to. It was a terrifying notion.

The tents were put up without discussion, within the boundaries of where the way station once stood. Here the dwarves had probably once stopped travelers in the Deep Roads, inspecting their goods or perhaps taxing them. Or maybe the station was built to watch for invaders? He really had no idea. When the First Blight struck, it had hit the dwarves the hardest. The darkspawn had swallowed up the Deep Roads, and the dwarves had retreated all the way to Orzammar, sealing up all entrances to the tunnels and leaving everyone stuck on the other side of those seals to their fate.

What must it have been like, to have realized that there was no escape? To have the darkspawn wash over you like a tidal wave, drowning everything in their path and wiping out almost an entire culture? The dwarves apparently never doubted that the Blight could return again, and had always afforded the Grey Wardens far more respect than anyone else. His own people were less dependable, naturally. They tended to forget what wasn't right in front of their faces.

Not that Duncan was better than the rest of humanity, judging them from his high perch. Far from it. He'd simply seen enough in his time that he could imagine with a fair degree of accuracy just what humanity was capable of. On most days he'd say that a Blight washing over the surface might not be such a bad thing, swallowing up humanity and perhaps belching and spitting it out for good measure.

Maybe he should sit down and make up a list of all the good things that would get destroyed at the same time—like cookies. The darkspawn would wipe out all cookies from the face of Thedas. That would be bad, and alone made this entire endeavor seem more worthwhile.

"Why are we stopping already?" Maric asked him, approaching quietly from behind. Duncan noticed that the man looked a bit feverish in the torchlight, sweaty and pale. The Deep Roads did not seem to be agreeing with him much. But then, who would they agree with, exactly?

"We'll be on the darkspawn soon. A lot of them."

"Really? I don't— Oh."

"We can sense them ahead," Duncan reminded him. "I expect the next bit is going to get exciting." He tried to sound braver than he felt.

Genevieve paced at the edge of the camp relentlessly, and her tension slowly infected the rest of them. There was little talk, and after the others had eaten their meal of dried rations and flat wine they had huddled closely around the small campfire—something that the Commander only reluctantly allowed. None of them wanted to admit that despite their exhaustion, the idea of closing their eyes while surrounded by that oppressive darkness was almost unbearable. The flames were warm and bright, and it was a little easier to pretend that they were not miles under the earth in their presence.

Even so, it didn't take long for the gloom to settle over them like a pall.

Julien and Nicolas played an Orlesian game on a large rock, something that required ivory pieces moved around on a checkered board. Duncan had seen the wealthy playing it from time to time, but had no idea what the rules might be or what it was even called. It seemed to require intense concentration, the two warriors furrowing their brows a great deal and stroking their chins quietly.

It was a game that suited the pair, probably. Duncan had thought them brothers when he first joined the order, but it turned out they were just comrades that preferred each other's company, and mostly kept to themselves. Duncan had rarely heard Julien speak more than a handful of words, and it was usually to calm Nicolas down.

That was something Julien could do when almost nobody else could. There was a gentleness to his manner that contrasted sharply with Nicolas's brusqueness and quick temper.

Kell sat across from Duncan, solemnly carving more arrows with his belt knife. His quiver was already full, yet still he applied himself to the task. No doubt he thought he'd need all the arrows he had and more soon—he was probably right. Hafter crouched next to his master, gazing up at him adoringly and probably wishing that he could somehow help with his task.

The rest of them just stared into the flames. Every time Genevieve paced past them, everyone froze. It wasn't anything overt: Julien and Nicolas paused in their playing, deliberately not looking up from their board, and the others held their breath. Her steel gaze washed over them and then moved on. She didn't say it outright, but it was obvious she thought it would be better simply to pick up the camp and keep traveling if no one was going to sleep.

It slowly became unbearable. Duncan's body cried out for sleep, and he found himself nodding off several times only to jerk himself back up. The fire was blissfully warm, the only source of anything decent in this Maker-forsaken place. He wanted to pick it up and hug it close. Maybe that would warm him up and stop the shuddering, which was now almost constant.

"Are you all right?" Fiona asked him, the sound of her voice initially a shock. He turned and stared at her fuzzily, at first not quite absorbing what she had said, before he finally nodded. "Would you like to play a game?" she offered. "I have some cards in my pack; I could dig them out if you—"

"No." He shuddered again, almost a spasm, and rubbed his hands vigorously next to the fire. The others stopped and stared at him, exchanging quiet looks.

"Are you sure?"

"Yes! I'm sure!"

The quiet descended again, and Duncan almost regretted his refusal. He rubbed his hands even more by the flames, noting how remarkably pale they were. *Funny*, he thought. *I spent half my life wishing I could be pale just like all the other children, and it turned out all I needed to do was freeze to death in the Deep Roads.*

"Perhaps I should build the fire up more," Kell offered.

"I'm fine!" Duncan snapped.

He could feel Fiona staring anxiously at him, though she hesitated to speak. So he wrapped his arms around himself and leaned close to the flames, trying not to look as miserable as he felt. From the awkwardness he felt around him, he doubted he was very successful.

"You know," Maric suddenly spoke up, warming his hands in the fire beside Duncan, "back during the rebellion, we had a ritual the night before a battle. We would pass around some dwarven ale. See who could take the largest swig."

Utha grinned and made a gesture with her hands. Kell paused in his whittling, his look bemused. "She says that's not really ale."

"You're telling me! I think they make it from fungus. It's black as pitch!"

Duncan groaned. "You drank that?"

The King winked at him and reached into his cloak, drawing forth a large silver flask. The dwarven rune emblazoned on the side of it was clear for everyone to see, and a few whistles of appreciation floated around the fire. Even Julien and Nicolas were interested now, grinning as Maric opened it up. The smell of something sickly sweet filled the air, like a skunk that had crawled under a shed to die and slowly rot in the heat.

Fiona laughed, covering her mouth with a hand. "Oh, that's foul!"

"My mother started the tradition," Maric said, lifting the flask to his nose and taking a sniff. He sighed in delight, as if the odor was wonderful and not putrid in the slightest. "She'd met up with a dwarf that had crossed the Orlesians. I think I was fifteen. I forget his name. Curliest beard I'd ever seen. Anyhow, he traveled with us for a time and he gave us an entire keg of dwarven ale as a gift."

The man's smile suddenly became fond, his eyes sad. Duncan had to think to remember that the mother the King spoke of had been murdered—right in front of him, so the story went. He wondered if that was true. "None of the men wanted it, but Mother was so stubborn she refused to waste anything, especially a gift. So the next night before battle, she brought out the keg and dunked a cup inside. Drank the entire thing in front of all her commanders, and then dared them to do the same."

He laughed then, a hearty and joyous laugh that slowly became tinged with sadness as it trailed off. Hesitating only a second, he brought the flask to his lips and took a long swig. Duncan felt his nose crinkling in disgust as the King gulped not once but twice, and then stopped, smiling madly as he made a satisfied "Ahhhh!" sound.

Utha made an impressed gesture. "I agree," said Nicolas.

"I was the last one to drink that first night." Maric smiled, his voice strained as if the ale had stripped his throat raw. "I had one sip and I vomited all over the campfire." He turned and offered the flask to Kell with a slight raise of his eyebrow.

The hunter regarded it dubiously, and then with the slightest sigh he put down his half-completed arrow and his belt knife and accepted the flask. He held it to his forehead and bowed in the King's direction, a gesture of thanks.

"I trained with the Ash Warriors," the hunter said. He stared into the flask as if he was certain that something was going to crawl out of it. "They believe it is necessary that one die before battle. If you cannot see your death and acknowledge it, it will take you unawares. Before my first battle, they bled me with shallow cuts and then salted my wounds until I finally screamed in agony." He grinned suddenly. Duncan had never seen the solemn man actually smile before, now that he thought of it. "When I did, they all laughed. They had taken bets, you see, to see how long I would endure."

Kell took a long swig, and merely wiped his mouth afterwards without any indication whether he liked the taste or not. "My lesson was not to do everything your comrades tell you to simply because they find it amusing. A lesson I obviously did not learn very well." He winked at Utha and passed the flask to her.

The copper-haired dwarf examined the rune on the flask carefully. She made several hand gestures toward Maric.

"She says the rune is . . . I can't decipher that, sorry," Nicolas said, confused.

"It's the mark of House Aeducan," Maric stated. "King Endrin gave it to me."

Utha appeared impressed. She took a long drink, gulping several times, and when she finished she lowered the flask and paused before letting out a long and completely unladylike belch that reverberated around the cavern.

Smiling proudly, she made gestures that Nicolas again translated. "I cannot taste it, of course, but I remember this foul brew well enough. My father loved it, and belched after every drink because he knew it annoyed my mother. He had to hide the bottles from her, and she would always send me to find them. I always did. He used to call me Little Spoilsport."

Kell gave her a serious look. "You've never spoken of your parents."

She nodded sadly. "They died. Darkspawn."

With that, she passed the flask to Nicolas, who eyed it warily. "My parents threw me out of their home when I was barely a man. I lied to the seneschal at Fortalan to get him to accept me into one of the outlier units. The first time we headed into battle, I was so frightened I wet my tunic."

Julien's eyes went wide with delighted shock. "You didn't!"

"I did. After the battle, I was called Puddle. The name stuck." He took a swig and his face twisted with pure disgust. "That's awful! Why would anyone drink that?" He quickly handed it to Julien.

The dark-eyed warrior frowned. "I have no amusing tale," he said in his quiet voice. The man's Orlesian accent was pronounced. Not for the first time, Duncan wondered if Julien was originally part of the Empire's aristocracy. If so, he had to wonder just what had brought the man into the Grey Wardens. Duncan's experience with Orlesian nobility told him that they rarely paid heed to such quaint notions as duty, but perhaps he shouldn't paint them all with the same brush?

"Sure you do," Nicolas teased him.

"No, I don't."

"What about that night in Val Mort? Before the darkspawn raid?"

Julien blushed, glancing at the others as if he wished he could crawl away somewhere. "That's not an appropriate tale, Nicolas. And it wasn't my doing."

Nicolas roared with amused laughter. "The others bought him an elven whore!" He paused, looking at the mage across the fire. "Apologies, Fiona."

She snorted. "Whatever. Your mother was a whore."

"So she was!" He looked back at Julien, taking great pleasure in his friend's discomfort. "He'd made the mistake of telling us he'd never been with a woman, see. So we made sure to fix *that* before he faced darkspawn for the first time."

Julien's face was crimson. "She was a sweet girl."

"She robbed him blind! Took all his coin and ran out the window."

The quiet warrior grinned then, nodding even through his embarrassment. "She was still a sweet girl." He took a long swig, shuddered at the evil taste, and then attempted to pass it to Fiona.

The mage declined. "I'm not drinking that."

"Oh, come on," Duncan urged her.

She grudgingly relented. Taking the flask, she held her nose and took the slightest sip. Immediately she gasped and began convulsing and making retching noises. Flailing with the flask, she tried to pawn it off on Duncan, and he took it from her while laughing. The elf fought hard not to vomit, and the others joined in the merriment.

"Oh, very kind," she finally gasped, her voice raspy. "Thank you for finding it so bloody funny that I've been poisoned!"

"Poor Fiona," Nicolas chided her. "Such a delicate flower."

"Go hump your horse." She giggled and wiped her mouth several times, as if that could remove the memory of the taste. "Ach! It's like liquid death."

Duncan smirked at her. "That was quite the show you put on there."

"No show required. Taste it yourself and you'll find out."

"Uh-huh," he said disbelievingly. He let the subject drop and turned his attention to the flask, giving it a prudent sniff. That was a bad idea. He flinched, his nose twitching like it had been set on fire. "I'm not sure I want to, now."

"You have to," Maric chuckled. "We all did."

Not everyone. Duncan glanced over at Genevieve, who stood off at the edge of the ruined outpost. She leaned against one of the walls, her back toward them. She had to hear them laughing and carrying on. Part of him wanted to call her over, invite her to join them. But she would refuse, naturally.

"I've never been in any big battle," he said, "but there was this one night where we were preparing to rob the Marquis . . . oh, I forget his name now. Wealthy bastard, though. Lots of guards, too, which made robbing his manse very risky."

Utha made a disapproving face.

"What?" he protested. "We were poor! He was rich! It was only fair."

"Sounds fair to me," Fiona laughed.

"So we were going to head out, all of us nervous and sweating like a bunch of elven whores in a chantry—"

"What is *with* all the elven whores?" Fiona complained.

"—and I remembered that I forgot my rope. So I ran down the steps to get it and I slipped. Fell down an entire flight of stairs and landed on a cat."

"You landed on a *cat*." Maric stared at him incredulously.

"A big cat. He was a local one, lived on the streets and chased dogs. We used to call him Rabbit."

Kell cocked an eyebrow. "Why Rabbit?"

"It had big ears; I don't know. Anyway, it scratched me so badly I was furious. I chased that thing down four city blocks, throwing stones at it. Little bastard was fast. Then I fell into a well."

"A well," Nicolas repeated.

Duncan shrugged. "I was a lot less graceful back then." He smiled ruefully at the memory. "The others didn't know where I'd gone, and I sat in that well for three days until a guardsman heard me yelling and pulled me up. Threw me in the gaol for the night, but at least I got a meal out of it." He chuckled, and it trailed off into a sigh. "Stupid cat."

"Didn't the others come looking for you?" Fiona asked.

He shook his head. "They died. Somebody tipped the Marquis off and all his guards were waiting for them. I was lucky I wasn't there, or at least I thought I was. Because only I survived, all the other guilders thought I was the one who'd tipped him off." There was a subdued silence at that, but Duncan merely grinned and raised the flask to the others. "To lost friends."

"To lost friends," they chimed in. He braced himself and took a swallow of the dwarven ale. It was like choking back the leather sole of an old and sweaty shoe that had been pounded into paste until it was slightly watery and grey. The others stared as he tilted the flask back, and after a series of audible glugs he finished it off.

The others clapped, impressed. Duncan handed the King back his flask, suddenly feeling very ill and shaky.

"Brave lad," Maric said.

"Thanks," Duncan grunted. After a moment he lurched to his feet and ran off to the corner of the ruin to vomit everything in his stomach onto the stones. Then he heaved a bit more, as the others grinned with amusement.

When the heaving was finally done, he looked back and gave them a saucy grin and a victorious thumbs-up. They applauded him vigorously, and he had to admit he was pretty damned pleased with himself.

He noticed, too, the appreciative look that Fiona shot King Maric. The man just shrugged it off with a shy smile.

Genevieve left her spot by the wall and walked back to her tent, sitting down on a large rock just outside. Duncan watched as she began taking out her weapons and laying them out around her for cleaning. It was a ritual he had watched her do often in the months that he'd known her.

The Commander paused and ran a hand through her white hair, yawning. She looked exhausted, he thought—not just physically but emotionally. She seemed aged, too, like her years were rapidly catching up with her. He supposed the thought of following after her brother when she had already written him off as dead must be difficult.

Duncan had never met Bregan, having joined the order months after the man had left for his Calling. He knew plenty about the man by reputation, however. His presence had lingered among the Grey Wardens long after his departure. His sister mentioned him often. The others had spoken of him, as well, and far more enthusiastically. Duncan always had the impression that most felt Genevieve didn't measure up to her brother as Commander, though it was never spoken of openly.

"Duncan," Genevieve remarked wearily, noticing him staring at her. She rested her head in her hand. "What are you doing?"

He wandered over to her, leaving the others behind. He could hear them talking again, Kell noisily stoking the campfire to keep it going. "I just thought these dwarven ruins might like some of their ale more than I did," he said with a wink.

She chuckled, and then took stock of some of the weapons she had laid out. The sword was the most impressive of the bunch, an elaborate two-handed blade that sparkled even though they were well away from the fire. Its magical runes were almost invisible, but one could make them out in the darkness. It had been her brother's, she'd told him once, handed over when he left into the Deep Roads.

Then she paused, and it seemed as if she remembered something awkward. "Ah. About what happened back at the tower . . ."

"It was just a girl!" he protested, the blush already creeping into his cheeks. He just knew she would bring this up eventually, and already had a defense all planned. "Surely *that* isn't against the Grey Wardens' rules as well, is it?"

Genevieve arched a brow, her look one of clear disbelief. "So you followed the girl up there, did you? In order to lie with her?"

"It's what . . . young men do, right? Or so I hear."

"Mm-hmm."

"What? It could happen."

She leaned back, folding her arms and fixing him with a level gaze. Duncan knew that look. It was the sort of look that could lead to things like getting one's head smacked against walls. "So what were you *actually* doing up there, prior to your . . . run-in with the young woman?"

He sighed in exasperation. "Looking around for something to steal."

Her eyes narrowed. "From the mages? Are you mad?"

"No risk, no reward. That's what I keep telling myself, anyhow."

Her face tensed, and it looked like she had a few things she was going to tell him herself. But then she waved them away with a flash of annoyance. He supposed it didn't mean much where they were, especially well after the fact. "At least you weren't caught," she muttered. "Though the flagrant risks you take are completely unacceptable."

"We're all going to die, right?" He chuckled, but he was only half joking. "Whether I die now or later doesn't seem all that risky to me." Genevieve picked up on his tone right away, and her expression darkened. She said nothing and nodded gravely, her attention returning to her sword.

Duncan supposed it was a little unfair to throw that in her face. She was far closer to her Calling than he was, and no doubt acutely aware that whatever happened down here, she would be following the path of her brother soon enough. He turned to go.

"Wait," Genevieve called after him. "I think it's time to explain your duty to you."

He paused. "My duty? Watching after the King? Is there more to it than that?"

Her mouth thinned into a grim line, and Duncan's flippant mood evaporated. She was utterly serious now. He moved in a little closer and crouched down near where she sat. She barely noticed him, formulating the proper words in her head.

"It's entirely possible," she said slowly, "that what we do here will fail. You know what the Grey Wardens thought of all this. They don't believe Bregan has been captured, none of it."

"I believe it," Duncan averred. He meant it, too. Genevieve could be many things, but in the short time he had known her, foolish and gullible were neither of those things. If those who had known her longer denied her visions for their own reasons, more fools they.

She nodded at him, her eyes showing a flash of gratitude. "The point is that we could die. There are only a few of us here, and despite what any of us believe, the chances of us actually finding Bregan before the darkspawn realize we are here and react is small."

"What do you want me to do?"

"If something has truly changed within the darkspawn, the threat of a Blight occurring is great indeed. If we cannot stop them from taking that information from Bregan, my job will be to assess the likelihood of them using it. At that point, your job will be to get King Maric back to the surface."

"By myself?"

She nodded. "You're stealthy. The King far less so, but you know better than any of us how to move unseen. I'm counting on you to take him."

"Don't you mean Kell? He's a hunter, he could—"

"I'm counting on *you*," she reiterated.

He gulped. Tall order, that.

"His nation will need him," she continued. Genevieve picked up her blade and balanced it lightly on her knee. She ran an admiring finger down its length, seemingly fascinated by the details etched into its steel. "They will need a leader who has seen the threat of the Blight firsthand, who believes in it. King Maric could help alert all of Thedas and bring the Grey Wardens great credibility in whatever follows."

"But what if . . . ?" Duncan let his question hang, feeling guilty even for thinking it.

"There is also the possibility that I'm wrong," Genevieve stated evenly, finishing his thought without any sense of accusation. She glanced up at Duncan, eyes dangerous. "That Bregan is dead, and I've made a terrible error in bringing us here. Or something worse."

"Worse?"

"If what King Maric learns could harm the Grey Wardens, could make us look like fools and prevent us from carrying out our duty, then you must make certain he never reaches the surface at all."

Duncan gasped in disbelief. "You mean . . . ?"

She held her chin thoughtfully, her thoughts distant. "He may try to escape. Whatever his reasons for joining us, however, the die is cast. If he must disappear down here in order for us to claim whatever story we wish on the surface, then that is what we must do." Noticing Duncan's wide-eyed look, she affixed him with a steely stare. "Consider the situation: There is a danger here, but I do not know what that danger encompasses, or what someone like Maric might learn in the process. We have a higher duty, Duncan. The Grey Wardens protect the entire world, not just one small nation."

He nodded slowly, his heart racing inside his chest. "I . . . I understand."

Genevieve smiled compassionately, if sadly. She reached out and placed a comforting hand on his shoulder. "I know you can do this. I am counting on you to see it through, if it comes to that."

He nodded again, uncertain what he should say, if anything.

She let her hand drop. "Go. Get some sleep. Tomorrow we will have more immediate matters to think about, yes?"

Tomorrow they headed into the lion's den.

Nodding breathlessly to the Commander, Duncan turned and left before she could say anything else. She trusted him, *him*, to watch the King in more senses than just the one. She wanted him to do it, and not Kell or Fiona or anyone else.

Probably because he was capable of murder, and she knew that. The thought settled coldly onto his heart. It didn't repel him, however. He knew the Grey Wardens weren't out to do anything more than defeat the darkspawn, no matter what it took. Sometimes that meant doing terrible things.

If it came to it, he would murder King Maric. He wondered if even Fiona, who expressed such dislike for the man, was capable of that. Probably not. For all her anger, she was a good person.

While he was not.

6

Maker, my enemies are abundant.
Many are those who rise up against me.
But my faith sustains me; I shall not fear the legion,
Should they set themselves against me.

—Canticle of Trials 1:1

Bregan couldn't be sure how much time passed in his cell. His mind was often clouded by a haze of pain, and he would drift in and out of sleep without any reference to mark whether a day had passed or a night. The hours had become fluid, lost to the darkness and despair he found himself submerged within.

Often when he awoke from his restless sleep, there would be a moment of confusion when he thought he might actually still be at the Grey Warden fortress in Montsimmard, that the ordeal of his captivity had all been but an unpleasant nightmare. A part of him waited for the familiar smells of the cypress and linen, searched for the faint moonlight coming through the shutters in his chambers, even though the rest of him knew better. Perhaps it was his mind hoping beyond hope, refusing to accept his circumstances.

It was strange to him, for if he had been asked he would have said he associated no fond memories with the fortress, despite it having been his home for so many years. Being part of the Grey Wardens was not something that had brought him joy. It had not been a misery, precisely, but rather a life he had *endured*. He had not resisted the pull that had brought him down that path, but neither had he walked it willingly.

The idea that now his mind yearned to send him back there seemed to him almost like a sick joke.

Genevieve would have argued with him. She had always believed their position within the Grey Wardens to be a great honor. The day he had been made Commander of the Grey, her eyes had shone with quiet pride while he had somehow felt smothered, trapped. Still he had done it, assumed the command and the responsibilities that came with it while his sister shook her head at what she perceived as his obstinacy.

And somehow it had translated into popularity among the men he had commanded. Bregan had never seen himself as being particularly more worthy than any of them. They had all made the same sacrifice as he, all taken that foulness into themselves just as he had, to fight against a threat that most of humanity thought was long past. He sought out no distinction for himself, and readily passed on the accolades offered by his superiors to those men who were actually deserving of them, and for that the Grey Wardens had loved him.

Genevieve had never understood that, either. His sister was all stiffness and duty, and she erected a barrier between herself and those she commanded. Bregan was the only one she let past that, and there were times he knew she resented his popularity. She thought he sought it out, that he deliberately cultivated their loyalty, and refused to believe him when he said that wasn't true.

Perhaps it was because that was what she would have done? Perhaps his sister had always craved popularity among the other Wardens, and would have gone to great lengths to get it if she thought it was possible to achieve. They both knew that would never be, however. People were like weapons to her, a means to an end. She preferred them to be equally hard, unyielding, and predictable, and was always surprised when they were anything but.

Knowing that she would need to carry on as Commander after him had been almost more difficult than any other reality visited upon him by the Calling. It would have killed Genevieve to see the men mourn, and to know that when her time came in the near future they would never mourn her in the same way.

The thought of his sister jarred him into the present. He'd dreamed of Genevieve as he slept, a haze full of pain and delirium, but even through it all he imagined she was out there calling his name and desperately searching for him in the utter darkness that had swallowed them all. A strange dream to be sure, but he knew well enough to consider the possibility that it might have been something more.

Had she followed him into the Deep Roads? Was she thinking to rescue him?

A panic gripped him. He opened his eyes and sat up sharply, fully expecting to find the darkness of his cell. Instead, however, he was greeted by light. A diffuse yellow glow permeated the chamber, almost smothered by the shadows but still enough to keep it from absolute darkness. The stench of corruption filled his nostrils once again, as if he were surrounded by meat on the verge of turning, but somehow it did not seem as potent as he remembered.

The humming sound, however, was stronger even than before. It was no longer something muted and distant; it was everywhere. It was behind the walls and under the floor; it filled the shadows and caressed his skin. There was a terrible beauty to it now, an awful yearning that pulsated within the sound, a tugging that pulled at the edge of his consciousness and yet frightened and nauseated him at the same time.

The humming had eclipsed any sense he had of the darkspawn. Any attempt he made to reach out with his mind to sense where the creatures were found only a wall of beautiful sound instead. Like a weed, it had insinuated itself into his consciousness, blocking out anything useful.

He was seized by the irrational impulse to scratch his hands across his face, to gouge away the flesh and bone and drag the humming out of his mind physically. The notion made him laugh, a mad giggle born of hysteria that was defeated almost before it made its way out of him.

"You hear it, do you not?" came the calm voice of the Architect, seated not five feet away from him on a rocky outcropping next to the wall.

Bregan was startled by the darkspawn's presence, and uncertain how he could have missed it even in the dim light. Had it crept into the cell while his mind wandered? Had he slept, and not even been aware that he slept?

A single glowstone hung next to the creature, the source of the illumination, and its gnarled staff lay across its robed lap. He had the impression that the creature had been waiting there for some time. Watching him, perhaps? Or probing into his thoughts with its magic? There were spells that could do that, forbidden magic that he didn't doubt in the slightest a darkspawn emissary might possess.

But if that were so, there was also probably nothing he could do. His thoughts would already have been violated, and his secrets stripped from him. He had already tried to escape, only to end up back where he began.

He shuddered, belatedly remembering that he was now mostly unclothed and yet covered in makeshift bandages over much of his chest and legs. He did not recall what had happened after he had been taken down by the rush of darkspawn attackers, had felt their teeth biting into his flesh. He was not even sure how he had survived.

His skin itched terribly underneath those bandages, but he resisted the urge to peel them off. A single tattered fur blanket had been provided to cover him, and he collected it around himself as he slowly sat up fully. The pain throughout his body was dull but insistent, as if his body protested against this unfamiliar movement. The sluggishness made him wary. There was a thickness to his blood, a deliberateness to his heartbeat that made him feel like something alien was crawling inside of him and sapping his strength. Just what had the darkspawn done to him?

"You may as well use whatever magic you have to pry open my mind, if you haven't done so already," Bregan growled. "I'm not going to tell you what you want to know."

The Architect blinked slowly, registering surprise in those milky-white eyes that continued to stare so incessantly. "Even if I could do such a thing," it said politely, its words clipped and even, "what makes you think that is the goal I seek?"

"Because that's what you darkspawn do, isn't it?" The words came out of Bregan as a croak, and his vision swam. He felt dizzy and groggy. The beautiful humming reached a crescendo, an orchestra of insistent sound that threatened to tear his mind apart. It crashed against him in multiple waves before finally receding. It took all his effort just to remain seated, sweat pouring down his forehead as his heart slowly thumped within his chest. "You dig . . . you search, for where they're kept. . . ."

"The Old Gods," the Architect offered.

Bregan nodded. The humming had withdrawn into the shadows again, but its power still made him shiver. The whispers inside that sound . . . if he paused, he was sure he could almost make out what they were saying. He was determined not to try. He covered his face with a hand, steadying himself. "You can't fool me," he gritted. "I know that's what you want. What other reason could you even have to keep me here?"

The Architect peered at him closely. It reached up with a scarred, puckered hand and ran a finger thoughtfully along its chin. Bregan continued to sweat under this scrutiny, shaky and exhausted while simultaneously trying not to let the darkspawn see just how weakened he was. He had no idea if he was successful. Probably not very.

Slowly the emissary got up, its brown robes rustling softly. It used the blackened staff for support as it leaned in to study Bregan even more closely. He shuddered, revolted by the creature's dead eyes. His flesh crawled and he wanted to pull away, but he couldn't even summon the strength for that much.

"You did not answer my first question," it said softly.

He cleared his throat and glanced at it, perplexed. "I don't . . ."

The Architect straightened, rubbing its chin again in an oddly human gesture. Bregan noticed the number of pouches and odd devices hanging from the loose hemp rope tied around its waist. One of them looked like a petrified skull formed into some kind of amulet, the skull having once belonged to something vaguely reptilian. "I suggested that you heard the call. You do, do you not?" It seemed more intrigued now even than before. "In fact, I will wager that you hear it more clearly now than ever."

"You mean the humming, the music."

"The Old Gods beckon, as they always have." The Architect turned and paced to the other side of the cell. The shadows cast on the walls by the glowstone danced ominously. "That is what you hear. To my people, it is a call that we cannot ignore. It whispers to our blood and compels us to seek the Old Gods out. We search and search for their prisons, and when we find one, we touch the face of perfection and thus desecrate it forever."

The darkspawn hung its head. Because it was facing away from Bregan, he couldn't see its expression properly, but he got the impression that the creature was filled with sadness, or perhaps regret. Could that be possible? The darkspawn had attacked all other life in relentless wave after wave, without mercy or quarter sought, for centuries beyond counting. Were they capable of regret? He had to admit that prior to meeting this particular one, he had assumed a large number of things about them that seemed to not be true. Just how not true remained to be seen.

"The face of perfection?" Bregan asked. "The Old Gods are dragons."

The Architect chucked with amusement. "Is that all they are, human? Is that such a small thing, then? Are there so many such creatures in the surface lands that they are not something of wonder?"

It was, in fact, quite the opposite. Dragons had been hunted nearly to extinction, and in truth had only begun to reappear in recent years. Even then, the Old Gods were things of legend, ancient creatures that predated even the Tevinter Imperium and might have been considered myths if the fact that a great, corrupted dragon leading the hordes during each of the Blights had not provided compelling evidence of their existence.

"I do not know what an Old God truly is," the Architect admitted. The creature's milky eyes stared far off into the distance, and Bregan realized it was listening to the humming. The sound rose as if in response, a song of beautiful whispers that caressed against Bregan's mind and made him shiver. He clenched his teeth to keep it at bay and was only partially successful. "I have never seen such a creature in my lifetime. Nor do I know if doing so would be beneficial. All I know is that the call of the Old Gods is a thing of perfection." It turned to look at Bregan again, its expression indiscernible but its tone soft and sad. "We are things of darkness, human. You know this better than any other might. To us, the call is the only light we shall ever know."

He stared at the darkspawn, this creature with its diseased flesh and its razor-sharp teeth, its dead eyes and the black talons on the ends of its spindly fingers, and he didn't know how to respond. For a long minute they remained in silence, Bregan sitting and watching the emissary as it seemed lost in thought. He wondered if it wasn't all too easy to start ascribing human motivations to it. It looked roughly humanoid, after all. To imagine that it might have feelings similar to those of a human would be a mistake. He had to remember that.

"Didn't you say it compelled you?" he asked.

The Architect nodded sharply. "That it does. Most of my kind are helpless before the call. They search because they must."

"Most of your kind," Bregan repeated. "But not you?"

"Nor, I suspect, you."

"I am not a darkspawn."

The creature stepped forward again, its interest renewed. "The same taint runs in your blood as in ours, Grey Warden, yet in you its effects are diminished. The question that comes to my mind is whether you have always heard the call of the Old Gods, or has that only happened since the corruption's advancement?"

"Advancement?" Bregan blinked in confusion.

The emissary gestured languidly toward him, and Bregan abruptly realized that it was pointing at his arms under the blanket. His throat became parch-dry as he brought them out and examined them more closely in the glowstone's yellow light. They were half covered in dark blotches. At first, he wondered if that was some kind of injury, or perhaps a bloodstain. But then he noticed the texture of the skin within those discolored areas: rough and withered, just as darkspawn flesh was.

"We regenerate quickly," the Architect explained in a neutral voice. "It is why we have never developed healing arts as your people have, I suppose. It seems that while the effects of the taint are slowed within you, they have advanced to the point where you have experienced this one benefit, at least."

"Benefit," Bregan exclaimed in horror. He dropped his arm out of the light, feeling his flesh crawl and bile rise up in his throat. He fought against the sudden urge to start ripping his own skin from his body.

The Architect reached out with a hand to comfort him, but he pulled away from it reflexively. He slammed up against the wall behind him, his breath coming in short and panicked starts. He wondered what the rest of his body under the blanket looked like. The itchiness he felt in his skin under those poultices, the thickness in his blood—was he covered in those blotches now? Was he slowly transforming into some kind of monster?

Is that what happened to Grey Wardens when they lived too long? When their resistance to the taint finally gave out once and for all? Had the very first Grey Wardens long ago discovered this horrible truth and devised the Calling so that future generations could avoid seeing it for themselves?

"I am sorry," the Architect said, and for once Bregan believed it. It withdrew its offered hand and simply stared at him uncomfortably as he sobbed. The tears came explosively, in gasps, and they shook his whole body. He burned with shame to be crying in front of the enemy, but he just couldn't help himself. The grief that welled up inside of him was overwhelming, compounded by the grogginess he felt and the maddening song that continued to tickle at the corners of his mind.

He had been called here by the Old Gods, too, he realized. It was their song that had lured him into the Dark Roads, that had told him his time was up. He was just the same as any of these darkspawn.

"I . . . only began to hear the humming recently," he finally explained. His voice was almost a croak, barely audible, but the Architect listened with intent fascination. "Once a Grey Warden hears it, that's when we go on the Calling. That's when we go to our deaths."

"An appropriate name, if an unjust end."

"There's never been anything just about it," Bregan blurted out. "I never wanted this. I never wanted to become a Grey Warden at all."

"No?"

"No." He spat out the word, avoiding looking the darkspawn in the face. It was stupid of him to say such things to this creature. Did he think it would have sympathy for him? Was he looking for sympathy? Because if he was, down here in the Deep Roads wasn't a good place to find it.

Almost belligerently, he found himself not caring. "I joined the Grey Wardens because I didn't have a choice. The one who recruited me . . . he wouldn't have taken my sister unless I went, too. He said I was the one he really wanted, despite the fact that it was her dream." He felt ashamed at this strange need of his to explain, but he continued anyway. "I told him that she would push herself harder than any other recruit he could hope for, that she would be the greatest Grey Warden they'd ever known. But he didn't care. He thought I would do better."

The emissary tilted its head. It was a look Bregan had seen on insects, or even dogs that were bewildered by some odd activity of their master's. He found it somehow pleasing that not everything the Architect did made him seem human. "That was a compliment, surely," it offered.

"It was a cruel fate. Either I joined the order or my sister would have ended up a soldier somewhere. A member of some city watch, or perhaps a guardsman's wife. And she would have been miserable, because becoming a Grey Warden was the only thing she'd ever wanted. I couldn't do that to her."

The confession left Bregan breathless, and he almost doubled over, shaking and weak. It was not as if his sister had never known this. They had been close their entire lives, and he had seen that knowledge deep in her eyes. If anything, it had made her more driven. They had never acknowledged that fact openly. It was never spoken of, never even alluded to despite the fact that they both knew the truth.

Some things, however, are easier to say in the shadows. Spoken here, they would never hurt Genevieve, and while it shamed him to admit, still it felt good. While every other part of him crawled with the taint, like he was some dirty and infested thing, a part of him deep down felt oddly liberated.

"You humans do strange things."

He laughed bitterly at the darkspawn's confusion, as honest as it appeared to be. "Yes, I suppose we do. I don't suppose you have brothers and sisters?"

"We are brethren." It blinked, its answer hesitant. "All of us, the same."

"But you're not the same." Bregan fought back a surge of the distant humming once again, clenching his jaw from the effort. "You said yourself the Old Gods can't compel you. You talk. You're not like any darkspawn I've ever seen."

The creature nodded, again hesitant, but said nothing.

"Why is that?" he insisted.

"I have asked myself this same question," the Architect said. It paced away again, its tone becoming troubled. "Do you think I have not? The darkspawn have been born in these depths, one generation after countless others before it, and each of my brethren is no different than any that have come before. And then came I." It drummed its long fingers along the staff, studying its own movement as if some kind of answer could be found therein. "Perhaps humans are similar? Perhaps from time to time one of you is born that is an aberration, different for no other reason than its pieces did not all fall neatly into place as they should?"

"Some would say it is the Maker's will, but yes. We are the same way."

The Architect did not immediately respond. Eventually it nodded, pleased. "Perhaps it is also similar among your kind that such aberrations rarely prosper. They are weak. Unfit. They are cursed by that which makes them different, and difference cannot be tolerated."

Bregan sighed. "Yes. Sadly, that is also true."

"But sometimes it is not a curse." The Architect walked toward the cell's door. Bregan couldn't be certain, but he thought he detected a hint of steel coming into the creature's normally cultured voice. "Standing on the outside allows one to see things from a new perspective, a perspective that the rest of its brethren lack."

"You have that perspective, do you?"

"I do." It opened up the cell door, which groaned in protest but appeared to be neither closed nor actually locked. "Would you come with me, Grey Warden?" it asked politely, turning back to regard Bregan where he sat against the wall.

"You aren't worried I'll try to get away?"

"I am worried for your sake. My ability to intervene when it comes to my brethren is limited, and regeneration will only do so much."

"Meaning I could still die."

There was a bitterness to Bregan's tone that the darkspawn detected. He could see it in the way it looked at him guardedly. "Is that why you fled the first time?" Its tone was pointed. He supposed it wasn't really asking a question so much as making an observation.

He sat there for a long minute, staring off into the shadows. Sweat beaded on his forehead, and his skin felt clammy and all too warm. The faint humming call in the distance prickled against his thoughts, and he absently noted just how hungry he felt. His stomach groaned with its emptiness, and yet he couldn't stand the idea of eating anything. The very thought of it made him want to retch.

The Architect continued to watch him, apparently having nothing better to do. He supposed there was really no point in avoiding such questions. "I had hoped I would be killed, yes," he admitted. "That is why I went on the Calling in the first place, after all."

"There are easier ways to die, human."

His grimace deepened. He stood, reluctantly allowing the soiled furs to fall away from him and down to the floor, and looked down at his body. All he wore were his bloodstained and filthy smallclothes, and every part of his skin that wasn't covered by the greyed cloth bandages was corrupted. It was like a network of black mold working its way across his entire body, and everywhere it touched he could feel a hot buzzing underneath the flesh. It was difficult to look at.

So instead he strode toward where the Architect waited, picking up the glowstone as he went. "I'll try not to run away this time, then," he grumbled. "But I'm not promising anything." He felt exposed and too vulnerable, but tried not to let it show. Though the taint might have made its mark upon his flesh, he was far from weak.

The darkspawn said nothing and instead turned and went out into the hall. Bregan followed. As he watched the back of the creature's robes, its bald and scarred head, he wondered faintly if he shouldn't simply try to kill it. He might not be able to escape, that was true, but perhaps he could take out this thing and whatever threat it represented. The fact that it was an emissary and thus commanded great magical power was one thing . . . the fact that it was also uniquely intelligent among the darkspawn, that was quite something else. It might even be his duty as a Grey Warden to kill it, just to be safe.

Yet he didn't. He remained close behind the Architect, holding the glowstone out before him and watching the alien light it cast on the ancient dwarven halls. He wondered why the emissary wasn't more concerned about its safety. Perhaps it had some sort of magical protection, something that would strike at Bregan if he so much as laid a finger upon it?

Or perhaps it simply knew better than he did that he wasn't going to do that.

They walked for a short time through the ruins, all of it tainted almost to the point of being unrecognizable for the structure it once had been. Now it was a darkspawn nest, a thing full of black tendrils and sacs of corrupted flesh. The fact that he could no longer reach out with his mind and detect the creatures he knew to be out there disturbed him greatly. The humming surrounded him now, presenting a blank wall that his mind slammed up against.

It wasn't long before the halls opened up into a vast chamber of some kind, the limits of which extended far beyond the reach of the glowstone. It was a point at which the dwarven stone carvings ended, that much he could see. The floors and walls were broken here, as if some force had simply torn the rest of it off and left it open to the underground beyond. Bregan could see natural rock, and the light gave it a sense of wetness, a great mass of something black and moist that filled up the shadows, with many things moving all around. In fact, the great mass of noise made him think of an insect hive. The smell of it was acrid and overwhelming. He couldn't place what any of it might be, and wasn't sure he wanted to.

The Architect turned to him, its milky eyes wide and unreadable. "Do you see?"

"No, there's not enough light. But I—"

His objection died on his lips as the emissary lifted up its dark staff. A deep purple glow surged forth from it, and suddenly Bregan saw the entire cavern clearly. It was vast, a great underground chamber that stretched out farther than he could possibly see, and it teemed with darkspawn. Thousands upon thousands of the creatures toiled, all so closely intermingled it seemed as if a mass of black maggots writhed in some festering carcass. The organic strands covered everything, great hives of it strewn like nerve clusters and dangling amid the horrific workers that moved among the shadows below.

Were they digging? He had the impression that the masses of them were all engaged in some sort of industry, all united in moving great portions of the rock out of the cavern and expanding it even further. Yet there were no sounds of tools crashing against stone, no hammering sounds or grunts of exertion. All he could hear was a rhythmic groan, a keening pitch that it seemed each of the darkspawn contributed to. The sound of it made his skin crawl, and he realized that the chorus in the distance responded to it. Like a cat that arched its back to meet a brushing hand it became ecstatic; it surged and almost overwhelmed his senses.

The world swayed around him and he felt himself stumble, only to have a strong hand grab his arm and steady him. His heart beat rapidly in his chest, and for a long minute the only other sound next to that powerful song was his own labored breathing. In and out. In and out, slow and controlled. He felt flushed, sweat pouring down his face.

He was ill. Perhaps he was dying.

"Be calm," the Architect urged him. The purple glow from its staff ebbed and suddenly the vast cavern was cloaked in shadows once again. But now Bregan knew they were out there. He could feel them moving, their tainted forms bumping up against each other as they swarmed over the rock like ants. The fact that he couldn't see them now almost made it worse.

He pulled away from the emissary's touch, his breath rough as he leaned against the nearby rock wall for support. He stomach lurched, and had there been anything in it he might have vomited. As it was he heaved painfully a few times and fought to gain control over his revulsion. The smoothness of the rock, the coolness of its surface, felt good against his skin. He curled up against it, tried to ignore the blackness that trailed across it. Closing his eyes helped, if only for a moment.

"A curious reaction," the Architect observed. Bregan opened his eyes and saw the creature watching him with clinical fascination. It made no move to approach him, content merely to let him convulse. Sweating and exhausted, he let himself slump down to a sitting position on the floor.

"There are so many," he breathed. He really didn't know what else he could say.

The Architect nodded solemnly. "The Old Gods call to them and so they search. They search because they have no choice. All who hear the call must obey, in the end."

"Except you."

"And you." It inclined its head.

Bregan sat against the wall and tried to ignore the great, dark chamber that he knew was beside him. He wanted to retreat back to his cell, somewhere small and safe where he could pretend that there wasn't a monstrous swarm all around him. Yet that, too, would be a weakness.

He wiped the sweat from his brow with a shaky hand. "So what is it you want from me, then?" he asked, his voice quavering. "You want me to help them? You want me to tell you where the Old Gods are, to speed this all along?"

"So you do know where they are." The creature seemed intrigued, but not surprised.

He laughed, a bitter bark that devolved into a fit of mad giggling that only left him hoarse in the end. The emissary seemed unmoved by his mirth. "Are you saying you really didn't know that? Isn't that why you brought me here?"

The Architect lowered itself onto its haunches to look Bregan directly in the eyes. Its brown robes rustled around it, and it placed its staff gingerly down on the ground. He didn't want to look the creature in the face, but he couldn't help himself. Those milky, dead eyes commanded his attention. They seemed so oddly serene, almost sincere in their concern.

"I did not bring you here to begin the Blight," it said carefully, emphasizing each word so there would be no misunderstanding. "The numbers of my brethren grow with each passing year, and given enough time they will find one of the ancient prisons. They will unlock it and the cycle will begin anew. This will happen whether you were to tell them where to look or not. I have no desire to see it happen sooner."

Bregan was flabbergasted. For a moment he could almost ignore the incessant humming that threatened to crack open his head and crawl inside. He stared at the darkspawn in amazement. "Then what do you want?"

"I wish to end it." The Architect stood and walked to the edge of the cavern, and stared out into it with eyes that Bregan was sure could see far better in the darkness than any human. "My brethren have been subject to this impulse since our creation. We rise to the surface and struggle to eradicate your kind, and each time you drive us back and we begin again. This will continue until one of us is victorious, yes? Until one of us is eradicated forever, if such a thing is even possible?" It turned and looked to Bregan, a cool intensity gripping its every word. "But what if it didn't have to be this way?"

"What other option is there?"

The creature crossed the gap between them quickly, crouching down with a look of such fervent excitement that Bregan almost recoiled. It clutched at his hand, holding it firmly. "In your blood lies the key," it whispered. "Yours is the middle ground between human and darkspawn, the path to true peace."

Bregan stared at the Architect, not quite certain he understood. "Middle ground?"

"Your kind will always be at risk from mine so long as our taint spreads and infects," it insisted. "And my kind will always seek to destroy yours so long as the call of the Old Gods continues."

"But I don't understand. There's no way those things can change."

"Can they not?" It seemed surprised. "You are human, and yet you are immune to the taint."

Bregan held up his arm. In the soft light of the glowstone, the trail of corruption along his flesh was only too evident. "Not anymore."

"You are not dying. You are *changing*."

The word sent a shiver down his spine. The creature said it as if this should not be alarming in the slightest, but the truth was that not thinking about what was happening to him was the only way he could keep from going mad. His mind shied away from images of those outside the order that had fallen sway to the darkspawn's plague. Those that did not suffer an agonizing death at the hands of the sickness became ghouls, beings whose shattered minds were subject to control by the darkspawn. They became pawns, even servants, until finally they withered away and perished.

Would he begin to obey eventually, just as they did? Would he be in that cavern soon, digging along with all the other creatures, mingling his flesh with theirs? "It . . . it doesn't matter"—his words stumbled together—"there's no way that the rest of humanity could become immune. Not unless they became Grey Wardens."

"Yes." The Architect nodded as if this point should be obvious.

Another shiver ran down Bregan's spine. Sweat ran into his eyes, and for a moment he felt faint. "But becoming a Grey Warden means drinking darkspawn blood. Most of those who do it die. Only a few of us ever succeed."

"Yes"—it nodded again—"many of your kind would very likely perish." Before he could protest, the creature raised its hand. "You exist halfway between human and darkspawn. If the rest of your kind could be made as you are, they would have no reason to fear my brethren."

"Other than the fact that the darkspawn keep trying to kill us?"

"That, too, would need to end. Humans and darkspawn must meet each other in the middle." It paused and studied Bregan carefully, as if watching for a reaction. Oddly, he found himself having very little reaction at all. He sat against the wall, listening absently to the droning hum that seemed to vibrate inside the very stones, and waited for the sense of horror to come. It didn't.

Shouldn't it? Unless he was somehow mistaken, the Architect was suggesting unleashing the darkspawn taint on humanity at large, putting each and every human through the same kind of torturous test that allowed one to become a Grey Warden . . . those that survived, anyhow. Which wouldn't be many. There was a reason only the strongest and hardiest were chosen to join the order. Few others had any hope of surviving the process.

Was such a thing even possible? Should he not be angrily demanding answers from the creature? Part of him said he should be horrified and enraged, and that he should find out the details behind this plan. He imagined it involved some brand of darkspawn magic, but what, exactly? Shouldn't he want to know?

As he sat there, chin on his chest and listening to his own hard and ragged breathing, he found that he didn't. Was it not the job of the Grey Wardens to seek an end to the darkspawn threat? And when had they ever actually been close to succeeding at that goal? Each time the Blight came, it brought with it a war that came that much closer to wiping out humanity altogether. Each time the world had to scramble to save itself, and each time it had barely managed to succeed.

How many more times could it do so? Would the next Blight be when the darkspawn finally succeeded in wiping out all life from the surface of Thedas? How many would die then?

Bregan suddenly recalled the man who had inducted him into the order. Kristoff had been a grizzled and uncompromising warrior, all hard edges and frowns. He had been Commander of the Grey for many years before succumbing to the taint. Bregan had accompanied him down to Orzammar, feasted with him at a table full of boisterous and drunken dwarves, and then watched him walk out into the Deep Roads.

At the time, Bregan had been overcome with grief. For all his taciturn manner, Kristoff had been his only real friend within the order. He'd allowed his student to care for his horse and sweep his quarters, knowing that Bregan would rather do such tasks than carouse with the other recruits. He'd played queens with Bregan on a dusty old board and sparred with him indoors when it rained. It was Kristoff's recommendation that named Bregan as Commander of the Grey after him, despite Genevieve's unspoken jealousy at the promotion, and Bregan had accepted it only because Kristoff had demanded he do so.

What he remembered of his grey-haired mentor that final night, however, was the man's relief. While it had been all Bregan could do to choke back embarrassing tears, Kristoff had been calm and composed. The sense of serenity around him was palpable, all the grumbling tension that was present for all the years Bregan had known him completely gone. He'd walked into the shadows of the Deep Roads, head held high as if a weight had been lifted from his shoulders, and stopped only to give his former student a few final words of advice.

"You will guard them," he'd said, "and they will hate you for it. Whenever there is not a Blight actively crawling over the surface, humanity will do its best to forget how much they need us. And that's good. We need to stand apart from them, even if they have to push us away to make us do it. That is the only way we can ever make the hard decisions."

At the time Bregan had thought, *What hard decisions?* There had been no Blight in centuries, and at worst the order dealt with darkspawn raids that popped up on the surface from time to time. The hardest decisions a Commander of the Grey was forced to make were which recruits could be given the test to join the order. It was never an easy thing, as even the hardiest of them often perished, but it seemed hardly worth Kristoff's words.

The Grey Wardens watched and waited as they always had, but now the order was but a shadow of what they had once been during the wars of long ago. Late at night in the quiet of his cell, Bregan had allowed himself the private luxury of believing that the days of the darkspawn were well and truly done.

At least, he had believed that until now.

"You say nothing," the Architect murmured uneasily.

"What should I say?"

The emissary gathered its robes closer around itself and circled Bregan warily. It seemed to be watching for some sign, its pale eyes intent. "My experience with humans is limited," it admitted. "What you will or will not do at any given moment is a mystery to me. Your kind is often irrational. Yet I was expecting . . . anger, perhaps?"

"And what am I feeling now, do you think?"

It blinked. "I would say that you are sad."

Bregan felt leaden. His thoughts became fuzzy, and for a brief moment it seemed as if the mad humming was a world away. He simply sat there in the quiet shadows, sweat running down his moist and corrupted skin as the robed darkspawn looked down upon him. How very unreal this all was, somehow. "Can you do it?" he finally asked. "This thing you plan. Can you actually do it?"

"Not alone." The Architect offered no further elaboration, and he wasn't sure that he would get any even if he pressed. Part of him wondered, in a much removed fashion, if perhaps he should attack this darkspawn after all. If he had thought the creature dangerous earlier, now it might possibly be the most dangerous thing in the entire world.

He did nothing. He sat there and stared down at the cracked floor, chipped away by an eon of wear. Once there had been stone tiles there, delicately inlaid with a geometric design typical of the dwarves. He'd seen something much like that within a bathhouse in Orzammar. Perhaps this had once been a similar place? He tried to imagine it filled with bright lamps and steamy tubs and curvaceous dwarven noble-hunters giggling behind their fans. Instead he conjured only images of corrupted flesh and pools of stagnant foulness. A cancer had taken over this place, a dank sickness that grew in secret until it spilled out onto the surface.

That was the truth, wasn't it? The world was sick. Since their inception, the Grey Wardens had fought back the symptoms time and time again. But they had never defeated the disease. Maybe the time had come for a more radical treatment.

The Architect beckoned to him with a black and withered hand. "Come with me, Grey Warden." It did not wait to see if he followed, but Bregan did not hesitate this time. Groaning with effort, he pulled himself up off the floor and stumbled after the emissary as it walked away from the cavern and went back the way they'd come.

They didn't return to the cell, however. They spent a fair amount of time crossing a maze of passages, some small, others huge and supported by crumbling arches that Bregan could barely see the tops of. He quickly lost track of where they headed, doing his best to fight against the gnawing weakness inside him and to keep the emissary within range of the glowstone's light. For all the fact that it didn't seem to exert itself, it moved so quickly he began to fear that he might actually get left behind.

Twice they encountered darkspawn. Once it was but a handful of the short genlocks. The second time it was an entire group of hurlocks, one of them a powerful alpha, armed and armored in metal that glistened like dark obsidian. Bregan tensed both times, expecting to be attacked, but the creatures did nothing more than make wary hisses and keep their distance. At first he thought it was him that they reacted to, an enemy Grey Warden in their midst. But then, as he watched their reactions more closely, he realized the truth.

It was the Architect they feared.

The emissary paid them little heed, merely holding out his gnarled staff threateningly as he passed among them. They backed off, making angry thrumming noises from deep in their throats, like dogs confronted with a clearly superior hound and salvaging what little of their dignity they could as they pulled their tails between their legs. Bregan was amazed, and found himself disconcerted to be so universally ignored.

Did they see him as a darkspawn, now? So full of corruption running through his veins that he wasn't even distinguishable as a Grey Warden? That idea disturbed him far more.

After a time, Bregan began to perceive that they were moving upward. They climbed a long flight of stairs, an ascent that left him gasping and shaking with exhaustion, and then entered a long tunnel that seemed to slope toward the surface. The stone there was mostly still free from the darkspawn taint, and he began to wonder just how far they had traveled. He had the impression that the dwarven ruins remained unbroken around them, that they had not moved into natural caverns, but who could truly say how far such ruins spread? Some of the oldest thaigs, according to the dwarven Shaperate, had been larger than Orzammar itself. Now they were all part of the festering underground world occupied by the dark-spawn.

He fell into a daze, focusing more on putting one foot in front of the other and keeping up with the Architect—who said nothing. Their travel was utterly silent, with only the beautiful strains of the humming tugging at Bregan's senses. He tried to tune it out. When he finally started to wonder just where it was they were going, he resigned himself to the fact that there was no point in asking. The Architect was moving and he was following.

Then the emissary finally stopped, abruptly enough that Bregan almost ran into it. He looked up and saw that the tunnel had come to an end. They were at an entrance of some kind that opened up into a larger natural cavern beyond. What little he could see with the glowstone told him this was natural rock, mostly untainted. The faintest breeze crawled across his skin, cool and welcoming, and only belatedly he realized that it signified fresh air. They were near the surface.

The Architect held up a calming hand as he spun about. "It is not as close as it seems," it cautioned in its usual calm and civilized tone. "The ducts that still exist here bring the air down from the surface. But it would be a simple matter to reach the surface from here."

Bregan stared at the creature suspiciously. "And why did you bring me here?"

"If you had attempted to flee again when we were still among my brethren, they would have stopped you. They listen to me at times because they fear me, but I am not the same as them and they know this."

It took a moment for the idea to sink in. He was exhausted, his legs burning now that he was standing still. The fiery itch underneath his flesh clawed at his tendons. The Architect turned and stared out into the cavern, the glowstone highlighting every fold of the withered flesh on its skeletal face. If Bregan were to guess, he'd have suspected that it felt pensive. "You want me to flee now?"

"Is that still what you wish?"

"Would you let me go?"

"I would."

That answer stumped him. He looked out into the shadowed passages where the Architect stared and wondered what the darkspawn saw there. Bregan had come to the Deep Roads to die. If he left, he could still do that. He could continue his Calling, as planned.

But if all he wanted to do was die, then there were simpler ways to do it. Even the Architect had told him that, and it was true. So perhaps he didn't want to die. Perhaps he could go to the surface, if it was truly reachable. He could warn the Grey Wardens about what this emissary planned, give them time to find a way to stop it . . .

. . . but should he?

Ignoring the idea that he would be attacked the moment he showed himself on the surface, his skin as corrupted as any mad ghoul's, it occurred to him that perhaps there was actually something to the emissary's plan. The death of so many was a horrific thought, yes, but if it meant survival? Stopping the Blight was a

Grey Warden's true duty, and even if Bregan had never wanted that onus originally, it was all he truly had left now.

"This thing you have planned," he began slowly.

"Yes?"

"You aren't just unleashing something on humanity? You said that the darkspawn needed to meet in the middle as well, yes? You must have a plan for them, too."

"We can speak on that, if you wish."

"But the idea is to end the Blights? Forever, so they never happen again."

The emissary turned and regarded Bregan for a moment, its expression unreadable. The large pale eyes blinked and it leaned heavily on its gnarled black staff. He ground his teeth, wondering if maybe this wasn't the creature's plan all along. Take him down into the depths, let the corruption gnaw away at his sanity until finally . . . what? Until he finally admitted that maybe the Grey Wardens never had all the answers? They did what they could to protect the world from the unthinkable, but possessed no solution save the constant sacrifice of young souls to the taint? Nothing Bregan had been taught could ever have prepared him for this.

"That is the idea, yes," the Architect murmured.

"And what do the other darkspawn think about this? Do they agree with you?"

"They cannot. I must make this decision for them."

Bregan found himself slowly nodding. He looked out into the cavern and felt another brush of cool air across his skin. It would feel good to be on the surface, he thought. By now there would be snow on the ground, and the icy breath of the wind would be welcome against his flushed, burning skin.

And then he thought of Genevieve, his white-haired sister with her stern glare. He remembered his dreams and wondered if she was indeed searching for him. If he went to the surface, she might even find him. And what would she say, if she saw him now?

"Let's talk about it, then." The words spilled out of him unbidden, yet as soon as they were said Bregan knew that it could be no other way. The whispers within the distant humming grew louder and more insistent, calling out his name from the shadows and tugging at his mind.

And he ignored them.

The Architect bowed low, respectfully, and then gestured back the way they had come. Bregan adjusted what little clothes he had left and began to stride purposefully down the passageway, back into the depths, and this time the darkspawn followed him.

7

Let the blade pass through the flesh,
Let my blood touch the ground,
Let my cries touch their hearts. Let mine be the last sacrifice.
—Canticle of Andraste 7:12

It was impossible to tell the time in the Deep Roads, but Maric
suspected that they couldn't possibly have rested more than a handful of hours. He had only slept in fits and starts, himself, and whenever he did awake he was aware of the Grey Wardens' commander
pacing outside.

It wasn't long afterwards when Genevieve finally stirred them
from their tents, her tone insistent. No doubt she had waited until
she simply couldn't take it anymore. Young Duncan grumbled, but
a deadly look from her silenced the lad. Maric would have laughed
had he not been certain he would have received a similar reaction.

The Grey Wardens began to efficiently pack up the tents. A hush
had descended over them. Whereas the previous day had been filled
with Duncan's amiable chatter, among other talk, now there was
only tense silence.

They insisted on packing up Maric's tent for him. He'd started
to do it himself, but Utha interjected herself between him and the
tent. He'd spluttered in protest, but the dwarf had simply ignored
him. And how did one argue with a mute, anyhow? So reluctantly
he'd given in, and it was probably just as well. The others had the
process down to a science.

Kell ventured ahead, the large hound bounding after him. Maric had wondered how wise it was to bring an animal down into the Deep Roads, but it was increasingly obvious that Hafter was no ordinary creature. He and the quiet hunter appeared to share a bond that went beyond that of master and servant. Kell rarely needed to give the dog commands. Hafter never went too fast or got too excited, either. He was as cautious and suspicious as the hunter, keeping an eye on every shadow. It was quite easy, in fact, to stop thinking of Hafter as merely a dog.

The only person other than Maric who appeared to have nothing currently to do was Fiona. She stood nearby, pointedly ignoring him, the beacon of white light from her staff providing the only illumination in the ruin now that the campfire was extinguished. Its flickering glow cast shadows on the ruin's walls, a virtual puppet's play cavorting high above them. Since she was holding the staff, the shadow behind Fiona was the largest, looming high over her as if about to pounce. How fitting that the fiery elf should cast the most dominant shadow, he thought.

Fiona bristled under his scrutiny. She made as if to ignore him, but finally she could take it no longer. "What is it?" she demanded.

"I'm wondering why you aren't doing anything."

"I *am* doing something."

"Making it glow? Wouldn't a torch suffice?"

She glanced toward her staff, doing her best to suppress a smirk. "No, not that," she said. "That barely takes any effort. I'm keeping an eye on the darkspawn. Someone has to."

"An eye?"

"So to speak. They've been getting closer. The brooches that Remille gave us seem to be working so far . . . it doesn't look like they know we're here. But we can't take any chances. As soon as they spot us, they're going to tell the rest of the darkspawn."

"Couldn't you kill them before they do that?"

The mage's amusement grew, and she arched a brow at him.

"They're connected to the rest of the darkspawn through the taint. Whatever one knows, they all know."

"How inconvenient."

"The brooches will keep them from tracking us, but if they become aware of intruders they will begin to swarm. It will be better if we can keep them unaware of our presence for as long as possible. Kell's gone to see how many there are."

"Won't they see him?"

She chuckled. "No. They won't see him."

A few more minutes and the tents had vanished into the Grey Wardens' backpacks, and the rest of the camp along with them. The smoldering campfire and the disturbance to the layers of grime and dust that covered the ground were all that provided evidence of their passing. Genevieve passed out torches to Duncan and Utha, and as soon as those were lit, Fiona allowed her staff to stop shining.

A good thing, Maric figured, as its brilliance would have alerted the darkspawn from miles away. He had to wonder just how many torches they had stored. He remembered there being phosphorescent lichen to offer light in some places, but that was irregular and difficult to count on. The idea of being stuck in smothering darkness down here in the depths was discomfiting, to say the least.

Genevieve wasn't interested in discussing the state of their supplies, however, and with an intense look she waved to everyone to follow. The speed of her gait made it obvious that she wanted to make up for lost time, and knew exactly where she was going.

The hours that followed were exhausting. Time crawled by slowly, and it was all Maric could do to keep up with the torches ahead. They were two points of warm light, slowly bobbing in passages so thick with shadows it felt almost as if they were swimming in them.

It wasn't anywhere near as cold as it had been up on the surface, but there was still a chill in the air that worked its way past Maric's armor and made him shiver. Duncan was too distracted to complain about it, at least. The lad kept his eyes peeled nervously, as did the others, with one hand on his daggers. Maric supposed that if the darkspawn were closer, those daggers would very likely be in his hands rather than in their sheaths.

The stillness was as maddening as he remembered. Nothing moved in the darkness except them, and despite the fact that they tread quickly on hard stone they made very little sound. It was like walking on a field of snow; every whisper was absorbed and every step was hushed. The fact that no one spoke now made it worse.

Sweat poured down his forehead and his legs ached, but he didn't fall behind. Genevieve pushed them through the long tunnels mercilessly, one hour blending into the next. On the few occasions when they reached a fork in the Deep Roads, she would irritably call for Maric to be brought forth and he would look around and try to remember which way they had come the first time.

He would have thought that after so many years it would be harder, that he would struggle to recall the path. Things had changed here, after all. The spread of the darkspawn corruption was worse, for instance. It didn't matter. He had no trouble at all remembering the way. He might as well have been here last year, or perhaps a few months ago.

Fiona caught his eyes once. She noticed his grim expression, perhaps, or the way he looked off into the distance. She said nothing, though she appeared curious. He ignored her and turned away.

Eventually Kell returned, the hunter and his hound emerging from the deep shadows of a side passage so suddenly that Maric jumped.

"What did you find?" Genevieve asked, waving at the others behind her to halt.

The man's unnaturally pale eyes almost seemed to glow from

under his hood. He shouldered his bow and then gestured toward his leather jerkin. Maric noticed black blood there for the first time, splashed violently across much of the front. "I was forced to kill a few," he muttered, obviously displeased with himself, "and the others I led away. None saw me, but they know something is here that should not be." He turned his head and stared off down the passage, his eyes piercing deep beyond the shadows. "There are more coming, now."

The Commander frowned, but did not seem upset. "That was inevitable."

"It is worse. There is a large group directly ahead."

"Then we will need to detour."

Maric raised his hand. "Err . . . this is the route we went last time. If we get off of it, I don't know that I'll be able to bring us back."

Genevieve scowled, staring off in the direction of the approaching darkspawn. She appeared to be weighing the options carefully, the torchlight making her face glow. Finally she gave a sharp nod. "We don't have any choice, for now. Kell, we're going to rely on your direction sense to find us a way around."

"Yes, Commander."

"Oh, Maker's breath," Duncan swore softly. Genevieve pointed a finger at the lad without even looking his way and he clamped his mouth shut, looking sour as he did so.

They turned down the side passage, the hunter leading them now. All their weapons were out, and so Maric decided to follow suit. He drew his longsword, its blade pale dragonbone and etched with runes that glowed a bright sapphire. It drew the immediate attention of the others and they ground to a sudden halt, staring at him in surprise.

Utha stepped forward, eyes wide, gesturing sharply.

Julien frowned nearby. "She wants to know where you got

that," he explained.

"I found it here in the Deep Roads," he admitted, "in the hands of a long-dead dwarf. I offered to give it back to the dwarves, but King Endrin refused."

Utha nodded, and made another hand gesture that didn't need to be interpreted. She was impressed. The others nodded approvingly, and turned to keep moving. Duncan hesitated, however. "Does it always glow like that?" he asked.

"No. It's reacting to the darkspawn, I think." He held it out toward the wall, something he'd done when he first found the blade, and watched the reaction of the Grey Wardens as the corruption covering the wall recoiled away from the blade like a living thing. The stone beneath was now bared, sapphire light shining over it.

"Sounds handy," Duncan muttered.

"I used to be lucky that way. Magical swords lying around, people racing in to rescue me at the last moment, bumping into dwarven legions in the middle of the Deep Roads, that sort of thing."

The lad stared at him, apparently assuming he was joking. "Well, let's hope your luck continues, then."

"Let's hope."

They pressed on, almost running now. The clinking sound of their metal armor was added to the thump of their packs and the tread of their boots on the rock . . . and off in the distance Maric could hear a humming. It was a deep sound that reverberated throughout the passage, a dread whisper that seemed to come from all directions at once.

He remembered it only too well. Darkspawn.

Without speaking, they broke into a full run. Twice Kell urgently gestured to the rest of them to switch directions into a side passage, the last time bringing them through a hole in the wall into a natural cavern. Maric felt uneasy about leaving the Deep Roads. The floor was uneven and slick, and the cavern led downward sharply. Would they even be able to find their way back?

There was little time to think about that, however. They sped through the dark caverns, and when they eventually reached a fork in the path, Genevieve called for a halt. As they waited, panting for breath, she waved for the torches to be doused. That was a bad sign, Maric thought to himself. Duncan and Utha quickly smothered the flames, which had already burned very low.

Fiona raised her staff, and with a whisper it began to glow once again. She kept the light dim, however, so it barely shone farther than their immediate area. Moving in these caverns would be difficult this way, with all the loose stones and debris lying about. That seemed less important than the rapidly approaching drone of the humming.

It made Maric's skin crawl. Next to him, he could see Duncan nervously fingering the hilt of one of his daggers. The lad's dark skin glistened with sweat, and his eyes flickered back and forth in agitation as if watching for something to jump out of the shadows.

Why they had stopped running, he didn't know. The entire group seemed frozen in place, holding their breath as they waited. The tension was almost unbearable. "What are we waiting for?" he finally demanded.

Nicolas jumped, startled, and frowned at him angrily.

Genevieve held up a hand to Maric, but didn't look back at him. Her intense gaze was elsewhere, as was Kell's and several of the others. They were all staring off into the darkness at something only they could sense. "We are waiting to see if those ahead will pass," she explained, her voice low.

"We are caught between two groups," Kell whispered.

Julien made a holy sign in the air before him. Maric could see the sweat running down his brow. "*Maker, my enemies are abundant,*" the man intoned, "*but my faith sustains me; I shall not fear the legion.*"

"There may be a way . . . ," Genevieve began uncertainly, but then paused. She glanced at the hunter and he nodded. Gesturing for his hound to follow, Kell immediately spun and began sprinting back the way they had come. She ran after him. "Quickly," she ordered.

They raced back through the caverns. Maric wanted to ask why they were heading back, but they were going too fast. He could only assume that whatever they had sensed ahead was worse than what was behind them.

"Maric, when the battle begins, stay back with the mage!" Genevieve shouted back to him as she ran. "Guard her! Duncan, stay with him!"

He barely had a moment to let the command sink in when the fight began. With a great war cry, the white-haired woman surged ahead, sword lifted high. Nicolas and Julien flanked her, the former with spiked mace and shield and the latter with two-handed blade. The three of them fell upon a line of darkspawn who appeared in the staff's white light almost as if from nowhere.

The tall hurlocks hissed in outrage, bringing to bear their own jagged-looking and primitive weapons as they suddenly recognized their ancient foe. They were too late, however, and the heavy warriors carved a path of carnage through their ranks. The humming sound grew loud and angry all around them. Darkspawn ichor fountained from gaping wounds as steel sliced easily through corrupted flesh.

Maric backed up, his runed longsword held warily before him. Duncan stayed close by, crouched low to the ground with both his daggers out. It was a feral pose, Maric thought, one that spoke of a quick and dirty fighting style.

Fiona stepped forward beside him, the glow of her staff intensifying until it was brilliant enough to light up the entire passage. "No point in hiding it now," she growled. She put out a hand against Maric's chest. "Stand back."

Holding up the staff, she spoke a few soft words under her

breath. Her eyes closed and the aura of magic intensified around her. He stepped back as ordered, and as he did so a ring of power surged forth from the mage. The air wavered slightly, filling with an unnatural sheen, and as the ring rushed down the passage and passed through the darkspawn ranks they appeared to slow slightly. Their weapons moved as if the air itself had become thick and sluggish. The Grey Wardens, however, were not impaired.

Genevieve and the other warriors pressed forward, grunting with effort as they hacked with their heavy weapons. All three of them were veterans. Their blows were careful yet powerful, and they wasted no more time on a single opponent than was absolutely necessary, kicking back a mortally wounded darkspawn with a boot if need be to make room. Neither Genevieve nor Julien seemed hindered by the lack of room for their large blades. They switched effortlessly between parries and jabs, even striking with the hilt when need be. Nicolas used his shield not only to protect himself, but to block attacks aimed at the other two whenever he could. His mace struck rapidly, its blunt head crunching jaws and breaking hands so that his opponents dropped their weapons.

Each of the three stayed aware of the other two, keeping their distance even and ensuring that none of the darkspawn passed their line. Their attacks were effective. The darkspawn reeled back, the alien humming taking on an angry and growling tone now. The warriors pressed forward, black ichor staining their armor and their faces, and for a moment it looked as if the trio might actually hold the narrow cavern on their own.

It was not to last.

Nicolas shouted in rage as a large hurlock crashed forcefully into his shield, sending him skittering back several feet on the uneven stone. He tripped and fell backwards, the creature frantically leaping on top of him and biting at his face with its great fangs. Julien spun around, eyes wide with alarm, and hacked the creature almost in half with one swing of his enormous sword. But the damage was already done.

Several short genlocks surged past the prone warrior, snarling with delight as they raced toward Maric and the others in the back. They were slowed by Fiona's spell, but not enough. Genevieve moved to try to quickly close the gap left by Nicolas's fall, but she couldn't. Julien was too busy trying to keep the darkspawn from overwhelming him and Nicolas, swinging his blade in wide arcs around him, and she simply couldn't hold the line on her own. More darkspawn rushed past them. Their line was broken.

The first genlocks made to throw their spears, but several arrows thunked loudly into their heads before they could attack. They went down, squealing in pain and clawing madly at their faces. Kell stepped forward, frowning as he nocked more arrows and fired them as quickly as he could into the oncoming force.

Utha dropped her pack and prepared to run to meet the darkspawn herself. Maric wondered what the dwarf planned on fighting with, since all she wore were her brown robes and leather gauntlets. He'd never seen her carry a weapon. Did she fight with fists? Is that what the Silent Sisters did?

"Utha, wait!" Fiona called out.

The dwarf quickly jumped to one side as the elven mage stepped forward, holding her hands out in front of her. With a look of concentration and a whisper of magic, a corona of flame surrounded her hands and then rushed out in a jet to burn the approaching darkspawn.

For a moment the cavern was lit up bright as day. The front darkspawn roared and writhed in agony as the fire engulfed them. The magical flames spread along the ground, sending up a cloud of black smoke that threatened to choke the passage. The darkspawn behind those in front were similarly burned, and hissed in rage, but continued to run forward despite their injuries. They leaped over their burning comrades, eager to reach Fiona before she could cast another spell at them.

Utha launched forward as soon as the path cleared. Her face remained serene as she met the first genlock that rushed at her. Planting one foot, she did a spinning kick that caught the short creature full in the face. Bones crunched under her leather boots and it staggered back.

Not pausing a second, the dwarf raced toward it. She grabbed the genlock's crude metal pauldrons and vaulted over its head, not letting go, and when she landed on the other side she used the inertia to throw the creature over her and into three more several feet away. The entire group went down in a tangled mess.

A tall, heavily armored hurlock hissed in fury and raised its blackened sword high to strike down at the dwarf. She dodged aside, the blade striking sparks on the stone, and then she sank low and swept her foot in a wide arc under the creature's feet. It toppled easily. Calmly she leaped on top of it and struck with a rigidly straight hand—not a fist, Maric noted—at its throat. Her fingers dug deep into its withered neck with a sickening crunch, and it flailed uselessly and tried to knock Utha off.

She was already gone, leapfrogging from him onto the back of another. Before that one could even react, she had her arms locked around its head and with a great heave and a twist snapped its neck.

More darkspawn were rushing toward her now, and Maric watched in amazement as the dwarf dropped to the ground and began striking out with her feet and her hands. Each kick was precise and measured, each strike of her elbow or her palm was aimed for maximum impact, and yet she moved almost too quickly for Maric to follow. He'd never seen anyone fight like that, ever.

Finally, a hurlock successfully grabbed Utha's robe from behind and hauled her back. She gritted her teeth and prepared to twist out of its grasp, but before she could do so, the grey warhound leaped on it from behind. Hafter growled angrily as he bit into the hurlock's neck with his powerful jaws, pulling it off the dwarf completely. Black ichor flowed as the hound tossed the creature to the side.

A genlock ran at Hafter with a spear, but two arrows streaked from the shadows and sunk into its chest, sending it flying back. Kell appeared, pale eyes glaring angrily at the creature that had dared attack his hound. The hunter's hood had fallen back, revealing a clean-shaven head decorated with elaborate black tattoos that Maric thought looked much like those worn by the Avvarian hill folk.

Kell quickly shouldered his bow and drew a flail from his belt. It was a mean-looking weapon, a spiked metal ball attached to a chain, and the man immediately began attacking several darkspawn that ran toward him. His strikes were careful, each swing flinging the spiked ball into a new opponent, where it landed with spectacular effect. Then the ball would be yanked out of the reeling creature and sent hurtling into a new one.

Hafter immediately ran to Kell's back, spinning in tandem with his master's movements and snapping at any creature that got too close. One large hurlock tried to stab at him with a spear and the hound locked onto the creature's arm and dragged it to the ground. He growled loudly and flung the hurlock about in his jaws, almost as if it were a rag doll.

"Maric!"

The shout from Duncan jarred his attention. More darkspawn had surged past Genevieve and the others, though the amount of carnage he could see from that direction told him that the warriors were doing their utmost to fight back toward them. Fiona pointed with her staff and sent blasts of magical energy firing into the surge of approaching darkspawn, but it barely slowed them down.

Duncan leaped at them. As the first hissing genlock charged with a battle-axe raised high, the young Grey Warden stabbed at its chest with his pair of daggers. The silverite blades slid through the corrupted black metal of the creature's chest plate as if it were made of little more than soft fabric. Duncan's body crashed into the genlock and knocked it down, with him still on top of it.

Another darkspawn spun around, its dead eyes focusing on Duncan as it sliced down with its axe. The lad jumped up agilely, avoiding the strike and letting it land instead on the head of the hapless genlock below. In the air, Duncan lashed out with the daggers at the new attacker, cutting a clean gash across its throat and sending ichor spraying.

Even as the young man landed again he was already spinning about low and cutting into the legs of creatures nearby. Maric noticed he went for the critical spots with those short blades, though whether it was his training or simply instinct he couldn't tell. The daggers plunged into gaps in the darkspawn's crude armor, slashing tendons and severing ankles. He stabbed at any back that was turned, barely pausing to see the creature go down as he turned to face the next.

"Fun, isn't it?" Duncan laughed madly toward Maric as he scrambled over a tall hurlock and thrust a dagger deep into its eye. The creature roared in agony and teetered back into another crowd of darkspawn, taking the thief out of sight.

Maric had his own problems now as a pair of hurlocks charged him with spears. The flesh on their bald heads looked almost rotted, he thought, withered and covered in suppurating sores. The large eyes were milky pale, filled with hate. The last time he had journeyed through the Deep Roads, he and Loghain and the others had almost died at the hands of darkspawn. They were surrounded and overwhelmed until a unit of deep-delving dwarves known as the Legion of the Dead had appeared. Would he be so lucky again this time? Somehow he doubted it.

Fiona gestured with one hand and a white blast of powerful energy lanced out from it. When it struck one of the charging hurlocks, it froze it to the spot, covering it with thick ice and frost. With a cry of effort she thrust out her other hand and a fist-sized, sparkling rock flashed into existence. It sped toward the frozen creature and shattered it into a thousand chunks of frozen gore.

The second attacker didn't notice the loss of its companion, or even slow. It hissed, low and deadly, and kept coming at Maric. Swiftly he jumped to the side and cut its spear almost in half, his enchanted blade easily slicing through the weapon's shaft.

Undaunted, the darkspawn threw the pieces of its weapon down and turned to leap on Maric, fanged mouth gaping wide. He was prepared, however, and was already spinning around to slash the creature across its chest. Its armor offered no protection to the dragonbone, and ichor sprayed from its wound as it squealed in pain. He didn't let it suffer for long as he hacked it down.

The time it took to do so was almost too long, as a pair of gen-locks charged him from the side. Their weight bore him down to the ground and one of them bit deep into a shoulder. Maric gritted his teeth at the sudden agony, and even in the urgency of the situation he could sense the corruption spreading out from his injury like some burning acid soiling his blood. Hopefully the First Enchanter's potions worked as promised.

He struggled to throw the creatures off, but they were too quick and surprisingly strong for their short height. He brought his sword hilt up sharply and bashed one in the jaw, the bone crunching and fangs flying out of its mouth. The creature grunted in pain and loosened its grip, and he was finally able to throw it off.

The other genlock reared up and flashed its bloody fangs, ready to sink them into Maric a second time, but before it could do so a bolt of energy hit it square in the chest. The flash of light dazed Maric for a moment, and he covered his eyes. Stars swam before him, and while he heard the sounds of combat going on around him, it all seemed to pass in slow motion.

Then he shook his head as his vision cleared. The genlock was gone. He jumped back to his feet, bringing his longsword to bear, and saw that several hurlocks were swarming Fiona. Duncan was successfully keeping the attention of several others on himself, but the mage was about to be borne down by sheer numbers.

Before he could move, however, he heard Fiona cry out a word of power. A thunderous wave of magic rolled out from her, brilliant enough to cause the darkspawn to squeal in pain and cover their eyes, and the entire cavern shook violently from an earthquake. Maric and the darkspawn, and many of the others around him, tumbled to the ground. Rocks shook loose from the ceiling, several larger pieces barely missing him.

As the dust settled, he looked up. The short elf stood there in her glittering chain armor, shoulders back and seemingly ten feet tall in her victory. Sweat poured from her brow, and her spiky black hair was plastered to her face. Her grin was one of excitement, however, and she was flushed. Her eyes caught Maric's and she winked at him impishly. He found himself chuckling in response, almost despite himself.

Fiona lifted up her staff high over her head, the white light emanating from it suddenly intensifying as the mage gathered her concentration to deal with the darkspawn around her, who were just now beginning to recover their feet.

The staff's light flickered suddenly as a pair of arrows sprouted from the mage's chest. Her eyes went wide as she looked down at them, a bright red bloodstain quickly spreading on the chain mail.

Her face twisted into outrage. "Bloody bastards!" she swore.

Another arrow flew at her and only barely missed her head. She stumbled to the side, clutching gingerly at the arrows stuck in her chest with her free hand. Maric spun around and spotted the culprit: a pale-skinned genlock not ten feet away from him, standing on top of a large outcropping of rock and using a crude-looking, blackened shortbow.

Springing into action, Maric charged toward the creature. He swung his longsword in wide arcs around him, forcing a path through the melee. He saw Duncan, fighting expertly with his daggers, wounded with several severe-looking gashes. Red blood mixed with black on the lad's dark leathers, yet he didn't slow. Instead Duncan snarled, baring his teeth and assuming a savage countenance that Maric found surprising as he charged into yet more opponents.

He had no time to stop and help, however. A new darkspawn, this one a tall hurlock with heavy golden armor, lurched into his path. He parried a blow from its massive sword with his own, sparks flying as the blades met, and then began a series of exchanges with it. The creature was no true swordsman, however, and it wasn't long before Maric outmaneuvered it and cut it down.

He moved on quickly. The pale genlock archer had unleashed several more arrows, and now noticed that Maric was running toward it with his glowing longsword raised. The first arrow it shot at him missed, and the second he deflected with his blade—accidentally, really, though he imagined it looked otherwise.

Watch as King Maric cuts shooting arrows out of the air! Nothing can stop him!

The third arrow caught him in the abdomen, landing with staggering force. So much for not being stopped.

Gathering his strength, he made a final rush toward the archer, leaping up onto the rock where it stood. The creature hissed at him defiantly, and he ran it through without a second thought. Gushes of ichor flowed down his sword blade and the front of his armor. The creature twitched, dropping its bow and emitting a harsh rattle from deep in its throat as it died.

As the genlock slid from his blade and fell from the rock, Maric turned and slipped on its blood. Rather ungracefully he bounced off the side of the rock and landed on the stony ground, a leg twisting painfully underneath him. He managed to hold on to his longsword, but even then he only barely kept it from cutting his own head off. More stars flashed before his eyes, and agony burned throughout his entire body.

Watch as King Maric tumbles to the ground like a fool! See him bounce!

A shadow reared in front of him, and he opened his eyes only to see a hurlock standing over him, ready to bring a battle-axe down upon his head. He tried to lift his blade to fend off the attack, but he was propped up against the rock and in completely the wrong position. He had no leverage.

Kell appeared out of nowhere behind the hurlock. With a shout the hunter brought his flail down directly on the creature's head, half crushing it and sending a splatter of bone splinters and gore showering out over Maric and the stone behind him.

He felt stunned. He barely noticed the creature slump to the ground, and didn't respond immediately when the hunter stepped forward to offer his hand.

"Your Majesty?" Kell asked, his voice tinged with concern.

Maric belatedly allowed himself to be helped to his feet, his leg threatening to buckle painfully under his weight. Looking around, he realized that the last few darkspawn were being dealt with. Both Utha and Duncan had come to Fiona's assistance, although the mage was quite wounded and covered in blood. She seemed less weakened, however, than she was thoroughly angered by her predicament. Nicolas was nearby, being supported by an anxious Julien, though it was difficult to tell which of them was more wounded since they were both coated in black ichor.

Genevieve moved around to the few darkspawn on the ground still struggling, determinedly plunging her blade into their hearts and finishing them off. "We do not have long," she growled loudly. "The other group of them is coming this way." After stabbing another darkspawn, the creature gurgling in pain and then collapsing into silence, she turned and caught Fiona's attention. "Healing. Do as much as you can, and quickly."

The elf nodded tersely, her face sweaty and pale. Duncan and

Utha both helped her sit down on a rock, careful not to touch the two black arrows that still stuck out of her chest. The dwarf knelt down in front of her, concern evident on her face as she made several hand gestures.

Fiona took a shaky breath. "Do it."

Utha put one hand on her shoulder, and with the other she grabbed the end of one of the arrows firmly. Fiona flinched and shut her eyes, but did not shy away. Duncan stood next to her, holding her shoulders to keep her steady even if he looked like he was about to be sick.

With a firm jerk, the arrow came free, its wickedly barbed head appearing along with a spurt of dark blood. Fiona cried out in anguish, a throaty and animalistic sound that made Maric shudder. She doubled over, only to be pulled back up by Duncan to keep her from bending the other arrow. She seemed even paler, if that was possible, and the red stain on the front of her chain armor was rapidly expanding.

Maric made to go over to help her, but a hand on his shoulder stopped him. It was Kell, his hood restored and his flail back in its sheath. The hunter looked pained as he gestured to Nicolas. "Come, he will need our help."

Hafter limped alongside them, filthy and with ichor literally dripping from his muzzle, but mostly unharmed. Lucky dog. Nicolas had collapsed back down to the ground, clutching futilely at his blood-soaked chest plate, and it seemed that Julien was too injured to properly get him up on his own.

"How bad is it?" Kell asked him.

Julien appeared frantic. He was kneeling down, trying desperately to get Nicolas onto his feet with only one arm, the other clearly broken. Nicolas, meanwhile, appeared dazed and barely aware of what was going on around him. "I don't know!" the dark-haired warrior responded, looking up at Kell with panicked eyes. "We need to get him to the mage! He'll bleed out!"

Pulling on Nicolas as he was, the man almost seemed to be doing more harm than good. Kell glanced at Maric, and Maric understood immediately what the hunter wanted. Crouching next to Julien, he spoke reassuringly and slowly removed the man's hands from his friend. The words didn't matter so much as their tone seemed to work, slowing down the warrior's panicked breaths and urging him to collect himself as Kell dragged Nicolas away.

"I don't . . . she needs to help him!"

"She will."

Maric's words were punctuated by another bloodcurdling scream from Fiona as the last arrow was yanked from her stomach. This time the mage did fold, clutching at her chest and shaking with exhaustion. Utha could do little more than look on in sympathy. Fiona gasped and spasmed as she attempted to control her agony enough to stand. Duncan stood back as she finally did so.

"I'm fine," she gritted weakly through her teeth. With a wave of a hand, a warm blue glow suddenly suffused her entire body. She sighed loudly as the pain was lifted from her, arching her back as the magic worked its way through her body. Maric watched, impressed, as several of the smaller cuts along her arms slowly closed and healed. When the spell was finished, the glow disappeared and Fiona collapsed limply. Duncan rushed forward to catch her before she hit the ground, and with a grin he tapped her on the cheek.

"Hey there," he said with a chuckle. "No passing out just yet."

"I know," she groaned.

Utha passed the lad a potion in a white bottle, which he immediately pressed to Fiona's lips. The mage made a sour face but drank as bidden, and then coughed severely as whatever had been inside jolted her upright. She shuddered convulsively once. Then she opened her eyes and looked around, still splattered in blood and pale as a sheet, but the weakness seemed to have been driven from her.

"See?" Maric patted Julien on the back. "She's fine. Nicolas will be fine as well, once she gets to him. I've been injured like that a few times, myself. Nothing handier than having a mage around to patch you up."

The warrior looked embarrassed and allowed himself to be helped back up to his feet. "I apologize, King Maric. I must look like a foolish old woman to you."

"It's just Maric . . . and don't be ridiculous. You two are obviously friends. I happen to know what that's like, believe it or not."

Julien paused, giving him a look that he wasn't quite sure how to read. Perhaps he thought Maric was being disingenuous? Eventually the man smiled a bit sheepishly, reassured. Without saying anything further, he ran to help Kell with his friend.

Genevieve watched Maric carefully from across the passage. She wiped the gore from her face with a length of cloth, but her eyes remained fixed on him. Her look was tense, he thought, and perhaps dangerous. The others hovered near Fiona, helping the mage gather her strength for healing spells, and only their commander stood apart. It was just a matter of a few feet, but it may as well have been miles. Maric had to wonder if it had always been that way for her.

Healing was doled out quickly, even as they listened to the sounds of the alien humming growing louder and louder in the tunnels. The other darkspawn were getting closer, and from the growing tension in Genevieve's pacing, Maric assumed that there must be more on the way from other directions now, as well.

The magic that Fiona provided had its limitations. It could mend flesh and restore a degree of health, but it could only do so much for severe wounds. Julien's broken arm remained weak, and while Nicolas could walk, it seemed certain he had internal injuries that would continue to plague him. Fiona herself clearly was not fully recovered. Utha hovered around her, wringing her hands nervously the more the mage pushed her limits.

When the time came for Maric's turn, Fiona was already shaking and coated in a fresh sheen of sweat. This was sapping what little reserves of mana the mage had left, he could tell. When she raised her hand to touch his forehead, he stopped her.

"I'm not badly injured. I'll be fine."

She arched an eyebrow curiously. "Is that supposed to impress me?"

"It's supposed to save your strength, actually."

The elf appeared taken aback. She hesitated, her dark eyes meeting his for a moment, before touching his forehead despite his protest. "Let me worry about my strength." Her tone was gruff but her fingers were gentle, brushing his skin lightly as the tingle of her magic began to wash through him. He tried not to stare at her, and instead concentrated on the aura of sapphire light that surrounded him.

His twisted leg felt better immediately, if not completely repaired. The puncture wound in his gut left by the arrow similarly stopped bleeding. While he was still not whole, the spell left him feeling a thousand times better. He smiled his appreciation at the mage, and she shot him a dubious look and said nothing in return before moving on.

Genevieve had them traveling again within minutes. They moved almost as quickly as before, or tried to, as the various injuries served to slow them down considerably. They were also exhausted, Fiona most of all. Still, the Commander spent her time constantly urging them to move faster and faster. Despite the wounds she herself must have suffered, she seemed unimpaired and drove herself by sheer force of will alone.

Fear worked to speed them, as well. Maric didn't need supernatural senses to tell that the darkspawn were closing in on them no matter how fast they moved. The humming was constant now, and he almost expected to spot a horde of darkspawn waiting around every turn.

They reentered the Deep Roads proper, dropping back into the dwarven passages through a great crack in the walls that could very well have been caused by some natural tremor. It looked to Maric like any other part of the Deep Roads did: dark and forbidding, with broken statues of the dwarven Paragons and the darkspawn corruption spreading over it all. How would they find their way back to the proper route now?

He didn't have time to think about it, as it soon turned into a chase. Genevieve's cries became frantic and they broke into a full run. Exhaustion burned his muscles as they pushed and pushed, taking one turn after the other. He began to hear more than the humming off in the shadows: Now he heard the hisses and clanging of metal, the shouts of true pursuit.

They left the Deep Roads again, though this time there was little choice. The passage simply seemed to sever—not neatly, either, but like a broken limb with the jagged edges of bone still protruding from the flesh. Beyond the broken stone lay only a wide natural cavern, the floor a sizable drop down. Whether the passage picked up ahead at some point again was impossible to discern through the darkness. Perhaps the entire thing had caved in here, but why?

They couldn't turn back. Going down was the only option. With the sounds of the darkspawn still approaching, Genevieve led the way by making the leap into the cavern. She landed and remained crouched for a moment, her sword held at the ready as she scanned the shadows for any sign of life. Nothing moved.

The rest of them followed immediately after. Maric landed hard on his sore leg and hissed in pain. The others ignored him, remaining still as they scanned the shadows. The only thing that the light on the mage's staff revealed around them was great chunks of rubble.

There was also the acrid smell of brimstone. Maric found it almost overpowering. Was there some kind of natural spring nearby?

"What *is* that?" Duncan complained.

"Quiet!" Genevieve snapped. Her sword remained out, her eyes at once so wary and so exhausted that they looked positively murderous. She obviously was convinced they were not alone. Duncan's jaw closed with an audible click.

Her caution was infectious, and while they moved forward into the unknown darkness of the cavern, they did so only slowly. Fiona held up her staff and made it shine brightly enough to show where they were more clearly. This was definitely some kind of natural fissure, and they could see the jutting bones of other passages up above at several junctures. This great cavern lay between the Deep Roads, or around it. It was difficult to tell.

The sound of something odd crunching under his boot heel caught Maric's attention. He looked down, and noticed bones.

The others saw them just as he did. Fiona breathlessly lifted her staff up again, and it illuminated many piles of bones. Not human bones, Maric was relieved to see. Nor darkspawn bones, either. These were animal bones, most of them old and covered in dust.

There was a pack animal called a bronto that roamed the Deep Roads, formerly tame beasts that the dwarven Shapers had engineered long ago and that had gone wild when the darkspawn had destroyed the dwarven kingdoms during the First Blight. Maric had never seen one himself, but there were supposed to be herds of them still roaming underground. These were bronto bones, he suspected. Piles and piles of them. A whole cavern so full that it blanketed the stone.

"Is this some kind of graveyard?" Fiona asked, her voice small.

Kell shook his head. He crouched down and picked up one of the larger fragments. The fact that it was jaggedly split was obvious. Something had torn it apart. Many of the bones had suffered similarly. Without comment he tossed the piece aside and nocked an arrow on his bow. His pale eyes looked around intently.

They were all quiet, waiting.

"Do you hear that?" Duncan finally asked.

Each of them cocked their head, listening. There were only silence and shadows. It had also grown warm, Maric found. He had assumed that the warmth he felt was a result of all the running and sweating, but now that they were still and he was calmer, he realized it was something else. Mixed with the sulfurous stench was a dry heat wafting in the air.

"I don't hear anything," Genevieve growled.

"Exactly! Where are the darkspawn? I can barely sense them!"

The Commander seemed stunned not to have realized it herself. They stood for a long minute, doing nothing, before she finally waved them to proceed. "We need to find a way through. Whatever reason the darkspawn aren't following us, perhaps we can use it to our advantage."

The rest of them appeared reluctant but said nothing. They followed her quietly, picking their way through the field of bones as the cavern slowly opened up into something even larger. There was light here, too. It was dim at first, the faintest glow of lichen clinging to the walls, but eventually it increased to the point where Fiona's staff wasn't even needed. Maric was reminded of the great caverns that the thaigs were built within, but here there were stalactites and stalagmites instead of dwarven buildings. There were fissures pumping out steam, and he thought he saw faint streams of lava behind large rocky outcroppings. Their orange glow added to the dread ambience.

There were also more of the bones littering the entire chamber. Many of them were blackened, jumbled atop piles of dark ash. Several of the fissures sent clouds of steam pumping up along the rocky walls. The smell of brimstone became almost overpowering.

Kell's hound began to growl fearfully, its hackles raised.

Genevieve stared into the distance, trying to peer past the faint haze of the steam as if she could command whatever secret this place held to reveal itself. Nothing came. Without looking at the others, she waved them forward. "Look for a way through."

As they began to spread out, however, Kell suddenly hissed, "Stop!"

Genevieve turned back, annoyance clear on her face—which instantly turned into alarm. The hunter stared upward, his eyes wide and stark with fear. She followed his gaze at the same time as Maric did, as they all did, and they saw what it was that had kept the darkspawn from pursuing them. Something descended down upon them from above, something large. Something with great, leathery wings.

"Dragon," Kell breathed.

8

The Old Gods will call to you,
From their ancient prisons they will sing.
Dragons with wicked eyes and wicked hearts,
On blacken'd wings does deceit take flight,
The first of My children, lost to night.
—Canticle of Silence 3:6, Dissonant Verse

"Wardens!"

Genevieve's shout of warning was unnecessary, and came too late as the black-scaled high dragon crashed down onto the ground amid them with cataclysmic force. It roared as it did so, a blast of sound so furious that Duncan covered his ears. He screamed, the pain unbearable, but he couldn't even hear himself. The ground shook under his feet from the force of the dragon's impact, and a rush of air from the dragon's wings beating hard sent him flying off his feet.

The world spun around him as he tumbled and skidded along the ground, until finally he slammed into a column of black rock. Agony blazed through his back. Gritting his teeth, Duncan forced himself to get back to his feet. A wave of dizziness swam over him, but he managed to keep his bearings.

The others had been scattered the same as he had, though the ones in heavy armor had not traveled quite as far. Already the high dragon was spinning around with surprising agility to attack them.

It stomped down onto Julien with a taloned foot, pinning him before he could rise, and turned its sinewy neck to glare directly at Genevieve with a head that was twice as large as the woman herself.

She did not retreat, standing resolute with her sword poised before her, eyes warily locked onto the dragon's. The creature snorted black smoke angrily, as if it was enraged by the presence of these intruders in its lair. It breathed through its huge fangs, each yellowed tooth as long as an arm, as it stalked carefully around Genevieve. She kept her sword ready and faced the dragon, her face grim determination.

The dragon stepped off Julien, and the man groaned in pain. Nicolas darted in, quickly dragging the man away to a rocky ridge nearby. There was too much dust and dirt stirred up by the dragon still clouding the air to see much of anyone else.

"Get yourselves to cover!" Genevieve shouted. Her voice drew the dragon's ire and it darted in to snap at her with its great jaws. She rolled to the side, her speed impressive despite her bulky armor, and slashed at the dragon's long neck with her sword. The point cut through its thick black scales, but not deeply. It was enough, however, that the creature reared up high and roared in outrage.

The entire cavern shook as the Commander darted forward, her greatsword held out to stab into the dragon's chest. She never got that close, however, as it swiped her aside and sent her hurtling along the ground.

The other Grey Wardens were reacting now. Duncan saw Nicolas rush in, bashing the dragon on its rear leg with his mace. Julien joined him a moment later, limping as he attacked with his sword. So, too, did Utha appear on the creature's other side. She had pulled out her double-club, a dwarven weapon he had seen her use from time to time, which consisted of two lengths of steel connected by a short length of chain. These she spun around her with dizzying speed, and she rapped the dragon's scales with a wicked blow.

Kell appeared, as well, leaping up to higher ground with Hafter bounding beside him. The hunter restrained the dog from running down to join the fray, and began carefully firing arrows aimed at the dragon's vulnerable head.

The dragon ignored the arrows and spun around with lightning speed. Its long tail swept Julien and Nicolas off their feet, sending them crashing to the ground, and only barely missed Utha as she did a somersault to avoid it. It fixated on the dwarf now, stamping down hard several times in an attempt to crush her. Each time the dwarf danced agilely out of the way.

Duncan pulled out his daggers and dashed forward to assist the others. The heat in this cavern was incredible, and already he was sweating profusely. It would be unfortunate if he got swept by those great wings into one of the lava streams—Duncan had never seen lava before in his entire life, but it wasn't hard to imagine how unpleasant it would be to end up dropped inside it. About as unpleasant as being chomped on by those giant dragon teeth, no doubt.

Are we really planning on fighting this thing?

Genevieve appeared out of the haze and smoke and charged beside him, her sword raised high. They didn't exchange looks and merely ran together toward the dragon's flank as it was preoccupied with Utha. Duncan gulped as they got closer. The creature loomed high overhead, far larger than it had looked from a distance. Far faster, too. It was long and lanky and quick. How in Andraste's name did it live down here?

Dragons were supposed to have been extinct, hunted into oblivion—or at least they were thought to have been until one was spotted over the Frostbacks at the beginning of the Dragon Age.

Was this that one? Was this where dragons came when they weren't flying about and razing the countryside?

Genevieve plunged her sword deep into the dragon's hide. Duncan did the same with his daggers, the silverite easily cutting through the scales. Bright dragon blood spurted from the wounds. His blades didn't cut anywhere near as deeply as the Commander's, but hopefully they were enough to cause the beast some damage.

Apparently they were. The dragon reared up again, roaring thunderously and bringing bits of stone plummeting down from the cavern's ceiling. As it spun around, Genevieve's sword yanked out of the creature's hide, coated red with blood. Duncan's daggers were almost torn from his grip and he had to pull hard to free them. The dragon opened its maw wide, and for a moment there was the sound of a great intake of breath.

"Look out!" Genevieve shouted.

She leaped on Duncan and pushed him to the ground, burying him under her heavy armor. The air was knocked out of him, and for a moment he felt confused. A moment later he realized why she'd done it: The dragon was breathing flame.

The blast of heat hit them first. Duncan cried out, but found the air forcibly ripped from his lungs. For a moment he couldn't breathe, and then the fire washed over them. At the same time, however, something else struck them. A wave of freezing cold from the other direction, something that made Genevieve's armor frost up and the air suddenly fill with boiling steam. The heat was searing and painful, but shockingly they survived. The flames were gone.

Genevieve pulled herself off of him, and he rolled aside quickly. He saw then the reason for their escape: Fiona had appeared, her staff held high over her head and flaring brilliant blue streams of power from the stone at its tip. She looked radiant, surrounded by a corona of magic so cold Duncan could feel it from where he lay.

The dragon could feel it, too. It bellowed in fury and launched itself at the mage, flapping its wings hard enough that Duncan had to struggle not to be blown away once again. Three arrows streaked toward the dragon's head, and one of them hit home in its eye. The creature shrieked and spasmed in midjump, and it crashed down next to Fiona and slid along the ground.

One of its wings nearly hit the elf, but she ignored it and instead collected her will. She channeled power through her staff, and the icy aura around her suddenly burst out in all directions. Instantly the entire cavern was filled with a freezing storm. Wind and snow blew in all directions, and the temperature dropped so rapidly that Duncan could see his breath.

It figures she would bring the damned winter down here, too, he grumbled. The dragon reacted wildly to the spell. It writhed in place, obviously in agony and beating its wings uselessly against the ground as it tried to escape from its millions of painful icy tormentors.

Maric appeared next to Fiona and charged the dragon as it spun, slashing with his enchanted longsword, which bit deep into the creature's hide. Another indignant shriek, and this time the dragon pushed itself to its feet and launched itself high up into the cavern. With several beats of its great wings it retreated to the shadowed recesses above them.

Genevieve stood unsteadily, covering her face against the blizzard. "Grey Wardens, to me! Regroup!" Her voice was almost lost to the howling winds, but the others heeded her call even so and ran toward her.

Duncan remained crouched low to the ground, trying to see through all the blowing snow to discern whether the dragon was about to swoop back down on them again. Perhaps it was gone for good? Perhaps they delivered it enough of a bloody nose that it had retreated to lick its wounds?

"Is it going to come back?" Fiona shouted as she arrived, her thoughts echoing Duncan's.

Kell dropped down from the boulder, Hafter barking angrily. "We should get back to the Deep Roads! Quickly, while there's still time!"

"No!" Genevieve growled. "Our difficulty will be no less there!"

"Than with a dragon? Are you mad?"

Julien and Nicolas approached, an injured Utha limping not far behind, and they looked surprised as they saw their commander cross the distance toward the hunter and grab the front of his leathers in her gauntlets. Her face was contorted with fury, yet he met her gaze levelly, staring at her with his pale eyes. Hafter growled menacingly at Genevieve's feet.

"We are *not* leaving," she insisted. "We fight. We will win."

"We should be facing darkspawn—"

"We should be finding my brother!" she snarled. "That is our mission! We find a way through this place, back to Ortan thaig! Or we die trying!" She turned a glare to each of the Grey Wardens in turn, challenging them to contradict her. None of them looked away, but none of them spoke, either. When those blue eyes fixed on Duncan, he shrank away a little. She really meant them to fight the dragon if it came back.

"Then what is your plan?" Maric demanded. He stood beside Fiona now, his runed longsword glowing faintly in the blowing snow. "Do you even have one?" he continued, his tone harshly accusing.

Genevieve's face was steel. She had no time to respond, however, as another cry sounded from the upper reaches of the cavern. The dragon was returning.

"Move!" she cried.

They scattered. Duncan ran as fast as his legs would take him, covering his face to protect it against the icy winds of Fiona's spell. He could sense the great mass of the dragon overhead, and for a moment he was certain that it was about to come crashing down on top of him, or worse, swoop down and snatch him off the ground in its talons like a hawk would a rabbit.

The creature landed somewhere behind him, however, and uttered another ear-splitting roar. He stumbled and half fell behind a column of rock. Lava swam in a narrow channel nearby, the blowing snow causing great waves of hissing steam to rise from its surface.

Getting his legs underneath him, Duncan turned and chanced a look around the edge of the column. He could definitely make out the dragon through the blizzard, but only as an extremely large and indistinct shape. It was clearly spinning around, its long neck darting down to snap at something below it, though who it was he wasn't sure.

Swallowing hard, he gathered his courage and ran out again. The high dragon came clearly into view as he approached, all muscle and grace and covered in glossy black scales. He might even have called it beautiful had it not been so dangerous.

The dragon bellowed again, its long tail lashing wildly behind it. Its wings beat madly and added to the flurry of the winds. The sound of its roar amplified in the cavern to the point where it was painful to hear. Duncan winced and tried to keep running forward despite the ringing in his ears.

The creature was having difficulty dealing with all the combatants. From what Duncan could see, the others had surrounded it on several sides. Every time the dragon attempted to concentrate on a single opponent, the others would move in to strike. So, too, did Kell's continual barrage of arrows keep distracting it from its intended target. He saw Utha dancing about near its legs, and Genevieve stabbing deep into its flank. Its black scales were heavily streaked with blood, presumably its own.

The dragon snapped down at Genevieve, and she only barely dodged out of the way. Two more arrows struck its neck and caused it to flinch. It snorted with rage and spun its entire body around, the thick tail swinging low on the ground and flinging Genevieve away. Duncan had to leap to avoid it, and heard the Commander land hard on the uneven rocks behind him. There was a snap like something breaking, and he heard her gasp in sudden pain.

Berserk, the dragon rushed at the outcropping where Kell stood with his bow, its maw open wide. Fiona fired a bolt of lightning at the creature, and it roared in pain as it was struck, but it was now too intent on its tormentor to be dissuaded.

Hafter bolted forward from his master's side, racing down the side of the rock before Kell could stop him. The hound barked furiously and charged at the dragon, but it barely even slowed down. With one great swipe of its forearms it struck the hound and sent him flying. Hafter yelped in pain as he crashed with incredible force against the far stone wall of the cavern, and then slid down to the ground below, where he lay still and silent.

Kell shouted in rage, his cool demeanor finally broken. He fired three arrows in quick succession at the dragon's head, and one of them struck true near its eye. It reached the hunter and snapped him up in its jaws, carrying him into the air. The man screamed now in agony, and even from where Duncan stood he could hear the sounds of ribs breaking as the dragon bit down with its enormous jaws.

"Kell!" Fiona cried out from below.

Duncan got near enough to the dragon's rear to stab into it with his daggers. He drew blood, but it only had to twitch its tail to send him stumbling down to the stone again. Dazed, he sat up, only to have the tail slam into him like a brick wall. He skidded several feet and then rolled, finally smacking his head hard against a stalagmite. His vision swam, and for a moment he couldn't tell which end was up.

When he raised his head, he saw King Maric charging at the dragon, his longsword with its blue glowing runes raised high over his head. He stabbed it deep into the creature's flank, just above one of its forearms, and that was enough to make it scream. It dropped

Kell out of its mouth, the man little more than a limp rag doll of blood and broken bones from what Duncan could see. Fiona ran to his side.

The dragon angrily spun on Maric then, its mouth open wide and dripping with red blood. The intake of breath was audible even from where Duncan lay, and for a moment the King stared up at the creature. There was nowhere for him to run, and nobody was nearby to distract the beast further. As the dragon glared down at him, Duncan saw him stare back and see his death in the creature's eyes.

And then the dragon blew its gust of flame.

Maric's eyes went wide with disbelief as the flames struck an invisible barrier in front of him. Instead of engulfing him completely, they passed around him harmlessly. He looked around and saw Fiona not a few feet away, her hands still raised from the spell she had cast.

"Get back, you idiot!" she yelled.

He stumbled away as the dragon stomped one of its legs, attempting to crush him underneath. It stomped again, this time catching his cloak and tearing it off his back. Nicolas and Utha appeared out of nowhere on its other flank, and for a moment the beast was torn between trying to attack the fleeing Maric and turning to face its new attackers. With a roar of pain and frustration it spun about, batting Nicolas aside almost instantly.

Fat lot of good I'm doing over here!

Duncan picked himself up off the floor, wincing from the sharp stab of pain he felt in his leg but refusing to let it slow him down. The dragon had its back to him again, and he needed to take advantage of that position this time. They could keep hacking away at this giant beast all day. It wasn't going to die unless they hit something really critical—like its head.

He raced across the stone, watching as Utha once again danced away from the dragon's attacks and struck at it when she could with her double-club. He saw a bright flash of blue light as Fiona laid a healing spell on Kell. When he reached the creature's tail, he didn't slow down, and tried to pretend that what he was doing wasn't completely idiotic.

Oh, don't turn around! Don't turn around!

Grinning madly, he stepped onto the thickest part of the dragon's tail and kept on running. It was difficult with the blowing wind and snow, and harder still as the creature jerked and moved underneath him, but somehow he managed to keep his balance as well as his momentum. Arms held out at his sides and shouting in near panic, Duncan sped up along the dark ridges of the dragon's spine.

"Duncan, you fool!" he heard Genevieve shouting from somewhere behind him. "What are you *doing*?"

It was a good question. One he didn't really have time to think about. The dragon was only just now becoming aware that there was something on its back. Fortunately, both Maric and Utha pressed their attack just then and kept the creature from attempting to deal with him.

He tried not to look. He kept his feet pumping and his eyes on the scales beneath him. He tried not to notice just how far down the floor was from this height. Terror thrilled through him, his heart beating wildly in his chest.

Then he slipped. For a split second, Duncan thought he was going to fly off and that this madness would have been for nothing. His heart leaped up into his throat. By reflex he managed to stab one of the silverite daggers into the base of the creature's serpentine neck. It went deep and lodged into bone, and impossibly he hung on to the hilt for dear life as the dragon reared up high and roared in pain.

The world spun dizzyingly around him. The dragon flapped its wings, hard, and with a great leap it went up into the air. His stomach plummeted, and he had to fight the overpowering urge to vomit. There had been entirely too much vomiting lately, he thought. No more vomiting!

The air whipped past his face, his black hair fluttering wildly. He tried to haul himself up toward the dagger, but it was all he could do just to hold on and breathe. He could barely see anything, as the light was almost completely gone. The dragon hit something and he was almost pulled off, and he realized it had landed on something high up in the cavern, perhaps on whatever ledge it had retreated to the first time. Then the dragon leaped up again, roaring as it beat its wings and flew.

Something whizzed by his head in the darkness, and for a moment Duncan didn't realize what it was. Then something else passed right over him and he recognized the tip of a stalactite. Was it trying to brush him off? A third one seemed like it was about to successfully do so, and he strained hard to pull himself up onto the dragon's neck and out of the way. Still, it banged hard into his leg and he winced at the flash of pain.

Then the dragon descended again. Summoning his strength, Duncan raised his other dagger and stabbed it a bit farther up along the creature's long neck. It twitched and attempted to dislodge its rider, but he now had two handholds. Scrabbling hard with his legs, he managed to wrap himself around the neck a little better. Now let it try to get rid of him.

It landed somewhere once again, the impact slamming him against the dragon's scales and nearly knocking the wind out of him. There was light from nearby lava, enough that Duncan could see the creature attempting to twist its head around. Its long neck was lithe, but not enough to allow it to reach where he actually was. Several times it snapped close, and he saw those giant teeth clearly and smelled the reek of brimstone and carrion on its breath. He hadn't even considered the possibility of it biting him off its own back! What if it had been able to do that?

The dragon was still moving, but now Duncan had the purchase he needed. Pulling one of the daggers out, he stabbed up ahead of the other. And then repeated this process. Quickly he ascended the dragon's neck this way until he was directly behind its head.

Now it thrashed him around. He had to hug the neck close, warm scales pressed against his cheek, and hang on for dear life. His stomach heaved left and right, and he would have vomited had there been anything in his stomach to expel. Fighting against the inertia and the winds whipping by him, praying to the Maker that he wouldn't be flung off across the entire cavern, he pulled one of the silverite blades out and then stabbed it directly into the dragon's head.

He could feel it hitting bone and cutting through, and bright blood spurted out over his arm. The dragon threw its head back and roared, but rather than dislodging him, this very movement forced Duncan to push the dagger in deeper. It went in even past the hilt, more blood and gore gushing out of the wound. He felt muscles twitch convulsively in the creature's neck. It tried to leap up into the air again, only to crash down so that its entire neck hit the ground.

He simply couldn't hold on. He lost his grip on both of his blades and was thrown off, hitting rock with such force that he heard his arm break. He screamed aloud as he rolled along the ground and skidded to a halt.

When he opened his eyes, he found he was back in the effect of Fiona's spell. Wind and ice whipped about, and for a moment Duncan couldn't see anything in the dim orange light of the lava. Where was the dragon? Where had it gone? How could he not see something so incredibly large?

Then it appeared, emerging from the blowing snow like a giant apparition. Its dark head was streaked with its own blood, and it roared in fury as it charged toward him. Every instinct told him to run, but he was too broken from the fall and too gripped in terror. As that great head descended down upon him, Duncan clenched his eyes shut, waiting for the inevitable . . .

. . . and then felt someone grab him from behind, yanking him backwards.

He saw Julien, battered and caked in blood. The wounded warrior picked him up and physically threw him back, and for a moment he felt himself sailing through the air as if in slow motion. He could see the high dragon behind Julien, its head snapping at the ground where Duncan had been only a moment before.

And then he crashed back to the ground, rolling away, and the pain flared up in his broken arm until his vision became little more than white fuzz. He fought against the agony and opened his eyes. The dragon reared on Julien now, clearly furious that the man had denied it its vengeance. It lunged down at him, and while Julien fought to bring up his sword to meet its attack, he was slowed too much by his injuries.

The dragon's head closed around his body, teeth closing in and crunching loudly. Duncan heard Julien scream in agony. Then the creature pulled the man up in his mouth and flung him up in the air behind him. The broken body sailed out of sight into the blowing wind and shadows.

The dragon slowly turned back to stare at Duncan, its black eyes narrowing in pure hatred. He gulped and began to scramble backwards, but before he could even get far he saw Genevieve charge the dragon from its side. She ran into view, soot covering her armor and sweat pouring down her face, the effort showing in every step. With a great cry she swung the sword hard against the base of the dragon's neck.

Blood fountained forth from the gash. The creature bellowed its fury and lunged its head down at its attacker. Genevieve was ready for it, however. Bracing herself, she shoved the greatsword up into the onrushing maw of teeth, the point of the blade driving into the back of its throat and piercing its head.

The inertia drove her back, and she slid along the ground several feet until one of her metal heels caught in a large crack in the cavern floor. She screamed in exertion as she pushed back against the weight, holding her ground. The dragon twitched violently and attempted to pull its head up and away. The blade remained impaled within its mouth, however, and as Genevieve held on she was yanked off her feet.

The creature floundered, its strength dissolving as bright blood gushed out of its mouth and down Genevieve's arms. It crashed down again, slamming her hard against the ground, but she doggedly held on. The impact drove the sword even more deeply into the dragon's head, and its whole body spasmed in response.

It tried to gnash its teeth, but couldn't quite close its mouth around the blade. Small blasts of flame guttered forth from the back of its throat, licking at Genevieve's face. It tried to claw at her, but the creature almost seemed too disoriented. It kept trying to rise and ended up only thrashing its wings uselessly.

Slowly but inexorably, she gained her feet and pressed her blade forward until her arms were well past the dragon's great teeth. It spasmed again, ribbons of blood streaming out of its black eyes. And then, just as Genevieve screamed in rage at the strain of holding against the creature's impossible strength, it collapsed to the ground.

Its wings settled, and its entire body twitched once and then was still.

For a moment Duncan almost couldn't believe it. The blizzard began to dissipate, and a hush descended over the cavern. He heard only Genevieve's labored breathing as she knelt down by the dragon's head, shaking with pure exhaustion. Weakly she braced a foot against its snout and pulled her blade free with a sickeningly wet sound. Dark red blood gushed out of its mouth, pooling at her feet. The dragon's eyes were still open, but they were blank. It was definitely dead.

They had won.

Duncan heard quiet footsteps approaching and twisted around to see who it was. Utha held her chest gingerly and favored one leg, her robes covered in streaks of blood, and ran quickly over to the Commander. Genevieve did little more than nod curtly and wave away the dwarf's concerned hand on her shoulder.

"I need to catch my breath," she gasped. Wearily tugging off one of her gauntlets, she wiped her sweaty brow with the back of her hand. "See to the others."

Utha glanced over to Duncan, but he pointed off toward the far end of the cavern. "Go that way," he suggested to her. "Julien got thrown over there; he's probably hurt really badly." She nodded and ran off.

Fiona and Maric were not far behind. Neither seemed too hurt, though the King looked battered and all but covered in foul ash. They both ran over to Duncan, the mage bending down to help him sit up. He winced as sharp pain radiated from his broken arm. There was blood covering the leather straps, and no way to tell if that was his or the dragon's. Truth be told, he didn't care to inspect the injury too closely. It felt bad.

"Are you all right?" Fiona asked

"Do I look all right?" he snapped, cradling his arm in front of him. The pain intensified for a moment and he hissed sharply through his teeth, closing his eyes as he rocked back and forth.

Maric whistled in appreciation. "I can't believe you rode that thing!"

"It was idiotic!" Fiona snapped up at him. "He could have been killed!"

"He looks alive to me. Plus, it worked."

Duncan held up a bloodied, shaking hand to distract the pair from their bickering. "Hello? Wounded here?"

The elf snorted in anger, frowning tightly as she turned back to see the extent of his injuries. When she touched his arm too strongly, he flinched and twisted away from her reflexively. That brought its own agony, enough to make him fall back to a prone position and writhe on the ground. Had he shattered the bone? It bloody well felt like it! It was like liquid fire burning through his veins.

"All right, then," she breathed. "A spell it is." She was pale and sweating, with dark circles under her eyes from the exhaustion, but still the mage collected herself and began to cast. She firmed her grip on his shoulder, whispering arcane words under her breath. The blue aura of power surrounded her and flowed into him, bringing with it a cool, blessed relief that made him gasp out loud.

He could feel his flesh mending, even feel some of the bones moving about inside his arm. That should have been painful, but it wasn't. The sensation was merely odd, his senses numbed as the magic danced its way along his body and tickled at his fingertips.

"We have some poultices," Maric commented. "Potions, too. You shouldn't waste your strength, Fiona; you look exhausted."

She didn't stop. "We may need those. I may not be here to cast these spells later."

He didn't argue, and instead looked around the cavern. Duncan followed his gaze and noticed Kell limping toward them. The hunter looked quite a sight, completely caked in dirt and blood, his leather jerkin torn with several long gashes in it along his side. He'd lost his hooded cloak, and his head was coated in blood, but for all that Duncan supposed he looked rather healthy for having been inside the dragon's mouth not minutes earlier.

The man wasn't looking their way. Instead he was casting around anxiously, looking toward the far reaches of the cavern. "Hafter?" he called. Normally such a shout would have been enough to bring the hound bounding toward him, but there was absolutely no response. Not even a bark or a whine.

Fiona looked up sharply. "Oh no! Hafter!"

Just then, Kell noticed a shape against one of the far walls. It was where the dog had been flung by the dragon, and from where Duncan sat it looked like he had not moved at all. He was just a heap of lifeless fur collapsed at the base of the wall, a small stream of hissing lava not two feet away. The hunter limped in that direction, ignoring his pain as he sped to see to his companion.

Fiona completed the spell. "Are you going to be all right?" she asked Duncan anxiously. He nodded and tried to get up. The pain was still there, and his arm was stiff as a board, but he was much improved. Maric helped him, while the elf ran off to join Kell, her tattered blue skirt swishing.

With Maric's assistance, Duncan limped over to where the pair of them knelt by Hafter's body. It looked certain that there was nothing that could be done. The dog didn't move, and Kell's face was anguished as he ran a shaky hand along his fur. Duncan had never seen the man look so helpless.

"Is he—?"

"No." Fiona shook her head. She sighed in relief, and Kell closed his eyes in silent thanks. Perhaps he prayed; Duncan really couldn't say. He'd never known the hunter to offer thanks to the Maker—or any other god, for that matter—but perhaps this was a special occasion. "He's badly hurt, but I think my magic will be enough to restore him."

She began to cast her spell, and as the blue glow spread across the hound's body, Hafter suddenly twitched. His dark eyes opened, and when he saw Kell kneeling above him, he whined plaintively and thumped his tail weakly against the stone floor. The hunter patted his head and urged him to remain still while the spell did its work.

"Lucky dog," Maric chuckled, to which Duncan could only nod.

An anguished cry from elsewhere in the cavern interrupted them. Fiona's spell fizzled to a halt as she looked up, and the rest of them turned around. At first Duncan couldn't see where the sound was coming from, and then he noticed Utha on the far side of the cavern next to a large, rocky outcropping. In the dim light of the lichen he could see that the cavern floor sloped up to that point and led back the way they came. The dwarf was very still, and it took him a moment to realize that there was someone crouching on the ground next to her.

It was Nicolas, holding a limp and bloody Julien in his arms.

"Fiona!" Duncan cried, though it was unnecessary. The mage looked to Kell and the hunter nodded quick assent. She collected her skirt and dashed quickly across the cavern toward the others. Duncan limped slowly, Maric helping him along, and he saw that Genevieve was walking there, too.

The elf got to Julien's body, and it took a moment to pry the grieving Nicolas off of him. The blond warrior was disconsolate, tears streaming down his face as he begged his friend to hold on. Utha looked sorrowful, but when she put a compassionate hand on Nicolas's shoulder, he shrugged it off angrily.

"Just help him!" he shouted at Fiona.

She nodded, shaken, and laid her hands on Julien. The blue glow of her healing spell surrounded him, but as Duncan drew closer he suddenly saw the warrior's state. Julien's body was twisted and broken, his head at an odd angle from the rest of him. Blood covered his armor and was pooled around him, and one of his arms was almost completely ruined. It was nothing more than a bloody red mass, held together by the fragments of his armor.

If Fiona had gotten here earlier, then perhaps . . . but from the way Julien's neck looked, it was possible he had died instantly. Duncan *hoped* he had died instantly. The man's eyes were open and staring, but strangely calm. Like there was nothing wrong with him in the slightest. Duncan shuddered and looked away.

Magic continued to pour from Fiona into the body, but very little seemed to be happening. Some of the gaping wounds on Julien's body were closing, but no color was being restored to his pale skin and he didn't move at all. Tears welled in the mage's eyes as she intensified her concentration.

"Do something!" Nicolas insisted. "Why is nothing happening?"

"I'm trying!" she sobbed.

Genevieve stepped forward. Her expression was stone, and she touched Fiona's shoulder. "Stop," she ordered. The elf looked up at her uncertainly, but there was no ambiguity in the command. The spell faltered and then ceased entirely.

"No!" Nicolas shouted. He knelt down again and cradled Julien in his arms, trying to support his head carefully even though the neck was clearly broken. "No, you can't stop! He'll be all right! He just needs healing!"

"He's dead," Genevieve said. Her voice was flat.

More tears streaked down his face, mingling with the splatters of blood. "You don't know that!"

"Look at him, Nicolas. He is gone."

For a second it looked like the warrior might rebel. He shook with rage, and then his anger quickly dissolved into tears. Trembling now with anguish, he lowered Julien's head back to the ground, and then pressed his face into the man's chest plate. His desolate sobs racked his entire body, his hands touching Julien and then recoiling. Duncan couldn't watch. The others hung their heads, and for a time all they heard in the hushed cavern was the sound of Nicolas's grief.

Fiona looked up at Genevieve, her face streaked with tears. "Are you sure you don't want me to try . . ." Her voice faltered, and there was nothing more to say.

"Magic cannot bring someone back from the dead." Genevieve gestured back to where Kell still sat. "Go and help the dog. We will need to move soon."

"No!" Nicolas roared, jumping up. "We're not leaving him here!"

"We must. The darkspawn are on their way; can you not feel it? We must use what advantage we have." She put a gauntleted hand on the warrior's shoulder, looking at him directly. For a moment she hesitated, and compassion broke through the Commander's steely facade. Tears of grief welled up in her eyes. "My friend," she began, her voice faltering. Nicolas stared at her in incomprehension, and it was clear that though Genevieve searched for words to comfort him, she found none.

Then she quickly blinked away the tears and resumed her aura of command, the moment of grief past. She removed her hand from his shoulder and nodded at him brusquely. "Say your farewells," she ordered him, "and do it quickly. We move out as soon as we're able."

He collapsed to his knees, the tears driven from him and replaced with a stark blankness as he stared down at Julien's corpse. The Commander turned and walked back to Kell without further comment, and Fiona slowly got up and followed her.

Duncan looked at Maric beside him, but the man simply stared uncomfortably at the ground. He had barely known Julien. Duncan himself had only known the warrior for a few months, but the others? Utha and Nicolas had been his constant companions for years, if not more. The dwarf knelt down next to Nicolas and put her hand on his shoulder, and this time he didn't pull away. He just stared, stricken.

There had been a lot of death back in Val Royeaux. Duncan had grown up on the streets, and it wasn't uncommon for people there to simply disappear. Sometimes they were arrested, vanishing to some dank dungeon never to resurface again. Sometimes people got sick and there was no medicine to help, and sometimes there were murders. He'd known a young girl, a fine pickpocket who'd taken a fancy to him once, that had been struck by a nobleman's carriage and had her leg broken. She'd lain there in the street begging for help and been ignored, and by the time she'd finally crawled out of the mud and into a nearby alleyway it had only been to die from blood loss.

So death was no stranger to him. Still, this was the first time he'd seen a Grey Warden fall in battle in the months since he'd joined the order. It seemed at times like they were indomitable, warriors and mages that simply could not be taken down by any force in Thedas, and yet here was evidence that it simply wasn't so.

He stepped forward, placing a hand on Nicolas's other shoulder, and was about to offer a comforting word when the man jumped up and spun on him. The sudden apoplectic rage in those eyes sent him stumbling back.

"You!" Nicolas snarled. Though Utha tried to restrain him, he ignored her. "Julien died saving your pathetic life. He should have let that creature snap you up."

"I didn't—," Duncan stammered.

"What were you doing, leaping on it? Do you think there are no consequences for your actions? You act the rash fool and look what becomes of it!" He gestured down at Julien, new tears streaming from his eyes.

"Hey!" Maric protested. "He brought that dragon down!"

"He brought Julien down, too," Nicolas growled. The blond warrior glared at Duncan, and there was nothing but accusation there. Nicolas was absolutely right, after all. The image of Julien pulling him away from the dragon's jaws played in his head: It should have been him lying there, neck broken and twisted around. It should have been him who'd paid the price for his bravado, but instead someone else had stepped in and paid it for him.

His eyes met Utha's, and the dwarf stared back at him in silent anguish. She was the most compassionate person he'd ever met, and yet she didn't move to intervene. She closed her eyes and lowered her head. She agreed with Nicolas. She didn't need to say it;

he could see it as plain as day.

Duncan retreated, the force of Nicolas's hatred driving him back. Maric shouted his name, but he turned and ran. The glow from the lava grew dim, and before he knew it he'd run out of the cavern and into the darkness, away from the others. The shadows welcomed him, drawing him into their embrace, and all he could do was to keep on running.

9

Here lies the abyss, the well of all souls.
From these emerald waters doth life begin anew.
Come to me, child, and I shall embrace you.
In my arms lies Eternity.

—Canticle of Andraste 14:11

Fiona glanced at Maric as he walked beside her. "You didn't need to come with me," she muttered. "I am perfectly capable of finding Duncan by myself."

"I know that," he said.

"I have a spell that will lead me right to him."

"So you told me earlier."

"And if I were to sense any darkspawn coming, I'd go back."

"I know that, too." He looked at her seriously. "I also know there's more than just darkspawn down here. I've had firsthand experience with such creatures. You shouldn't be alone out here any more than Duncan should."

She couldn't really argue with that logic, so she sighed and turned her attention back to the tunnel ahead. Maric had been frustratingly agreeable since they'd left the dragon's cavern. He was being respectful of the Wardens' loss, she supposed, and that was unexpected. There were times when she thought Maric a fool, a man who seemed to get by on his irreverent charm instead of acting as she would have expected a king to act. And then there were times like this when he seemed thoughtful and competent, and she could see perhaps a sliver of the leader his reputation claimed him to be.

Which was the real man, then? It was impossible for her to tell. So instead she tried to ignore him and concentrate on their task. Frustratingly, she found it almost harder to ignore Maric when he was quietly following beside her than when he was chattering away. Surely he'd planned that.

They walked for a short time through a winding passage, the white light of her staff showing the way even though it probably was unnecessary. There was a lot of the phosphorescent lichen down this path, which at least meant that Duncan hadn't wandered this far completely in the dark. If he had, what he had done would have been suicidal on top of being extremely foolish. She was still going to kill him when they found him.

And if she didn't, Genevieve certainly would. The Commander had been livid when she'd learned Duncan had run off. There had been a moment where she very nearly ordered them to move on, leaving the lad behind to fend for himself. Fiona had seen the thought cross the woman's mind, and only reluctantly had it been discarded.

The darkspawn weren't on them yet, after all. They had a little time, if not much. Fiona had volunteered to retrieve Duncan, if she could. The fact that Maric accompanied her made it less likely they would return to the dragon's cavern only to find the others gone, but it was not impossible. The King's knowledge of the way to Ortan thaig was far less useful now that they were essentially lost.

"Look at that," he murmured, pointing down to the ground. There were patches of colored moss, purple and grey mostly but also bits of orange. The walls in these caves were moist, and the air was humid and smelled of musty greenery. Strange how they had just left behind a cavern with streams of lava and here was already something completely different. She'd expected mostly stone and more stone down here in the underground, but there was much more. It was full of life. Indeed, there were *dragons*.

"It's just moss," she said.

"No, I mean it's not corrupted. Do you notice there's very little evidence of the darkspawn around here? Ever since we left the Deep Roads."

"They probably don't come this way often, thanks to the dragon."

"Do they need to? The corruption spreads everywhere, I thought."

She had to admit he had a point. As they'd descended, the taint had become so thick it almost choked the air, and yet here there was almost nothing. Perhaps it was the lava and the heat, burning the corruption away? Perhaps it was the presence of the dragon. The Old Gods were said to be ancient dragons, after all. There could be a link.

As they approached a cave opening ahead, she heard the sound of running water. They stepped into another large cavern, and from where they stood on the edge of a small cliff they looked out over what had to be some kind of underground lake. The water was cloudy green, lit from beneath by phosphorescent rocks until it shone like an emerald on the rocky ceiling. It had an eerie beauty to it, she thought.

The acrid smell of brimstone clung to the air, and the echoing sound of dripping water surrounded them. How far the cavern went on she couldn't tell. At some point it was all just a greenish haze mingled with the mist.

Maric stood at the edge of the cliff and stared out at the water, awestruck. He said something under his breath that she didn't quite catch.

"What's that?" she asked him.

"*Here lies the abyss, the well of all souls. From these emerald waters doth life begin anew.*" He raised an eyebrow when he saw she didn't recognize the quote. "It's from the Chant of Light."

"I didn't have a very religious upbringing," she responded wryly. Which was an understatement, but how could he know what it was like in the alienages? There were no chantries there, and when the priests came it was with alms and many words of benevolent advice for the poor elves and their lost, wicked ways . . . and a large number of wary templars to guard the priests from harm.

"Oh. It's where Andraste goes to speak to the Maker for the first time. It's where she convinces him to forgive mankind. It was supposed to be this beautiful temple deep under the earth surrounded by emerald waters. I guess I always imagined it looked like this."

"I doubt there's a temple here."

"I know, I just . . . never mind." Blushing slightly, he pointed out a natural path that led down the side of the cliff. "Do you think Duncan really came down this way? This far?"

She nodded. "So it seems. We're close, however."

They made their way down the path, which turned out to be little more than a collection of embedded stones at several points, some a fair distance apart. Fiona was still quite drained from all the spellcasting and found it difficult to maneuver with her chain garments and her heavy skirt. Twice Maric needed to steady her before she slipped on the dewy mist that clung to everything, and he helped her down to the next ledge. She curtly thanked him, feeling more like an ass each time.

At the bottom was a shore comprised of mud and slabs of rock mixed in with strange white formations. It was as if misshapen statues dotted the edge of the lake, all of them in the process of melting down into sludge. Perhaps it was sulfur or lime; she couldn't really say. The formations were surreal, however, and oddly sad. Even with the constant dripping sounds, the entire cavern seemed somehow muted.

"Wait," Maric suddenly said.

"What? Do you see him? He might be nearby . . ."

The man rubbed his chin and fretted for a moment, and her curiosity was piqued. She stopped and stared at him, allowing the light of her staff to wink out. There was enough light from the glowing water to see by, after all, even if it cast everything in an odd shade of green. She was getting tired of trying to maintain the concentration.

"I want to thank you," he blurted out.

"Thank me?"

"For saving my life. When the dragon breathed its fire, you could have let me die, but you didn't." Was he blushing? It was difficult to tell in the green light, but the way the man stammered and avoided looking at her, it seemed like he might be. Now it was her turn to be amused.

"Do you think I would let anyone die, if I could stop it?"

He shrugged. "Less 'anyone' and more me in particular. You've made it pretty clear that I'm not your favorite person. Not that I'm arguing with you, really, I just . . . appreciate that you did what you did. I know you didn't have to."

"I see." She laughed softly at his discomfort. She probably shouldn't, but she couldn't help herself. "Whatever I may think of you, King Maric, I don't want you to die. I did have to do it, and there's no need to thank me."

"No, there is." He finally managed to meet her gaze, his look completely earnest. "I will find a way to repay you. I promise."

Fiona's objection died on her lips. She wanted to tell him that he could keep his promise of repayment. She didn't want any human lord to "owe" her anything, especially since the chances that he would actually see such a notion through were next to nothing. What was a debt to an elf, or a mage, to such a man? Especially since there was no debt to speak of.

But she couldn't tell him that. And she didn't know why. For a moment there was only hushed silence on the green shores of the endless lake.

Then she shuddered and the moment ended. He looked away, embarrassed, and she turned around. "If you like," she agreed, shrugging. She imagined he was good at empty gestures. It was part of his kingly charm, no? With any luck he would simply forget the matter. In fact, that's what would most likely happen.

They walked along the shore, weaving a circuitous route past the white formations. Another sound joined the echoes of dripping water in time: a strange murmur that seemed to come from all around them. Maric suggested it might in fact be the water, but she wasn't so sure. The water rippled, making the green lights dance upon the ceiling, but there were no tides or splashes or anything else that might make such sounds. She sensed no darkspawn, but that didn't mean there weren't other things living here.

When they found Duncan, it was without warning. The young man sat on a particularly large formation next to the shore, this one a great blob that almost looked like a ship. The "prow" hung over the water, and there he sat with his feet dangling over the edge, staring glumly out into the distance.

They approached, but Fiona didn't want to step onto the formation. The white surface looked slick, almost slimy. Who knew just how stable it really was, as well? The stench of salt assaulted her nostrils.

"Duncan?" she called to him softly.

He didn't look. "Came to get me, huh?"

"I wanted to come. Duncan, this is silly. Why are you doing this?"

"They don't want me to come back." He sighed, staring down into the murky depths beneath him. "Genevieve, maybe, but not the others. And I don't want to go back."

"So you'd prefer to wander around down here in the dark?"

"It's not so dark," he chuckled, though it was flat and bitter. For a moment the greenish light shining up from the water intensified, almost as if responding to his words. He stared down at the glowing patterns formed by the ripples, fascinated.

"But it's dangerous. Genevieve almost ordered us to leave."

"She should have. *I* would have."

Fiona looked to Maric for help, but the man merely shrugged helplessly. He barely knew Duncan, but she'd assumed they had formed some kind of connection during their days traveling together. Still, what was he supposed to say? He stared at the lad with compassion, maybe even with understanding, but he remained silent.

She grabbed on to the nearest outcropping of the white structure, testing it to make sure it wasn't going to collapse under her weight. It was surprisingly solid, and at the same time it felt vaguely coarse and slimy, as if its surface were made out of sandy sludge just short of dissolving entirely into goo. It left a pale, gritty residue on her fingers as well. She pulled herself slowly up, feeling the heels of her boots sink into the muck, and gingerly made her way to where Duncan was sitting.

"Be careful," Maric called after her.

She knelt down next to Duncan, careful not to sit in the sludge as he was. It was plastered all over his leathers, she noticed, like he had been wallowing in it.

They didn't speak for several minutes. Fiona just looked out over the green water as he did, admiring the play of the light upon the ceiling. The strange murmuring continued, ebbing and flowing just as the lake was. She noticed odd shadows moving beneath the water, as well. Fish, here? The source of the sounds, perhaps?

She reached out with her Grey Warden senses and felt nothing. Nothing at all. The thought that after so much corruption in the tunnels they would be here and it would be completely free of the taint was worrying, but she put it aside for now.

"I suppose I'll need to go back?" he asked her.

"Not unless you think you can reach the surface on your own."

"Probably not."

With a sigh he stood up, wiping his hands on his tunic. She

stood, too, and led him back to where Maric waited anxiously. Maric reached out and helped them both down, one after the other, and then turned to regard Duncan cautiously.

"Are you all right?" he asked.

The lad shrugged. "You know, I never wanted to become a Grey Warden. I probably shouldn't have been one. Genevieve made a mistake in picking me, I think."

Maric's brow furrowed in puzzlement. "I think you mentioned that once before. Why didn't you want to become a Grey Warden? You didn't volunteer, you mean?"

"The Wardens have the Right of Conscription," Fiona explained. "It dates back to the First Blight, a long time ago. Everyone was so grateful to the order for finally defeating the darkspawn that they gave them a number of powers, one of which was the right to recruit anyone they wished. If the order wants you, you're recruited. End of story."

"I hadn't heard that."

"It's not a right they invoke much these days. It's been so long since the last Blight that some people think the order isn't important any longer, that the darkspawn will never return to the surface. The order has to be careful not to push anyone too far. That's how we've become so few."

Duncan dug out a cloth from his belt and wiped irritably at the white sludge that clung to his boots and his jerkin. She noticed that wherever he wiped it off, the black leather was stained to a murky green underneath. Suddenly she was relieved she hadn't sat down in it.

"Genevieve pushed it with me," he said. "I was going to be executed."

"Executed?" Maric asked, surprised.

"I'd murdered someone." The lad glanced away, shadows crossing behind his eyes. Fiona could see them, and wondered if Maric could see them, too. She knew what a hard life could drive someone to do. She knew only a little of what Duncan had been through, enough to feel sympathy for him. "I'd already been thrown in a dungeon to await my hanging when Genevieve came to see me. They let this armored woman into my cell, and the way she looked at me, I thought she was supposed to be my executioner. I thought maybe they'd decided to just have me beheaded right there."

"That'd be an easy mistake to make. Your commander is a grim, grim woman."

"But instead she sat me down and explained to me that she could take me out of there. She could make me a Grey Warden, and if I survived the Joining I'd be a warrior, I'd fight for a noble cause for once."

"So you said yes."

Duncan's face became solemn. "I said no."

"An odd choice, waiting to be hanged as you were."

The lad squirmed, looking uncomfortable. For a long minute he didn't say anything, but just when Fiona was about to call a halt to the conversation and suggest they return to the others, he sighed. "The man I killed was a Grey Warden."

"Ah."

"He caught me robbing his room at the inn. The owner had tipped me off, assuming the fellow was going to be gone for a while. I didn't even know who or what he was. He drew his daggers and warned me to give back the ring I'd found, but I refused. It was valuable, I could tell, and I'd rightfully taken it."

Maric grinned. "Rightfully being used in the loosest sense there?"

"I'd been starving. The winter had been hard." He frowned thoughtfully. "I'd never killed anyone before. I wouldn't have killed him then, either, but the fight was so long. He was so determined to get that ring back, he wouldn't stop. I'd meant to just put my knife to his throat, to force him to submit. . . ." He trailed off, sighing again.

Maric seemed confused. "Why did you care so much?"

"You think I should enjoy killing someone?"

"No." The King looked puzzled. Fiona glared at him, warning him off this subject, but he ignored her. "The first man I ever killed was out of desperation. I bashed his head open on a rock. I didn't enjoy it, either, but he'd left me no choice."

"He thanked me." Duncan's voice became a whisper as he remembered the moment. "I'd cut his throat, and he was bleeding over everything. I was desperate and trying to cover the wound, trying to stop the blood, and he got this look on his face like he was grateful. Like he was at peace. He grabbed my shoulder and stopped me and I looked straight at him, and then he thanked me." The lad ran a hand nervously through his black hair and turned away. "It . . . stuck with me. What kind of man would thank someone for murdering him? What kind of life must he have had? The watch burst in and arrested me. They dragged me in front of a judge and he was the one who told me the man had been a Grey Warden."

"So Genevieve recruited someone who'd killed a member of her own order?"

"She said it was impressive, the fact that I'd managed it at all."

"But you refused."

He chuckled ruefully. "I just wondered if being a Grey Warden would make me like him. Or like her. Would I be thanking someone someday for cutting my throat? I couldn't do it. I even told her what he'd said, and she just nodded and left my cell without saying a word."

Maric looked at the lad incredulously, but said nothing. Duncan shrugged and cleared his throat, seemingly nonchalant. "It didn't matter. She showed up at my execution the next day and told them she was invoking the Right of Conscription before they could get the noose around my neck. Boy, they didn't like that."

Fiona snorted. "No, they sure didn't." She remembered the controversy that had sparked, not just with the Lord Mayor but also within the order. They thought that Genevieve had gone mad. Recruiting the murderer of one of their own? And not only recruiting him, but against his will? The Commander had been typically adamant, however. She had gone to that cell to see what kind of man Duncan was, and had seen something in him that she had never explained to anyone.

Duncan had had a difficult time of it when she'd first brought him to the fortress at Montsimmard. None of the others had wanted to associate with him, so he took his meals alone in his cell. Kept mostly to himself. As the most junior member of the order, Fiona had been forced to see him through his Joining. She had initially refused to do it, but Genevieve hadn't cared. In the end, Duncan had been a surprise. She had expected him to be a worthless criminal, and instead he'd turned out to be something quite different.

She put her hand on his shoulder. "Nicolas is grieving. He's not thinking rationally. You can't take what he says so personally, Duncan."

"Even if he's right?"

"Hey," Maric interrupted. "You brought that dragon down to the ground. If you hadn't done that, it could have killed any of us."

"Yes, but it should have been me. I jumped on its back; it should have been me it snapped up, and not Julien."

Fiona could see the guilt in him. It broke her heart a little. She reached up and brushed the dark hair out of his eyes, and he ignored it. "So we should be happier if you died, instead?" She smiled sadly at him. "Oh, Duncan. He saved you, and I bet he'd do it again if he had the choice. And you would have done the same for him."

The lad looked dubious. "Maybe," he mumbled.

She pushed him, smiling, and he allowed himself to be moved. The three of them quietly began walking back up the shore, but Maric suddenly hesitated.

"That Grey Warden." He looked at Duncan curiously. "Why

didn't he just give you the ring? Was it that valuable?"

"He'd bought it to give to the woman he was going to marry," came the flat response. "He never got the chance to."

"His name was Guy," Fiona added. "Genevieve was his fiancée." Maric's eyes widened with mute surprise, and that effectively ended the conversation.

They said nothing further as they made their way up the path back to the top of the cliff. The murmurs followed them for a time, and then grew silent. If the sounds belonged to any creatures other than whatever fish could live in a sulfuric lake, they remained hidden within the shadows.

When they finally returned to the dragon's cavern, the others were waiting for them. The dragon's carcass sprawled across the rocks, looking somehow smaller than she remembered. Its stomach was mostly cut open now, as well. Bloody entrails spilled out onto the ground, Kell standing amid it all busily prying black scales off its flank with a belt knife. Fiona imagined he had opened the belly up to try to retrieve some of the dragon's bones. They were highly prized, as Maric's enchanted blade demonstrated. She had no idea if the bones were as hard in their natural state. Probably not, as it seemed unlikely that anyone could remove them if they were.

Hafter barked excitedly around his master's feet, though the hound had a pronounced limp and was nowhere near as quick as Fiona knew him to normally be. Kell looked down at him and grinned, and then sliced off a large chunk of the dragon's flesh with his belt knife. He tossed it to Hafter, and the dog pounced on it greedily and began chewing away. It was fitting somehow, she thought.

Genevieve turned and watched as they entered, frowning severely. Fiona saw the body of Julien nearby, wrapped tightly in his black cloak, with Nicolas still kneeling beside him. The warrior glanced up and scowled when he spotted Duncan. Utha put her hand on the man's shoulder to restrain him and he visibly deflated, his face twisting into silent grief that he then hid by turning away. The dwarf, at least, looked apologetically at Duncan. Whether the lad saw it or not, Fiona couldn't say. He kept his face completely blank.

"It's about time that you returned," Genevieve snapped. "The darkspawn are growing brave. A pair of shrieks attempted to sneak in here, and we were forced to kill them. More will almost certainly follow."

"Well, we're back," Fiona stated. "Duncan didn't go far."

"Sorry," he mumbled.

Genevieve glared sternly at the lad, her jaw clenched and her lips pressed thinly together. He didn't look up to meet her gaze, but Fiona suspected he felt the disapproval anyhow. How could he not? It radiated from her in palpable waves. "What was that?" she snapped at him. "Do I need to fear you running off even here in the Deep Roads, Duncan?"

"I'm not going anywhere," he said, though it hardly seemed convincing.

"You should have let him go," Nicolas muttered, just loudly enough to be overheard. Genevieve's eyes widened in outrage and she turned to stare at him, but the warrior stared back at her defiantly. "What is he doing here with us?" he insisted. "He's some gutter rat you picked up in Val Royeaux. A murderer! A thief! He doesn't belong in the order."

"I say he does," she seethed.

"His presence demeans us all!"

In a flash, Genevieve darted toward Nicolas and cuffed him across the face. Her heavy gauntlets made the blow far more severe than it might have been otherwise, and the man reeled back onto Julien's wrapped corpse. The others stared in shock as she towered over the warrior, her face red with fury. Nicolas stared up at her in dismay, covering his cheek almost reflexively.

"Control yourself!" she roared. "The boy brought down the dragon. He did his part, as did Julien. If anyone is demeaned, it is you with this pointless display."

An awkward silence settled among the group. Utha stepped forward, her look anxious, and she made several gestures to Nicolas. Fiona couldn't see what they were, but it was clear they were meant to calm the man down. He glanced nervously at Genevieve, who remained towering above him, but she ignored him and instead turned to look sharply at each of the other Grey Wardens in turn.

"The time has come for us to move on. Let us do so—quickly."

"No," came the firm response. It was Kell. The hunter stood up slowly from the dragon's corpse, wiping his knife on the scaleless flesh of the creature's belly before sheathing it on his belt. He turned around and met the Commander's look with a calm, resolute expression. "We have come far enough, I think. It is madness to proceed."

"You are not the commander here," she said, her voice low and dangerous.

"And you are not acting as a commander should." He gestured toward Maric, who appeared to be watching the confrontation intently. "We have the King of Ferelden with us. He is not someone whose life should be thrown away lightly. If there is no chance of us succeeding, we must return him to the surface."

"What we *must* do is prevent the Blight."

Kell shook his head sadly. He removed the leather gloves he wore, now coated a dark and ugly red from the dragon's innards. "But we are not doing that. There is no chance of success for us here, Genevieve."

"You are wrong."

"Am I?" His pale eyes narrowed. "If a Blight truly comes, our duty now is to see the King safely back to the surface and help his people prepare for it. We waste our efforts seeking a man who is likely beyond our reach."

"I do not believe that."

"Why? Because the rest of the order did not believe in your visions?" He held his hands out in supplication, his voice pleading. "I believe in your visions, Genevieve. Let us heed them and meet the coming Blight with our eyes open."

She stared at him silently, her face cold stone. Fiona shivered, and wondered where this was going to lead. All of them tensed and watched the Commander with dread. She reached down and slowly pulled her greatsword from its scabbard, the metal grinding softly. She held the blade before her, not taking her eyes from the hunter. The threat was implicit. "Not while there is a chance to stop it. I say that chance exists, and if it requires the sacrifice of each and every last one of us, we will continue down this path until I say otherwise."

Kell appeared unimpressed. His hand moved cautiously to the hilt of the flail at his side, but he did not draw it. Hafter, sensing the confrontation, growled and raised his hackles. He bared his fangs at Genevieve and his master did nothing to restrain him. The moment dragged on.

Utha stepped between them. The dwarf held her hands up at Genevieve and Kell, and then angrily began signing at Kell. It was too fast for Fiona to follow, but he seemed to understand. He frowned thoughtfully. "You agree with her? After all this?" he asked.

The dwarf nodded solemnly. She gestured again, and this time Fiona did understand it. *Too much has been sacrificed to turn back now.*

"I agree with Kell," Nicolas chimed in. He stood up, glowering.

He looked to Fiona and Maric, as did Utha and Kell. Genevieve did not. She stiffened, refusing to acknowledge that a consensus was being sought to determine her right to command. Fiona wasn't certain what the woman would do if that consensus was not in her favor. Would she go on her own? Would she try to kill them? Fiona hadn't been part of the order long enough to know what the protocol was in a situation like this. There probably wasn't one. In the face of the darkspawn threat, mutiny was normally not an option.

"I am here to help you Grey Wardens," Maric said slowly. "You know more about the darkspawn than I ever could. If there's a chance to save Ferelden from the Blight, I'm willing to risk my life to do that. But if there's not, that's for you to decide."

"Idiots!" Duncan suddenly blurted out.

All eyes turned toward him. The lad was furious in a way that Fiona had never seen before, almost shaking. He turned accusingly toward Nicolas. "We killed a dragon. A *dragon*! And you want to turn around *now*? What do you think Julien would have said to that?"

"Don't tell me what Julien would have said." Nicolas's words lacked heat, however, and he stared at the floor.

"You all want to turn tail at the first sign of trouble? Then go. Make Julien's death mean nothing, if that's what you want. I didn't even want to join the Grey Wardens, and now I know why. You're a bunch of bloody cowards!"

Kell's brows rose, but he said nothing. Nicolas, too, remained silent.

"I should never have let you run me off," Duncan continued, his face turning red from rage. "I jumped on that damned dragon's back, and you know what? It was worth it! None of you had the damned balls to do it. You think those Grey Wardens of old that you talk about, the ones that stopped all those Blights, you think they did that by playing it safe?" He stormed over to Genevieve and planted himself by her side. She did not acknowledge him in any way, her face remaining inscrutable. "If Genevieve is the only one with the guts to see this through, then I'm going with her. Me, the *gutter rat*."

The last was spat at Nicolas. The warrior winced and closed his eyes. Utha looked between the two of them and shook her head sadly, but made no move to intervene. Kell arched a brow at Fiona, the silent question obvious.

She shrugged. "I think Duncan's said it all, hasn't he?"

In the end, neither Kell nor Nicolas argued with the decision. Genevieve accepted their return to the fold without further comment. Fiona doubted that she would forget, however. She never forgot anything.

They traveled down the passages where Duncan had gone, after Fiona pointed out that there were other paths that way that went in different directions. They couldn't return the way they'd come, after all, not without encountering the darkspawn and beginning the very battle that they had fought the dragon to avoid. So they needed to go forward, and hopefully find a way back to the Deep Roads and a route to Ortan thaig. Privately Fiona wondered if these caves didn't simply keep going down forever. Maybe there was no way back now, and would have been no way back even if Kell had gotten his way.

She kept those thoughts to herself.

At Maric's suggestion, they carried Julien's body with them. With his body still wrapped in his cloak, they hefted him up on their shoulders and took him the short distance to the emerald lake. It was difficult getting him down the narrow path from the cliff, but the Grey Wardens carried the burden without complaint. Even Genevieve said nothing, despite the delay.

At the shore of the lake, standing amid the white pillars, they released Julien's body and allowed it to float out onto the green waters. Chantry tradition demanded that bodies be cremated and their ashes properly interred, but there was no way for them to build a pyre, and burying anything in the stone was impossible. Better this than leaving their comrade in the cavern and to the mercies of the darkspawn horde.

They watched the body for a time, each of them shrouded in silence. Fiona hadn't known the man very long, but she had always appreciated his quiet nature. For a warrior he had been remarkably thoughtful. He had never treated her as anything other than a fellow Grey Warden, and for someone who was both a lowly elf as well as a mage, that meant a lot.

Nicolas knelt at the water's edge and hung his head in agonizing grief. The others pretended not to notice, to let the man preserve at least a shred of his dignity.

"*Here lies the abyss, the well of all souls,*" Maric intoned. "*From these emerald waters doth life begin anew. Come to me, child, and I shall embrace you.*" He walked to Nicolas's side and put a gentle hand on the man's shoulder. Nicolas looked up at Maric with gratitude, tears welling in his eyes.

"*In my arms lies Eternity.*"

The body slowly sank beneath the surface.

10

With passion'd breath does the darkness creep.
It is the whisper in the night, the lie upon your sleep.
—Canticle of Transfigurations 1:5

Bregan opened his eyes.

Something had changed while he slept. How long had it been? It was pitch-dark in his cell, just as it had been when he had closed his eyes what seemed an eon ago. The Deep Roads were a single night that stretched on into infinity.

Somehow he suspected that a great deal of time had passed, however. The burning under his flesh had ebbed, to be replaced by a strange iciness. He poked his skin and found it heavy and sluggish, and wondered, if he poked hard enough, whether the resulting dent might simply remain. His limbs felt detached, as if they didn't quite belong to him.

So, too, had the humming lessened. Then, as he listened to it there in the blackness, he realized that wasn't quite true. It was stronger. The far-off chorus had become a powerful symphony, a great swell of beautiful music that no longer pounded to get inside his head but instead tickled at the edges of his thoughts. It was far easier to ignore, but now he found it distracting. He found himself losing his train of thought whenever he listened.

He shook his head, refusing to be enticed, and sat up. The furs on which he had lain had been changed at some point. How, he wondered? They were thicker now, coarser. Feeling around in the

DRAGON AGE: THE CALLING   215

dark, he also found some clothes folded neatly nearby. They were not his. They were made of a rough, scratchy material he didn't recognize, perhaps dwarven. That made him wonder if they would even fit.

He stood up slowly, wincing at the aches he felt throughout his body. There was little pain, however. Running his hands over his bare skin, he noted that most of the bandages and poultices were gone. He was whole. His flesh was rough, however, as if he were covered in thick scars. Strangely, it also felt like he was touching someone else's skin. It was as if he was numb. And cold, too, even if he did not shiver.

Carefully feeling through the clothing pile, he picked out what seemed to be a pair of trousers. That would do for now. They fit well enough even though, as he had suspected, they were indeed too short in the legs.

Where had the glowstone gone? He remembered that it had not been present when he returned to the cell, but not why. In fact, he remembered very little about returning to his cell at all. He had come alone, that much he knew, but what had happened with the Architect? He had a vague recollection that they had spoken, but his impressions were distant. Had it done something to his mind?

The idea should have alarmed him more, but it didn't. He supposed it was possible that this, too, could be the result of magical meddling. But he doubted it. If the Architect had wanted to erase his memories or otherwise use magic to alter his mind, there had been far better opportunities for it to do so.

No, he had come back here willingly, to sleep. He had been exhausted. His limbs had been weighing him down like lead, and the incessant humming had nearly driven him mad. He remembered these things, and the slumber reaching up to drag him into oblivion almost before he touched the ground . . .

. . . and then nothing. No dreams, for perhaps the first time in many years. Grey Wardens always dreamed, the price of sharing the fringes of the darkspawn hive mind. Yet now, nothing. Blissful unconsciousness.

Bregan waited for a time. He felt around a bit more on the floor and discovered no weapon, nor any armor. Perhaps he was still not trusted? It didn't matter, really. The habit of keeping a weapon with him was something born of a lifetime spent as a warrior, a lifetime of preparation for a war he would never get to fight.

It was a lifetime he had despised.

How glorious simply to realize that. He wanted to leap around and shout it out loud. Certainly there was nothing stopping him—but who would care? Let his sword rot wherever it had ended up.

After what seemed like an hour spent pacing around the small chamber, he realized that he was waiting for the Architect to appear. It was an odd thing to discover. The darkspawn was not his friend, after all. He had chosen to remain, yes, but he still wasn't certain why. Ostensibly he thought it was important to end the Blights, but the same part of him that had always hated being a Grey Warden wondered why he even cared about that. What did it matter to him now? Was he not the walking dead, his own suicide postponed by the Architect's plan?

These thoughts made him strangely impatient. He found himself listening to that far-off music, the calling that reached in and cradled him each time he began to pay attention to it. It almost made him swoon, and each time he felt forced to shake it off. There were more important matters to deal with.

Bregan walked to the metal door and discovered it unlocked. It creaked open loudly, the sound reverberating throughout the hush that permeated the place. He almost expected a hue and cry to begin, and darkspawn to come rushing to restrain him, but none did. The quiet returned, punctuated only by the rise and fall of the distant chorus.

As he edged out into the hall, he realized that things were coming slowly into focus. He was making out the rough edges of the wall in front of him, and he could almost see the door he had just opened. It was as if he was walking in a deep forest, his eyes only just now becoming accustomed to the faint moonlight sifting in through the branches and revealing a shrouded world of trees and roots and rocks. Here there were only ancient stone walls and debris, however, and no light at all to which he might become accustomed. How was he able to see anything?

As he blinked and stared into the slowly receding shadows, Bregan realized that something was approaching. He froze, terror racing through him, and cursed the fact that his ability to sense darkspawn appeared to have fled him completely. It was a shriek, one of the tall and lanky creatures that the Grey Wardens had always considered the assassins of the darkspawn. They used stealth to their advantage, striking from the shadows and rending an opponent to ribbons with wickedly long claws. Their battle cry was a terrifying shriek—hence the name—that he had heard only once before in his life, and even then it was only in the distance as a lone one of these creatures stalked a forest, picking off any Warden it could find in the darkness.

The thing hunched down as soon as it spotted him, baring its long fangs in a threatening grimace. It hissed, brandishing those signature claws, but did not advance. Bregan tensed, a lone bead of sweat making its way inexorably down his brow. The shriek then calmed. Perhaps it had decided it was not about to be attacked? Bregan could not be certain. Whatever the reason, it cautiously loped its way past him in the hall, keeping its dead eyes trained on him as it did so.

And then it was gone, disappeared back into the shadows. He waited, his heart racing, and wondered if it would return now and strike him from behind. But there was no surprise attack. It had simply passed him by. Bregan was alien enough to have caused it suspicion and even alarm, but not enough to be considered a threat.

He shuddered. He felt chilled, and the strangeness of his skin made him wooden. For a moment he was almost overcome by the desire to claw at his flesh, and to keep clawing at it until he peeled it back and scraped his way past whatever sludge had made its home just under the surface. And then that moment passed. His fear ebbed, and a sense of detachment returned.

If he could see, even poorly, perhaps this was a good time to explore.

It felt strange, walking around the remains of the dwarven fortress. The encroachment of the darkspawn corruption was enough that some areas were either completely impassable or impossible to determine what their function might once have been, but others seemed remarkably untouched. He found what might have been a kitchen, with a fire pit now encrusted with black moss and dirt surrounded by rusted pans and even knives. He recognized a counter and assorted barrels and cabinets all tossed about, as if some great calamity had turned the entire kitchen upside down and then simply left it to be overtaken by dust and time and the taint.

Indeed, that's very likely what had happened here. What use would the darkspawn have for a kitchen, after all? Nothing the Grey Wardens had ever found gave them reason to think the darkspawn ate anything. The taint sustained them.

That thought brought to mind the fact that his own hunger had vanished. He had eaten nothing for days, and yet now he felt . . . full. Not sated, precisely, but unpleasantly filled with something that precluded actual hunger. The idea was disturbing, and he tried to turn his mind away from it.

He wondered where the dwarven bodies were. Had it been so long that even their skeletons had turned to dust? Had the darkspawn removed them? Had the dwarves all fled before the darkspawn had taken over this part of the Deep Roads? It occurred to him at the same time that he had no idea what the darkspawn did with their dead. There were no bones to be seen, yet he imagined they had to perish from natural causes like any other living creature. If they lived here, then where did they die?

Perhaps *lived* was too strong a word. There was no evidence that the darkspawn occupied the ruin in the same sense that humans or dwarves might have. There were no sleeping quarters, no places where they kept belongings. He knew that they were capable of forging equipment and building structures when they needed to, but if they did such things, they certainly didn't do them here. Darkspawn clearly passed through and patrolled the ruin, but otherwise it felt very empty indeed.

As Bregan moved about the abandoned halls, he slowly realized that he could hear a new sound over the chorus. It was a strange, insistent scratching. He couldn't place what it might be, only that it felt out of place amid the shadows and the gloom. Curiosity slowly overcame his apprehension. Cocking his head to listen, he felt his way around the halls and searched for a way to zero in on where it was coming from.

It didn't take long to find. The light he noticed before anything else, a bright beacon shining through a far-off doorway that immediately hurt his eyes even though he was only seeing it from a distance. He had to put up his hands and blink through tears before he acclimated enough to approach. The closer he got, the more the dazzling light pained him. The sound became clearer, however—it was someone writing, as if with a quill. Interesting that he was able to pick that up from so far away. Fighting through his discomfort, he made his way to the doorway and looked inside.

It was difficult to see through the glare, but even what Bregan could see shocked him. The room he looked into was a library, not corrupted in any way and filled beyond capacity with books. There were great, wooden shelves lining the walls, each of them bursting with haphazardly stacked tomes. The books did not restrict themselves to the shelves, however. They littered the floor in tall piles that looked as if they might teeter over at any moment. Some lay open, others were leaned against the wall, still more formed a mountain of texts on an elaborate stone desk that took up much of the central chamber. The entire scene would not have looked out of place in some cultured dwarven nobleman's estate in Orzammar, were it not for the disorganized chaos.

The Architect sat at the stone desk, an ornate lacquered chair rising high behind him. Bregan could see a quill pen in the creature's hand, the feather busily twirling about as it wrote in a large, leather-bound ledger. The source of the blinding light was the glowstone, now hanging from the Architect's chair and filling the library with flickering shadows. He didn't remember the stone being so incredibly bright, certainly not enough to hurt his eyes.

The darkspawn noticed him standing in the door and paused in its writing. It appeared surprised to see Bregan, raising what might have been eyebrows had it had any hair in the desiccated flesh on its head. As soon as it realized his discomfort, it glanced at the glowstone and made the connection. With a wave of its gnarled hand, the stone's radiance dimmed—enough to elicit a sigh of relief from Bregan. The pain was gone, and he could now see clearly into the room.

"My apologies," the Architect offered.

"I woke up and you did not come."

It nodded. "You have been asleep. I had no way of knowing for how long. I took the glowstone so I could write, and because I knew you would become more . . . sensitive when you awoke."

Bregan frowned in confusion. He stepped gingerly into the library, marveling at the array of shelves along the wall. A tall stone ladder was hooked up to a runner that went the entire length around the room, allowing one to reach up to the very top of any of the shelves. A dwarven contraption, surely, but, unlike everything else he'd seen in this ruin, it was in excellent shape. "I don't understand," he finally said. "How long was I asleep? A day? More?"

"I do not know what a 'day' is."

"You don't?" Bregan waved absently at the shelves. "It doesn't explain that in one of these books somewhere? I got the impression you read them."

The darkspawn sat back in its chair, steepling its fingers as it watched him with great interest. Bregan somehow got the feeling that he had intruded on this creature's sanctum, and yet it retained its polite and cultured air. Those eyes widened with alarm every time his hands came close to touching one of the books, however. Was there something there it didn't want him to see? Or was it possessive of its treasures?

On closer examination, Bregan noted that most of the books were yellowed and falling apart. Many of them had been poorly rebound and repaired, probably by the Architect itself. No doubt its concern was that he would damage them accidentally.

Had these ancient tomes been here all along? Or did the emissary collect them from throughout the Deep Roads? He tried to imagine this creature voyaging to ruined thaig after ruined thaig, sifting through rubble for dwarven books that hadn't completely disintegrated in the passing centuries. There couldn't have been many. The few with legible text left on the binding were written in dwarven, and thus beyond Bregan's ability to decipher. What topics would interest such a creature, he wondered?

"I have read them," the Architect replied. "Some of them I have read many times. There are many things they speak of that I do not understand."

"A day is one of the ways we measure time. The sun falls and it becomes night, and when the sun comes up again a day has passed, twenty-four hours in total."

"Ah." It seemed pleased. "I have read of these things, but I had no way of knowing of their connection. Thank you for providing me this information."

"You're welcome." Bregan walked up to the great stone desk,

carefully navigating his way between the stacks of books scattered on the floor. Several of the tomes were quite large, he noticed, and one leaning against the desk was almost as wide as the desk itself. Its pages were cracked and so tarnished yellow that the delicate writing was almost indecipherable. It wasn't dwarven but rather Tevene, the language of the ancient magisters. Arcane writing. "You said I would be more sensitive when I awoke. Did you mean to the light? Why would I be more sensitive?"

The darkspawn studied him quietly for a moment, cocking its head to the side as if confused. "Do you not remember?"

"Not well, no. But something has changed."

"You complained that the calling of the Old Gods was driving you mad. I offered to speed up the progression of the taint within you, and you agreed."

Bregan froze. The chill of his skin, the change in the buzzing, the strange sensations . . . what had been done to him? "What do you mean, I agreed?" The alarm in his voice made the Architect stiffen. It regarded him with concern, but did not move from its chair.

"I was not entirely certain that I would be able to," it explained. "But you insisted. I will admit to a certain fascination with the idea. The possibility that your change could be accelerated, and the changes that would incur. Some I could guess." It gestured to the glowstone still hanging on the chair, now giving off only a dim orange glimmer. "It was no brighter than previously. It is your tolerance that has altered."

Bregan stood there, stunned. He had *asked* for this? Slowly it dawned on him that for all the strangeness, the constant humming was no longer driving him mad. It had become something beautiful and strange now instead, and it was he that had transformed into something alien. He felt it. He felt the change under his skin.

He held his hands up in front of his face. The dark stains he had seen on his flesh previously had spread. They had spread until his skin was little more than mottled and dark with it, the areas where it had changed now withered and rough, much like the darkspawn's flesh was. His nails were long and black, almost talons.

Shuddering in horror, he allowed his hands to drop. "I want to see my face."

The darkspawn cocked its head again. "How do you wish to do that?"

"A mirror. Give me a mirror."

"I know of no such device."

He slammed a fist down on the desk, sending several of the more precariously stacked books tumbling off. "Something reflective! I need to see myself!" he shouted furiously.

It seemed nonplussed and slowly gathered its brown robes and stood up from the chair. Without a word it turned and left the room, leaving Bregan standing where he was. He felt foolish. He felt angry. What had he done? Was the emissary simply leaving him, offended at his behavior?

Did he really think the creature had done this to him without permission? No. No, he didn't. If it had wished to experiment on him, it could easily have done so before. He had asked for this, and even as he considered the idea a vague recollection of it swam across his mind. He had been in pain. The humming had been everywhere, even inside him. He had wanted it gone.

It took several minutes before the Architect returned. It held up what appeared to be a round, steel shield. A thing of dwarven make, yet so covered in the dark tendrils of corruption it would be impossible to see anything in it. He glanced in confusion at the emissary, yet it ignored him. With a gesture of its hand a great black flame burst into being upon the metal.

Waves of heat emanated from it, making Bregan realize just how chilled he actually was. He was standing in the chamber with only a pair of trousers on, yet it was not the temperature that made him cold. He knew that.

He watched as the black fire crawled its way along the shield's surface, scouring it clean. Within moments the brilliant sheen of the metal on its inside surface had been revealed. It wasn't quite a mirror, but it would probably do. The Architect unceremoniously handed it over.

Bregan expected the shield to be burning hot, but it wasn't. It was barely even warm. Enchanted, he assumed. Not that it should be a surprise—who knew how many treasures the dwarves had left in these tunnels when their kingdoms had crumbled? All an enterprising darkspawn had to do was find them.

He held the shield up and looked into it. The minute details were indistinct, but the condition of his overall face was obvious: The taint now covered it all. His white hair had fallen out in clumps, and now there were only scattered strands and wisps of it left amid the withered and blackened flesh. His lips also seemed to have peeled back from his teeth, leaving him with a permanent skeletal grimace.

The rest of it could not be made out, and perhaps that was for the best. Bregan let the shield drop, a numbness coming over him. He had seen ghouls like this. Infected people that had survived long enough for their bodies to be ravaged by the course of the taint. Now it had finally caught up with him, as well. Strange that he didn't feel more upset. The shock had worn off, leaving only a sense of inevitability.

"You are angered?" the Architect asked him carefully.

"No."

"There is another chair behind you, against the wall, if you wish to sit." Bregan turned and found that, sure enough, a simpler stone chair was where the emissary indicated. It was buried under a mound of rolled-up scrolls and weathered tomes. He walked over and cleared it off before sitting. The aged stone protested under his weight. It was almost too small for him, built for a dwarf, but he didn't care.

"I want to talk about your plan," he stated.

The darkspawn sighed, but appeared unsurprised. It walked back around its desk and settled into its chair. The light of the glowstone wavered as if in acknowledgement of its presence. "Yes, it is time," it finally said.

Questions percolated through Bregan's head. He had been too crazed and exhausted to ask the Architect about his plan when he'd returned earlier, or at least he assumed that had been the case. There was nothing more he could do about his physical condition, after all. Really, he owed the Architect thanks for sparing him a long and agonizing process—one that the Grey Wardens had started when they inducted him into the order long ago. It was finished. He should feel relieved, if anything.

"You plan on unleashing the taint on the surface?"

"Those that survive," it began slowly, "will become immune to the taint, as the Grey Wardens are. This is an immunity they would pass on to their offspring."

"But they would be tainted. Like I am now."

The creature nodded, as if this was something it had already considered and that didn't bother it in the slightest. "That is so. I told you earlier that darkspawn and humanity would need to find a middle ground. That is humanity's part. Your people would endure a great change."

Bregan sat in the chair for a minute, mulling this over. It should have bothered him more, the idea of initiating genocide on such a scale. But this would be protecting them, too, would it not? He was doing as he had originally been tasked, as all the Grey Wardens had been tasked: End the Blights. Save the world. So long as that was what was happening here, he couldn't ignore the result simply because of the cost. When he considered the loss of life during the First Blight alone—in fact, was he not sitting in a ruin that was evidence of all that had been lost? What sacrifice was too great for the sake of survival?

If it were possible to end the Blights.

"So you need my help. To bring about this change in humanity."

The Architect spread its hands. "Not at all."

Bregan was floored. He almost jumped out of his chair, and only calmed himself as he noted the tension in the darkspawn as it watched him. He took a deep breath and settled back into the stone seat. "But why did you bring me here, then? I assumed you needed to know what I know. Now you're saying you don't?"

"I do need to know what you know," it said, clearly pleased that Bregan had managed to restrain himself, "but it has nothing to do with humanity. That part of my plan will proceed without your assistance." It tapped its chin thoughtfully. "I know little of your kind, and often your reactions are surprising to me, but I had surmised that even though a Grey Warden might wish to end the Blights as much as I, you would hesitate to strike such a blow against your own kind to do it." It peered at him, suddenly fascinated. "Am I wrong?"

"You aren't wrong." Bregan noticed the way the darkspawn looked at him, the way it wrung its hands and leaned forward in its seat. Was it excited? Normally the creature seemed so cultured and passive, the idea that it might be emotional about anything was odd. "So I assume you need my help with the other part of your plan. Dealing with the darkspawn."

"That is so."

"Are you planning genocide against your own kind, as well?"

It nodded. "What I intend will inevitably lead to such, yes."

Now Bregan was intrigued. Somehow he had assumed that the Architect's plan for the darkspawn would be more lenient than his plan for humanity. "But there's more to it than that?"

"My kind are subject to the call of the Old Gods." It leaned back in its chair, looking off into the distance as it spoke. There was almost a religious fervor to its words, a belief in its holy mission that came across very strongly. The fact that Bregan could find such belief here, in the shadows of the Deep Roads, was at the same time intriguing and a little frightening. "So long as the call continues, it does not matter if our numbers are depleted. They have been depleted before, and yet each time we have rebuilt and each time we have done it with only one purpose in mind: finding the prisons of the remaining Old Gods to free them."

A slow realization began to dawn on Bregan. "So you mean to . . ."

"To find and kill the remaining Old Gods, yes." The creature smiled, an expression that turned into more of a toothy grin on its puckered and twisted face. It looked positively demonic when it did that. "And you know where they are."

Bregan didn't bother trying to hide the fact that it was true. He'd surmised that this was what the darkspawn sought back when he'd made his first attempt to escape. What else could he provide that this creature didn't already know or already have access to?

To have it admitted, however, made him squirm. There were only a few within the order that knew the locations of the ancient prisons. He didn't even know how that information had been acquired, or of what use it might be. Knowing the location of the prisons didn't mean that the Grey Wardens knew how to reach them, after all. Those destinations were far beyond the reach of men.

"How do you even know that?" he finally asked.

"You are not the first Grey Warden to enter the Deep Roads."

That made Bregan pause. Of course there would have been others. The Calling had been a tradition within the order since the First Blight. In the years after the first darkspawn invasion of the surface, fewer Grey Wardens died in battle. They lived longer lives and realized at the same time that their vaunted immunity had a time limit. Somehow he had assumed that he had been the first to have been captured, though there was no reason to.

How long had this been going on?

"These other Grey Wardens . . . they told you this? Willingly?"

The Architect stared at him, its animation gone as it considered its words. At least, that was what Bregan assumed it was doing. "Most of your kind that enter the Deep Roads die, even though I attempted for a long time to prevent that. The darkspawn do not always do my bidding, as you have seen, and even if they did, it is not always possible to take a Grey Warden alive."

"I don't doubt it."

"There has only been one, one that I was able to find and who spoke to me in time. It was he who told me of the Joining, and he who told me of the knowledge that one such as yourself might possess."

"And where is this Grey Warden?"

"He is dead." The Architect's tone was flat, perhaps even sad. Bregan considered the possibility that this man it spoke of had been a friend of some kind. Was that possible? It seemed perhaps it was. "By his own choice. He could not endure the transformation as you have. It was beyond his tolerance."

"Ah."

"I knew that one day you would come." Now the darkspawn's fervor returned, and it stared at Bregan intensely with its milky eyes. "And I knew that when you came, I would be able to bring you here, and that you would see the true purpose that lies before us."

"You knew it?"

"I had a vision."

Bregan shuddered, and he found himself growing even colder than he had felt before. Vigorously he rubbed his arms in the chair. Darkspawn dreaming seemed bizarre indeed. Was the Architect speaking of a prophecy? Did it believe in the Maker? He was almost frightened to ask, but the more he thought of the implications, the more agitated he grew.

Yet the thought of ending the Blights . . . according to the Chantry, it had all begun with the Maker. Mankind had intruded into heaven and destroyed it with his sin, and the Maker had thrown those men back to earth to become darkspawn. So was it not fitting that visions, the very handiwork of the Maker, be involved in the Blights' end? Perhaps the Maker had forgiven mankind at last?

The very idea . . . could it be true? It made his heart beat quickly, made him nervously tap his foot on the floor.

"And, let us say I considered telling you where the remaining Old Gods were," he said slowly. "How do I know this isn't just some ruse for the darkspawn to do what you yourself say they are compelled to do: Find the Old Gods?"

"That is an excellent question. I do not know how it might be possible to convince you of this, but my intent is not to awaken the Old Gods. My intent is to slay them. Their call must come to an end."

Bregan sat back in his chair, letting out his breath slowly. Kill the remaining Old Gods? Prevent another Blight from ever occurring? Set the darkspawn free from their compulsion? Were these things even possible? He didn't know. Yet in his heart he knew he had already made his decision, when he had turned back into the Deep Roads with the Architect instead of escaping to the surface.

He didn't even need to say it. The emissary watched him closely and was silent; it knew that Bregan was going to help. Perhaps its vision had told it that and it had known this all along. Bregan knew a little of visions. He knew of the Fade, and what it meant to walk its roads. He knew that sometimes the Maker worked in mysterious ways. More mysterious than Bregan could ever have guessed, if there was truly some purpose to him being where he was and having suffered as he had.

"If we are to do this thing," he sighed, "then there is something you should know. I believe my sister is coming. With other Grey Wardens. I think she knows I am still alive."

The darkspawn didn't ask how he knew. It merely nodded. "Yes, I am aware."

"You are?"

"I am." It leaned forward in its chair, staring at Bregan intensely. "We will need to prepare for their arrival."

It didn't take long for Maric to discover what the murmur they'd heard at the underground lake had actually been. The sound arose again behind them as the group passed through a long and narrow cavern lined with stalagmites. Now that it wasn't coupled with the echoes of dripping water it was much clearer, and sounded almost as if there were people hidden in the shadows whispering to each other under their breath.

"What *is* that?" he asked, stopping to look behind them. All he could see, however, was more impenetrable darkness and more rocks. The sound stopped immediately, as if reacting to the sudden scrutiny. He tried to peer into the darkness, half expecting to see bodies scurrying out of sight. But there was nothing.

Kell paused beside him, also turning to look. Maric wondered if the hunter's strange eyes saw more than his did. Hafter stopped at the same time, sniffing experimentally at the air and uttering a low and menacing growl. Finally Kell pointed at one of the stalagmites just on the edges of the light given off by Fiona's staff.

Maric watched, but didn't see anything unusual about it. Just as he was about to ask, he suddenly noticed movement. The "stalagmite" unfolded, revealing a serpentine creature with a long and wormlike neck that ended in a maw full of sharp teeth. Its mottled skin was almost perfectly camouflaged to match the stone around it. It spun on them and hissed threateningly from afar, and then bounded off into the shadows with alarming speed.

Hafter growled again, eager to chase after the creature. The hunter restrained it with a small gesture. "The dwarves call them deep stalkers," he whispered. "Were we fewer, or they more numerous, they would have already ambushed us." He pointed to several other stalagmites nearby, and now Maric began to see the subtle differences. He noticed where the creature's limbs folded up under its carapace, where it tucked its long neck under its body. Hidden in plain sight, the disguise was almost perfect. He could have reached out and poked them, they were so close.

"They're just going to let us pass?"

"They will follow, for a time, hoping for one of us to stray. The sound you hear is them communicating to each other, telling of intruders to their domain."

"We heard that back at the lake."

The hunter looked at him with amusement. "Then you're lucky you did not remain there longer. No doubt they were calling for more."

"Lucky," Maric repeated. Duncan had sat there by himself next to that lake, no doubt presenting an enviable target to these deep stalkers. He was the lucky one, probably.

They continued on in silence. A pall hung over the group now, and they all seemed eager to find their way back to the Deep Roads, if such a route existed. Utha stopped as soon as they left the cavern, kneeling and putting her hand to the ground. She had done this several times already, closing her eyes as if she could feel something within the stone that none of the others could. Dwarven stone-sense, Maric suspected, though it had been many years since he had seen it used.

When she stood, she made a signal to Genevieve and led them down a new passage confidently. The Commander did not question her, and had said little of consequence since they'd left the lake. Nicolas, too, had been sullen and withdrawn, stumbling along without even a hint of preparedness should they need to fight. Duncan kept far away from the man, remaining miserably to the rear of the party, which Maric figured was probably smart of him.

He allowed himself to fall back to where the lad walked, and for a while they traveled together silently. Duncan refused to look at Maric, and though Fiona shot Maric a dangerous look of warning, he remained where he was.

"How are you feeling?" he finally asked.

Duncan seemed puzzled. "How should I be feeling?"

"I don't know. That was quite the impressive outburst back at the cavern."

"Yes, well." Duncan shrugged, obviously hoping that Maric would simply let the conversation drop.

"You remind me a little of myself, you know."

"Really? Maybe I should have myself fitted for a crown, then?"

Maric ignored the sharpness in his words. "When I fought in the rebellion, I wasn't much older than you are now. I was never sure of myself, always questioning whether I was good enough or strong enough to be king. Every loss was agonizing because I was the one who caused it."

Duncan snorted. "Seems like you made out well enough."

"I know they call me Maric the Savior. I don't know who started that. Probably Rowan, come to think of it. She always encouraged the adoration of the people, because she believed it was important."

"I don't know who that is."

"My wife, the Queen." He tried to keep his voice flat. From Duncan's curious glance, he suspected he wasn't very successful. "She died. Two years ago, now."

"I'm sorry," Duncan said earnestly. "Did you love her?"

"I did. I do." Maric cleared his throat, studiously looking ahead. "There was another woman before her, however. An elven woman by the name of Katriel, the very one who led us to Ortan thaig when I was in the Deep Roads. She saved my life, but when I found out she was a spy and had cost us the battle at West Hill, I killed her. I ran her through."

Maric could feel the lad's speculative look, and was suddenly glad for the dim light as he was sure his color was rising. Why he was suddenly talking about this, he wasn't certain. He had never talked about it to anyone before, not since it had happened. Perhaps he was being foolish.

"I'd heard about that," Duncan said carefully. "Some of it, anyway."

"No doubt. Loghain made sure word got out, so everyone knew that justice had been done." He turned and looked at Duncan directly. "My point is that it wasn't justice. I was furious and felt betrayed. I felt responsible for all the people who had died because I was the one who trusted her. I couldn't forgive her. I murdered her, and I never regretted anything more in my life."

"Oh."

"We all make mistakes, Duncan. Some of them are going to cost others dearly. What's important is that your intentions were good, and that you learn from what you've done." He attempted a wan smile. "I wish I'd known that a long time ago."

They walked side by side for a time, both of them staring off into the shadows in awkward silence. Finally the lad looked at him, and for a moment Maric could have sworn the lad actually looked bashful. "Thank you," he said quietly.

Maric nodded and smiled. There was nothing more he could say.

"Hold!" Genevieve suddenly shouted from the front.

They all stopped, Kell drawing his bow and nocking an arrow almost instantly. Utha was ahead of them and gestured to the others to join her. They moved up, and as Fiona cautiously brightened the white glow from her staff, what the dwarf had found was revealed.

An entire section of the cave ahead of them had collapsed, and was almost impassable. What was far more important, however, was that past the hole in the cavern wall appeared to be a section of the Deep Roads. It would require them to climb up the rubble and squeeze through a fairly narrow aperture, but the signs of dwarven architecture beyond were unmistakable.

"It's a way back," Fiona breathed.

"I thought it seemed like we were headed up," Duncan said, and Utha nodded her head in agreement.

"Are there darkspawn up there?" Maric asked.

"No," Fiona offered, the faraway look in her eyes telling him that she was casting out her Grey Warden senses. "Not nearby, anyhow." The elf tapped the onyx brooch attached to her chain shirt. "It looks like the gifts from the Circle are proving their worth. We've lost them for the moment."

Genevieve seemed unconvinced. "Perhaps," she frowned, "though it is odd. Normally they swarm like a horde of bees when disturbed." She drew her greatsword, the blade flashing in the staff's glare, and approached the rubble cautiously with it in hand. Waving for the others to follow her, she began her ascent.

It was a slow process to get through the hole in the wall. In the end, they needed to clear some of the rocks at the top of the pile to make room for those with bulkier armor. Utha was the first through, and she gave the all clear from the other side.

It was good to be back in the dwarven passages, Maric thought. He noticed almost immediately, however, that the signs of darkspawn corruption had returned. There was an almost marked transition from the natural caves they had just left. Why was that? Was there something about the Deep Roads that made them more susceptible to this strange infestation? There he saw the familiar trails of black filth and the clusters of fleshy sacs lining the walls. The crumbling statues, too, looked much like every other part of the Deep Roads they had been to. They could be anywhere.

Genevieve looked about grimly. "Do you recognize anything?" she asked Maric.

He shook his head.

"Then we proceed."

They traveled for hours, Genevieve pushing them mercilessly, as if she expected an attack from the darkspawn at any moment. The other Wardens, however, seemed content that this was unlikely. They had slipped the noose, as it were, and if the darkspawn were searching for them anywhere it was back in the network of caverns they had just left. This appeared to bring no comfort to their commander, who became more tense the longer they traveled.

Twice they passed tunnels that branched off from the main route, the entrances marked with great stone archways. Utha signed that these were abandoned thaigs, though any indication of which ones they had been was now scoured away by time and the encroachment of darkspawn corruption. The dwarf stood at the entrances and stared sadly into the shadows beyond, clenching and unclenching her fists. Maric had to wonder what it must be like for her, to know your people once ruled a great empire that had been reduced to a shadow of its former self.

Much later they came upon a section of the Deep Roads that had mostly collapsed into the caverns below, leaving a gaping chasm filled with little more than cobwebs and darkness. The wall on one side remained intact, along with a narrow ledge at its foot just barely wide enough to walk along. They eyed it with suspicion, but Utha seemed convinced that it was well enough supported that they could cross it one at a time, if there was anywhere to reach. The light from Fiona's staff was not enough to extend all the way to the other side. They could only assume that there even *was* another side.

Genevieve went first, overriding objections by saying her armor was the heaviest present. If they couldn't get her across now, they wouldn't be able to do so later. Kell tied a length of rope around her, but Maric doubted the rope would even hold her properly if the stone on the path gave way. It offered little more than peace of mind.

Still, she went across without a moment's hesitation, flattening herself against the wall and sliding slowly along the ledge until she disappeared into the shadows. The rope represented their only indication that she had not fallen. Quiet minutes passed as they watched the rope carefully and Kell slowly let more and more of it out. Just when it looked like they were about to run out of rope, it jerked sharply. Twice. She was across.

Maric was one of the last to go, and it was an experience he was not likely to want to ever repeat. Slowly sliding along the narrow ledge, one barely got any indication that there was even a floor beneath. In that darkness it felt like he was suspended, and that he would pitch forward into the vast pit before him at any moment. He couldn't see how deep it went, but he could feel it. He needed to stop once, pressing his head against the wall and closing his eyes to keep the world from spinning around him. Only the insistent tugging of the rope kept him moving, inching on toward the pinpoint of light on the other side.

When he finally stumbled off the ledge, he was sweating and trembling. Kell grabbed him and Fiona ran up. The warm glow of her staff was probably the most welcome sight he could possibly imagine.

"Are you all right?" she asked, concerned.

"I didn't fall in," he chuckled.

The elf frowned severely at him. "Is that a yes?"

"Err . . . I suppose so, yes."

She snorted derisively and turned on her heel, walking away. Maric glanced askance at Kell and the hunter merely shrugged. He couldn't explain it, either.

They pressed on, entering a new portion of the Deep Roads with tunnels that looked higher than he remembered. They trudged through portions that were flooded with shallow, brackish water and others that were so thick with the corruption they needed to cut a path through the black film. Maric's sword was particularly suited for this, its runes glowing brightly as he forced the foulness to part before him. At one point they passed a hall lined with dwarven statues, most of them crumbled or covered in lichen and moss to the point of being unrecognizable.

Just when Maric felt like he was about to collapse from fatigue, he noticed a set of runes on one of the walls almost covered by dust and debris. "Wait!" he called out.

Genevieve ordered a halt and turned, concerned. He ran up to the wall, scraping it clear with his gauntlet, and smiled as he recognized a number of the markings. It had been years since he'd seen them, but he remembered them clearly. "I know these," he exclaimed. "We passed by these! I mean, I did, when I was here before . . . we came this way!"

"Are you sure?" Genevieve asked skeptically.

"They could just look similar," Duncan added.

Utha stepped forward and inspected the runes carefully. She made a series of motions at the others, and he didn't need a translation.

"It doesn't say anything about Ortan, right? It mentions another thaig?" At the dwarf's cautious nod, he turned around and studied the tunnel carefully. There was more overgrowth and corruption here, but that had been the case ever since they'd entered the Deep Roads. The layout tweaked his memory, but he couldn't tell if that was because he actually remembered this place or because so many of the passages were similar to each other. "If I'm right, there should be a crossroads ahead, with even more runes on the walls."

The Grey Wardens blinked at each other, uncertain what to make of Maric's pronouncement. Without another word they turned and began marching ahead. Within minutes, they reached the crossroads he remembered. There were lava flows here, channels in the walls carved by the dwarves and at one time filled with glowing lava to provide light. The area was covered in random debris, much of the roof having collapsed, and, as he had predicted, more large runes were carved into the walls.

Maric smiled broadly. "See? Just like I said!"

The exhausted relief on the faces of the others was obvious. The idea that they might not have simply been wandering aimlessly all this time was a welcome one. Only Genevieve seemed more disturbed by their luck than reassured. She eyed the pillar suspiciously and regarded Maric with a raised brow. "Do you know the way to Ortan thaig from here?"

It took only a moment of thought. "That way." He pointed. "I remember we came the other way, and then Katriel . . . we saw those runes. That's how we knew where we were going."

She pondered carefully. "How long?" she finally asked.

"Less than a day."

With a curt nod, she unshouldered her pack, tossing it to the ground. "Then we rest here." When the others hesitated, staring at her in disbelief that she didn't intend to push on, she shrugged. "For whatever reason, the darkspawn are not near. We must take advantage, while we can. Don't bother setting up tents. We won't remain long."

Considering he was ready to collapse, Maric didn't offer an argument.

11

The first of the Maker's children watched across the Veil
And grew jealous of the life
They could not feel, could not touch.
In blackest envy were the demons born.
—Canticle of Erudition 2:1

Duncan felt like he was little more than a pile of bruises as he walked alongside the others. They'd had barely a handful of hours to rest, enough time to strip off some sweaty leathers that he felt like he'd been wearing for weeks and to rub magical ointment on his wounds. Fiona had passed it around, and they'd all taken a turn by the fire. It had been a litany of painful hisses, grunts, and relieved sighs.

His arm remained stiff and sore, but Kell had inspected it and declared that it was no longer broken. Fiona's spell had done the trick, and the ointment had managed to relieve much of the ache that had been plaguing him since the battle. He experimentally flexed and unflexed his hand, frowning at the fact that it seemed difficult to make a proper fist. But he could, and that was what mattered.

Hafter was the only one of them who'd slept well. Almost as soon as they'd set up the fire, the hound had curled up at his master's feet and was snoring within minutes. Duncan liked how the dog's feet twitched, and how he would occasionally huff like he was about to bark in his sleep. A dog's dreams were probably about running through sunny meadows and barking at squirrels, which was the sort of dream that Duncan wouldn't mind having himself.

Then he remembered that Hafter was tainted just the same as the rest of the Grey Wardens. Perhaps his dreams were just as dark, and when he ran, he ran away from the frightening shadows that always lurked at the edges of a Grey Warden's mind.

He hoped he was wrong, for the dog's sake.

Genevieve led the way down the passage, tense and quiet. She was eager to get to Ortan thaig as quickly as possible now, and would brook no further delay. The others tried to keep up, but even so she pulled farther and farther ahead. They exchanged glances with each other, clearly wondering if she even cared that she was putting such distance between herself and the rest of her party.

Probably not, Duncan suspected.

He edged closer to Fiona and walked at her side for a time. The mage looked marginally less pale after some rest. Genevieve had strictly forbidden her to use any more magic to speed up the healing of the others, and though Fiona had complained, Duncan had to agree. All their major injuries had already been dealt with. She needed her strength, especially if Ortan thaig was as dangerous as Maric claimed.

He had told them all what had happened the last time he'd been there. Giant spiders, deformed by the taint, had swooped down upon them from a sea of spiderwebs that had obscured the upper reaches of the thaig. To defeat them, they'd burned the webs down. Duncan wondered if there would still be spiders there. He shuddered at the thought. He didn't like small ones, and the thought of meeting ones as big as he was, poison dripping from their mandibles, was downright revolting.

"I need to tell you something," he whispered to Fiona.

Nearby, Nicolas shot him an annoyed glare and sped up his pace to pull ahead. There was going to be no forgiveness there, Duncan saw. The warrior had been sullen and bristly by the campfire, barely attending to his own wounds and not even removing his soiled armor when he had the chance. He'd elected to take the first watch without question, stiffly walking off as the others looked after him in pity.

The elf was regarding him with interest. "What is it? Is it about Maric?"

"No!" he snorted. "What is it with you two?"

She sighed in exasperation. "Fine. What do you have to tell me?"

"It's about Genevieve." He glanced toward the Commander, and could barely see her off in the shadows ahead. It was as if the thaig were drawing her magnetically, and the closer they got to it the faster she was compelled to move. "She left the camp during the night. Not to go on watch, either. I mean she snuck off."

Fiona looked puzzled. "Snuck off? What for?"

"That's what I wondered. So I followed her."

"And she didn't see you?"

"I happened to be a very good thief in Val Royeaux before you lot came along, you know."

"Point taken. What did you see?"

"She didn't actually go very far." He hesitated, suddenly not sure he should be relating the story, after all. Perhaps Genevieve would view it as an invasion of her privacy. He had been snooping on her, though at the time he told himself he was just making sure she'd be safe. But now that he'd brought it up with Fiona, there wasn't any point in stopping. "She went just down a ways from the crossroads with a torch. Then she began taking off her armor."

"You watched her strip?"

"No! I mean . . . well, yes, but it wasn't like that. I thought that maybe she just wanted some privacy. I was going to turn around and let her be, and that's when I saw it."

"Saw what?"

"I thought it was a bruise." He remembered only too well the patch of discoloration that had extended all the way from the Commander's bare shoulder down the side of her ribs and almost to her thigh. He had been alarmed at first, especially at its intensity. Too dark to be a bruise, he'd wondered if maybe it had been a burn from the dragon's fiery breath. Had she been hiding her injury this entire time? Why would she? "It wasn't, though. I don't think Genevieve knew what it was, either. She held the torch close to take a good look in the light."

"And what did she see?"

"I thought . . . I thought it looked like darkspawn flesh."

Fiona stared ahead, pondering this information as they walked. For a moment, Duncan regretted telling her. He hadn't been sure what to think when he'd seen the "bruise." He'd been horrified, and from the look on Genevieve's face, she'd felt the same. He had the feeling, however, that it hadn't been the first time she'd seen it. She'd known it was there, and had hidden it from the rest of them.

"It could just be an injury," she offered. "An old injury."

"I don't think so."

"What else could it be?" She turned to look at him sharply. "Do you think she caught the plague? She's a Grey Warden, how can that be?"

He shrugged. "I don't know."

Maric walked up to them suddenly, effectively interrupting their conversation. "What are you two whispering about so urgently?" he asked, trying to fight against a yawn and losing the battle.

"It's nothing," Fiona said too quickly.

"I was just telling her how tired I was," Duncan cut in. "We didn't get much sleep before Genevieve was kicking us all up. I could have sworn I'd just shut my eyes."

Kell walked close, his bow unslung and at the ready. Hafter

padded along amiably beside him. "I, for one, am glad we did not sleep more," the hunter muttered.

"Really?" Maric asked.

"The dreams were difficult to bear." Kell's eyes darkened and he looked away. Hafter glanced up at his master, whining quizzically.

Utha stepped toward them, making several agitated gestures with her hands. Fiona sighed and nodded her agreement. "I was the same. The dreams came as soon as I closed my eyes, like I was drowning in them." She closed her eyes and shuddered at the memory.

"Perhaps it is being within the Deep Roads?" Kell asked.

Maric shrugged. "I haven't had any dreams. Besides the usual, I mean."

"Grey Wardens always have dreams," Fiona explained. "It comes with being part of the darkspawn consciousness. They've been getting worse since we entered the Deep Roads."

"Each night has been worse than the last," Kell added grimly.

"Not me." Duncan put up his hand. "I've been fine."

Fiona regarded him with a suspicious eye. "Are you sure? I thought for certain . . ."

"No. Just the normal sort of cheese dreams."

"Oh! I get those," Maric chuckled.

"Really? Fiona was using these spells to turn the darkspawn into giant pillars of stinky cheese, and I kept thinking, 'Why stinky cheese, of all things? I hate stinky cheese.' But she wouldn't use a different spell and got really angry at me."

"You mean like that?" He indicated the elf, who was indeed glaring at them with seething disapproval.

"You are both idiots," she grumbled, rolling her eyes.

"I think it was more that she just really liked stinky cheese," he told Maric. "She kept taking a big bite out of each pillar. All I could smell was feet."

"That's disgusting."

"That's what *I* said!"

Genevieve's appearance ahead of them cut off all conversation sharply, like a splash of cold water. They all stared as she stormed back toward them, her demeanor cold fury. "Why have you slowed?" she demanded. "We are there." Without waiting for a response she turned back.

They rushed to catch up, and quickly discovered that she was correct.

Fiona held up her staff and let the white light shine intensely into the cavern they entered, and that still didn't reveal it all. Duncan felt like they were disturbing a tomb, a great cavern full of the skeletons of ancient dwarven buildings long since settled to their quiet decay. He could see hints of crumbling walkways, great columns and statues fallen to the ground and shattered, gutted buildings, some of which climbed almost up to the vaulted ceiling high overhead.

Once this had been a bustling city, and now it was completely silent and still as a graveyard. A thick black dust had settled over everything, and the upper reaches of the cavern were nothing more than a grey cloud full of strange clumps. If that was all a result of the webs being burned down so many years before, they hadn't been rebuilt. Perhaps the giant spiders had moved on? They could always hope.

"Ortan thaig," Maric breathed. Duncan noticed the distant, haunted look in his eyes. He got that way every time he thought of his last voyage in the Deep Roads. It made Duncan wonder why the man had agreed to come back here at all, despite the urgency of their mission.

Genevieve had her greatsword held out before her warily. All of them had their weapons in hand now, in fact, staring into the still shadows as if they expected a swarm of monsters to come rushing out at them. "Has anything changed?" she asked Maric.

"Fewer cobwebs."

The Commander gestured to Kell, who moved forward and knelt, studying the thick layers of dust and dirt that covered the stone. Hafter paced around him, snuffling at the ground with his nose and sneezing. "There has been much movement through this cavern. Most of it has been very recent, and dark-spawn."

"And my brother?" she asked.

The question hung in the air, and Kell paused. He stared at the ground with his pale eyes, as if he could see patterns in the faint tracks that none of the rest of them could. Duncan suspected that was probably the case. The hunter had a sensitivity to the taint that went far beyond any tracking ability he might have learned during his time with the Ash Warriors. He was always the first to sense the approach of darkspawn, and he could discern between the various breeds by their scent alone. Some of the Grey Wardens even used to claim that Kell could do the same with them, sense who was who from afar just as if they were darkspawn. If so, the hunter never commented on it.

"Your brother has been through here," he finally agreed.

"Where?"

He arched his brow at her. "I am accustomed to his particular scent, Genevieve, but even I cannot track him through all the others. He has been here; that is all I know." He gestured at the ground, and even Duncan could see that the piles of black dust and dirt had been disturbed by many pairs of feet. Darkspawn feet, presumably, though apparently not all.

Genevieve frowned in frustration, and she searched the distant shadows of the thaig helplessly. Then her features hardened and she set her jaw, turning back to regard the others. "Then we search every inch of this ruin until we find some trace of him."

"How do we know there even is a trace?" Maric asked. "He could have just passed through. He could have been chased through, for all we know."

"Then let us find out where he ran," she growled. Hefting the greatsword onto her shoulder, she turned and marched into the ruined streets of the thaig. The others followed without question.

For a time they moved carefully through the narrow passages between buildings. Some of the walls and walkways had collapsed, leaving large chunks of rubble strewn in their way, but much of it had not. It was a testament to the skills of the dwarves that many of these rune-covered arches and delicate statues were still standing.

The light from Fiona's staff bathed everything in a harsh glare, but left many shadows. Everywhere Duncan looked there was darkness just beyond the edge of the staff's white glow, waiting behind statues and in doorways, obscuring the secrets this place kept. He imagined that Maric's spiders still hid in those depths, watching them progress with their many dark little eyes and waiting until they had proceeded too far in to retreat.

He rubbed his arms, feeling suddenly cold, and Fiona shot him a dark look. She held her staff at the ready, alertly watching for signs of attack. They all were. The only sound they could hear besides their muffled steps in the dust was Hafter's growling. The hound's hackles were raised, and he appeared to find every building they passed worthy of staring down.

Only Maric didn't seem ready for combat. He held his longsword loosely at his side, walking among the others and staring up at the walls around them with wide, sad eyes. He'd told them of the spiders, yes, but what else had happened here? Was he thinking of the elven woman, the one he'd loved? Was he thinking of his wife?

They passed a stone arch, one where the wall around it had collapsed, leaving only the cracked and dusty curve of the arch standing alone. Large runes had been carved along the top, and Utha stopped and stared up at them, her face grim and unreadable.

"What is it?" Kell asked her quietly, walking up behind her.

She made several gestures, most of which Duncan couldn't understand. But he recognized one of them: *family*. This must have belonged to the house she came from, he realized, a part of her family's legacy. Kell nodded in understanding and patted her shoulder. She continued to stare up at that arch, quiet determination in her eyes.

They entered what looked like it had once been an outdoor amphitheater, the steps now falling apart and the stage now littered with darkspawn bones yellowed with age. There were so many strewn amid the debris that Duncan marveled at them.

As they passed through a narrow alleyway, Nicolas found a crevice in one of the walls that led into an old armory. It was huge, the stone forges still upright and looking almost as if someone could walk up and stoke the fires even now to get them going again. The rest of it was in ruins, barrels falling apart and metal tools rusting on the ground. There were pieces of things that might have been used for forging metal, and impressive-looking weapons, now pitted and tarnished, still hanging on the walls.

One of the forges was excessively tall, reaching all the way up to the stone ceiling and covered in runes all down the side of its chimney. It looked more like a giant oven, Duncan thought, with strange holes perforating its side at regular intervals.

"It's for dragonbone," Maric mentioned behind him. "They get the bone so hot they need to pour water through the holes to cool it off. You see where it goes through the floor there? That goes down to a lava pit." He grinned at Duncan. "Or so King Endrin called it when he showed me the one in Orzammar. He said it hadn't been used in centuries."

Duncan peered into one of the holes. He saw nothing but darkness, and no obvious mechanism for opening up the forge. "Maybe your sword was made here."

"Maybe it was."

They moved through the armory and forced open the rusted doors, discovering what must have once been some kind of central square just outside. The staff's light revealed evidence of a battle from long ago, one that the passage of time had not completely eradicated. Some of the barricades still existed, slabs of stone and benches and other large items that had been dragged to close off access from the nearby lanes. Most of these had fallen apart. Or the walls around them had disintegrated. Or they had been torn down by whatever force had attacked the people here.

For here they remained. Even amid all the dirt and dust, Duncan could see the shards of bones and pieces of rusted armor and weapons—and none of it was darkspawn. There was a stone fountain in the middle of the square, the statue of a horn-blowing dwarf still standing in its middle. It was overgrown with lichen and thick black moss, much of which had died when whatever water had been within the fountain had disappeared ages ago. The concentration of bones was thickest around there. A last stand, perhaps, the defenders forced to put their backs against the fountain as they fought the darkspawn invaders to the bitter end.

It was a sad scene. Duncan tried not to picture the desperation that these dwarves must have felt, abandoned to their fate. They had fallen here, and whatever injured or survivors there had been had no doubt been taken away by the darkspawn, while the others just remained where they fell. They decayed here as the years passed and the dust settled, the fountain went dry, and nobody at all marked that they had died.

Utha stepped toward one of the barricade piles and began pulling at one of the larger flat slabs of stone at its base. It refused to budge and so she pulled harder, putting her back into it, and this was when Duncan realized she was crying. Silent tears were streaming down her face as she attempted to pull the slab free, her frustration mounting.

Nicolas went to assist her, and the dwarf stopped as soon as he got close. He gave her a compassionate look and bent down to help, and after composing herself she continued her task. Kell joined them and within moments the trio had worked the slab free. Genevieve watched quietly, not objecting to this strange practice but still eager to move on.

They slowly dragged the slab to the fountain and together lifted it upright so it leaned against the stone. Sweating with effort, Utha removed her black cloak and threw it over the top of the slab. It settled there, and she stared up at it silently.

They all did. It was a poor marker, perhaps, but it was better than nothing.

Utha wiped at her tears and shook off her grief. If she offered up a prayer to her Paragon ancestors, she could only mouth them to herself. Duncan would have been tempted to say a prayer to the Maker, but he didn't have King Maric's facility for such things. He didn't know a single line of the Chant of Light, and besides that he had no idea whether the dead dwarves would have even appreciated such a tribute.

They moved on. In time, Kell led them to an abandoned campfire. How he found it, Duncan hadn't a clue, but as they got near he pointed it out. A small campfire at the base of a tall obelisk, completely undamaged by the passage of time. The obelisk shot up like a finger in the dark, completely smooth on all sides, the top of it obscured in shadows.

Genevieve ran over, eagerly searching around the campfire for anything left behind. There was nothing, though from the way the dust was disturbed it looked like someone had slept on a bedroll there very recently. She turned and motioned to Kell, although he was already running over to join her.

After a moment of kneeling by the fire, he looked up at her and nodded. "He was here. This camp is recent."

"Is there any indication of where he went?"

"No. He slept here, however, so clearly made it this far without meeting the darkspawn."

"Is that possible?" she asked, troubled. "They would have sensed him. A lone Grey Warden moving through the Deep Roads should draw darkspawn like flies."

"Nevertheless, here he was."

Maric stepped forward. "Are you certain it was darkspawn that captured him? Or that he's even been captured? You said he was alive, and maybe he is, but I don't see the darkspawn trying to take any prisoners."

Genevieve spun on the King, and for a moment Duncan thought she was going to attack him. Her rage slowly died down, however, and she turned back to stare at the gutted campfire. Her eyes became hollow and haunted. "No," she finally admitted. "I don't know that for certain."

For a long minute the group remained quiet. There was not a single sound in the dark cavern, and only the faintest musty breeze—air that was brought in through whatever masterpiece of dwarven engineering remained in this place, Duncan assumed. He wondered what other sorts of creatures could be down here that might have captured a Grey Warden, and why they might do so. And if it was darkspawn, why would they suddenly start acting in a way they never had before?

Genevieve cast about in all directions, looking far off into the cavern. What she was searching for, he really couldn't tell. A clue? A feeling, anything? So much of the thaig was shrouded in shadow, she likely couldn't see very much. The skeletons of buildings hovered around them, silhouettes of sturdy statues and the tattered estates of what had surely once been great dwarven families. They didn't have time to search it all.

"There," she stated firmly, pointing off into the distance.

Duncan looked to where she was pointing: In the shadow-filled end of the thaig, barely seen at the edge of their light, was the remnant of a great palace that had been carved into the rock.

It might have been beautiful once, pillars and promenades leading up to a set of grandiose gates that towered high over any visitors, but now it was little more than a husk, a series of broken steps and debris and gaping holes carved into the wall that led deep within. The old palace was covered in strands of old ash and dirt, and who knew what lay inside that dark warren of tunnels?

"You've *got* to be kidding," he muttered under his breath.

"But why there?" Kell asked carefully.

"Because that is where he would go," she stated with certainty. "If he came here, that is where he would head." Without saying another word she began to march in that direction. The others looked at each other uncertainly, but one by one they followed her. There was little choice, really.

"We're stumbling around blindly," Fiona whispered, scowling. Duncan glanced at her but didn't comment. They weren't blind, really. They were following Genevieve's vision, but it felt more and more like they were stumbling after a ghost. He wondered if their commander really knew where she was going anymore, and he suspected the others wondered the same thing.

It took them several hours to make their way up finally to the palace ruins. The land sloped upward the nearer they got, and yet the amount of debris became so thick it was impossible to remain on the roads. Entire buildings had collapsed here, choking the paths and forcing them actually to climb over the piles of masonry rather than trying to go around them.

As they reached the foot of the main steps leading up into the palace, Duncan began to realize just how enormous it truly was. The stairs alone towered high above them, requiring a climb of over a hundred feet, much of it on steps that had long ago cracked and crumbled away. They were littered with pieces of stone that had fallen from above and bits of bone and rusted metal that might have once been bodies.

One of the intact pillars lining the stairs was easily hundreds of feet high, almost reaching the top of the cavern. Its surface was a spiderweb of thick cracks, and he wondered whether if it crumbled, the palace's vaulted ceiling would come crashing down on top of them. The ceiling might once have held breathtaking frescoes. Now it was stained and burned, with only a hint of the beauty that it had once had.

Several of the other pillars were already crumbled, and at least one enormous section of a pillar lay in their path. Clearly when that had come crashing down, it had caused great destruction and created a giant crater in what was once a marble landing in front of the gigantic palace doors.

Only one of those doors still remained, and it lay open and askew as if it was just barely hanging on before it, too, tumbled to the ground. It might have been bronze, Duncan thought. Now it was stained with an ugly green patina, and covered with coarse lichen that completely obscured whatever fancy inscriptions and carvings decorated its surface long ago.

Beyond it lay only shadows. He saw hints of giant webs; gossamer strands of it now hung from the ceiling. The group exchanged wary glances when they saw a blackened husk just inside the door, and only upon coming closer did they see it was one of the giant spiders about which Maric had told them, its legs curled in close to its body like a twisted rib cage. How long it had lain there they couldn't say, but it was long enough to be as covered with dust as everything else at the entrance.

"Perhaps you got them all," Duncan breathed, still staring in horror at the spider.

"We didn't think so," Maric said. "We heard them moving the next day. Or at least we thought it was them."

Genevieve poked the husk with her sword, and with a hard push rolled it over. Its head became visible, and Duncan saw that its mandibles were easily large enough to cut off a man's head. Thankfully its many eyes had long ago shriveled up and been covered by dust. He didn't want to see them. "You thought the spiders kept their nest in this palace?" she asked the King.

"We never came up here to see."

"We haven't seen any live spiders since our arrival," she said thoughtfully, more to herself than to anyone.

Kell knelt down, running his hand through the layer of dust on the ground and then rubbing it between his fingers. "Someone has been through here recently," he murmured.

"Was it my brother?" Genevieve demanded.

"I do not know." His brow furrowed with confusion. "The trail is odd. It was definitely just a single creature, either the man we seek or a darkspawn. Only . . ."

"It is enough. We go inside." She began to pass through the doorway, her sword held out cautiously in front of her as she looked up and around at the hanging web strands.

"Wait, I don't . . ."

"Come," she ordered. Duncan ran to catch up to her, and he heard the others following. His heart thundered in his ears, sweat dripping down his face as they slowly moved into the depths of the dwarven palace. He didn't know what they would find inside, but the fear that gripped him claimed it would be nothing good.

Somehow he had imagined that the webs would just get thicker and thicker until they reached the heart of some nest, with some great monstrous spider queen to greet them. But it wasn't like that at all. The webs began to disappear not long after the entrance, and while they found a few more shriveled spider corpses, those, too, ended. The shadows closed in around them, the air getting thicker and thicker. The sounds of their labored breath and the echoes of their slow footsteps on the stone were all he could hear.

They entered an enormous gallery, lined with dwarven statues and large paintings that had blackened and fallen apart from the passage of time. The staff's light only revealed a small part of it, but it seemed like it went on forever, great marble pillars shooting up to a ceiling he couldn't even see.

The sound of their footsteps changed suddenly. It became a loud crunching noise, as if they were crushing gravel underfoot. "Look," Kell said.

Duncan looked down. The floor of the gallery was all but covered in a sea of bones. Darkspawn bones. Many of the skeletons were still intact, the corrupted flesh long since dried up until it was a leathery sheath. They still wore their blackened breastplates and weapons, as well. A great battle had occurred here, these darkspawn pressing inward toward . . . what, exactly? And what had killed them all?

Their numbers grew greater the farther in they walked. It was possible to pick a path among the bones, but not easy. Duncan began to identify dwarven skeletons among the darkspawn. They had been outnumbered. Dozens and dozens of darkspawn for every defender. He saw one dwarven corpse still in its rusted armor, surrounded by a pile of darkspawn bones in a way that made it look as if they had all died while the creatures had been tearing the dwarf apart. All at once. That couldn't be right, could it?

"This is bizarre," Maric said beside him, mirroring his thoughts as he looked around. Duncan simply nodded. "And her brother came through here?"

"There is a trail," Kell commented from nearby.

"But is it his?"

The hunter looked at Maric with his pale eyes and said nothing, the answer in them clear: He didn't know. Genevieve was not letting that stop her, however. If anything, she was speeding up as she moved through the gallery, almost as if she fully expected to find her brother on the other side.

Duncan had his doubts. Could anything be alive in here other than them? If Genevieve's brother was here, how could he not have heard their approach? Their crunching steps were echoing loudly in the gallery, a cacophony that seemed violently at odds with the serenity of this graveyard. He had heard stories of skeletons possessed by demons that would get up and lash out at anything living—he half expected these bones to do just that, rising to silence the intruders in their shadowy domain.

A pair of giant stone doors loomed ahead of them, appearing out of the gloom like twin monoliths towering over the bones below. The doors had been battered inward by some great force, and it was easy to see what that was. There were huge darkspawn corpses in front of the doors, massive things that must have once been twelve feet tall with great, curved horns protruding from their skulls. They were called ogres, if he remembered, but he'd never actually seen a living one.

Their battering rams lay next to their corpses, wicked-looking hunks of metal that they must have used to force in those doors. How long that had taken, one could only imagine. Days, probably. There were all sorts of debris on the other side of the doors, some massive barricade that the darkspawn had finally broken their way through and poured past, dying by the hundreds as they did so.

Genevieve approached the doors cautiously, her eyes wide as she strained to peer beyond them. With a wave of her gauntlet to Nicolas, she sent him around the other side of the ogre corpses. Nothing stirred.

"More light," she ordered Fiona.

The mage frowned, and with concentration her staff suddenly flared into brilliance. Duncan squinted and covered his eyes. Suddenly he could see all the dead skeletons in the gallery, stretching out for hundreds and hundreds of feet behind him. An entire army. He could make out the runes carved into the pillars, and the great beams still crisscrossing the ceiling a hundred feet overhead.

Beyond the doors lay a round, domed chamber. The first thing Duncan noticed was the throne that sat on a stone dais in the center of it. The second thing was the sea of skeletons. They were dwarves, all of them, a layer of bones so thick it was impossible to see the floor. The dais itself was bare, but one lone skeleton sat on that throne. A single, silent witness to the carnage, now covered in a layer of dust.

One by one, the group moved into the chamber. They picked their footing carefully among the fallen bodies, staring around with wonder. The hush was palpable. It was as if they were stepping foot into something dark and terrible, where the light from Fiona's staff seemed harsh and unwelcome.

"Look at them all," Fiona said in awe.

The skeletons in the room were thickest near the doors. At first his assumption had been simply that the dwarves had been fighting the darkspawn as they'd burst through the doors, the last-ditch defense of their dwarven ruler. But where were the darkspawn corpses inside the throne room? There were none.

Utha made a gesture, her eyes wide. Kell nodded. "I agree. This is too strange."

"We should go," Maric said quietly.

"No," Genevieve snapped. Sword out, she began to move closer to the throne. "There is something here. I can feel it."

"Something, yes," Maric shouted after her. "But not your brother!" She ignored him.

Duncan walked to the corpses that were right next to the door, kneeling down to get a closer look. Fiona was behind him, also intrigued. He noticed that only some of them still had weapons, now rusted and useless. The rest of them had nothing. Outside in the gallery, the skeletons were all still holding their blades, or their blades were nearby, but in here the weapons were just somewhere on the floor.

Fiona breathed in sharply. "Look on the doors!"

In the light he could see it clearly: The inside of the doors were covered in *scratches*. Long, shallow scratches everywhere. Some of the skeletons still reached up with their limbs, still clawed at the door. It was the same on the wall by the doors. Some of the finger bones were worn down to the knuckles.

These dwarves hadn't been fighting the darkspawn. They had been trying to get *out* even as the darkspawn were battering their way in. Something had frightened them so terribly they had tried to claw their way out with their bare hands. And then they had died. All of them, at once. And the darkspawn had died with them.

What had happened here?

Something was terribly, terribly wrong. Duncan turned around and saw Genevieve stepping up onto the dais, with Maric and the others just behind her. She seemed transfixed by the single dwarven skeleton that sat on that throne. It seemed to recline there, in a stone chair that was far larger than it was, as if it had simply fallen asleep with its arms still on the rests. It wore an elaborate black helmet, with small horns and an iron face guard, and black chain armor still draped across its bones. And there was not a single other corpse within thirty feet of it.

The dwarves had been trying to get away from the throne.

"Wait!" Duncan called out.

Genevieve stopped and turned back, curious, and he watched in horror as the skeleton on the throne beside her suddenly moved. It lifted its head, its eye sockets alight with a red, sinister glow. A thick power swelled in the shadows around them, a susurrus of voices in their ears as an old magic took form.

The Commander wheeled on the skeleton, her eyes wide with terror, and held out her sword threateningly. "Get back! Get back!" she shouted to the others. Utha and Kell backed up slowly, the hunter with his bow drawn. Hafter stayed at his side, growling menacingly. Maric and Nicolas remained at Genevieve's back, drawing their weapons.

YOU HAVE COME. The voice both came from the skeleton on the dais as well as rang out in Duncan's head. He could feel it slithering into his mind like an eel, like something that left a disgusting trail behind it that made him shiver. *I HAVE WAITED, AND AT LAST YOU HAVE COME.*

Nicolas roared in rage and charged at the skeleton, his shield up and his mace high over his head. The skeleton waved a hand at him and a surge of power sent him flying off the dais, crashing hard to the ground amid the skeletons.

"Nicolas!" Genevieve shouted.

WHEN THE DWARVEN PRINCE CALLED TO ME, I GRANTED WHAT HE DESIRED. AND I HAVE WAITED IN THE DARKNESS FOR ONE TO TAKE ME BACK INTO THE LIGHT, AND YOU HAVE COME.

"Never!" Genevieve shouted again. "I will never!"

Duncan raced toward the dais, pulling out his daggers, with Fiona running at his side. Already she was gathering a corona of power around the head of her staff, whispering words under her breath. Magic was filling the entire chamber, but he wasn't sure it was all hers. The light was dark and greenish, prickling at his skin and filling his body with a strange heaviness.

NOT YOU. The skeleton turned now and pointed at Fiona, extending a long and bony finger out at her. She skidded to a halt, gasping out loud as a liquid blackness enveloped her. *IT IS YOU.* The staff dropped from her hands, its white glow winking out completely, her eyes widening in shock.

Maric rushed at the skeleton and it lashed out with its other hand, sending a bolt of lightning that threw him back, forcing him to jerk and spasm on the ground as electrical energies sparked over his entire body. He screamed in agony.

Two arrows sped at the skeleton, lodging in its bones uselessly. Genevieve lifted her sword up high. "Attack it! Destroy it!" She rushed at the creature, leaping over Maric on the ground, with Utha immediately behind her. Duncan turned to help Fiona, reaching out to try to free her from the black power that had her in its thrall, but it was so freezing cold that it burned his hand. He recoiled, hissing in sudden pain.

I KNOW WHAT YOU DESIRE. The skeleton lifted both its hands now and the greenish glow in the room intensified. Duncan felt it affecting him, draining his energy. He stumbled to one knee, his head suddenly full of cotton like he had just woken up from a deep sleep. On the dais, Genevieve and Utha also stumbled to their knees. Kell dropped his bow, wavering, and Hafter whined in confusion. *I LURED YOU HERE WITH THE PROMISE OF THAT DESIRE, AND YOU CAME. AT LAST I SHALL BE FREE OF THE DARKNESS.*

It was all Duncan could do to keep from collapsing to the ground. Sweat beaded his forehead and he dropped both his daggers. His vision swam. He saw Maric trying valiantly to pull himself along the ground toward the skeleton, clenching his teeth with effort. Utha fell, unconscious, and Genevieve was not far behind her.

Dismay filled Duncan as he saw *something* rise up out of the skeleton, like gossamer wisps of smoke that lifted up from its bones and swam across the air to sink into Fiona.

The elf threw back her head and let out a horrible, keening wail. Her entire body tensed, her hands flying out at her sides. Her skin became a pale white, and then began to change. It bulged, and twisted. Her body grew, and took on a hideous form, her head becoming something gnarled and fanged even as she shrieked in torment.

And then the transformation was done. A demonic abomination now stood where Fiona once had, a thing of rent flesh and claws, its gender no longer even apparent. The thing's eyes glowed with menace, and it regarded Duncan with amusement. It waved a hand at him.

SLEEP.

The world became grey and fuzzy, and the ground rushed up to greet him. He slept. Despite every fiber of his being fighting against it, still he slept.

They all did.

12

Though all before me is shadow,
Yet shall the Maker be my guide.
I shall not be left to wander the drifting roads of the Beyond.
For there is no darkness in the Maker's Light
And nothing he has wrought shall be lost.

—Canticle of Trials 1:14

Sunshine poured through an open window, the yellow silk curtains ruffling gently in the breeze. It took Maric a moment to realize he was in the palace at Denerim. He inhaled deeply, amazed at how wonderful that air smelled, how warm the feeling of sun on his bare skin was. It was so easy to forget about these simple pleasures when you were miles underground in the Deep Roads. . . .

The Deep Roads. The thought rankled, and suddenly he wondered why he was at the palace at all. Shouldn't he be with the Grey Wardens? The memory slipped away like quicksilver the more he tried to focus on it. Had he been dreaming?

He was in his own bed in the royal chambers, wearing only crisp linen sheets and not heavy silverite plate armor. The mahogany vanity that had been a gift from the Antivan royal family dominated the wall. His grandfather's dwarven-made spectacles sat on the small desk, retrieved at great expense from an Orlesian nobleman in Nevarra, and next to them was the cumbersome tome on King Calenhad that he had been slowly making his way through for the last year. He had no talent for reading, and the scholar's language was dense enough to make the effort difficult. Maric was stubborn, however.

He was where he was supposed to be. Why did he think he had traveled off on some adventure, chasing after an ancient order that didn't even exist in Ferelden any longer? The entire idea was ludicrous.

Someone shifted in the bed next to him and he froze. Rowan was dead. There shouldn't be anyone—

"Maric?" came a muffled, sleepy voice.

Panic gripped him, and his heart began beating rapidly. He stared with wide eyes as the woman lifted her head from her pillows. The honeyed curls were just as he remembered them, tousled and not quite covering her elven ears. Wide emerald eyes blinked at him as she smiled. "You're a strange one to look at me so," she chuckled. "Did you have a bad dream?"

Katriel. It was Katriel, the elven spy he had killed fourteen years before.

"I . . . don't know," he choked. "Maybe I did."

She made a moue and reached up with one hand, brushing his hair away from his eyes. The gesture was like something out of his distant memory, and yet so strikingly familiar. He took her hand and held it firmly against his cheek. She even smelled the same. How had he forgotten that? Tears welled up in his eyes.

"Oh, Maric," she said, her concern suddenly real. "You did have a bad dream! Oh, my darling man. Always the sensitive one, tsk."

He held her hand to his face a moment longer, frightened that if he let it go she would slip away. But finally he fought down his tears and looked at her. "How did you get here? I don't understand."

"I came to bed after you were asleep. I hope I didn't wake you."

"No, I mean, what about Rowan?"

Her brow furrowed in puzzlement. "Rowan is in Gwaren with Loghain, as she should be. We do not expect them to arrive in

Denerim until tomorrow. Have you lost track of the day?"

"Expect them?" He rubbed his head, confused. "But . . . Rowan is dead."

Katriel sat up in the bed now, the sheets falling away and revealing her nubile body and pale skin as he remembered them. She hugged him close, sighing sadly. "Is that the dream you had? Oh, Maric. Don't you remember? She was very sick, yes, and we were so frightened, but Loghain pulled her through it."

"Loghain pulled her through it," he repeated. An empty place in his heart ached, making its presence felt. He remembered it only too well.

"You know what he's like." She frowned, brushing his hair aside again. "There she was, wasting away and hovering near death, and the bastard was yelling at her, shouting that he would storm the Fade itself to retrieve her if she died. You were so angry at him."

He couldn't respond. He gulped, and his throat felt tight and dry. She cupped his cheek in her hand and looked at him warmly. Once he could have drowned in those emerald eyes. "I was proud of you. I never liked that bastard, and I don't know why you put up with him. Still, he held Rowan's hand for days, refusing to sleep or eat. They say his will was so strong she could not refuse it, and she survived."

"Is that all it took?" he croaked quietly.

"Shhhhh," she purred, leaning in close and planting a soft kiss on his lips. He felt numb and didn't respond. "Don't let it bother you so. Your queen is here, my love. Will you not let me help you forget that terrible dream?"

Maric allowed himself to be pulled down on top of her. She kissed him again, and this time he responded, slowly at first but then with more vigor. The feeling was so real, so potent, he couldn't deny it.

How often had he wished for just this very thing? The opportunity to go back and undo what had been done, to make it right.

This was as it should have been. It would be so simple just to allow it to happen. Deep down he knew that here it would be possible to forget that he had ever murdered this woman, that he had ever married Rowan and then watched her die while his best friend became colder and colder with each passing year. Here, being a king would not be a chore, and as he looked into Katriel's eyes beneath him and saw her crooked grin, he found it so very tempting.

But there was another elf. Almost unbidden, the memory surfaced of Fiona, taken over by the demon and transformed into an abomination. Her agonized screams still rang in his ears, and even though that other lifetime slipped through his fingers like a half-remembered dream, that part tugged insistently at his conscience.

He had made Fiona a promise.

"I can't," he whispered, disengaging from Katriel. He moved over to his side of the bed and got out as she stared at him in confusion, clutching the sheets to her chest.

"But why? What is wrong?"

"This isn't real." He refused to look at her, refused to look into those green eyes. He remembered looking into them when he had run his sword through her chest, not quite believing he'd done it even as he watched her life slip away. In those eyes he had seen such utter disappointment. She had hoped to reach him, to appeal to his mercy even though she knew it was hopeless, and he had met her expectations completely. Yet even though this life felt completely real and enticing, he couldn't stand the thought of Fiona out there suffering. He had to act.

"Maric," she said softly behind him.

He refused to turn around, clenching his fists from the effort it took.

"Maric," she said more firmly. "Look at me." Reluctantly he turned. Katriel stared at him sadly, as if she knew they were about to part. "We could have a life here," she said. "You don't need to go back to that other world. You can stay here."

"Stay here and pretend, you mean."

"Is it pretend?" She smiled wanly. "What is reality, Maric? What is it, really? You could be happy. Why do you believe so strongly that you must do what makes you unhappy? Have you not earned a little joy?"

Katriel reached out a hand, waiting for Maric to take it so she could draw him back into bed. Her eyes pleaded with him. He hung his head, his heart breaking, and her hand slowly dropped.

She didn't cry. He turned and walked out of the room quickly, before he changed his mind. The hollowness in his heart felt like it had become a bottomless pit that nothing could ever fill. He shut it, closed it off, and forced himself to become numb. It was something he had done for so long it almost came easily to him now. Numbness had become second nature.

As soon as he stepped out the door, the world changed. He was on a twisted landscape dotted with disconnected walls and doors, as if someone had spread out the pieces of a building without any knowledge of their relation to one another. More incredible by far was the sky, a vast sea of blackness with swirling ribbons of white crossing it. Islands floated above him, some large and seemingly an arm's length away, and others distant.

Everything had a strangely unnatural sheen, the corner of his vision fuzzing as if none of this were distinct enough to be real. He watched as the patchwork walls slowly moved, forming different configurations in front of him and then slowly reassembling themselves. One wall quietly disintegrated into the ground, disappearing entirely. Small floating lights caught his attention, bright wisps speeding across the landscape not far from where he stood.

This was the Fade. Men came here to dream, and supposedly only mages were able to cross it while awake, but here he was. Had he fallen asleep? Had the demon trapped him here somehow, and that was why he remained even though he was awake? What was happening to his body in the real world?

None of his questions had answers. He stood there on that plain, feeling a dry breeze brush across his face. At least his proper armor and clothing had reappeared upon leaving his chambers. That was something. His chambers, and the rest of the palace with it, had simply disappeared. As had Katriel. He looked around but saw no trace that any of it had ever existed, and felt a pang of regret for what he had lost.

But it hadn't been real, had it? She had been a dream conjured up for his benefit, intended to hold him here. He had to hope that meant there was a way out.

But how does one leave the Fade? Looking around, he realized he didn't have the faintest clue where to go. There were no pathways that led beyond the terrain on which he stood. He saw no structures, no glowing portals or anything of the kind. Just the doorways that led . . . where, exactly? Beyond what Fiona had spoken of that night outside the Deep Roads, he knew nothing of the dream realm.

"Lost already, I see," murmured a voice behind him.

He spun around and froze as he realized it was Katriel. She looked as he remembered her best, in the sturdy leathers she had worn during their travels in the Deep Roads. A dagger sat in her belt sheath and her blond curls fluttered in the breeze that swept across the field. Katriel regarded him now with an amused look, but appeared content to wait for him to speak.

"You . . . you're not here," he stammered.

"Apparently I am."

"But you're not Katriel."

"So sure of that, are you?" She walked toward him, her amusement dissolving into an annoyed frown. "I know you well enough, Maric, and you're no scholar. You know as much about the Fade as you do about winemaking. You need my help."

"Your help," he repeated dumbly.

She arched a brow at him. "Do you think you can make it through the Fade on your own? I led you through the Deep Roads, once. I can lead you through here. If that's what you really want."

Maric retreated several steps. This looked like Katriel and sounded like Katriel, but this wasn't some dream of his any longer. She had to be some kind of demon, something that had followed him out of his dream once it failed its mission. Now it was trying to lure him back. His heart beat rapidly in his chest as he drew his sword, brandishing it at her warily. "Get back," he growled. "You are trying to trap me again. But I won't stay; I need to get out of here!"

Katriel seemed unimpressed, glancing at his blade with barely concealed contempt. "That's not truly your sword, Maric. You must realize that."

"I'm willing to take my chances it'll still cut you."

She nodded, smirking ever so slightly. "Maybe so. What do you intend to do, then? Run about aimlessly? Pinch yourself until you wake up? Loghain is not here to save you, love. You need my help."

"I'll not be led anywhere by a demon!"

"Oh, yes." She glared at him pointedly. "Good idea. You wouldn't want to run headlong into someone's sword, after all."

Maric staggered back. The way she looked at him so knowingly with those green eyes cut him to the quick. Yet it couldn't be possible, any more than it was in the dream. "I left you in that dream," he insisted. "I had to! I made a promise. . . ."

"Yes, I know," she said sadly. Katriel sighed and walked up to him, patting him softly on the cheek. "I couldn't offer you happiness. Not before and not now. So instead I will help you do this, if this is what you really want."

He felt torn. "What I want," he said resolutely, "is to get out of here."

"Out of the Fade." She nodded. The elf turned and gestured toward the terrain around them, and Maric realized she was indicating the various doorways that dotted the landscape. "There are ways out all over the place, Maric. Unfortunately they won't help you much. You're being kept here unnaturally."

"By the demon."

Katriel began striding purposefully toward one of the disembodied doorways. Uncertain what to do, Maric followed behind her. He glanced at the barren field around him. Whatever Katriel really was, she was right about one thing. At best he would have wandered the Fade, hoping to stumble across something useful.

She reached the door and stood beside it, facing him. He stopped, wondering what it was she planned. He kept his sword out, just in case.

"Let me make this simple," she said. She twisted the door's handle and opened it. There was nothing. It was an empty doorway, and Katriel even stuck her hand through it to emphasize that fact. "This doesn't lead anywhere. Unless you want it to." She closed the door again and then opened it . . . and this time Maric fell back as the doorway led to a verdant forest. He could see blue sky, sunshine, even hear the birds. It was a portal carved into thin air.

Katriel closed the door again. "It's not a door," she stated, getting his attention with her hand. "It's a transition, a symbol. It could be a transition to the real world, where you would suddenly wake up and start to forget all about this, but you can't go there. Not while the demon holds you."

"Why are you telling me this?" he asked.

She sighed, and smiled at him, but ignored his question. "You need to confront the demon. Only a part of it crosses the Veil into the real world, just as only a part of you is here." She waved at the door. "You can reach the demon, if you want to badly enough."

"Is it asleep?"

"No. This is its realm. It still has power, enough to kill you." At

Maric's questioning look, her gaze hardened. "This was your plan, Maric. I didn't say it was a good one. I'm simply helping you however I can."

"By sending me to my death."

"Isn't that what I do?" Katriel's tone was bitter, and she looked away from him, staring off into the distance. For a moment she looked vulnerable, broken. This was as Maric remembered her, and his heart ached. He wanted nothing more than to reach out and comfort her. When she glanced back at him, however, the hardness returned. "You can locate your companions the same way," she offered. "They are trapped in a dream, as you were."

"Won't they break out of it?"

"Not everyone is as willing to deny themselves what they want as you are, Maric." There was pity in her green eyes, he saw, and suddenly he doubted. He didn't know everything that could be; nobody did. A part of him wanted desperately for her to leave him, to return back to the dream that he had left behind. But an even larger part wanted her to stay. Perhaps he hadn't truly left her behind at all.

"I'll try," he muttered.

It might have been a foolish thing to do. If Katriel was deceiving him, if she was really some spirit trying to send him back into the demon's clutches or even to his death, then so be it. He couldn't stand there and call Katriel a liar. Not after what he had done to her. He would rather be nowhere at all.

He turned the handle.

The street was much like any busy street in the poorer quarters of Denerim, Maric thought, though he was certain this was nowhere in Ferelden. Orlais, he suspected, from the snippets of conversation he picked up from the passing crowds. The shops were packed closely together here, the plaster over the brick cracked and fading, and the signs of poverty were everywhere. The rain came down lightly from the grey skies overhead, enough to stir up the dust in the cobbled streets and bring with it a wet, musty odor that assaulted his nostrils.

Was he still in the Fade? It seemed that he was, even though the change had been abrupt. This was a place just like his palace chambers had been, a figment or even a dream.

He nodded at several old washerwomen busily collecting rumpled linens from their lines. They stared at his armor, scandalized that he would go about so openly armed and obviously considering calling for the city watch. Maric had no idea what that would entail in this dream world and he didn't want to find out, so he quickly hurried on.

There was one shop in particular that seemed somehow more *present* than the others. Its plaster was less faded, and there was color there whereas every other part of the street seemed muddy and grey. He noticed a box of carefully tended herbs in the windowsill, and light blue curtains that fluttered in the breeze. The door to the building was painted a sharp red, and closed, but a pair of barn-style doors stood wide open to a workman's shop within.

He could hear the sound of hammering, and surmised that the place belonged to a carpenter. It was easy enough to see with all the sawdust on the ground, and sawhorses standing next to a pair of unvarnished chairs. They were well-made, too, sturdy and thick. More furniture lay just inside the doors, including an upended table and a half-painted dresser. This was a busy place.

The hammering stopped. "Duncan! Bring in everything before it gets rained on, for Andraste's sake!" The voice was deep and strong, the sort Maric associated with a large man. It also had no trace of the Orlesian accent. In fact, if he didn't know better he would have said it was Fereldan.

"Blast it, boy!" the voice thundered again. "Where have you gone off to?" As Maric approached the shop, the source of the voice suddenly appeared at the entrance. It was a giant of a man, pale-skinned with a thick beard and dark hair pulled back into a ponytail. He wore a large smock covered in sawdust and old streaks of paint. Grimacing, the man snatched up a chair in each hand before he noticed Maric.

"Oh! Sorry, my lord," he said, eyeing Maric uncertainly. "Were you looking to buy something? I was just bringing this in out of the rain."

"It looks like fine furniture. You're a master of your craft."

The man bobbed his head, smiling a bit bashfully. "Thank you, my lord. You're from home, I see. We don't get many Fereldans here, especially not in this part of the city."

"You're from Ferelden?"

"From Highever. My son barely remembers, but I will never forget." The man then noticed the slowly increasing rate of rainfall and suddenly looked abashed. "And here I am keeping you out in the rain! Please, my lord! Come in!" He retreated into the shop, carrying the large chairs with him as if they weighed little more than feathers, and Maric followed. He suspected a man that big could probably have hefted a half dozen more, perhaps on one shoulder.

The shop was small, with more chairs and other assorted bits of furniture piled up around the wall than it could feasibly contain. There was space enough for a workbench, covered with bits of wood and shavings and a wide assortment of metal tools, as well as a large table turned upside down on a pair of sawhorses. It would be a fine piece, the legs curved and gently inlaid with the fine floral carvings Maric had seen on similar Orlesian pieces. It was the sort of table that would be welcome in any noble estate.

The carpenter noticed where Maric was looking and his grin broadened. It was a grin that Maric had seen on Duncan, come to think of it. "For the Marquise," he said proudly. "Special commission."

"You seem very busy."

"My son and I work hard. We've done well, I think."

A door that led from the shop to the interior opened, and a dark-skinned woman walked through. She had a mop of frizzy black hair on her head and kind, almond-shaped eyes. Care had worn lines on her face and brought wisps of grey at her temples, but she was still pretty, he thought. From the bump he saw under her dress, it was obvious that she was pregnant. "Oh!" she said, startled to see Maric. "I thought you were closing the shop, Arryn." Her Rivaini accent was strong, but her command of the King's Tongue was perfect.

"This man is from Ferelden, Tayana."

She nodded at Maric politely, though her eyes held a slight suspicion. She did not believe he was here actually to shop for furniture. "How do you do, ser," she said.

"I'm actually looking for your son." At the startled looks from both of them, he quickly added, "Provided that Duncan is your son, of course. Maybe eighteen years? Black hair?"

The man's smile evaporated. "What has he done?"

"Arryn?" the woman asked uncertainly.

"Go inside, love," he told her. She glanced at Maric fearfully but then nodded and retreated inside the house. The man looked at him sternly. "What has my boy done? He gets into trouble from time to time, my lord, but he is a good boy. We do the best by him that we know how."

"I'm sure that you do." Maric felt guilty deceiving the man, and letting him think he was someone important. Not that it was a deception, entirely. *And he's a dream-father, too, let's not forget that.* "I need to speak to your son. I'm afraid it's important."

The man nodded slowly. "Let me find him, then." He went inside, and Maric waited. Rain pelted the roof above. Several carriages thundered by on the cobblestones outside, and he faintly heard a woman calling for her children to come inside. A flash of lightning was followed by the first peal of thunder.

In time, the door opened again and the burly man reappeared, this time accompanied by a sullen-looking Duncan. The young man looked drenched, as if he had just come in out of the rain, wearing a set of black trousers and a white shirt soaked right through.

Duncan stared at Maric in surprise, and then looked up at his father. "I don't know this man. I didn't do anything to him!" he said defensively.

"That's enough!" His father pushed him into the shop.

Maric cleared his throat. "Actually, I would like to speak to him alone."

"Alone?" The man looked angrily at Duncan, who rolled his eyes and sighed. Finally the man nodded at Maric. "As you wish." With a warning glare at his son, the man turned and went back inside, closing the door firmly behind him.

Duncan folded his arms and stared challengingly at Maric, but said nothing. There was no sense in his eyes that he knew who he was looking at, not even a little. Maric cleared his throat. This might not be very easy. "I suppose you don't remember me?"

The lad squinted his eyes. "Should I?"

"We haven't known each other long."

"You have me mistaken, I think."

"No, I don't." Maric gestured to the shop around him. "I know this may be a bit hard to believe, but I don't know how else to explain it to you. This isn't real."

"What? Of course it is!" Duncan stepped back, looking at him like he was insane. Maric wondered if maybe that wasn't true. The whole idea of the Fade was incredible. How do you explain to someone that they are in a dream? What if someone had come up to him a year ago and suggested such a thing?

Sadly, a part of Maric wondered if he wouldn't have simply felt relieved.

"No. This is a dream. This isn't real."

Duncan turned toward the door, but Maric caught his shoulder and spun him back. The lad was furious now, but there was also something else in his expression. Was it doubt? Maric seized upon that. "You know what I'm talking about," he insisted. "You are a Grey Warden, Duncan. We are in the Fade, in a dream, sent here by the demon we encountered in the dwarven palace. Don't you remember?"

Duncan pulled himself out of Maric's grip, and backed up sharply enough to bang against one of the shop's wooden walls. A nearby pile of chairs rattled loudly. "No!" he snarled, suddenly enraged. "That never happened! That . . . that was a dream!"

"*This* is the dream, Duncan."

"No!" he shouted. He charged at Maric, fists flying, but Maric caught his wrists and together they fell onto the Marquise's table in the center of the shop. The table went flying off the sawhorses, crashing to the ground with an enormous racket as two of the legs broke off. Duncan was on top of Maric, struggling to free his fists as his face contorted into fury, and Maric barely fended him off. Finally he threw him back.

"Don't be stupid!" Maric snapped. "You know it's true! I can see it!"

Duncan fell back onto the floor, hitting his head against another chair and sending it flying outside into the rain. He sat there, stunned.

The door into the house flew open and Duncan's father charged out with a carpenter's hammer in one hand, his face filled with concern and fury. "What is going on here?" When he saw Maric lying on the damaged table, and Duncan not a foot away, he immediately charged at Maric. Those strong hands grabbed the neck of Maric's breastplate, lifting him off the table as if he weighed nothing at all. That powerful face was just inches away from his own, red with rage. "Why have you brought trouble to my home?

Get out of here!"

"Father, wait," came Duncan's quiet plea.

It was enough to make his father pause. Still holding Maric aloft, he turned and scowled at his son. "Did you cause this, then? Duncan, I thought I taught you better than that."

The look that Duncan suddenly gave his father was at once so hopeless and so sad that Maric knew the lad realized the truth. "You did," he said quietly. "You did teach me better."

"And what is your excuse, then?"

"You died," Duncan whispered. His eyes glistened brightly, and he wiped at them, turning away. His father's fury dissolved instantly, and he lowered Maric back to the table on the floor as if he were little more than an afterthought.

"Son," he said, his voice thick, "it doesn't have to be like this."

"It already is."

The lad turned back to his father, his eyes bleary with tears, and the two of them stared at each other quietly for a moment. His father sighed sadly, and Duncan closed his eyes. And just like that the entire shop vanished. It was simply gone, replaced by an open plain and the island-filled sky of the Fade above.

Duncan barely seemed to notice. He was in his black leathers and his Grey Warden tunic once again, the twin daggers at his sides. He stared at the spot where his father had been, tears rolling down his cheeks. "I really thought—" His voice caught, and he swallowed hard. "I really thought it was them; I thought it had all been some nightmare."

"I know."

"I was so relieved. That I hadn't been stuck, alone . . ."

"I know."

Maric tensed as he saw Katriel approach from nearby. He had half assumed that she would simply be gone, that maybe her appearance had just been another dream. Yet there she was, striding toward them and regarding Duncan with an amused expression.

The lad frowned and followed his gaze, turning to spot her with a degree of surprise. He backed away warily, going for his daggers, but she held a hand to show she was unarmed. "The new Loghain, I take it?" she asked with a slight grin. Duncan turned and looked incredulously at Maric.

"This is Katriel," Maric told him with a sigh.

"You mean . . . ?"

"Yes, *that* Katriel."

"But isn't she . . . ?"

"Dead?" she answered for him, giving Maric a wary look. "That's the rumor. I've come to help. If you prefer to think of me as something unpleasant, that's fine. It would be no worse than what I was in life."

Duncan seemed confused. "We can't trust her!"

"She led me to you," Maric told him. Then he turned to Katriel, trying not to meet her gaze. It was a torment to see her like this, to have memories dredged up that he had thought long-buried. "We need to find the others," he told her.

She nodded, and gestured down a desolate path lined with tall statues. "There is another doorway in this direction. It will take you where you need to go."

Maric and Duncan stood in the Frostback Mountains. A wind rushed past them, cold and brisk. Maric looked up at the impressive snowcapped peaks looming high overhead. The snow on the ground was thick, almost coming to the top of their boots, and from the dark clouds it looked likely that a storm was to come.

"Oh, great," Duncan mumbled. "More snow."

Maric glanced at the lad but said nothing. He had left Katriel behind, as before. Either she couldn't follow them or chose not to; Maric wasn't certain. He found that his thoughts kept returning to her. If she was a product of his dream, how did she leave it? Why was she helping him against the demon that created her? Perhaps she was another demon, an enemy of the first? Or was he simply being misled? So far her information had been useful.

A part of him wondered if it was possible that she was actually Katriel. They said the dead passed through the Fade on their way to the Maker's side, and sometimes lost their way. Perhaps she was a ghost. It was a dangerous and frightening thought, and he tried to push it out of his mind.

A steep path led up the side of the mountain and they followed it, shivering in the wind. The trees here were thick evergreens, crowding the path and forcing them to push many low-hanging branches out of their way.

When the path turned a corner, a vista opened up before them. These were the Frostbacks at their most breathtaking: great mountains reaching almost up to the sky, a vast forest in the valley below leading to a frozen lake that he could see with crystal clarity. Had the lake not been ice and snow, it would almost have been possible to leap into the water, so long as one didn't mind bouncing on the crags a few times. And provided hitting the water from such a height didn't simply kill one outright. Still, it was impressive.

"What is that?" Duncan murmured.

Maric turned to see what he was looking at, and realized the path continued along the cliff around the mountainside and ended at a walled holding. It was a grey, somber-looking fortified settlement, perched on the edge of the cliff and seemingly built half into the mountain. There were men on the walls, he saw, with long hair and beards and thick fur cloaks, already pointing at the two strangers on the path. Dogs began to bark as an alarm was raised.

"They don't seem that friendly," Duncan remarked dryly.

"They are Avvars. Hill folk. They're not apt to like us much."

"Should we fight?"

"No, let's wait to see what they do."

It didn't take long for three men to stream out of the gates, tall warriors with stern frowns commanding vicious-looking warhounds that barked and growled and strained against their leashes. That they didn't simply unleash the hounds on them must mean they were willing to talk, he hoped.

The trio stopped just short of Maric and Duncan, staring at them suspiciously as they held back their dogs. The leader was an older man with grey hair well past his shoulders, but even so, he was powerfully built. He had the air of authority, as well.

"Lowlander," he growled.

It wasn't exactly a question, but Maric nodded. He thought it best to remain polite. The Avvars had a long history of warfare with the "lowlanders" in the Fereldan valley, and had stubbornly refused to join the kingdom when King Calenhad had united the teyrns centuries ago. The years since had just made them more determined to remain apart.

"Why have you come?" the man demanded.

"We are looking for a man by the name of Kell," Maric said. The looks the men exchanged told him they knew exactly who he was talking about. This wasn't surprising. So far it seemed like each of these dreams had been centered completely around the person doing the dreaming.

Did people have different sorts of dreams? Ones where they were innocent bystanders to events, irrelevant to the larger scheme of things?

"You seek Kell ap Morgan? Why?"

"That's something I'd need to speak with Kell about." It wasn't an answer that these hillsmen liked, and he saw them bristle at his temerity. Duncan raised his eyebrows at Maric, clearly thinking that they were about to get into a fight and not altogether opposed to the notion. Luckily, the grey-haired leader spat at his fellows and halted their rage before it got out of hand.

"We shall see," he grunted. Nodding for the others to follow, he turned and began to walk up the path back to the holding. The others ran after him, yanking hard on the warhounds to get them to come. Maric and Duncan were left either to follow or remain behind. It wasn't much of a choice.

"They smell like urine," Duncan complained, though without force.

"You can stay here, if you like."

They went inside the holding, and were greeted immediately by a crowd of curious hill folk. The children were filthy and feral, staring with wide eyes as they chewed on their fingers. The adults were little better. These were people who lived from day to day, clinging to this mountain like stubborn weeds and subject to a wide assortment of disasters, from disease to poor hunting years to violent feuds with neighboring holdings. The Avvars were born to harsh misfortune, as well as inured to it.

The buildings outside the caves were low but remarkably well-built. These were not primitives, Maric reminded himself. They knew of masonry and mining and traded with the dwarves to acquire fine weaponry and other supplies. Each of the doors had a hide stretched over it, which was then decorated with brightly painted runes.

The totems in front of most of the buildings were also typically Avvarian. Stone idols built to honor their gods, if Maric remembered correctly. The only one he knew of was the Father of the Skies, to whom the Avvars returned their dead, leaving their bodies out on the rocks to be picked clean by the birds. He supposed that was no stranger than burning one's dead, though he was curious what they did with the bones.

The men led Maric and Duncan across a dirty courtyard littered with dog dung and hanging furs, toward a larger stone building. It was little more than a hut, really, but it was wider than most of the others and had an impressive carved eagle head over the door. Someone important lived there.

The grey-haired man went directly inside, and when Maric went to follow him the other two Avvars interjected themselves, crossing their arms and glaring at him firmly. No access just yet, then.

They waited in the courtyard, a group of dogs coming up and snuffling at their legs curiously. These were not well-kept animals like Hafter; they were almost wolves, and covered in matted fur that reeked of wet. Duncan gagged and covered his mouth, but Maric just smiled. Being Fereldan, he had been around dogs since he was a child.

Nearby, a group of children looked around a corner at them with fearful expressions. One brashly threw a stone at Maric, missing by a wide margin, and then the whole group of them ran off giggling in terror. The pair of guards at the door took no notice of any of it.

When the grey-haired warrior reappeared, he had beside him another: This was a younger warrior, wearing a reddish fur cloak and with long brown hair and a short beard. As Maric saw the intense, pale eyes, he realized that this was Kell. A Kell with hair, and sporting tribal tattoos up and down the length of his bare arms, but there was no mistaking the man's taciturn demeanor.

"Kell?" Duncan asked, gasping.

The hunter's eyebrows shot up. The grey-haired warrior glanced at him, frowning heavily. "The lowlanders say they have come to speak with you, Jarl. Do you know of them? We can feed them to the dogs."

Kell studied Maric and Duncan closely, those pale eyes traveling over them carefully. Maric saw no hint of recognition, but that meant little when it came to the inscrutable hunter. Duncan put up his hand as if to speak, but the grey-haired warrior growled him down. What happened if Kell decided that he wasn't going to speak with them? They were surrounded by a holding full of seasoned hillsmen that could cut them down instantly.

"Let them come inside," Kell finally said. He seemed hesitant, but stepped aside and gestured for Duncan and Maric to enter the stone hut. The other men present appeared startled, but deferred to Kell's wishes and gave way.

The hut's interior was uncluttered, with thick furs covering the floor and a large, high-backed chair made of logs. This was an audience chamber of some kind. Maric knew the sort. Several longbows and animal heads were displayed prominently on the wall. One of the heads was from a giant bear, its roaring mouth wide enough to engulf a man's head. An impressive trophy.

Maric could see little past a curtain that hung in an interior doorway, but saw the hints of another room beyond. He also heard the distinctive cooing of an infant, as well as the sounds of a young woman's soft humming. She quieted, and Maric got the impression of someone peeking curiously through the curtain, but could make out no details.

Kell sat down in the chair, resting his chin on his fist as he studied them again. "I saw you both in a dream," he murmured, "and now you are here. How can this be?"

"That wasn't a dream," Duncan snapped. "This is."

Maric wouldn't have leaped right into it like that, but perhaps it was just as well. The hunter looked at each of them in turn, no doubt wondering if they were joking with him. Seeing that they weren't, he frowned. "This is no dream. You are standing here before me, in my hall and in my holding. This is reality."

Before Duncan could respond, Maric held up his hand. He stepped forward and touched Kell's shoulder, looking into the man's eyes. There was confusion there. He wasn't certain that what they were saying was the truth, and perhaps that was enough. "Do you remember that dream?" Maric asked him. "You were a Grey Warden, just like Duncan here. We encountered a demon that trapped us in the Fade." He waved at the room around them. "That's what this is. This is your dream."

A dark cloud passed over Kell's face and he jumped up from his chair, pulling his shoulder from Maric's grasp. Disturbed, he walked over to the curtain leading into the other room, but stopped short of opening it. He bowed his head and listened for a moment to the crying of the child next door. "How did you get here, then?"

"You can end the dream," Maric told him. "That's what I did, when I realized what it was. And I came looking for you. We can't stay here, and Fiona needs us."

"Fiona," Kell tested the name out. "The mage."

Maric nodded. "We're asleep, I think."

"We could be dead. This could be the Beyond." Kell seemed almost hopeful. "You could both be demons sent to tempt me from my final rest."

"Is that what you think?" Duncan asked him.

The hunter thought about it, and then closed his eyes. "No," he said grimly. "I know what happened to this place, to its people." His eyes were bright as he opened them and took one final look around. "I will not accept a lie."

The infant in the other room suddenly began to wail, and Kell flinched as if struck. He stood there, his face ashen as he listened. None of them moved. "Do you need to say good-bye?" Maric asked him cautiously.

He shook his head. "No," he rasped. "I did that long ago."

The man was replaced by the figure Maric knew: clean-shaven and bald, with the hooded cloak and the hunter's leathers. His eyes shone from beneath his hood with grim intensity. A moment later the hut vanished, replaced by the empty landscape of the Fade.

The three of them walked through a door into a dwarven home. The ceiling was low, and the air filled with the smell of coal smoke and meaty dishes. A large family lived here; solid dwarven chairs were mixed in with children's toys and rolled-up furs and a table covered in vellum scrolls. Maps adorned the walls, at least one of them a map of Ferelden that Maric recognized. A large brazier filled with coals lent a warm orange glow to the chamber.

A dwarven child ran in, perhaps ten years of age with a mop of unruly coppery hair on his head. He skidded to a halt, clearly having expected someone other than a trio of three humans to be at the entrance, his expression turning from excitement to horror. "Mam! Pap!" he squealed. "There's cloudheads come!"

"Humans?" A matronly dwarven woman walked into the chamber from a dimly lit kitchen, wiping her hands on her apron. Maric could hear something bubbling in a large pot, and noticed several other children behind the woman looking past her skirt. The woman's black hair was streaked with grey and pulled back into a bun, and she wore spectacles. Much the same as Maric's grandfather had, he remembered. "By the Ancestors! It *is* humans!"

Several more people entered the room. An older man walked in, a fat dwarf almost as wide as he was tall, with a bald head and a bright coppery beard going halfway down his chest. He walked with a cane and possessed the air of a distinguished gentleman, perhaps a scholar. A fit young man walked beside him, his own coppery beard short but lovingly cultivated with braids.

The young man looked outraged at the presence of intruders and rushed forward, his fists out. The older dwarf grabbed his shirt and hauled him back forcefully. "Wait, Tam! Don't be stupid."

"Why are you here?" the young man demanded angrily.

The woman stepped forward, waving the children behind her back. They retreated into the kitchen but didn't go very far. The tension in the room made them terrified, however, and the woman wasn't far from it herself. She nodded cautiously at Maric. "We don't have anything someone like you would want, human. There's no reason for you to hurt anyone."

Maric put his hands up. "Please calm down. We don't mean any harm." He looked back at Kell and Duncan, who nodded. None of them wanted to start any trouble with these people.

"Then answer the boy," the man grunted. "Why are you here?"

"They have come for me, Father," came a new voice. Maric turned, and was shocked to see Utha enter the chamber from a short hallway. Her long braid had been undone to reveal a luxurious mane of coppery hair, and she wore a simple dwarven dress with a fine leather mantle. Her expression was forlorn. "There's no reason for you to be frightened. These are friends."

"Friends?" the older woman interjected, confused. "Since when do you know humans, Utha? What strange business is this?"

"I'm sorry, Mother, it would be difficult to explain." Utha turned toward Maric and the others and nodded. "I trust you are all well?"

"You can talk!" Duncan exclaimed.

"It seems that here I can, yes."

"And you remember us? You know who we are?" Maric asked her carefully.

"You are the King of Ferelden," she stated, reciting the fact with a sad sigh. "The men with you are Grey Wardens, as am I. Yes, I remember."

The dwarves in the room looked fearful and confused. The older man stepped forward, glancing at Maric as if he were a snake ready to bite, but walking up to Utha in order to take her hand in his own. "Utha, what are you speaking of? This is madness!"

She looked at her father, tears welling up in her eyes, and she reached up to fondly stroke his cheek. "I know it is, Father. It's time for me to go."

"Go? Go where?"

Her mother marched toward them, the woman's concern overriding her fear of Maric and the others. The rest of the family piled in behind her, babbling confused questions. "What do you mean you're going?" she asked. "Why would you leave with these people?"

Utha pressed her lips into a thin line, controlling the tears that clearly threatened to overwhelm her. "I must," she whispered, her voice thick. She hugged her father and then her mother, each of them returning her gesture warmly even if they didn't understand what she was doing. The children gathered around Utha, hugging her legs and shedding panicked tears as they realized what was happening.

"You won't stay for dinner, even? You and your friends?" her mother asked with faint hope, tears streaming down her face.

Utha kissed her mother tenderly on the cheek, saying nothing, and did the same to her stammering father. Then she turned to face the young man who stood grimly nearby. She began to speak to him, but a wave of grief held her tongue. She paused, collecting herself even as the young man stared at her, not comprehending.

"You fought well, Tam," she finally forced out. She made herself look him directly in the eyes, though it was clearly difficult for her. "I was very proud of you. Very proud."

"You . . . were?"

"Oh, yes," she said fervently. "I swore an oath to avenge you." She turned and looked at the others, new tears welling. "I swore an oath to avenge you all. And I shall." Her tone was resolute, and with that the chamber vanished. They were back in the Fade, standing in a field of impossibly tall rock pillars, and Utha stared off into the distance. She looked as she did before, dressed in simple brown robes with her hair braided down her back.

She turned back to the others, her eyes red from tears. She made several emphatic gestures, ending with her fist clutched over her heart. Her expression was so desperately apologetic that Maric didn't know what to say.

Kell walked up to her. They stared at each other for a long moment, and then she hugged him tightly around his waist. He stroked her hair fondly. "We do not blame you, Utha," he said. "You stayed as long as you could."

Duncan hung his head sadly. Maric looked at him and wondered if he thought of his own family. He saw Katriel standing not far away, watching the group but unwilling to join them. He wondered how terrible it would have been just to stay with her for a time, to enjoy that lie just a little bit longer. He longed to talk to her, to make her understand. . . .

But these were thoughts he needed to banish. He had made a promise. Their lives hung in the balance.

They needed to move on.

A cabin made of logs stood at the top of a hill, amid a verdant forest that appeared to stretch on forever under a clear blue sky. The trees here were enormous pines shooting straight up into the sky, rows upon rows of towering sentinels that made the cabin look like a tiny thing in comparison. It wasn't, of course. As they drew closer, they could see that the building was significant, with a large pile of chopped wood outside and a warm trail of smoke leading up from a chimney. A furry hide stretched over a drum next to the doorway, and a large fire pit still smoldered from recent use, a spit over it stained from whatever carcass had been roasted there.

"We are in the Arbor Wilds," Kell surmised, studying the terrain. "In the south of Orlais. Dangerous country. A difficult place to live, to be certain."

Duncan looked up, interested. "Dangerous? Because of the animals?"

"Because of the dryads."

"Whoever lives here seems to be doing fine," Maric noted. "And there's someone now." He pointed off in the distance toward the side of the cabin, where a shirtless man with short dark hair and a beard was busily chopping wood on a tree stump. They walked up the dirt path, the rhythmic sound of the chopping echoing over the countryside. A flock of crows burst into flight from one of the nearby trees, cawing loudly as they vanished into the sky.

The chopping sounds halted.

As the group came around the side of the cabin, they encountered the dark-haired warrior facing them warily with axe in hand, still sweating and heaving from his exertions. He looked on them as one might regard a pack of wild dogs, uncertain whether they were actually going to attack or slink away. Whatever he thought, he said nothing. It took Maric a moment to realize that he knew who this was.

"Julien!" Duncan cried in amazement.

The man narrowed his eyes. "Do I know you?"

"Of course you do!" Duncan replied. "We're—"

"Friends of Nicolas," Kell interrupted, placing a hand on Duncan's chest to hold him back. The lad looked confused for a moment before he realized why. This wasn't Julien. It couldn't be. Julien was dead.

"I find that hard to believe," he responded, holding up his axe a little higher. "Nobody knows we're out here, not even my relatives. You don't look like the normal sorts of bandits we get, but I'll tell you the same as I told the last: Leave now, or face the consequences."

"We're not bandits, I assure you," Maric told him.

"Then what are you?"

"If we could speak to Nicolas, that would be easier to explain."

Julien assessed them carefully. His gaze went from one to the next before he finally lowered his axe. It was done only reluctantly, and likely only because all of them kept their weapons sheathed.

"We will see" was all he said as he swung the axe hard into the tree stump, lodging it there. He walked back toward the cabin, snatching up a damp linen shirt from on top of the woodpile and throwing it over his shoulder.

The inside of the cabin was a single chamber, filled with evidence that it had been occupied for a long time. A stone hearth dominated the room, two worn chairs in front of it surrounded by several wine bottles askew on the floor. A bookshelf overflowed with dusty tomes, and a desk sat next to it covered with reams of papers, many of them crumpled into wads, and an elaborate quill-and-ink set made of gold. The kitchen was a mess of iron pots and dishes scattered about the stove, and beyond it lay a single sizable bed in the corner covered by several thick bear furs.

Nicolas sat inside in front of the hearth, the fire roaring and filling the room with warm light and a smoky smell. He wore a long black shirt and leather trousers, and stared into the fire with the air of a man weighing a heavy burden. He barely glanced up as Julien and the others crowded in through the door.

"You heard?" Julien asked him.

Nicolas continued to stare into the fire, his face haggard and worn. "I did."

"And do you know these people?"

Maric stepped forward. "Nicolas, I know this may be hard to believe, but—"

The blond warrior stood up, interrupting him with the heavy scrape of his chair as it was pushed back. He looked at Julien solemnly. "You need to leave me alone with them, Julien."

"What? You're mad! Tell me who they are first."

Nicolas walked toward him. Ignoring the presence of the others nearby, he took Julien's chin in his hand and kissed him tenderly on the lips. Julien seemed chagrined at first, and then accepted the gesture. It was sweet, and had the air of a couple that had been together for a great long time.

Maric glanced away, embarrassed by the intimacy, not to mention the fact that he hadn't quite realized the nature of the two warriors' relationship earlier. Not just comrades, then, and far more than close friends. The older Grey Wardens seemed unsurprised.

"I'm not mad," Nicolas whispered. "But you need to trust me."

Julien was clearly confused, but he reluctantly nodded. Giving one final suspicious glare at Maric, he said, "I'll be right outside, then." Marching across the room, he opened a large wardrobe next to the bed and removed his greatsword. It was dull and looked as if it had not been used in some time. The man hefted it onto his shoulder and walked back outside, still glaring the entire way.

Nicolas watched him go, frowning sadly. As soon as Julien was out the door, he sighed. "He doesn't know."

"But you do?" Maric asked him. "You know this is a dream?"

"I know this is the Fade. I knew it instantly. To see Julien alive, I knew it couldn't be true. I held his body in my arms. You don't forget that."

"Then we don't need to explain," Duncan said, relieved.

An awkward silence ensued as Nicolas turned back toward the hearth. He walked to the wooden mantel and ran his hand along its length, as if testing its smoothness. His eyes looked haunted, Maric thought, and for a long moment they all watched as he stood there. The only sound was the crackling of the flames.

"We'd talked about this," the blond man murmured. He didn't look at them. "Leaving the Grey Wardens, and coming out here on our own. We'd have a few years left before the taint caught up to us, and we could spend it with each other. We could truly be together." He gently ran his hand along the mantel again. "It was a fine plan, down to every detail. . . ." His voice trailed off and he became silent again, staring into the fire.

"You mean to stay," Kell said. It wasn't a question. The hunter and Utha exchanged a sad, knowing glance.

Nicolas nodded. "I mean to stay."

"You can't!" Duncan objected, his dawning horror evident as he realized what was being suggested. "You can't do that! You know that isn't him, right? It's a lie!"

"It's not a lie."

The warrior seemed resolute. Maric walked toward him and tentatively put his hand on the man's shoulder, looking at his eyes to get his attention. "But it is a dream. Your body is back in the real world, just like ours. If you stay here . . ."

"Then I die?" Nicolas smiled, abashed. "We knew it was possible one of us could fall in battle. I thought I was prepared, but I wasn't." He turned back to the mantel, unable to meet Maric's gaze. "I love him. Tell me I should return to a life where I can't be with him. Tell me this isn't better."

Maric couldn't tell him that. He let him go and stepped back.

"But—" Duncan looked around, his confusion only mounting as he saw both Kell and Utha accepting Nicolas's words just as Maric did. "You can't be serious! You have to come back. This is suicide!"

"I can think of worse ways to die."

"No! It's wrong." He ran up to Nicolas, making as if to push him back against the hearth. The warrior warily caught at the lad's leathers and held him with a strong hand, though Duncan didn't struggle much. He seemed more astonished than outraged. "How can you let the demon defeat you like this?"

Nicolas nodded slowly, closing his eyes as if the idea pained him. "Julien saved you," he sighed. "He did the right thing, I know that. I wish I'd died with him." Then he paused, opening his eyes and looking directly at Duncan. Tears streamed down his cheeks. "I did die with him. This has nothing to do with the demon."

"But—"

"Let me have my dream," he pleaded, his voice heavy. It was as much to Maric and the others as to Duncan. "Please, just let me have this one last thing."

Duncan looked like he was about to continue arguing, but seeing the expression on Nicolas's face, he visibly deflated. Finally he nodded. He didn't agree, even Maric could see that, but he couldn't argue in the face of that pain. He gave Maric a troubled glance and then turned and stormed out the door without another word.

Kell walked up to Nicolas, extending his hand. "You served well," he said. "You did your duty. Let it end here." Nicolas shook his hand heartily, the tears coming more quickly. He fought to control a sob.

Utha went to the warrior, looking up at him with compassionate tears of her own. She made no gestures, but simply took both his hands in hers.

"Thank you," he croaked, his voice near breaking.

Maric nodded at the man. Part of him felt disquiet at the idea of leaving Nicolas behind, a warrior who could still be of great help to them. But would it be better to demand that he follow them, fighting until he died some grueling death alone in the Deep Roads? Or worse, survived and carried on alone? It didn't seem as if Grey Wardens met happy ends even at the best of times. Perhaps it was better to choose your own.

The idea settled over Maric like a dark cloud as they left Nicolas behind in the cabin. Outside, Duncan waited with his arms crossed. The lad looked distressed rather than belligerent. It must be difficult to understand when death seemed like a thing very far away. Perhaps it was better that he didn't.

Julien solemnly watched them leave, and then returned inside the cabin to his love. This dream wouldn't end, and somehow that brought Maric a small amount of comfort.

"We need to find Genevieve," Duncan avowed.

Maric agreed, and together the group swiftly walked down the hill and out of the wilderness in search of the Grey Wardens' commander.

Time was running short.

13

Draw your last breath, my friends,
Cross the Veil and the Fade and all the stars in the sky.
Rest at the Maker's right hand,
And be Forgiven.

—Canticle of Trials 1:16

The guard studied the group with a wary eye as he peeked through the massive gate's shuttered window. The livery of a horned stag on a black background hung from the battlements. Duncan didn't recognize it, but he assumed it was Orlesian. The guard's accent seemed to confirm that. "M'lord doesn't take in travelers," he sneered.

Maric glanced back at the rest of them, clearly asking for ideas. They had spent the better part of the afternoon traveling through the marshes before they'd seen the remote outpost. It had appeared out of the mist, ivy creeping up its cracked stone walls and greyish moss hanging down. It was as if the marsh was busily trying to reclaim the place, and yet it endured nobly.

There was a single keep within the walls and a small courtyard, room for no more than perhaps a hundred men, according to Kell's estimation. The sort of outpost the Empire built on the fringes of its borders, watching for incursions even if none had materialized for centuries beyond counting. They were convenient places for out-of-favor aristocrats to be exiled, though Duncan knew that some noblemen took these frontier assignments seriously and tried to make an honest go of it. They brought law to the local villages and attempted to clear the wilds of outlaws and pagan worship. This place, however, looked as if it was barely holding its own against the murky marsh around it, and if there was any local population to speak of, they hadn't seen evidence of it. This was a cold and wet wilderness, full of snakes, and certainly an inhospitable place to build anything.

Duncan shrugged, and neither Kell nor Utha appeared to offer anything better. Maric sighed and turned back to the waiting guard at the window. "We're looking for someone. A friend."

The guard squinted at Maric. "We don't have no Fereldans here."

"She's not Fereldan. She's Orlesian, perhaps the captain of the guard? Her name is Genevieve."

"What's that? I don't know anybody by that name! She certainly isn't the captain, 'less he up and turned himself into a woman when I wasn't looking! Begone, all of you!" The guard made to close the shutter, but paused as someone behind him mumbled something indistinct. Duncan strained to hear but couldn't make it out. The guard merely grunted and looked back at Maric. "My friend here says the new seneschal's wife goes by that name. That her?"

"Most like, yes."

"What's your business, then? We've had our fill of travelers in these parts. We don't open up the gates for no one without His Lordship's say. So if you got some message to pass on, I'll take it and you lot can be on your way."

Maric paused, and Duncan could see his mind working rapidly—and coming up with nothing. The King of Ferelden was not much of a bluffer, it seemed. Duncan was hardly surprised. "Tell her that her brother is here to see her," he spoke up.

The guard pressed his face against the trap window, rolling his eyes around so he could clearly see who spoke. "That you?"

Duncan was tempted to say it was Maric, but the panicked look in the man's eyes said that wasn't likely to be a good idea. Too bad, as the only other person who could pass believably as Genevieve's brother would be Kell, and he was an even worse liar than the King. "Half brother." He nodded. "My name is Bregan."

The guard chewed his lip thoughtfully, eyeing Duncan's swarthy skin. Finally he grunted. "We'll see what she has to say about it, then. Wait here, you lot." The window slammed shut with a loud clack.

Maric frowned. "You sure that's a good idea?" he whispered.

"You got a better one?"

Utha made a complex gesture to Kell, and the hunter shrugged in response. "I don't know who this seneschal might be," he said to her. "I know very little about our Commander beyond her life with the order."

The dwarf nodded as if to say that she was no better off.

They waited in the mist for quite some time, listening to some unknown bird cawing off in the distant marshes. When the shutters clacked open again, it startled them all. "You there," the guard growled, looking at Duncan. "She said she'll see her brother. The rest of you can wait outside."

"Surely that's not necessary?" Maric asked. "We only—"

"It's the seneschal's orders." The guard slammed the window shut again and a moment later the gate doors creaked open. The courtyard beyond was mostly mud, with only one gnarled tree covered in hanging moss growing next to a smithy and a dilapidated stable. The stable appeared to contain few actual horses, and most of the foot traffic seemed to be between the keep and the larger tower next to the gate. There were a handful of soldiers in sight, all men wearing ill-fitting chain hauberks and the same stag-on-black livery as above the gate.

The weary guard waved Duncan inside, and he had little choice but to go. Maric met his gaze as he passed, and that look seemed to say, *It's all up to you now, lad.* Which was wonderful, really. Just excellent. Duncan should have learned a long time ago when to keep his fool mouth shut.

He waited in the mud as they closed the gate behind him. It made a loud and final *thoom* as it shut. The guard walked up to him and waved at another standing nearby. This was a much younger man, younger than Duncan even, with his armor looking as if it were made for someone much larger. His helmet kept falling in front of his eyes, and he kept needing to push it back up.

"Take this one up to the seneschal's quarters," the guard barked. "No dawdling!"

The younger guard bobbed his head nervously and began trotting off toward the keep. He didn't look back to see if anyone was following, so Duncan sighed and ran after him.

Their path took them under the keep's portcullis, so rusted he doubted whether it had been lowered in years. Tall reeds grew along the wall. Inside the keep things were much tidier, if dark. There were few windows, and the low ceilings made the passages feel cramped, but the young guard seemed to know where he was going. He urged Duncan to keep up with him as he steered clear of the small inner hall with all its tables and chairs and instead took them down a narrow side passage to a long set of stairs.

"So what is this place called?" Duncan asked as they climbed.

The young man looked at him, surprised. "This is the Garrote. Don't you know?"

"Is that really its name?"

"No," he chuckled. "I can't remember what it's called on the map. Even His Lordship calls it the Garrote. They say the Nahashin Marshes will choke the life out of you."

"Clever."

The stairs led up to the floor where Duncan assumed the lord and his family lived, as well as senior members of the castle staff. A tiny sitting room appointed with a thick Anderfel rug opened up onto several groups of cramped apartments. A young girl with red pigtails and a plain grey dress sat in the corner and looked up at them with interest, but the young guard ignored her and took them into one of the apartments.

The oaken door was open, and inside was another chamber, this one with barely room to move in. It was filled with a small desk piled with papers, with only a stool to sit on. Several swords leaned against a wall, and a lone lantern hung from a hook to offer a bit of light. Two doors led farther in, but both of them were closed.

"When you're done, ser, I'll be just down the stairs." The young guard spun on his heel and marched unceremoniously out the door, closing it behind him.

Duncan looked around the room. He didn't see much that reminded him of Genevieve, apart from the swords. She obviously wasn't the seneschal, so what was she doing here at the castle? Was she still a Grey Warden? Was she just part of the garrison here, or maybe a bodyguard to the local lord? He couldn't picture a proud warrior doing something so unimportant, but he supposed her dream was her own.

One of the doors opened, and Duncan turned to see a figure in noble dress walk in, distractedly carrying several long scrolls under one arm and trying not to drop them. This was no woman, however, but a man. He had piercing blue eyes and black hair with grey at the temples, as well as a distinguished-looking short beard. He stopped and regarded Duncan curiously, and Duncan suddenly realized who it was.

Guy. The Grey Warden he had murdered.

"You're not Bregan," the man said in a friendly, if puzzled, tone. He walked over to the small desk and unloaded the scrolls on top of all the papers already there. Several of them were pushed off and floated lazily to the ground. He studied Duncan again, scratching his beard thoughtfully. "I told them not to bring anyone else inside. Bregan is here, is he not? Does he not wish to see us?"

Duncan opened his mouth and tried to form words, but he couldn't. In retrospect, it should have been obvious that he would find the man here. Guy had been Genevieve's fiancé when he died. It's only natural that her fondest wish would be for him to have lived, and for her to have married him. Duncan knew almost nothing about him, however. For understandable reasons the other Grey Wardens had been reluctant to discuss the man with his murderer. He was well thought of, a good man who had known Genevieve most of her life, and who followed her into the order. That's all he knew.

Guy's puzzlement increased as Duncan remained silent, then he became alarmed. "Has something happened?" he asked in a hushed voice. "Bregan . . . he still lives? Has something happened to him?"

"No, he's . . . fine," Duncan managed.

"Ah." The man nodded and then looked expectant, waiting for the real explanation. He was interrupted by the other door opening and a woman walking in. She wore a long grey dress, and had long white hair that cascaded down her back. She was full-figured and kind-looking, her face worn with smile lines, and Duncan did a double take as he realized this was Genevieve. Not the warrior he knew, with her cropped white hair and hard, muscular features, but merely Guy's wife.

She smiled at Duncan, but seeing his stunned expression and his gaping mouth, she looked quizzically at her husband. "Is something amiss?" she asked him.

"I can't truly tell. I was told your brother was here, and I thought it a surprise so I didn't tell you. But now I'm not so sure."

"Bregan?" she exclaimed excitedly, her smile lighting up her face as she turned back to Duncan. "Is he really here? Is there news? Oh, do tell me! It's been ever so long since I've heard from him!"

The warm-hearted gushing was too bizarre. She might as well have grown antlers on her head; he couldn't stop staring. They were both waiting for a response, however, so he had to pull himself together. "I, uh," he stammered, "need to speak to Genevieve. Alone."

Concern crossed her eyes, and she glanced at Guy. "Bad news, then," he said grimly. "I need to speak with Lord Ambrose anyhow. Shout if you need me, love." He kissed her warmly on the forehead, though she hardly noticed, she was staring at Duncan so intently. With one final wary look his way, Guy walked out to the sitting room, softly closing the door to the apartment behind him.

Genevieve stared at Duncan with dread. He felt immeasurably better now that Guy was gone, but he didn't know what to say. "You don't know, do you?" he asked, hoping beyond hope that he was wrong.

If anything, her stare intensified. "I don't know what, exactly?"

"That this"—he gestured around him—"is a dream. It's not real."

She peered at him, trying to piece together what he was actually saying, as if it couldn't possibly be what she thought. Then she frowned. "This is what you came to tell me? Is this some form of joke?"

"It's not a joke. Don't you remember me? My name is Duncan."

"Is Bregan even here? Do you even know my brother?" Genevieve angrily strode past Duncan to the door behind him. "I'm not going to put up with such nonsense, I'll tell you that. My husband will have you put in the dungeon!"

"Wait!" He grabbed her by the shoulder. She spun around, not frightened but instead glaring at him in outrage. "Tell me you haven't had a dream where you were a warrior!" he pleaded. "A Grey Warden, leading the rest of us on an important mission!"

"That was just a dream." The doubt in her eyes, however, told him differently. She didn't pull away from his grip, and she didn't open the door to leave.

"Are you sure? How would I even know about your dream otherwise?"

"No, this can't be." She shook her head, and when she finally noticed that he was holding her shoulder, she pulled it free. She paced to the other side of the room, anxiously wringing her hands. "That dream, it was horrible! This must be some kind of trick!"

"You're the Commander of the Grey in Orlais. It's no trick."

"I haven't picked up a sword in years! There was a Grey Warden who came to our village when I was young, and he spoke about recruitment, but I was not good enough. My brother convinced me to give it up! No, I remember that clearly!"

"But it's not true."

"It is!" She shook her fist at him, her voice taking on a tone of desperation. "My brother is a chevalier, a general in the Emperor's army! He has a wife, and a son! He is nothing like the miserable man in my dream!"

"He is a Grey Warden, like you. Or he was. We're searching for him."

"No, no!" She turned away, putting her hands to her head as if she needed to keep it from exploding. Duncan was growing a bit worried that perhaps he was pushing too hard. But what else was he supposed to do? It's not like he could leave and come back some other time when she'd had a chance to think about it. "I saw him just two months ago! He brought my nephew, and he is so deliriously happy!" She stopped, stunned, and slowly turned back to glare at Duncan dangerously. "What about Guy? Are you saying that he doesn't exist, as well?"

He took a step back. He remembered that look. If there was anything about this woman who reminded him of the warrior he knew, there it was. Did that make it a good thing? He couldn't tell. "He . . . died."

"He's alive," she insisted, her voice steel. "You're trying to take my husband away from me, the one thing that has made my life worth living. The one thing I cherish above anything else!"

"I'm not!" he protested. "You don't have a husband!"

"Only because you *murdered* him!" she roared, her face red with rage. She made as if she were going to charge Duncan, her fists raised, but she stopped herself almost immediately. Her whole body shook with fury, but her eyes blinked with horrified realization.

"And how would you know that," he asked slowly, "unless you knew who I was?" He cautiously approached her. "Because you do know, don't you? You just don't want to know."

With a scream of rage, Genevieve dashed across the room, scooping up one of the swords leaning against the wall and spinning on Duncan. He saw the murder in her eyes and had his knives out even as she rushed at him. He parried her first blow, but her second almost tore one of the daggers from his hand. This was not the fighting of a woman who hadn't picked up a blade in years, but of a seasoned veteran.

"Stop!" he shouted, but she pressed the attack. Grimacing, she made one hard slash after the other, pushing him backwards until he almost tripped. In such close quarters his daggers should actually have had the advantage, but he didn't want to *hurt* her. Though he didn't want to get hurt, either.

Duncan darted his dagger out at the hand holding her sword, trying to disarm her, but she was too quick for him. Pirouetting, she bashed his forearm aside and then lunged forward, throwing him against the wall and shoving the sword's edge against his throat. It held there, pressing hard enough that he felt its bite against his skin. It made him choke, and he pulled his head back, trying not to swallow.

She peered coldly into his eyes, mere inches from his face. This was definitely the Genevieve he knew, despite her appearance. She could cut his throat in the blink of an eye, and he was helpless to prevent it. Could he be killed in the Fade? Would that mean his body would simply die back in the real world? A bead of sweat rolled down his forehead, the moment stretching into forever as neither of them made a single sound.

Finally she pulled back on the sword's edge ever so slightly. He gasped and swallowed hard. "Tell me why I shouldn't kill you," she demanded.

"You're the Commander! We need you!"

"This is a good life," she said, her voice low and filled with steel. "Bregan is happy. I am happy. Guy is alive. And most important, I've never had anything to do with the Grey Wardens and especially little bastards like you."

Her last words bit hard. He stared at her in disbelief, unable to formulate a response.

"What did you think?" she snapped. "That I would recruit the murderer of the man I loved as a reward? It was a *punishment*. I wanted to be a Grey Warden, but my brother made it a misery. He hated it, and knowing that he joined because of me made me hate it. You took away the one thing that allowed me to forget."

"I'm sorry. . . ."

"No, *I'm* sorry." She gritted her teeth, the anger making her shake. "I was so certain that you would die in the Joining, that you would get just a taste of what Guy and the rest of us had to go through. Enough for you to choke on. But you survived. The Maker played yet one more joke on me."

"But I thought—"

"You've proven useful," she cut him off, her tone ice cold. "You have some skill, and you get things done. You've made a fine Grey Warden." She sneered at him. "Congratulations."

They stared at each other a moment longer, and then she pushed herself away from him. "Go," she said. "Go back to the others and get out of here. I won't be *retrieved*, not by you. Not by anyone." He dropped down to the floor, coughing and choking and clutching his throat. He could feel blood where the blade had left a shallow cut. She stepped back, looking at him with a hateful glare, and he could do nothing but stare back at her blankly.

Was that what she really felt? He'd always wondered. He'd never thought she'd held any love for him after what he'd done, but to hate him so? Why keep him close, then? Why not send him away to some other Grey Warden fortress as soon as she became a commander? She had that authority.

"I don't believe you," he insisted.

She snorted derisively. "What do you believe, then?"

"I believe you're better than that. I look up to you. You saved me from that cell, and I know it's because you thought you were doing the right thing. I think you're just trying to make me leave."

Genevieve sighed, her face calming. "Then go."

"So you're just going to stay here, then? Live a lie?"

"I've had my fill of truth."

He nodded slowly, rubbing his neck and clearing his throat several times. It felt almost as if his larynx had been crushed. "So you're going to give up. Just like Nicolas."

She frowned, putting the sword down on the desk with all its scrolls and papers. More of them fell to the floor. Then she glanced up at Duncan. "What do you mean? What has he done?"

"He's with Julien. He refused to come with us. He'd rather die in the Fade."

A bit of sadness crossed Genevieve's eyes and she glanced down at the floor. "He deserves that much, if that's what he wants."

"Is that what you really think?"

"Why not?" she snapped irritably. "Would reality be such an improvement? Is it such a crime to be with the one you love? Let the man be with Julien. Let them both have some peace."

"But it's not Julien he's with."

"You don't know that. They say the spirits of the dead cross the Fade. I have no trouble believing that Julien's spirit would stay with Nicolas, if he found him here in the Fade."

Duncan paused. "Is that what you think Guy is?"

Genevieve stared off in the direction of the door, as if she could see through it. There was a yearning in her expression. A desire for something she had denied herself long ago. As a shadow slowly crossed over her eyes, he knew her answer. "No," she admitted bitterly.

An awkward silence ensued. Duncan picked himself up off the floor as she stood where she was, rigid and pointedly not looking at him. She hung her head, her mouth twisted into an unhappy grimace. The silence was interrupted as the door to the apartment suddenly flew open, and Guy rushed in.

"What's happening here?" he demanded, staring with alarm first at Duncan and then at his wife. "I was told there was shouting? Fighting?"

"Nothing's happening," Genevieve said flatly. She didn't look at him, either.

His gaze fell upon the sword on the desk, and his mouth thinned. He glanced at Duncan suspiciously. "Are you certain?" he asked Genevieve. "I can have this young man sent away; there's no need to have him here upsetting you, love."

"No," she said. Then she simply stood there, staring intently at the ground. Duncan wasn't sure what he was supposed to do next. Was he supposed to leave? Was she ignoring him now? Guy glanced at him with a mixture of confusion and questioning. He didn't know any better than Duncan did, but clearly he knew something was very wrong.

He leaned in close to Genevieve, putting a hand on her shoulder until she looked up at him. Tears reddened her eyes. "What's wrong, my love?" he pleaded. "Please tell me."

"I need to go."

"Go? Go where? When will you be back?"

Genevieve wiped away her tears and clenched her teeth. She put a hand on Guy's face, staring at him as if she was memorizing his every feature. Then she kissed him on the lips, tenderly. His brow knotted in confusion. "Soon, I hope," she whispered.

And with that the keep around them vanished. Duncan was almost startled by the transition, stumbling as the wall behind him faded away. They were back in a plain of rock, with the endless skies of the Fade overhead. Genevieve was in her heavy armor and her Grey Warden tunic, her white hair cut short once again. She stared at the ground, clenching her jaw, and did not move.

From not far away, Maric and the others ran up. "You did it!" he shouted.

"I guess I did," Duncan muttered. He kept his eye on Genevieve, however, and saw her close her eyes and collect her will. The hard edges had all returned, but then perhaps they had never quite gone away, had they?

Behind the others, he saw the elven woman with the blond curls, Katriel, slowly approach. Maric stiffened, spotting her at the same time that Duncan did. Genevieve noticed her, as well, and when she did she drew her greatsword in alarm.

"Wait!" Maric shouted, holding up a hand to stop her.

Genevieve didn't lower her sword. "Why? Who is this?"

"Someone I . . . once knew."

"Then it is a demon!" She charged toward Katriel, who remained where she was and barely looked at her attacker. Instead, she watched Maric with her sad green eyes. The elf had met them each time they had returned from a dream, and each time she had seemed more desperately sad. Maric was the same way. Duncan could see his heart breaking each time he saw her.

Maric ran after Genevieve now, catching her just before she

reached the elf. He grabbed hold of her armor and pulled her back, though it was a struggle. "Stop! She can help us!" he insisted. Kell and Utha looked on, concerned, but did not intervene.

The Commander stared at Maric as if the man were mad. "Help us? Have you lost your mind?"

He paused, and looked unhappily toward Katriel. For her part, she continued to simply watch him. Genevieve stepped back, scowling with disapproval but keeping her sword at the ready. Maric approached the elf closely, apprehensive and fearful all at once. "Will you help us? Face the demon?" he asked her, his voice small.

She looked at him, her expression pensive. "No," she admitted. "And you should not go to face it, either."

"Why not?"

"Because I love you." When he recoiled from her words, anguished, she rushed forward to him. Tears streaked down her face and she became frantic. "Maric, the demon will kill you! Don't go to your death, not for duty! Not always for duty!"

"I made a promise," he mumbled.

He tried to look away from Katriel, but she reached up with her hands and clutched at his chin, attempting to make him look at her and crying even more forcefully. He fought against it, but weakly, and when she finally looked him in the eyes, tears were streaming down his face, as well.

"Let them go and do this task," she whispered urgently, her voice racked with emotion. "Have you not sacrificed enough?"

"I need to save her."

"There are others to save. Others trapped in the Fade, living in an endless dream." She kept her eyes fixed on his, her plea desperate. "You mother is here, Maric. We could save her together. Please . . . don't go."

Maric flinched, his eyes filled with stark pain, but he didn't look away from Katriel. For a long moment there was only silence.

Then her expression slowly became resigned, and she nodded des-
olately. She took a deep and ragged breath. Duncan felt almost
embarrassed to watch, and even Genevieve turned away with a
grimace. "I understand," the elf whispered.

"I wish I could ask you to forgive me."

She reached up and tenderly brushed aside his hair with a sad
smile. "Forgive yourself," she said. "And forget me." Then she
turned around and walked away. Maric remained where he was,
watching her leave. He seemed calm, almost serene. Duncan wasn't
certain why.

It made him doubt. Maybe there were good spirits in the Fade
and not just demons. Maybe ghosts were real. Maybe the Maker
truly did watch over His children and helped the ones that needed
Him the most.

Or maybe it had all been one last trick to try to lure Maric away.

Duncan was suddenly glad they were going to face the demon
now. Let them get away from this place or die trying. He was tired
of nightmares.

The group walked into an elven alienage, a walled-off part of a
larger city. The buildings here were mostly hovels, crammed close
together and sometimes even on top of one another. It was a hap-
hazard pile of tenements and dirty shops, washing lines strewn
across the street sometimes going up two or even three stories high.
The street itself was mostly mud, the worn paths filled with stale
water and smelling of dung. The only spot of color in the entire
quarter was the central square, where a well-tended oak tree spread
its branches wide, its vibrantly green leaves forming a canopy that
left much of the ground beneath it dry. A wooden stage had been
built there, adorned with poles that were covered in bright blue
garlands. A place of celebration, Duncan imagined, even if there
was nothing on the dusty stage now.

The odd thing, he noted, was that there wasn't a single person throughout the entire alienage. The street was bare, and not a single elf poked his or her head out of any door or window. Dark clouds billowed overhead and threatened rain, but no one ran about to collect the laundry from the lines. Window shutters clacked rhythmically in the breeze. It looked as if the entire place was deserted.

Duncan drew his daggers. There was an unease to the silence, a strangeness to it that raised the hackles on his neck.

Utha squinted as she looked around and made quick gestures toward Kell.

"You are right," he murmured. "This seems very different from the other dreams, and it is not solely for the lack of people."

Duncan had to agree. There was a strange distinctness to his vision, here. It made everything look slightly unreal, as if he were seeing at it all through a pane of glass. Everything also appeared slightly washed out, and that wasn't just the dinginess of the elven homes. Even the sky was lifeless, nothing but grey clouds from one end to the other. He half expected the clouds to part and reveal the Fade sky with its floating islands on the other side.

"Then where do we find the demon?" Maric asked.

Nobody had an immediate answer. The iron gates leading out of the district were closed up tight. They were solid and forbidding-looking, as apparently the elves were not even permitted to gaze upon the rest of the city and its superior conditions.

Not that the slums of Val Royeaux were much of an improvement over this, Duncan thought. The fact that they were an improvement at all was bad enough—the alienage had the feel of neglect, like the buildings and its people were the refuse that was brushed off the rest of the city. The elves here obviously made the best of it they could, but he imagined even the most down-on-his-luck thief he'd run with in the slums would have turned up his nose rather than stay here.

As Duncan slowly scanned the area, he noticed that not only was the gate closed, but so were all the doors. All except one. A single innocuous building on the other side of the square had its door invitingly open. "Look there." He pointed.

They all did, and paused. "That almost seems too convenient," Genevieve muttered. Nobody argued with her, but quietly the group began crossing the square toward the door.

"Will Fiona be here?" Maric asked quietly. "Or just the demon?"

"I don't know," Kell admitted.

Genevieve motioned the Wardens to spread out. Kell and Utha went around one side of the great oak while she and Duncan went around the other. Maric kept up behind them. Nobody said a word, the only sound the wind through the eaves overhead.

As the group crept through the door, Duncan paused. The hallway just inside wasn't what he would have expected. It was wide, for one, and the walls were covered in the delicate paper he'd seen sometimes in the homes of the truly wealthy. Here it was decorated with petite roses, each one growing from a vine that stretched up to the peaked white ceiling overhead. The floors here were a polished wood, dark and rich and clean enough to eat off of.

"This can't be the same place we just entered," he muttered.

The others were looking around now, as well, their grips tightening on their weapons. "We went through a doorway, didn't we?" Maric whispered. "We could be anywhere."

"We are being led," Genevieve declared. "This is a trap."

"Do we have much choice?"

She had no answer for him. After a moment's hesitation the group moved forward again. It became obvious that this was an estate, the home of some Orlesian aristocrat. They passed a luxuriously appointed sitting room, a hallway that seemed to go off into a servant's wing, and even a conservatory complete with whitewashed doors that opened up onto a sunlit garden filled with flowered bushes.

All of it still had the same unreality that the alienage did, the feeling that everything wasn't quite right. Duncan noticed, as well, that the estate was similarly abandoned. The hallways should have been teeming with servants and guards, an entire staff bustling about to run the household, and yet there was nothing but silence.

"Do you hear that?" Kell asked quietly.

The group stopped in the hall. Duncan cocked his head and ever so faintly heard the sound of a woman crying. It might have been Fiona; it was too far away to tell and would have been impossible to hear if it wasn't otherwise so quiet. The hunter had good ears.

They moved on, Kell leading the way as he tried to find a path toward the sound. They passed through an open courtyard filled with verdant bushes and a marble statue of Andraste atop a burbling fountain. Opening a sliding window, Kell took them carefully into an empty kitchen. It was large, the sort that would have normally been filled with servants desperate to bake their bread and finish the evening meal, but there was no one. It didn't even smell as if it had ever been used. The sounds of the whimpering woman were definitely louder, however, and as the hunter brought them to the back of the kitchen they found a narrow flight of stairs leading downward into darkness.

The cries were coming from below.

"Do we go down?" Maric asked nobody in particular.

There was no answer. They had no way back into the waking world, no way to free themselves from whatever spell the demon had placed upon them. If this was truly a trap, then they had to walk into it with their eyes open and hope that they came out the other side.

Duncan felt growing dread as they descended single file. The stairs creaked ominously beneath their weight, and the air turned chill the farther down they got. His heart began to beat rapidly, and he had to force himself to keep moving. The stones around them changed, becoming natural rock. They entered a dank cave, the sound of the crying ahead echoing past stagnant pools.

This was no natural place, he thought. This was a memory, something so terrible that to Fiona it had become a dark cave filled with terror. He could feel it clawing at his senses, and could see the others feeling the same. Sweat poured down their foreheads, their eyes wide as they pushed ahead in the shadows. Fiona wasn't trapped in a dream filled with her fondest hopes—she was trapped in her worst nightmare.

A faint light appeared ahead of them, the cave opening up into a small cavern. It was bare except for a candelabrum of wrought iron standing in the center, the candles flickering and sending shadows jumping about the rocky floor. A man stood next to it with his back turned, his grey hair pulled into a genteel ponytail. He was dressed in the embroidered velvet jacket and high leather boots typical of an Orlesian nobleman, and carried a long leather whip curled in one hand.

What he was using the whip on was obvious. Fiona lay prone on the stone floor, facing away from them with her arms raised above her head and chained to the wall. Her head hung down limply, and the back of her robe was ripped open from so many whiplashes across her back that her skin was red with blood. Duncan would have thought her dead were it not for the quavering of her shoulders and her racking sobs.

"Did you think"—the nobleman sneered at Fiona beneath him—"that I was going to let the Chantry take you away from me? Whisk you off to the Circle of Magi, hmm?"

"I'm sorry, master," Fiona pleaded. Her head still hung down, almost touching the floor. Her voice was reduced to a broken whisper, and she continued to cry.

"You forget my connections! I can ensure they forget about

some little elven harlot! The mage who found you was mistaken, as simple as that!"

"Yes, master . . ."

"It's not as if I need you for any foul magical gift you possess, do I?"

"Yes, master . . ."

Although Duncan couldn't see the man's face, his rage was clear. He unfurled the leather whip and cracked it loudly. "You're not listening to me, foolish girl! I have had enough of your insolence! Enough!" He raised the whip up high, preparing to lash Fiona once again.

"Stop!" Genevieve ordered him. She moved into the small cavern, her greatsword raised cautiously before her. The others followed suit, keeping their distance from the nobleman and spreading out. There was no way of knowing what to expect from him.

He paused, not landing his blow, and instead turned to look at them. The nobleman was arrogantly handsome. His eyes were lined with black kohl, an Orlesian custom, but, far more noticeable, they glowed with a sinister purplish hue. He smiled, as if pleased. "Ah! And here they are at last. Found your way out of your dreams, did you? Well, throw away a gift if you will; I won't give you another."

"We do not need your gifts," Genevieve said, her tone deadly. She lowered her sword at him. "You will release Fiona, and you will release us. Do it."

He chuckled lightly. "Release my precious girl? I don't think so! I bought her fair and square! I have spent years raising her; I'm not about to waste all of that!"

"We know what you are, demon. There is no need to pretend."

He clucked his tongue reproachfully. "Do you think you are actually here? Do you think those are actual weapons that you have pointed at me? Who do you think is the master of this realm, and who the dreamer?" With a wave of his hand, Genevieve was thrown back with terrible force. She grunted as she slammed hard into the stone wall of the cavern, her sword clattering to the ground. He raised his hand, grinning, and she rose as if carried by the throat, kicking her legs and clutching at her neck as she choked.

Kell unleashed an arrow, and it lodged into the neck of the nobleman with little effect. Utha charged at him, Maric right behind her with his sword raised high, and the nobleman merely waved with his other hand and sent the two of them tumbling back along the floor. Kell shot two more arrows, both of them striking the demon harmlessly, before he took out his flail and charged as well.

"Really," the nobleman sighed dryly, "this is silly." Still holding Genevieve against the wall, he flicked his free hand at the hunter and sent him flying explosively back, falling hard to the ground near where Maric and Utha tried to regain their feet.

Duncan stayed back, his daggers at the ready. His first thought was to circle around and try to stab the demon unawares, but seeing how effective the others were being with their attacks made it seem unlikely that his would be any better. Instead, he edged over to where Fiona lay and gingerly touched her.

"Fiona?" he whispered. "Are you okay?"

She raised her head slowly, and he realized that was a very stupid question. Her back was bloody and flayed open, and as she looked at him with questioning, reddened eyes and a face stained with tears, he gathered she had no idea who he was and barely even registered that he was there.

"Here, let me try to get those manacles off you." He took her hands, noticing that her wrists were rubbed raw and bloody by the thick iron manacles that held them. It seemed like they might be simple enough to pick. He reached into his belt and pulled out his hidden lockpick.

"Away from her!" the demon roared, spinning on Duncan and thrusting out his hand to dash him away from Fiona. Duncan slid along the ground and bashed his head hard on a stone outcropping by the wall, crying out as agony burned through him. He groggily tried to sit up, and could hear the sounds of shouting as Genevieve and the others charged the demon again. Perhaps he had successfully distracted the creature? That was a comforting thought.

He got to his feet just in time to see Genevieve thrust her greatsword completely through the nobleman's midsection. It passed through cleanly, spilling no blood as it came out the other side, and he looked at her almost in disappointment. "Truly, is that the best you can do? Are such futile efforts supposed to impress me?" He reached out with a hand, his speed lightning quick and too fast for Genevieve to avoid, grabbing her throat and lifting her off the ground.

She gasped and batted ineffectually at his hand. "See? I can do this the old-fashioned way just as easily," he chuckled. "As soon as you dispense with this useless struggle, you can all perish quietly. Saving you for later was obviously a mistake."

Kell lay nearby, sprawled on the floor unconscious. Duncan couldn't see where Utha was. Maric stood near the demon, his head bloody, clearly laboring to lift his runed sword for another strike.

"Maric, don't!" Duncan shouted.

The demon spun his head around to spot Maric, and his other hand snatched Maric up by the neck the same way he had Genevieve. Maric gasped loudly, holding on to his sword and hacking as the demon lifted him off the ground. His efforts did little more than slash the creature's embroidered coat.

The nobleman glanced down at the slashes, his purple eyes flashing dangerously. "For that, you will need to suffer." Still holding Genevieve aloft with his other hand, he began to crush Maric's throat. The crunching sound was wet and unpleasant, and Maric let out a guttural cry of anguish that filled the cavern.

Suddenly another shout rang out, a feral scream of pain and rage. It was Fiona. She rose from the floor like a madwoman, shaking from the effort, her eyes wild, bright magical power coalescing around her fists. The demon paused and turned a curious eye toward her, but not before she unleashed an enormous bolt of lightning at him.

The flash of light blinded Duncan, and the thunder that followed almost threw him off his feet. He stumbled against the wall behind him, and when he opened his eyes he saw that Fiona had dropped down to her knees, her effort spent. The demon was on the ground, having dropped Genevieve and Maric both. His coat was completely burned away, leaving his bare chest smoking from the strike. He seemed dazed.

Duncan took his chance. He charged across the room, leaping into the air and landing directly on top of the nobleman before he could recover his bearings. *Let's see if this does something now!* He plunged both of his daggers into the demon's head as he landed, and they slid bloodlessly into the creature's eyes.

He roared in pain, flailing his arms about and unable to see. Duncan felt himself gripped by an invisible power and propelled high up into the air. He was bashed into the ceiling of the cavern, pressed there as if by some giant hand. He was being crushed, the air forced out of his lungs and leaving him gasping.

"That was a very foolish thing, little one!" the nobleman snarled, yanking one of the daggers from his eye. The purple glow in that eye was now sickly bright, shining out as if it was bleeding from a crack in his facade. He turned toward Fiona, an inhuman grimace on his face. "You wish to play, do you? You wish more lashes? When will you ever learn?"

"Never!" she spat. She lifted herself back off the ground, so weak she was shaking, her face contorted into nothing short of vicious defiance. "I will never suffer your touch again! Never!"

"We shall see," he snapped. Flames burned around one of his hands, black flames that filled the entire room with a stark coldness that made Duncan flinch. He pointed his hand at Fiona, the flames growing to even greater magnitude. She glared at him and did not back down.

Before the demon could act, however, Duncan saw a blood-soaked Maric rise up behind him. The King roared a battle cry as he swung his longsword and beheaded the demon in one stroke.

They woke up.

Duncan picked himself off the cold stone floor of the dwarven ruin, the skeletons still all around him. He saw the corpse of the dwarven ruler, the one who had been possessed by the demon, and it now sprawled lifelessly on its ancient throne as if it had never moved. The dead were simply dead once again, and he watched as the ruler's bones crumbled and slowly fell apart, whatever magic had held them together now departed. Within moments there was nothing on the throne except dust.

The ominous sense in the room was gone. He could hear the others stirring, and he saw Maric waking up on the dais. Right next to Duncan, Fiona stirred. She was back to her normal form, he saw, and none of the injuries she had suffered in the Fade translated to her body. None of theirs had.

She stared at her hands, almost disbelieving. "This . . . is the real world? I'm alive?"

"We all are," he told her with a grin.

She leaned over and snatched him up in a hug, crying tears of exhaustion and relief, and he held her close. He couldn't imagine what she had gone through. He didn't want to. It was bad enough remembering what he had left behind.

Not all of them recovered, however. While the others all began to rise, Nicolas remained sprawled where the demon had flung him, as lifeless as the ancient corpses around him.

Duncan found himself hoping that wherever Nicolas was now, his dream continued and he found the peace he wanted so desperately. Somebody should.

14

And as the black clouds came upon them,
They looked on what Pride had wrought,
And despaired.

—Canticle of Threnodies 7:10

Fiona felt relieved to get out of there finally.

The group all but fled the ruined palace after Kell reunited
with Hafter. The hound barked at his master repeatedly, almost as
if admonishing the fact that he and the others had left him alone
for so long. She wasn't sure if the hound had slept, or if he had been
somewhere with them in the Fade. Dogs dreamed, didn't they? Either way, he was clearly relieved, as was Kell. The hunter said little,
and just patted Hafter's head and smiled sadly.

They took Nicolas's body with them. It didn't seem right to
leave him amid all those dwarves who had died so horribly. Kell
and Maric carried him between them, neither speaking a word as
Genevieve led them out. Fiona followed along, hugging her arms
around herself and trying to regain some warmth. She couldn't stop
shivering. The more that nightmare lingered in her thoughts, the
colder she felt.

They left Nicolas outside the ruined palace, at the foot of the
long stairs. It took them a while to collect enough loose rubble to
pile on top of him until they had a cairn of sorts. Genevieve laid
his black cloak on top, and they hung their heads for a long moment. The cavern held nothing but oppressive silence for them.

"It feels wrong not to bury him," Fiona murmured.

"It was his choice," Genevieve snapped.

She couldn't argue with that. Nobody could. Were they supposed to march all the way back to the underground lake to allow Nicolas's body to rest with that of his lover? The idea had appeal, but they all knew it was impossible. The darkspawn would surely catch up to them long before then. This would have to do.

It seemed to her that there should have been some kind of discussion then. They needed to talk about what they had been led into, and where they were going. Fiona felt like there needed to be some *recognition* of what had happened, even if her mind screamed at her not to think about it. Every time she remembered that whip cutting into her flesh, her thoughts veered away violently. But the others seemed no better off than her, and so they all numbly followed after Genevieve as she led them back into the thaig.

For hours they stumbled through the ruined streets. Fiona barely noticed the city itself anymore, as wrapped up as she was in her own darkness. The dream had felt so real. The demon had impersonated the human man who bought her from the slavers that took her in after her father had died. She'd had no idea back then who those kind men really were, only that they offered her food and a warm bed to sleep in. Then an even kinder man came to take her from them, and she found herself in his luxurious home and thought herself the luckiest little girl in the entire alienage.

How very naive she had been. Count Dorian, as she learned her new master's name to be, had been in search of an elven whore he could keep as a pet, something he could put in a pretty dress and bring with him on one of his many trips to the capital, like baggage. The Countess had permitted him his new toy, and completely ignored Fiona as she went about her own dalliances. Fiona lived in that household a prisoner, invisible and not even knowing that any of it was wrong, only that she needed to please the Count or suffer his wrath. Often his wrath came whether he was pleased or not.

Escaping the man had not been easy. Fortune had brought her to the notice of an elderly mage on the streets of Val Royeaux, though the Count's fury when he discovered it had been immeasurable. She still flinched when she thought of how he had whipped her that night. He had gouged and bled her until she had pleaded for death, and he had denied her even that.

And then she had grown angry. She had dug deep down inside and demanded that whatever talent for magic she had, a talent in which she did not even truly believe until that moment, come forth and save her. And it had. She had killed the Count with raw magical force, and lay bleeding beside his corpse as exhaustion took her.

The demons had come, then. They had whispered soft things, promising that they could take all the pain away. So desperate was their desire to possess her they nipped away at her mind, and it was all she could do to lie there and cry silent tears as she resisted.

The Countess found her in the dungeon, unconscious and lying in a pool of her own blood. Almost dead. Why the woman had contacted the Circle of Magi to come and take Fiona away, she had no idea. She never saw the woman again. Perhaps the Countess had felt pity? Perhaps she had felt some gratitude for the elf who had finally slain her cruel husband and transformed her into a rich widow? She could just as easily have called on the watch, or let her die.

The Circle, sadly, had been little better. At least the nightmares grew fainter in time. She thought that she had finally put them behind her, but apparently it was not so. It felt like an old wound had been ripped open inside her heart, leaving it raw and bleeding.

They were just outside a field full of so much rubble and debris that it was impossible to tell what it all might have once been, when Kell picked up Bregan's trail again. The hunter held his hand up to call for a halt and knelt, running his fingers along the ground and closing his pale eyes. He lifted his head slightly as if catching a scent, and softly said, "I found him."

Everyone knew who he meant. The effect on Genevieve was electrifying. She almost pounced on Kell, demanding that he follow the trail immediately. He stared up at her, and for a moment Fiona thought he might challenge her authority once again. He didn't, however, merely nodded and stood to lead the way.

Genevieve almost vibrated, she was so intent. The change in her from the surly and silent commander that had left the ruin was marked. Was she still as keen as before on finding her brother? It seemed so, though Fiona felt like she had to remind herself why they were even down here. They had only been in the Deep Roads, what? A couple of days? It felt like forever.

Duncan walked beside her for a time. She looked over at him and he smiled sadly. He meant it to be reassuring, she assumed, but it just reminded her that his heart had been broken in the Fade as well. She didn't know exactly what he had gone through, but she knew enough. He looked older.

"Why did the demon want you?" he asked her suddenly.

"Because they become very powerful when they possess a mage."

"It seemed plenty powerful already."

She shrugged. "I don't know. It had sustained itself in our world so long, perhaps it had only a little power left. Perhaps a mage is all it ever wanted. It's in the nature of demons to covet what they can't have."

He nodded, chewing on the idea.

"Thank you for coming for me," she whispered to him.

"You shouldn't be thanking me," he said. She followed his nod and saw he meant Maric, who walked not far from them, too lost in thought to realize he was being discussed.

"Why? Because he killed the demon?"

"He's the one who broke out of his dream first, and came to get the rest of us. He insisted we had to save you. Without him, I don't know that I would have left my . . . I would still be there. For certain."

Duncan looked away, frowning to hide his pain. What sort of dream would hold a boy who had grown up alone in the slums of Val Royeaux, she wondered? She didn't want to ask, and instead clutched his hand and gave it a warm squeeze.

They reached the massive doorway that led out of Ortan thaig after another hour of picking their way through piles of stone and masonry. Maric indicated that he had gone through this door before, and that his group had first encountered darkspawn several hours afterwards. Fiona exchanged glances with Kell and Utha, although they said nothing. They sensed no darkspawn nearby. It seemed odd, after how the creatures had hounded them so far. Perhaps when the darkspawn picked up their trail again, she would be wishing for just this sort of oddness.

The great iron door had clearly been bashed in long ago by some powerful force. Ogres, she assumed. The great blue brutes were the workhorses of the darkspawn when they appeared, and whenever the attack on this thaig happened they would have almost certainly numbered among the horde. Still, it was impressive. She could almost picture the creatures swarming in through the breach, washing over whatever dwarven defenses remained like a dark tide.

Hafter sniffed among the rubble in front of the door, making anxious sounds. Then he lifted his head and looked into the shadows beyond the door and whined. Fiona was inclined to agree.

Beyond, they were back in the Deep Roads. It did not take long for them to start seeing the familiar signs of darkspawn corruption, so thick here they could not really make out the stone any longer. It was a sickening layer of skin that covered everything, and it felt unnerving, squishing as it did beneath her boots. The idea of touching it with bare skin made her shudder in revulsion.

There was also a new sound. Perhaps *sound* was not the right word, as she felt it far more than she heard it. She had been feeling it for some time, she realized. Sometimes it seemed like something whispering her name, or at least she thought it was her name. At other times it was little more than the softest, most alluring notes of a chorus carried to her from afar.

It had something to do with the darkspawn. That was all she knew.

They traveled for a long time. She wasn't even certain just how long, and kept her mind focused on maintaining the light from her staff and putting one foot in front of the other. Her mind cried out for rest, but she nearly felt glad for the fatigue. She suspected they all did, as their pace made it almost impossible to think.

Kell remained in front, his faithful hound keeping step, and he stopped every now and again to kneel and furrow his brow as he studied the invisible trail. How he could pinpoint a single Grey Warden amid all this darkspawn filth, Fiona couldn't begin to guess. But he did it. He turned down several passages and kept them going, until finally they reached another section where the dwarven masonry had collapsed, opening up into the inky black caverns below . . . the true home of the darkspawn, underneath the Deep Roads.

"There." He pointed.

Genevieve stepped forward, enough to gaze into the breach and see that the debris leading into the cavern below was indeed scalable. "Then we go there," she stated unequivocally.

"No, we do not. First we talk."

She brushed by him. "I am not interested in talking." She marched on ahead, scrambling down the rubble into the shadows below. Fiona went to follow, but Kell gave her a direct look and shook his head no. She paused, and so did the others behind her.

They waited. Genevieve could only go down so far before the lack of light prevented her from going farther. Fiona heard her eventually stop and sigh in exasperation. She turned around and marched back up the rubble until she stood in front of them. Her face filled with silent fury, she crossed her arms and glared at Kell. Hafter growled menacingly beside him, but he waved a hand to shush the hound.

"Is this to be another challenge, then?" she demanded.

The hunter studied her for a moment with his pale eyes, his expression reflective. The man was inscrutable at the best of times, and right now Fiona had no idea whether he was angry or simply concerned. "Genevieve, we have followed you," he said slowly, "as you rushed heedlessly into one danger after another. We followed you into the palace. This needs to change."

"We are not turning back."

"I am not speaking of turning back."

"The palace was not my fault," she insisted. "We were led there by an illusion, one that tricked you just as it did me."

"We were led there by your obsession and your lack of caution." He was picking his words warily. Duncan glanced at Fiona with alarm, although he said nothing. She had to agree. This wasn't likely to go anywhere good.

"And?" Genevieve demanded. "What do you propose, then? I am your commander. Are you attempting to replace me?"

"I have no interest in leadership," Kell replied. "But I am the senior Grey Warden here after you. It falls on me to ensure this task of ours is performed to our best ability, and that requires caution you refuse to provide."

"Maker take your caution!" she snapped angrily.

His eyes narrowed. "See reason, Commander."

Maric stepped forward from behind Fiona. "I agree," he said, his tone as reasonable as she'd ever heard it. "I'm willing to risk my life if it will save my country, Warden, but I've no interest in throwing it away."

"Is that what you all think?" Her eyes went from him, to Kell, and then to Duncan. They remained on the lad, though Fiona wasn't certain why. "You think I wish to throw my life away?" Duncan looked down at the ground, his expression awkward.

"I don't know," Kell responded. "We could all die. But if this is how we continue, we will die for certain."

She scowled at him, her jaw clenching. Her arms uncrossed and hung by her sides, her hands clenched into fists. "Thank you, Kell," she said crisply. "Your opinion is noted. Let us proceed into the cavern below."

He hesitated. "I think you misunderstand what I mean. You—"

Genevieve's gauntleted fist flew so quickly, Fiona didn't even see it coming. Kell did, however, and he leaped back, adroitly evading her swing. "I said we proceed!" she roared, her face red and shaking from berserk rage.

With a loud growl, Hafter launched himself at Genevieve. She had time only to cover her face as the hound barreled into her, latching its jaws around one of her gauntlets and bearing the both of them down to the ground. They landed heavily, sliding along the ground. The hound whipped his head rapidly back and forth, snarling as Genevieve struggled to get him off.

"Hafter! No!" Kell snapped.

The dog didn't listen. It continued to fight viciously, and even when the hunter moved in to try to physically pull him off he didn't respond. Finally Genevieve gave a great heave, shoving the large hound off of her.

Hafter landed only a foot away, Genevieve's gauntlet still in his mouth. He immediately scrambled back to his feet, dropping the gauntlet and ready to charge back at her again. Utha darted in and grabbed the hound around the neck. Hafter snapped at her in surprise, but then turned his attention back to Genevieve, fangs bared.

Kell held his hand out to Genevieve. "I apologize, Commander. He—"

The hunter didn't dodge the second punch. She struck him across the face hard, shouting in fury, and he stumbled back. Hafter barked loudly, outraged by the fact he wasn't being allowed to protect his master. Genevieve jumped up and ran at Kell, but this time Maric and Duncan were able to stop her. They tackled her from behind, and in her berserk rage she was almost able to get away from them. Her bare fist was pulled back to strike Kell, who stood stunned only a foot away, yet Duncan held it back.

And that was when Fiona saw it. All along the Commander's hand, and continuing down into her wrist and likely farther, was an ugly stain. The very sort of stain that Duncan had told her about earlier. It wasn't a bruise, or anything natural. It looked as if her flesh were rotting.

She gasped in shock.

Utha saw it, too. Then Maric and Duncan saw it clearly in the light. Genevieve noticed what they were doing and followed their gaze to her hand, and saw that its corrupted flesh was plainly visible. The fight simply drained out of her. She let her hand drop and went limp, and both Maric and Duncan stepped carefully away from her.

"What *is* that?" Maric asked, staring at her hand in horror.

Genevieve grimaced. She walked over to where the gauntlet lay and picked it up. For a moment she said nothing, wiping off the hound's spittle and ignoring the fact that Hafter growled at her viciously from nearby. "It is the darkspawn taint," she said, almost too quietly to be heard.

"But . . ."

"It catches up with us all eventually, Maric."

Kell stepped forward, rubbing his chin where Genevieve's fist had connected. He seemed chagrined but not angry. With a gesture and a serious look, the hunter quieted Hafter, and then tugged one of his own leather gauntlets off and held up his hand. A stain was visible all along his forearm, much smaller than Genevieve's but still prominent. "I have it as well," he said flatly.

Utha rolled up a sleeve of her brown robe. A series of dark stains traveled up much of the length of her arm. She made several gestures and Kell nodded. "It began when we came into the Deep Roads," he said, "along with the dreams."

Genevieve looked disturbed, her brow furrowing as she glanced from Kell to Utha. "I thought it was just me," she muttered.

"If you had spoken to us, we would have told you."

There was little she could say in response to that. She stood there, looking lost and uncomfortable as a long moment of silence passed. Fiona shot Duncan a quizzical look and he shook his head vigorously. He didn't have the same stains, then. Neither did she, that she knew of. Yet.

"Why is this happening?" Fiona asked, breaking the silence. "Is it because we're so close to the darkspawn?"

Genevieve chewed on the idea. "There is no record of Grey Wardens being affected this way. I thought my time had simply come. Perhaps there is something else at work."

"Such as?"

The Commander said nothing, merely staring at the ground. Kell replaced his gauntlet and was similarly quiet. Utha merely frowned. They didn't know, she realized. It wasn't a comforting thought.

"Then perhaps there isn't a Blight at all," Duncan suggested. As the others looked at him, he nodded at the idea. "We don't know for sure that the darkspawn are behind this. They're just here in the Deep Roads. This could be something else entirely, you said so yourself."

Genevieve nodded hesitantly. "Still," she said, "something is very wrong here."

"But we do not know it involves the darkspawn," Kell murmured, "or the Blight. Surely our only mission is to prevent a Blight from occurring. If that is not what is happening . . ." He let the thought hang in the air, and the Grey Wardens exchanged disturbed glances.

"But there is a Blight," Maric announced.

Fiona looked at the man, and saw him shy away from the curious looks of the others. "I didn't want to tell you this," he said hesitantly, "but there is a reason I gave you an audience when you came to Denerim. There is a reason I believed you."

"And here I thought it was the Commander's charm," Duncan quipped.

Maric ignored him. "After my mother died, Loghain and I were lost in the Korcari Wilds trying to get away from the Orlesians," he began, his voice solemn. "We met an old woman, a witch who saved us. She gave me a warning. She told me that a Blight was coming to Ferelden." There was something more to his story, Fiona could see it. But he stopped there, snapping his mouth shut.

Genevieve pondered the tale, and looked at Maric curiously. "A witch hiding in the Wilds? And you believe what she said?"

"There were . . . other things she said that were true."

"Magic cannot see the future, Maric," Fiona told him.

"But there are visions. Mages can see them; you said so yourself." He let out a long, ragged breath. "I don't know if I trust her. I paid a high price for the witch's words, however, and it just seems like too much of a coincidence if it isn't true."

Fiona saw the shadow behind the man's eyes. She didn't know the full story of this witch, but she could see that its implications disturbed him. And he believed in what he had been told. But that was not so incredible, was it? Fiona believed in Genevieve's vision. They all did. It was not difficult to believe that at the root of these visions lay the Blight, warnings against the coming disaster.

Genevieve nodded firmly. Her conviction had returned redoubled; Fiona could see the zeal burning in her eyes. "This is no co-incidence," she declared. "We proceed with the mission. Carefully." The last she said with a sour glance at Kell.

He shook his head, frowning. "We are exhausted, Commander. You are exhausted. We have been through a great deal. Let us take a rest before we head below."

"But we are here! We must press on, quickly!"

"The brooches continue to hide us from the darkspawn," Kell said, pointing at the onyx brooch on his vest. "And we will need our strength. We rest here."

Genevieve stared at him as if he gone mad, but finally she relented. "If you insist," she said stiffly. Without another word, she marched over to the nearest wall and unslung her pack.

It seemed they were stopping after all.

The dream, when it came, was similar to the hundreds of dreams Fiona had suffered since she'd become a Grey Warden. Before, however, it had always felt as if she was looking on the dream from afar, hazy and easy to forget. Now it was crystal clear.

Fiona stood on a battlefield littered with dead men. All of them were soldiers in heavy armor, knights wearing the griffon standard of the order. Each had been brutally slaughtered. The smell of blood and decay hung thick and cloying in the air, the buzzing sound of flies nipping at her senses.

Overhead, the sky filled with an endless, roiling black cloud. It looked like ink spreading slowly in water, a great stain that blotted out the horizon. She had been told about this. The first sign of the Blight, said the Grey Wardens, is found in the clouds. When the mighty dragon rises, its corruption touches the world and spreads.

She was alone on that field of corpses. All alone. The wind picked up, a sickly breeze that carried with it the stench of carrion. A gloom fell upon her, and she stumbled as she watched something rise from out of the field of bodies nearby. It was enormous. A great, black *thing* that was as cold and terrible as anything she could have imagined.

Fear pulsed through her. Her heart raced, and she looked away. She didn't want to see it. She threw her hands up in front of her eyes not to see it. Yet still she felt it coming. Her foot caught between two corpses and made her fall back on top of them. Dead flesh pressed against her and still she covered her eyes. Still she felt the darkness surging ever closer to her.

It was coming. And it was coming for her.

Fiona screamed in terror—

—and then awoke. It took her a moment at first to realize where she was, and that the darkness was expected. The campfire had died down to small flames, offering only the faintest illumination. She could see someone lying on the other side of the fire, facing away from her and shrouded in shadow. Perhaps it was Kell? Hafter lay nearby, easily identifiable by his mound of fur and his heavy breathing. Otherwise the silence was almost oppressive, as if it was closing in around her from all sides.

"Are you all right?" a voice whispered behind her. It made her jump, and a gentle hand touched her shoulder to calm her down. "I'm sorry. I just heard you thrashing."

It was Maric. Her heart beat a little too fast for her liking and she sat up. Sweat covered her face and had soaked into the padding under her chain, making it uncomfortable and itchy. The man looked up at her from beside the fire, his eyes bleary with sleep and his blond hair askew. His normally silvery armor was now dull with dried blood and grime. "I'm fine," she whispered back. "I apologize for waking you," she added as an afterthought, and heard him settle back to sleep.

Fiona stared into the fire. Utha was also nearby, sleeping quietly, as was Duncan. Genevieve was obviously on watch, no doubt out there in the thick shadows that lurked not a foot away. The group seemed so few now. She clutched her arms around herself and shivered. She hadn't thought it was so cold down here before. Perhaps Duncan's complaints were finally getting to her.

She picked up her staff and very quietly stood, not wanting to disturb the others. Utha stirred in her slumber, shivering and pawing her hands at some invisible enemy.

Fiona could sympathize. What the others were going through, she couldn't even imagine. As they had retired, she had carefully inspected herself as well as she could without completely removing her armor and her skirt. She found no traces of the corruption on her skin, and that was a relief. Really, there shouldn't be any. She had been a Grey Warden only a little longer than Duncan— her Calling was so far away she shouldn't even have to think about such things. Yet in Genevieve's own words, some other force was at work here.

With a bit of concentration she willed her staff to glow. Not so brightly as to wake the others, but enough so she could see where she was stepping. She didn't want to travel far, just enough to get some breathing room. The dream awaited her if she went back to sleep, or perhaps other nightmares even worse. It was better to walk.

She stopped at the edge of the cluster of rubble that lay strewn over the ground in the crumbled passage. Farther on there was only more of the moist darkspawn filth, and she didn't want to touch that again. She had seen enough of the corruption to last a lifetime, and somewhere off in the far distance was that strange sound, the beautiful whispering.

She didn't want to listen to it, but couldn't help herself. She closed her eyes and tried to pick out what the whisper was saying. Was it a song? Was it a name? It almost seemed that it was calling out to her, stroking her soul ever so softly. . . .

Fiona heard someone approaching behind her and she jumped. She turned around to see Maric approaching cautiously. "You can't sleep either, I see," he whispered.

"I thought you could."

"No," he said. Then, more emphatically: "No, not at all."

"I wish I hadn't tried."

Maric removed his fur cloak and spread it on a part of the ground where the rubble was mostly absent. He seated himself on the edge, leaning against the wall and issuing a tired sigh. Then he looked over at her and offered her a seat on the other side. She hesitated only briefly, propping her staff up against the wall. She didn't need to maintain direct contact to keep it lit, after all.

They sat in silence for a time. Finally Maric turned to speak to her, but before he could say anything she interrupted him. "Thank you," she blurted out.

Maric paused, tilting his head a little to the side as if she had caught him completely off guard. "What for?"

"For coming to get me. Duncan tells me that you were the first one to break out of the trap, and that you insisted on finding me." It was a bit difficult for her to get the words out, considering how rude she had been to the man on several occasions now. If he would simply stop staring at her, this would be much easier. "How did you do it?" she asked him.

He shook his head as if clearing it, and stared at her in confusion. "How did I do what? Find you?"

"How did you break out of your dream?"

"Ah." He nodded soberly. "I promised you that I would repay you."

"And you always keep your promises?"

"I try. It was enough to remind me that I couldn't stay where I was, even if I wanted to. I knew I had to try to help you, if I could."

His sincerity was enough to move her. Tears welled up in her eyes, and she wiped them away quickly, feeling even more foolish.

She had completely misjudged the man, it seemed. All the expectations she had laid on him for being this king and this figure of legend, and it turned out he was simply a good man. How unexpected.

Maric glanced away, allowing her a moment to compose herself. "Thank you, then," she repeated. "I . . . didn't expect you to repay me this way, or any way, but it means a great deal."

He nodded slowly, and then turned back toward her. His demeanor was completely serious, and his gaze intense. "I wanted to speak to you," he said, "to tell you something. That man from your dream. I am not him. I know what you think of me, but I am not like that."

"I know."

"I don't know what he did to you, but . . ."

"I was a slave," she answered, as easily as she could. "The Count bought me from slavers when I was seven years old, and I was his pet until I was fourteen." The words came out in a rush, and she felt the flush crawl up her cheeks. She had never spoken of this to anyone. It was a part of her life she had buried, pushed down into shadows never to be thought of again. Yet she felt like she had to tell him. "What you saw, that was my life until I finally murdered him and escaped to the Circle."

Maric's eyes were wide with horror. "I don't know what to say."

"What is there to say?" She shrugged. "Slavery is illegal in the Empire, but it still goes on. Nobody pays attention if an elf disappears here or there. Nobody cares what happens to us in the alienage. Wealthy, powerful men like the Count get to do whatever they like, to whomever they like, so long as nobody cares."

"I'm sorry."

"No need to apologize. I was lucky. I had the talent for magic, a curse for every other person and yet for me it meant freedom. It meant an escape to the Circle, the lone elf in the tower, uneducated and frightened of anyone who even came near me." She grimaced at the memory. "The mages were just men, I discovered. Capricious and sad and bigoted just like everywhere else. I swore I wouldn't let them keep me, and I escaped them, too."

"To the Grey Wardens."

She nodded. "Some people look on becoming a Grey Warden as a duty. Maybe even a punishment. Duncan had to be forced. I *begged* to be recruited." The memory was an unpleasant one. The Joining ritual that had followed it was even more so. Drink the blood of darkspawn, they said, and if you survive it will only be for a time. You will be a Grey Warden until the Calling comes at last. And she had drunk it gladly. And she hadn't looked back.

They sat there on the cloak, staring out together into the shadows. Finally it was Maric who spoke. "My mother was killed in front of me," he said quietly. "I had to become the leader of her rebellion, something I felt completely unprepared for."

"You don't need to tell me this," she murmured.

"No, I do." He looked at her, his expression grim. "There was an elven woman named Katriel. A spy from Orlais that I fell in love with, and she with me. She saved my life, and yet when I found out what she was, I didn't give her a chance. I killed her."

"I didn't know about that."

He chuckled ruefully. "You must be the only one."

"Was she . . . the one in your dream?"

He nodded. "I would have done anything to take back that day. Yet I couldn't. I had to go on, because Ferelden needed me. I married a woman who was in love with my best friend, because Ferelden needed me. And when she died I kept going, despite the fact that everything in my life felt empty, because Ferelden needed me." He looked at her again, his eyes sad. "Everything was because Ferelden needed me."

"Why are you telling me this?"

"Everyone has nightmares, Fiona."

She felt Maric take her hand, and he squeezed it. She was drawn to him almost magnetically, and found herself leaning to give him a tentative kiss. She pulled away only a fraction afterwards. He looked as surprised as she did, though not displeased.

Then she leaned in again, more urgently, and their kiss had passion. She felt him breathing against her, and accepted his arms as they closed around her.

She wanted this. She wanted to be with a good man, and forget for just a moment about where they were, and what had happened to them. She needed a moment's solace, and she suspected he did, too. Pulling away from the heat of his touch, she tugged desperately at her chain mail, undoing the leather straps that held it down. She pulled at the padded undershirt, sighing with relief as she finally got it off.

Maric hesitated. "Fiona, I . . . perhaps we shouldn't . . ."

She ignored him, reaching over and undoing the straps that held his breastplate in place. He seemed pained, struggling with himself despite his obvious desire. "But what about the others?"

"I don't care."

"But . . . here?"

"Forget where we are." She pulled the breastplate over his head and he let her, staring helplessly. When it was done, she started working on the straps for his pauldrons, and after a moment's hesitation he began to help. They tugged and pulled and twisted until slowly they got his bulky, heavy armor off.

She untied his stained and soiled undershirt and removed it, unveiling bare skin. He was covered in bruises and cuts, as no doubt was she. His eyes were locked on her with an intensity that threatened to burn her up. The King was a handsome man; she had to give him that. But not all handsome men were also bad men.

"Are you certain?" he whispered, his breathing husky. "There are . . . bad memories for me down here. I don't know if . . ."

"Shhhhh," Fiona hushed him quietly, putting a finger to his lips. He stopped and looked at her with such an ache of loneliness it almost broke her heart. She slowly stroked his cheek. "I am tired of pain. So *tired*. Aren't you?"

His answer came as he leaned in, his kiss gentle as if he thought her fragile. And then another followed, and then another.

Damned be the darkness, she thought.

She let the light of the staff extinguish.

15

And so we burned. We raised nations, we waged wars,
We dreamed up false gods, great demons
Who could cross the Veil into the waking world,
Turned our devotion upon them, and forgot you.
—Canticle of Threnodies 1:8

Genevieve moved alone through the underground tunnels.

She used a torch to light her way initially, but as she progressed farther into darkspawn territory she found that more and more of the tunnels were lit by the phosphorescent lichen that lined the walls like mold. For all she knew, it could even *be* mold. Perhaps the corruption that coated the stone like slick bile had its own growths, its own process of decay. Whatever the source, the sickly green light in the tunnels was eventually strong enough that she could extinguish the torch and move through the shadows without it. She could save it for later.

If later came at all.

This was likely to be a one-way trip. That truth had been staring her in the face for some time now, but she had refused to acknowledge it. Abandoning the others was the right thing to do. Bregan was her brother, and it was she who insisted that he was alive. This was her responsibility. The talents of the others had been useful, but it was better if she did the rest on her own.

Kell would wake up to find her gone, and rightfully judge that it was better to abandon the mission and return to the surface. It would be a difficult ascent for the others, but Genevieve was confident they could do it. She was less confident that she would succeed in reaching her own goal.

But she had to believe. She felt Bregan out there, felt him just the same as she felt the darkspawn. Every now and again she would turn a corner in the tunnels and would feel her brother's presence on the edge of her senses, almost as if his scent had been carried to her somehow on an invisible wind. Why she felt him now when she had only dreamed of him before, she didn't know. Perhaps it was because she was so close. It burned under her skin, the knowledge that he was near enough to touch.

Dizziness overcame Genevieve and she paused, leaning against the rough-hewn stone walls for support. The dark mucus there smeared on the shoulder of her armor, but she barely noticed. That infernal song! The more she concentrated on trying to feel where her brother was, the louder it became, the more it infused itself inside her very mind. It was maddening, and yet she steeled herself against it. She could *not* let it overcome her now.

She had begun to hear it weeks ago, before they even arrived in Ferelden. The faintest whispers at first, an odd humming that she assumed was a residue of the powerful dreams. And then she realized what it was. Her time had come, just as it had come for Bregan.

They had taken their Joining together, so she had known that it would not be long in coming, but somehow she had assumed she would have more time. The Grey Wardens had elevated her to her brother's rank knowing that it was a temporary measure, something sure to last less than a year or two at best, yet still she had been determined to prove them wrong. All those years of living in her brother's shadow and finally it was her turn to lead, and then the whispers had come and ended even that.

She hadn't told anyone. The Grey Wardens had ignored her warnings about Bregan, at best suggesting that the order would need to prepare itself if what she said proved to be true. The possibility of preventing the calamity didn't even enter into their minds. Such fools. If she had told them of the whispers, then they would have leaped upon it as an excuse to send her into the Deep Roads—alone, and to die.

Genevieve wiped the sweat from her brow. She stared at her steel gauntlet and watched it shake. She felt weaker than she had in ages, like there was a thick poison loose in her blood. It made her skin itch and she wanted nothing more than to strip off her armor and scratch until she stripped the flesh from her bones.

There was no stopping now, however.

Banishing the fear that curled like a serpent in the pit of her stomach, she pushed herself away from the wall and began to walk. Her balance wavered, but by pure force of concentration she made herself place one foot in front of the other. *I have come this far*, she thought. *I will not be denied now. I will stop the Blight.*

For what seemed like endless hours she trudged through corruption and the mire, the dim greenish light of the lichen sometimes becoming a glare that sickened her and at other times becoming so faint that she was tempted to relight her torch. She moved through the shadows, stopping at every junction of the tunnels to listen and see if the feeling of Bregan would return again. She pressed her mind outward, feeling for anything, and yet all she heard now was that alluring song off in the distance.

Where were the darkspawn? At one point the creatures had been hounding their every step, and her Grey Warden senses could tell they lay in every direction even when they weren't actively on top of them. Then they lost them in the lower caverns and, what? They had simply vanished.

She found it difficult to believe. No matter how effective the brooches given to them by the First Enchanter were, that shouldn't change how darkspawn behaved. As soon as the creatures got a hint of their intrusion, the activity should have built until the Deep Roads were buzzing like an angry beehive. Losing their prey should have only increased their exertions. The idea that the darkspawn might be looking in completely the wrong direction, and only there, was too bizarre.

Something was not as it should be. She felt frustration as she realized she was missing an important piece of the puzzle. What was making the darkspawn act so strangely? Assuming Bregan had indeed been taken captive, why do that now when they had never once done so in all the centuries the Grey Wardens had sent elder members of their order to the Calling?

Unless they had. Those who went to their Calling were never heard from again. What if they had been sent into the darkspawn's arms, and not to their deaths at all? Yet the order claimed it knew, and she had to believe.

The rocky passage opened up slowly, and she noticed smoother walls now. Architecture. Dwarven handiwork. The tunnels had circled around to an older part of the Deep Roads, then. Here the statues seemed to be absent, the craftsmanship less precise, the lava flows missing. What was it, then? The Deeper Roads? She had never heard of such a thing.

Almost without warning, she received a sense of darkspawn approaching. She tightened her grip on her greatsword and waited. Why hadn't she detected them sooner? Had they found some way to mask themselves from Grey Warden senses, just as the brooches masked the group from them? A sobering thought, to be certain.

She inched forward, sweat beading on her forehead. As her eyes tried vainly to pierce the shadows, watching for an attack, she realized that there was only a single creature coming. A lone stray, then? A forager, perhaps, unable to sense her through the brooch's cloaking?

She had to kill it quickly. Slay it before it became aware of her and she might be able to avoid alerting the horde that inevitably lay in wait.

Genevieve moved to the side of the tunnel, pressing against the wall behind a stone support pillar. It was hardly large enough to hide her, but the darkness shrouded her here. These creatures could see far better in the dark than humans could, but they were not immune to it.

Her heart thundered in her chest as she waited. She peered around the pillar, waiting for the darkspawn to show itself. The minutes passed. Sweat dripped off her forehead and ran into her eyes, but she ignored it.

Soon her patience paid off. A figure appeared in the distance, just barely discernible against the green haze of the lichen. It shuffled toward her, its raspy breathing clear in the vast and empty silence. A hurlock, then, she noted from its size. She readied her sword. Even a hurlock could be killed in a single blow if she was quick.

She pressed as flat against the wall as she could, stifling her own breathing and listening for the faint sounds of the creature's steps. It came closer . . . and closer. The crunch of a piece of nearby stone underneath its foot signaled the moment to attack. She stepped out from behind the pillar, preparing for the silent swing—

"Genevieve."

It was Bregan. He stood there in front of her, and she knew it was him even though he wore a black suit of darkspawn armor and was so covered with diseased flesh he could very well have passed for one of the creatures. His white hair was gone, and his eyes had reddened until they were the color of blood, but it was him.

She stopped in midswing, howling in dismay. Andraste's mercy, what had *happened* to him?

"Bregan?" she asked, disbelieving.

He nodded. He seemed calm, and those bloodred eyes flicked to her sword with interest. Genevieve lowered the blade and then dropped it to the ground. It landed with a dull clatter. Should she kill him? The knowledge he possessed needed to die with him, but what if he had already given it away? What if there was something he could tell her?

Looking at what he had become, part of her wondered if she should kill him even so. Her brother had sacrificed everything for her, even a semblance of a life. Could she do any less for him?

"We have kept the darkspawn away, for a time," he said. "I knew you would come, and I wanted you to arrive safely."

"Who is 'we'? Bregan, what has *happened* to you?"

He stepped toward her and took her arms gently in his hands. Both enthralled and horrified by those eyes, she was unable to look away. Of all the things she had imagined upon reaching Bregan, the idea that he wasn't some unwilling captive was not one of them. The idea that he might have turned into some . . . monster . . . was even worse.

"This is what we become," he said. "If you wait long enough, the taint spreads within you and becomes this."

"That's horrible!"

"No, this is freedom!" Bregan shook her emphatically. "We have a chance, Genevieve. A chance to do what no Grey Warden has ever done. We can *end the Blights forever!*"

The words sank in only slowly, and as she realized what he was saying she looked at him in puzzlement. "End the Blights? How?"

"It requires a sacrifice. A large sacrifice. But we have to be willing to make it." He seemed so resolute, his tone so certain. "Please, if you come with me, we can explain it to you."

"Are there other Wardens here?"

"There is a darkspawn emissary." He put up a finger to silence her as he felt her tense in response. "I know what you are thinking, and I thought the same, but he is not like any darkspawn I have ever seen. He is something different, an ally. Come, listen to him speak. That is all I ask."

"Have you gone mad?"

Bregan seemed to consider the question. He released her arms, and Genevieve stepped back, her mind whirling with questions. Maybe *she* was the one who had gone mad. Of all the times for it to happen, the strange music off in the distance swelled and pressed in on her mind. She tensed and fought it off. She had to know what this was, what had happened to her brother.

"Perhaps," he pondered. "I don't know."

She ran to him and took one of his hands in hers. His skin was cold and clammy, but she ignored it, looking pleadingly into his eyes. "Bregan, we have to get you away from here! Before something terrible happens!"

"And go where?" he asked. When she had no answer, he chuckled. It was a mirthless, cold sound. "Where could I go that I would not be killed instantly on sight by anyone who saw me? Where could you go?" He gently tugged on her gauntlets. She let him do it. They came off and revealed the stains of corruption below. "We are dead, Genevieve. Dead the moment we drank the blood in the Joining, in the name of stopping these Blights by any means necessary. That is the Grey Warden way, isn't it? And here we have our chance."

"But . . ."

"Did you actually come here to save me?" Bregan released her hands and she jerked them away, hiding them behind her back. "All this way, through darkspawn and who knows what else, to bring me home?"

"I came to stop you." She frowned, her calm returning to her by inches. "I came to prevent a Blight from occurring."

"Then prevent it." He held out a tainted, withered hand to her. She stared at it dispassionately, wondering if that was truly the fate that awaited her. Had the ancient Grey Wardens known that? Had this happened before, she wondered, and this was why they created the Calling? Death seemed like it would almost be preferable.

But she had to know. The order had a noble cause, one that had saved countless lives and would save countless more. She had wanted to be a Grey Warden since long before the recruiter even came to her village—and what if there was something to what Bregan said? Stopping the Blights. Forever. That was worth a sacrifice, was it not?

Genevieve took Bregan's hand. She was shaking like a leaf, and couldn't force herself to stop. "What . . . what about the others?" she asked hesitantly.

"I can't make promises about them."

"Are you certain this can be done, Bregan?"

He grinned, displaying teeth that were stained and eerily sharper than she had ever remembered them being. Like dark-spawn teeth. "I'm not certain about anything anymore," he said.

And then he led her away, down the tunnel and into the darkness as the distant music swelled into a chorus that drowned out everything else.

The group woke up only to discover that Genevieve had vanished during the night. It was not difficult to guess where she had gone. Kell cursed himself for a fool for even agreeing to her suggestion of standing watch, though Maric had other ideas on that front. She had left them asleep and unguarded. Anything could have come upon them in the night and slain them all—and for what? So she could follow her obsessive drive to locate her brother. He wasn't even convinced that this was truly about stopping the Blight, not to her.

But the others still believed. Duncan in particular seemed most aggravated by Genevieve's departure, storming about the campsite and ranting about how stupid she could be. It was an odd way to talk about one's commanding officer, Maric had to admit, and he wondered just what had occurred between the two of them inside her dream.

Utha watched the lad pace, and then indicated that they needed to follow after Genevieve. The others said nothing at first, staring at each other awkwardly, and Maric realized what they were thinking. Chasing after their commander was a Grey Warden concern. Indeed, even if they still thought that stopping the coming Blight was a possibility, that, too, was their concern—but not his. Maric had already performed his task, and they couldn't reasonably ask the King of Ferelden to follow them into what looked like certain death.

He looked at Fiona then, and found her studiously avoiding his gaze. He had woken up alone, and they hadn't exchanged words since. In fact, she said very little. The elf didn't seem angry, as far as he could tell. Perhaps she was simply trying to pretend it hadn't happened, or that it had been a moment of solace and nothing more. Perhaps he had spoken too much of Katriel. He had lain with his former elven love, too, in these Deep Roads; it was impossible not to see the comparison.

He told the Wardens that he would go with them, of course. There was no turning back now, any more than there had been after slaying the dragon. They were past the point of no return. Whether or not he believed in the witch's warning, he was committed to this path.

So they descended. Fiona led the way with her staff shining brilliantly in the greenish shadows, and they moved as swiftly as they could. The looks on the Wardens' faces told him everything he needed to know: The darkspawn had returned. Even he could hear the faint sounds of their approach, the distant droning hum getting louder by the minute.

"How long do we have?" he asked Kell.

The hunter stared intently off into the shadows, his pale eyes glinting dangerously. He unslung his bow from his shoulders and drew an arrow. Hafter growled angrily at his feet, hackles raised. Duncan drew his silverite daggers, grimacing as he, too, watched for an unseen enemy.

"It won't be long now," the lad murmured to him.

"So quickly? Where did they all come from?"

"I don't know. They're ahead and behind us."

"Is there a way to get around them?"

Duncan said nothing. Instead the group began to run. Fiona raised her staff and cast a spell of protection, a blue glow settling over each of them. Their urgent pace quickened as they reached an intersection of passages. Three directions availed themselves, each of them leading into more shadows and greenish haze.

Kell waved to them to stop, and keenly peered down each passage in turn. Maric's hand tensed on his sword, his heart thrilled with fear. The others formed a defensive position almost immediately, turning their backs to Kell and facing outward, weapons at the ready. The alien hum of the darkspawn seemed to surround them.

"They are down every passage." The hunter frowned ponderously. Hafter growled at the shadows, baring his fangs, and Kell absently reached down to soothe the hound with a gentle pat.

"So where do we go? Which way?" Duncan demanded.

Utha pointed directly ahead, and Kell nodded. "Yes. We cannot stay here. We need to find a more defensible position, for they are coming to us no matter which way we go."

"How did Genevieve get past them?" Fiona asked, frustration mounting in her voice.

The hunter ran ahead, not answering the question, and the rest of them followed quickly on his heels. It was possible that Genevieve hadn't gotten by them at all, Maric thought. She could be dead already, and they would never know. What he really wondered was how the darkspawn seemed to suddenly zero in on them so effectively when the Wardens were supposedly hidden by the onyx brooches they wore. Something was not right.

They raced ahead down the new passage, evidence of rubble appearing amid the darkspawn filth. Ancient statues lined the rocky walls here, most of them so crumbled and covered in blackness that they could barely be recognized as such. Had the dwarves existed even here beneath the Deep Roads? There was no time to stop and admire the scenery, however. They ran, breathing hard from exertion and panic. Maric stumbled on a patch of uneven rock and Utha darted in to steady him before he fell. He nodded his thanks to her and kept going.

The passage opened up into a cavern, and they immediately slowed. A structure fully filled half the chamber, a wide set of stairs flanked by tall statues leading up to a massive dais lined with tall pillars. The rocky wall behind the dais had been carved into a great, vaulted arch. Once this had been an impressive sight, perhaps a temple honoring some ancient dwarven deity, but now it was blackened with decay and corruption. So much of it lined the floor leading up to the stairs that it had gathered into black clusters, twisted sacs as large as a man. The clusters hung from the ceiling as well, slowly oozing filth down to the ground, where it collected in stagnant green pools.

Kell pointed to the dais. "We make our stand there." They didn't argue and began running up the flight of stairs. The filth was deep enough here that it enveloped Maric's boots and made a wet, sucking sound each time he pulled them free. The rancid stench stirred up by their movements was overpowering.

There was some kind of altar at the top of the dais, simple and flat and only as high as Maric's waist. At least he assumed it had been an altar. Now it was so covered by a bubbling, festering mass that he didn't even want to get close to it.

The group spun on their heels immediately, forming a defensive line at the top of the stairs and looking down on the cavern below them. All Maric could hear was their ragged breathing and the droning hum of the approaching horde. There was a hunger to it, the sound rising and falling almost rhythmically. Fiona raised her staff up high and it began to glow with such a dazzling brilliance, the entire cavern was lit up. Maric almost thought he could detect the horrified cringing of the corrupted foulness down there. Indeed, a faint hissing noise erupted from the chamber, and some of the tainted clusters exploded in a display of dark green goo.

Hafter began to bark furiously, but quieted at a gesture from Kell. Utha exchanged a dubious glance with the hunter and he nodded to her with a hint of a smile. He reached out and stroked her cheek fondly, the hound looking up at the action and blinking in surprise. Utha clutched his hand and held it to her cheek for a moment, her eyes moist, and then she let it drop.

Fiona glanced at the pair and then turned back to face the cavern, her expression resolute. "We're not done yet," she vowed.

"Sure looks that way," Duncan muttered.

Kell turned to him, studying the lad thoughtfully. "You need to leave us here, Duncan. Let us battle these creatures while you slip away."

"Slip away?"

"You are adept at moving through the shadows. Alone, you could possibly evade the coming horde. You could find Genevieve, if she lives, or even her brother."

"I think you overestimate my sneaking abilities," he snorted.

"You should try," Fiona said. "We don't know how many of these creatures are coming. Someone has to finish our mission, if it can even be done."

"I'm not leaving you here," he insisted stubbornly. "I'm not going anywhere."

"And if I ordered you?" Kell asked.

"Then I guess I would have to disobey."

The hunter grinned. "Then I suppose I won't do that."

They turned back toward the cavern and waited. The humming of the darkspawn grew louder and louder, and then the first ones spilled into the chamber. Several short genlocks bounded in, followed by a hurlock in massive black armor and carrying a deadly looking spiked sword. It hissed up at the dais, and the genlocks joined in, stopping and hissing with displeasure upon sighting their quarry.

An arrow sped across the air and struck the hurlock between its eyes. It collapsed without a sound. The genlocks roared and charged. More arrows flew and the darkspawn stumbled to the ground, dead before they even reached the stairs.

"I am running out of arrows," the hunter announced, drawing his bow again.

"I'm running out of clean smallclothes," Duncan responded.

More darkspawn surged into the cavern now, coming from both entrances. It was a wave of them, their humming filling the entire chamber and drowning out every other sound. Kell carefully fired arrows into the mass, and though each strike sent a creature squealing to the ground, it was clearly not going to be enough.

Fiona pointed her staff at them, her brow furrowing in concentration as a fireball issued forth and hurtled to the bottom of the stairs beneath them. The flaming sphere detonated at the front of the darkspawn ranks, sending the creatures flying and filling the cavern with a flash of magical flame. The creatures let out ear-splitting squeals of anguish, many of them engulfed completely and flailing as they fell to the ground on fire. The flames spread to the oozing filth that covered the cavern floor, and suddenly the ground itself was burning, smoke rapidly filling the air.

Maric was impressed. "How many more of those do you have in you?" he asked her. No answer was forthcoming as the elf swooned and fell backwards. He rushed forward and caught her, his heart jumping as he noted how pale she already was, sweat pouring down her brow.

She blinked rapidly and pushed herself back to her feet. "A few more," she gritted out. The darkspawn ignored their burning comrades, leaping over them and rushing through the flames even as they got seared. More arrows rapidly struck those at the front. Fiona let out a scream of effort and a second fireball launched itself into the darkspawn ranks, the blast sending a wave of heat and charred stench past Maric.

More were already pushing their way into the cavern, though it was getting difficult to see through the flames and the smoke. He coughed and blinked his eyes at the haze. It seemed the dwarven ventilation ducts were simply not as good here—or, more likely, they were gummed up with the same filth that covered everything else.

So be it. Better to suffocate than die at the hands of these monsters, if need be.

He darted forward as the first hurlock raced up the steps, its flesh scorched black and its translucent eyes filled with raw hatred. He knocked its blade aside with his own and then spun around, beheading the creature in one clean stroke. Ichor fountained from the stump, splattering over his armor, but he ignored it.

More darkspawn were already racing toward him. An arrow whizzed by his ear from behind, striking one of the creatures and sending it tumbling down the stairs. He lifted his sword and charged. With the more heavily armored Grey Wardens either dead or gone, it fell to Maric to hold the front line as best he could. If only the stairs were narrower.

Another fireball passed over his head as he met the first darkspawn blade, parrying it with a shower of sparks. He didn't see the blast of flame as the fireball hit its target in the distance, but the wave of sound and searing heat was almost enough to knock him back. Several of the darkspawn in front of him fell; he used the opportunity to plunge his sword into the back of one of their necks.

Thick smoke billowed into his face and he gagged, and then fell back as a genlock in spiked, tattered plate armor leaped at him and slammed into his chest. Maric grunted in pain as his head hit the stairs, and he watched with horror as the genlock gleefully reared up with its club and prepared to bring it down upon his head.

Utha tackled it, flying right over Maric. All he saw was a flash of brown robes and her long, coppery braid, and the creature was torn off of him. He jumped up just in time to see the dwarf striking down with her fist into the genlock's face beneath her, crushing its snout and sending both ichor and fangs splattering in all directions. Without pausing, she spun and kicked a charging hurlock in its chest and sent it hurtling back down the stairs.

More arrows flew overhead. Maric quickly raised his sword to defend himself as a pale-skinned hurlock attacked out of nowhere. It brought its large blade down in an overhand strike that he was only barely able to parry. The force of the blow rang through his shoulders. Grunting with effort, he pushed the darkspawn's blade up and off his own and then thrust the pommel into its forehead. Bone gave way with a sickening crunch and it squealed in pain, falling to the ground.

Duncan rushed at two hurlocks that attempted to race by Maric on the stairs, their swords raised as they hissed in rage. One of his silverite daggers slashed across the throat of one and it fell back, clutching at the gushing wound. The other hurlock swung its sword down, roaring, but he easily danced aside.

Dropping into a crouch, Duncan sliced the creature across its shins with his second dagger. The blade cut deep into its bones, and it stumbled to the ground with an angry squeal. Barely pausing, the young Grey Warden leaped up into the air and brought both his daggers to bear with a flourish. He landed on top of the darkspawn with a war cry, plunging both the daggers into the monster's head. It spasmed once and then was still.

Then another wave of darkspawn was upon Maric and he

couldn't see anything other than the opponents directly in front of him. He swung his longsword in wide arcs in front of him, less concerned with artistry than just forcing the creatures back down the steps. The blue runes on his blade were glowing more brilliantly than he had ever seen them before, and it seemed to make the darkspawn reel back the moment they came too near.

Acrid smoke got into his eyes. The foul stench of burned flesh threatened to overwhelm him. He sliced off the sword hand of a hurlock, sending its weapon flying, and then kicked it hard in its armored breastplate. Screaming, it fell back down the stairs, knocking several others down on its way and ending up impaled on the spear of one of its own comrades.

The stairs had become littered with darkspawn corpses, and enough of the creatures had reached the dais that it was becoming crowded and chaotic. Sweat poured down his face, his breathing labored from the thin air. He glanced over to see Kell not far away, his flail whipping around him in circles, its spiky head tearing out darkspawn throats. Hafter fought at his side, his fangs dripping black ichor and his fur matted with red blood that must have been his own.

Maric was wounded, as well. He felt the puncture in his thigh left by a spear that had managed to bypass his guard, and it was slowing him down. Even so, he couldn't stop. He swung his sword hard at a genlock that attempted to race past him, cutting it down. Then he spun about and impaled another genlock that raced at him with black blade raised high.

Where was Fiona? He looked around frantically for a sign of the mage, but saw nothing but chaotic fighting. He caught a glimpse of Utha fighting nearby, grimacing with determination and splattered in black ichor, but there was too much smoke and chaos for him to see much farther. He should have stayed closer to Fiona. He should have guarded her instead of rushing ahead.

Maric paused as he heard a new sound over the din: a guttural

DRAGON AGE: THE CALLING 353

roar, deeper and louder than anything he'd heard previously. He looked down the stairs and saw another creature appear. It was a massive, muscled thing with blue skin and twisted black horns, almost demonic looking. It spotted Maric and uttered a furious bellow, displaying razor-sharp fangs and emitting a spray of thick spittle.

"Ogre!" he heard Kell shout with alarm from nearby.

The creature raced up the stairs, overrunning its own darkspawn comrades and swinging its meaty fists to bash them out of its way. It had its milky-white eyes set on one target: Maric. Two hurlocks in front of him tried to get out of its way, but the ogre was impatient. It stepped on one, crushing it underfoot with a sickening crunching noise, and slapped the other aside so hard it went flying and slammed against the wall of the cavern.

Maric braced himself as the creature charged, leveling his blade in front of him and staring intensely. It roared another challenge and swung a massive fist down at him. He rolled to the side, barely avoiding the strike, and came up on his feet without taking his eyes off the creature. Chunks of stone flew from the stairs; a large crack was left behind. The ogre paused and turned its horned head toward him, glaring as if suddenly aware Maric would not be such an easy kill.

The creature ran at him and swiped repeatedly with its taloned hands. Any one of those strikes could tear his head off, he thought. He ducked under the first swipe and then rolled forward to avoid the second, slashing at the ogre's legs as he passed. The blade cut easily through the creature's thick blue hide, black ichor spitting from the wound.

The ogre twisted about to try to grab at Maric again. He only barely avoided its grasp, rolling to one side once more. More smoke drifted by his face and made his eyes water, but he kept the creature in sight.

Letting out an ear-splitting bellow, the creature reared up and then brought its fists down onto the steps below it with incredible force. The impact sent out a shockwave that shook the entire structure, and Maric was thrown onto his back. His ears rang from the sound, and as he shook his head he suddenly saw that the blue giant was above him.

It snatched him up in its meaty grip, easily hoisting him aloft. Maric still held on to his sword, but it was now locked at his side along with his arms. He struggled, but the creature only squeezed him until his armor dug into his flesh. The pain of his bones crushing together was unbearable and he screamed.

When he opened his eyes, he was eye to eye with the ogre. He saw every ridge on its twisted horns, every vein on its bluish hide. It grinned wickedly, the rotten carrion stench of its breath filling Maric's nostrils.

It could rip my head off with those fangs, he thought. *Or just crush me into a pulp. Not a bad way to die. Far better than, say, slipping on a puddle or eating a chicken leg the wrong way.*

He clamped his eyes shut, waiting for the inevitable. Suddenly a peal of thunder rang throughout the cavern and a bolt of lightning struck the ogre directly in the chest. Maric felt the heat of it, felt himself deafened by the wave of force and sound, and flew out of the ogre's hand as it was propelled backwards. It roared in pain as Maric tumbled to the stairs, falling awkwardly on one leg and wrenching it badly. Agony burned through him. He would have kept falling down the stairs had there not been a great number of darkspawn corpses already there to stop him.

Maric groaned, unable to move, and watched as the ogre slowly got back up to its feet. The scorch mark left by the lightning bolt covered much of its chest, still sizzling and smoking. It glared angrily toward the top of the stairs where Fiona stood, smoke still curling from the end of her staff. She looked like an elven goddess of vengeance, streaked with ichor and soot, her teeth bared in fury.

"That's right!" she shouted. "Come and get me, you blue bastard!"

The ogre roared up at her in response, bringing both its fists down upon the steps beneath it. The ground shook from the blow, and at first Maric didn't realize what it was doing. Then he saw: It was digging its talons into the stone. With a great wrenching groan, the ogre ripped up a large piece of masonry from the stairs, leaving an impressive gap. Stone chunks flew off, one large enough to crush Maric's head bouncing on a step not a foot away.

With a bellow of effort the creature heaved the masonry boulder up at Fiona. She lifted her staff, shouting as she summoned another spell. A white flare burned around her staff as another lightning bolt lanced forth from it, striking the boulder in mid-flight. With a resounding crack that filled the cavern, the boulder shattered into a cloud of dust and a thousand shards that flew in every direction.

Fiona stumbled backwards, pale and weakened, and the ogre began a lumbering charge up the stairs toward her. Maric pulled himself up to his feet, his leg burning with agony. He ignored it and began to race up the steps after the creature, taking two or three at a time.

The ogre got to the top of the stairs, towering over the mage. Though she held up her staff and made a feeble attempt to summon a spell, there were only swirls of light around her and nothing more. The ogre roared in victory.

Maric reached the ogre from behind and, shouting a loud war cry, he raced up the creature's large back, allowing his speed to carry him. He plunged the dragonbone longsword between its shoulder blades, the enchanted blade thrusting through thick hide and bone. He bore down on the hilt with his weight, pushing it even deeper until the sword shook from the effort.

A gush of cold ichor erupted from the wound, splattering on Maric's face. The creature squealed in torment, arching its back and clutching at the air with its taloned fingers. It tried vainly to reach for the impaled sword, twisting about frantically. Maric attempted to hold on, but the hilt was slick with ichor and he lost his grip. Tossed aside, he landed on the dais, his head cracking forcefully against the stone.

The ogre arched back even farther, screeching and trying to get at the source of its anguish. Maric could see the tip of his sword jutting from the front of its chest. Slowly it teetered back, and then toppled. It crashed heavily to the stairs and then began to tumble down to the bottom, picking up speed as it went.

A cloud of smoke surged across his vision, stinging his eyes. He could feel the heat of nearby flames, hear the sizzle and pop of the darkspawn corruption as it burned. He heard Hafter barking loudly somewhere off in the distance, and then Duncan shouted. He couldn't see anything at all. There was a ringing sound, too, and Maric realized it was his head. It throbbed dully and he couldn't move.

"Maric!"

It was Fiona's voice. He discovered that he had closed his eyes. The sounds of battle suddenly seemed very distant, as if they were happening somewhere else and not quite relevant. A sense of weakness and peace descended over him. His eyes fluttered open to find the mage looking down at him. Her face was pale with exhaustion, her short black hair coated in ichor that dripped down across her forehead. She was holding him in her arms, and he felt blood oozing from his head. She looked so frightened, he thought.

He wanted to comfort her, but couldn't. His hand felt leaden and not quite under his control, and while he tried to reach up to her, he missed her completely.

"Maric! You need to get up!" Fiona shouted frantically. Then her attention was drawn by something he couldn't see. She stared off, dread filling her eyes as the darkspawn humming suddenly got much louder. It filled the entire cavern, and Maric could almost picture another wave of darkspawn piling in from both passages.

"That's too bad," he muttered. "I'd hoped we'd gotten them all."

"There's no end to them." She looked weary, the fight all but gone out of her as she watched the darkspawn horde's inevitable approach. Kell yelled somewhere far off, and Hafter howled in pain.

He stared up at her and smiled wanly. Somehow it didn't seem so terrible. He felt bad for young Cailan, but he knew that Loghain would do right by the boy. Far better than he could ever have. He had felt a hollowness for so long, an emptiness that just grew worse with each passing year.

Yet here, lying in her arms, Maric felt strangely content. He looked up at Fiona's face and thought only how beautiful she was. Those dark eyes had seen so much suffering. He wanted to tell her that there was no more need to be frightened, that everything would be all right now.

And then a wave of magic struck them, a power colder than anything Maric had felt before. His vision clouded into a pure white, and then he sank into darkness. The only thing he found himself regretting was that he was alone.

16

Blessed are they who stand before
The corrupt and the wicked and do not falter.
Blessed are the peacekeepers, the champions of the just.
　　　　　　　　　—Canticle of Benedictions 4:10

"Duncan."

The word penetrated Duncan's brain only slowly, and it took him a moment to realize that he was gradually coming out of unconsciousness. Inch by inch he crawled up out of the fuzzy haze of pain that enveloped him. He remembered fighting. He remembered the ogre charging into the cavern, and then being overwhelmed by the endless waves of darkspawn. A spear had stabbed through his gut, gone right through him and out the other side. He remembered the blinding pain, the blood bubbling up out of his mouth and the creatures leaping atop him. And then—

—he started awake, sitting up far too fast. The pounding in his head became excruciating agony. He winced, pressing his hands to the sides of his head as if that might prevent his brain from exploding. That's certainly what it felt like was going to happen, anyhow. That's also when he noticed there were heavy iron manacles on his wrists.

"What the blasted . . . ," he muttered.

"Not so fast," the voice cautioned him. "We're all wounded."

Still pressing on his head, Duncan opened his eyes slowly. There was light in the small chamber, a harsh orange glow emanating from a strange amulet that hung near the door. It was enough to make his head throb, and he looked away into the shadows.

The voice was correct about one thing: He was bandaged. He could feel the thick bandages around his chest, all stuffed with some kind of material that felt warm and itchy at the same time. There were other strips of cloth wrapped around one shoulder and his left thigh, injuries he didn't even remember receiving even though they pulsated painfully enough now. The cloth used for the bandages looked yellowed and suspect. Best not to examine them too closely.

"How are you feeling?"

The concerned voice was Fiona's. He blinked several times, getting used to the amulet's glow, and saw her sitting next to him. The elf looked quite a fright, her hair matted with dried ichor and her chain shirt not only splattered but possessing several gaping holes. Her skirts were tattered and filthy. She, too, was manacled as he was, their restraints connected by rusty chains to a stone wall behind them.

The others looked no better. He could make out Kell in the dim light, one of his legs heavily bandaged and little left of his leather jerkin other than a tattered vest. Yellowed cloths covered much of his upper chest, dark stains seeping through in two spots. Hafter slept next to him, the hunter stroking the hound's head absently. The dog was unbandaged, but his fur was covered by enough wet, reddish areas that he was likely wounded as well.

Utha sat beside him with her arms around her knees. She had several cuts on her face, and her brown robes were almost black with blood and soot. The dwarf didn't look pleased, he thought, and she grimly examined her manacles as if she could find some way to break them open just with the intensity of her gaze.

King Maric was lying on the floor on the other side of Duncan. He was still unconscious, his head covered with a thick bandage soaked through by an alarming amount of blood. His silverite armor was dull and black, and covered in so many splatters of ichor and blood, he couldn't really tell if the man was injured anywhere else.

They were in a cell. A single, long chamber with stone walls and chains attached to the wall with solid-looking pitons. The amount of corruption covering the wall was extensive, tendrils spidering out in every direction, and he was glad the deep shadows hid most of it. The air was musty, heavy with the smell of blood and layered with an insidious foulness that crept inside him every time he breathed.

"Duncan, how are you feeling?" Fiona repeated. "You look confused."

"I am," he muttered. "How did we get here?"

"I don't know." She looked around the cell, her gaze lingering on the stone door. "We can't reach the door to test if it's locked, and with my hands bound I can't cast."

"You can't cast at all?"

"Nothing that would help us out of here." Her eyes flicked to Maric beside him, her face filling with anxious concern. "Can you please check Maric? He hasn't stirred, and I can't reach him."

Duncan turned toward the man, lugging his manacles closer—they were heavy—and pressed his fingers to the man's neck. There was definitely a pulse, weak as it was. "He's alive."

She breathed a sigh of relief. Kell glanced at both of them, frowning. "The song is very loud here, is it not?" he said.

"What song?" Duncan asked. He didn't hear anything at all; the cell was completely silent save for their breathing. He could sense the presence of darkspawn all around them, a whole sea of them almost right outside the door. Was there no end to these creatures?

Fiona looked at him archly. "You really don't hear it?"

"Hear what? There's no song."

She glanced at Kell. "I hear it very faintly, like something off in the distance. I thought maybe it was the darkspawn, but now I'm not so sure."

"It's the Calling," he said solemnly. Fiona stared at him, stunned, and Duncan felt the same way. The Calling? There's no way Fiona should be hearing that already, surely! Utha made several gestures at the hunter and he nodded. "I don't think it's just because we're down here, either. Something is happening to us." He indicated the spreading corruption over the visible parts of his chest and arms. There was a lot of it. If Duncan had seen the man walking down some street, he would have expected children to be throwing stones at him and calling him a leper, if not worse.

Horror dawned on Fiona's face. She raised her manacles and let one of her chain sleeves fall to reveal her bare arm. It was covered in several long scratches, and bloodied, but the corruption was clearly visible. It wasn't as extensive as Kell's, but it was there.

"I checked not even a day ago! This wasn't like that!"

"We are corrupting from within," Kell agreed. "Far more quickly than we should be." Utha beside him merely nodded grimly, turning back to stare at her manacles.

Duncan twisted himself around to try to look at what bare skin of his own he could. There wasn't much. Some of the leather straps covering his arms had come loose, but not enough for the armor to peel away, and while his trousers were ripped, the bit of skin underneath was too covered in dried blood for him to tell anything. His hands, however, were clear. "I don't see anything," he announced nervously. "And I don't hear anything, either."

Fiona shrugged. "You were the last of us to take the Joining."

That wasn't exactly reassuring. His Joining had been only months behind Fiona's, while hers had been many years behind Kell's and Utha's.

"So this is where darkspawn keep their prisoners, huh?" he asked, hoping to change the subject. "Do they have executioners? Are they going to come and question us?"

Utha made a rude gesture and Kell frowned at her. "He doesn't know," he gently reprimanded her. Looking back at Duncan, he answered. "They don't keep prisoners. The Grey Wardens know that the darkspawn are capable of simple industry, but they don't seem to care about questioning us or finding our plans. They aren't the most subtle creatures."

"Hate to contradict you, but we sure look like prisoners."

"I know." His pale eyes narrowed as he considered the matter, troubled. "I had hoped Genevieve might be here," he muttered.

Time passed slowly. Their weapons had been stripped from them, as had their packs, so there was nothing to eat and the store of healing poultices that Fiona had brought were now uselessly in darkspawn hands. Occasionally strange sounds would come from far off, loud ringing noises as if something was pounding against metal, and then a great groaning. They heard the darkspawn, too, hissing and moving about. It was faint, but they were definitely out there and leaving them alone, for whatever reason.

Maric stirred, in time. He groaned at first, and at Fiona's urging Duncan checked his bandages and ascertained that whatever muck was underneath them seemed to be working. The man's bleeding had stopped. Duncan gently shook his shoulder until he opened his eyes.

It took a minute of blinking before he finally turned his head and looked directly at Duncan. His eyes looked a bit unfocused, and he seemed confused. "Cailan?" he groaned.

Duncan chuckled. "Unless your son looks nothing like you, no."

More blinking. "Duncan?"

"There you go."

Sitting up was a slow process for him, and the same questions followed that Duncan had asked before. Fiona seemed relieved to see that Maric was awake, at least, and with the passing minutes he seemed to get stronger and stronger. "What was that spell at the end?" he muttered. "Who cast that?"

"It was an emissary," Fiona answered. "I didn't see it, however."

"They're the ones that can talk, right? Well, if we're lucky we'll see it eventually."

More time passed, and they took turns getting some sleep. Not that any of them rested much. The cell was cold, and their injuries ached. Duncan wanted nothing less than to rip off those bandages and whatever itchy mixture was applied to his skin beneath them. If darkspawn had truly mixed it together, he didn't want it on him. He could only imagine what it was actually doing, mixing with his blood. The idea made him want to vomit.

Eventually there were new sounds. They perked up as footsteps approached the door. *More than one set*, Duncan thought to himself. Three creatures, at least. Definitely darkspawn, as he could sense their taint. The door swung open with a loud, wrenching sound—though he didn't hear a key turning at all. Not locked, then? An odd cell, to be sure.

The first darkspawn who walked through the door was an emissary. Duncan had never seen one before, but the creature looked just as he imagined a darkspawn mage should: dirty robes, blackened staff, and a small, withered head complete with toothy grimace. As evil as it looked, however, it walked with a calmness and sense of self-awareness that spoke volumes of its intelligence. This was no simple, raving monster. He wasn't sure whether to be impressed or terrified.

The other two darkspawn who followed the first were much more heavily armored. They looked strange, however. Their withered flesh was not quite the same, and their eyes were bloodred rather than pale white. Were these ghouls, then? Neither had any hair, but even so, Duncan could see that one of them was clearly female—

He paused, shock registering even though he couldn't quite believe it. The female stared directly at him, her gaze intense. The hard lines of her face were familiar, as was the grim set of her jaw.

She wasn't wearing her Grey Warden tunic, but her armor still looked the same, simply tarnished now rather than silvery bright as it once had been.

"Genevieve," he breathed.

Maric's eyes went wide, as did the others' when they realized it was true. Hafter raised his head and growled nervously. "What has happened to you?" Kell murmured in disbelief.

Genevieve held a hand up to the robed emissary and the male darkspawn with her. "Wait," she said. Her voice sounded strange, Duncan thought. There was a sibilant quality to it, a faint hiss that accompanied her words. It made him shudder. She turned and knelt down before them, looking at each in turn with her bloodred eyes. "Please do not be frightened," she said.

"You're joking, surely," Maric scoffed.

"I know that my appearance is horrific. I know that your senses say that I am a darkspawn, but I am not. This is what a Grey Warden becomes, given enough time for the taint to ravage our bodies."

Kell looked up at the armored figure beside her with recognition. She nodded. "This is Bregan, my brother." Bregan nodded to them, but said nothing. They could only stare back, dumbfounded. Duncan had never met the man, so he'd had no idea what to expect, but this wasn't it. "And this is the Architect." She indicated the robed emissary, and it bowed politely.

"The Architect," Fiona repeated suspiciously.

"I was lucky to find you when I did," the creature stated, far more eloquently and softly than Duncan would have expected from a darkspawn. "My ability to direct my brethren is limited, and lacks efficiency. Once their bloodlust was aroused even I could not keep them from you. I apologize for how very close you came to perishing. That would have been unfortunate."

"You apologize?" Fiona glared at the creature.

Genevieve held her hand up at the emissary once again, frowning. "I know how this may look, but all I ask is that you give me the chance to explain as it was explained to me."

The group was silent. Duncan had no idea how they could even respond to that. He was too caught up in staring at the Commander, or his former commander, perhaps. One couldn't be a Grey Warden and a darkspawn both, surely. Her white hair was completely gone, and her flesh dark and withered. Yet the mad intensity had disappeared. It was replaced with a calm sense of iron purpose that suffused her entire demeanor. He wondered if the others could see it.

"I don't understand," Kell said slowly. "We were brought here, then? On purpose? And now that you have found your brother, your plans have changed?"

"They have not changed," she avowed.

"If you actually wish to speak with us, then free us. Why keep us prisoner?"

Genevieve exchanged a look with the Architect. Duncan couldn't see anything in the creature's expression, but she sighed heavily and turned back to the hunter. "Until we've had a chance to explain, this is for your own good."

"I see."

There was nothing else to say. "The Architect is not like others of its kind. It is not controlled by the same impulses, and wants to see the rest of its kind free as it is free."

The creature tapped its chin thoughtfully. "If we were not subject to the call of the Old Gods," he said, "there would be no reason for us to search for them. No reason for us to ascend to the surface, and thus no Blights."

Utha's head shot up, as if her interest had suddenly been gained. Kell seemed intrigued, as well. Fiona gasped. "No Blights? You mean not ever?"

Genevieve actually smiled, displaying rows of sharpened teeth stained yellow by corruption. "Do you see? The Architect has a plan, one that only Grey Wardens can see carried out." She took a deep breath. "We exist halfway between humanity and darkspawn, tainted but never controlled by it. The Architect has the ability to advance the state of our corruption, to push us to what we would become in time if we never went to our deaths as Grey Warden tradition commands."

"But why?" Fiona asked, horrified.

"Because the darkspawn ignore us now," Bregan answered. Genevieve looked up at him, and he stepped forward to stand beside her. He seemed fierce, resolute. His red eyes burned in his skull. "I know where the Old Gods are. The Grey Wardens have always known. The problem is that they have always lain well beyond our reach, in lands we are unfamiliar with, past a sea of darkspawn."

He paused to let the implication sink in. Utha made several agitated gestures, and Genevieve nodded eagerly. "If there were enough Grey Wardens like us, aided by a darkspawn who knew the underground, we could find the Old Gods and kill them before they were ever tainted. We could stop the Blights before they began and end the Calling."

"Thus freeing my brethren," the Architect added softly, almost reverently. The way it steepled its fingers together in front of its chest made it seem almost like a priest to Duncan. Was that intentional? Was it an act?

"You mean to tell this creature where the Old Gods are!" Fiona shouted.

"I already have." Bregan's answer stunned the group and they stared at him in shock. He folded his arms defiantly and refused to explain himself further.

"We have an opportunity," Genevieve explained slowly. "We can do what the Grey Wardens have existed to do for centuries, centuries which have been filled with Blight after Blight, each of which has slain countless people and threatened the destruction of our world. We can stop it!" She punched her hand into her fist emphatically. "As Grey Wardens we have sworn to do *whatever is necessary* to combat the darkspawn. We sacrificed our own lives the moment we took the Joining and drank that blood. The fact that the Architect even exists gives us a chance now to do the unthinkable!"

"*If* you trust this darkspawn," Maric suddenly said.

Bregan regarded Maric with a cool stare. The others looked at him oddly, as well, and Duncan knew why. Of them all, Maric was the only one who was not a Grey Warden. Was he even part of this plan? Duncan wanted to ask what they intended to do with the King, but then he remembered what Genevieve had told him the first night they'd camped in the Deep Roads: If the King ever learned anything he wasn't supposed to, he would need to die.

Perhaps it was better not to ask just yet.

"Yes," Bregan grudgingly admitted. "If we trust this darkspawn."

"And you do?" Kell asked.

"I trust his plan, yes."

"And I trust Bregan," Genevieve added, looking up at her brother with genuine affection. It was odd to see the expression on the face of someone so completely blighted, with those red eyes and withered skin.

"And how do we know you are not under some kind of mental control?" Fiona asked suspiciously. "Blood magic is known to control minds. You could be influenced by magic and not even be aware of it."

"If that were so," the Architect said, "then why attempt to convince you of anything at all?"

"Then tell me this," she responded. "If your 'brethren' are actually freed, does that make them better? Will they stop attacking the surface? Or the dwarves? Will they stop spreading disease?"

It appeared unfazed by the questions. "I am free," it stated simply. "This gives me the choice to act differently than others of my kind. Would you deny the rest of the darkspawn that choice?"

Fiona appeared taken aback by his response. Bregan leaned in. "It is one step," he said. "Only one step of several. Before those other steps can be taken, however, first we must stop the Blights."

"And what are those other steps?" Maric pointedly asked.

Bregan ignored him. He nodded to Genevieve and she stood. "We will not tell you everything. I know how this might seem, but we have little choice. I am willing to trust my brother and I will do anything if it means fulfilling my vow. You may not feel the same." She looked down at the ground and became awkwardly silent for a moment, considering her next words. "I appreciate that you came all this way with me. I truly believed you would turn about when I left you, but now that you are here, I need to ask if you will follow me a little farther."

A silence followed her words. Fiona eventually arched a brow at her former commander. "And if we don't?"

"Then here you remain," Bregan answered. "Until our task is done."

"And what about Maric?" Duncan blurted out. He regretted it as soon as he asked the question. The others looked at him curiously, especially Maric. Only Genevieve didn't look at him. In fact, she studiously avoided his gaze.

"He will be returned to the surface," the Architect said carefully. "In time."

"That's too kind," Maric remarked.

"Returned how?" Duncan insisted. "Alive?"

The darkspawn gave a hint of what might have been a smile. "To allies."

It didn't elaborate, and Duncan desisted. He obviously wasn't going to get an answer on this, either, though he had to wonder what sort of "allies" the creature could be referring to. Allies of

Bregan's, most likely. He noticed Genevieve shooting a curious look at her brother at the mention, but only for a second. Perhaps they didn't tell her everything, either? Curious.

Genevieve turned to go. "I will give you time to decide," she said. "In the end, if Bregan and I must do this on our own, then that is what must be." Bregan nodded to her, but as the three of them started to walk to the door, Utha suddenly slammed her manacles down hard on the ground. The ringing sound they made drew everyone's attention. The dwarf sat there, watching Genevieve and Bregan fervently. Duncan wasn't sure if she was furious or . . . something else.

She made several gestures with her hand. They were quick and punctuated. Certain. Her expression did not change. Kell, however, reacted with shock. "No, Utha!"

Genevieve knelt down in front of the dwarf, concern upon her face. "We can give you more time if—"

Utha made a simple, negating slice of her hand.

Kell shook his head at her, stricken. "No, you should wait. We could . . ."

She turned and gazed at him sadly. Duncan watched as she made a series of complicated gestures to the hunter, most of which he didn't understand. It was an explanation, however, something involving several chopping movements with her hand and a determined expression.

Kell, in turn, became more and more hopeless. And then finally he nodded, resigned. "If you truly think you must."

She made a nodding gesture with her hand. She did.

Genevieve watched Utha, torn, but then her face hardened. She looked up at the Architect behind her, and gave him a curt nod. He lowered himself with the aid of his staff to kneel beside Genevieve, his robes rustling as he did so, and held out a slender, withered hand to the dwarf.

Utha took it, her eyes fixed on the emissary and her jaw set.

Duncan expected for there to be some kind of incantation spoken, some ritual. But there was only silence. The Architect stared into Utha's eyes and nothing happened at first. Then black veins began to appear along her hand where the darkspawn touched her. They became darker and darker, the veins branching until her entire hand was crisscrossed with them.

The dwarf closed her eyes, shaking ever so slightly. Duncan watched as the black veins appeared on her neck. Then they spread to her face. Her shaking became more pronounced, and she clenched her teeth hard to keep her composure. Hafter woke up, sensing something, and when he noticed the emissary standing nearby and felt the strange magics at work, he began to growl menacingly. Kell put his hand on the hound's neck to quiet him. The hunter looked away and shut his eyes tight. He couldn't bear to watch.

A shadow formed around the Architect's hand, a black and amorphous mass that seemed to grow out of him. It got larger, and as it did the small chamber grew chill. Duncan shivered, and saw frost forming on the wall next to Utha. Her breath was coming out in white plumes, as it was for the rest of them. The shadow *crawled* off of the darkspawn's hand and onto the dwarf's, and there it slowly sank into her. Her flesh withered and curled, the air filling with the foul stench of decay.

Utha began to spasm. Still she fought against the agony that was burning through her. The stain on her skin spread, crawling up her neck and covering her face. Her coppery hair began to grey, and then it became white. Her long braid twisted and curled behind her, like a match that was burning itself into a cinder. Her eyes shot open, bloodred, and she opened her mouth in a sound-less scream . . . and what wisps remained of her hair simply fell out.

And then it was done.

Utha pulled her hand from the Architect's and doubled over, her body racked with shudders that grew less and less. The plumes of breath grew fainter until finally they disappeared and she was still. Duncan thought for a moment that she had died, but as she slowly sat up he realized that she was now simply cold.

The darkspawn nodded at her and lowered his hand. The chill in the air lessened almost immediately, although it did not disappear.

Everyone but Kell stared at Utha. The hunter averted his eyes and calmed Hafter as the hound whined in confusion. Fiona shook her head in disbelief, furious, but Duncan didn't know what to think. The dwarf was now as bald and tainted as Genevieve and Bregan, her eyes that same bloody red, but she seemed calm. She nodded curtly to the Architect and he ran a finger along her manacles. They opened with a loud clicking sound and dropped off her.

Nice trick. Duncan needed to learn that sometime.

The dwarf stood and walked forward to stand before Genevieve, not even looking back at the others. "Thank you," Genevieve said with the officious tone reserved for a good soldier. Utha nodded again but did nothing else.

Genevieve glanced toward the hunter. "And you, Kell?"

He did not look at her, and said nothing. Duncan could see from his troubled expression, however, that he was uncertain. The hunter closed his eyes, frowning deeply.

She looked to Fiona, though far less hopefully. "Fiona?"

The mage glared at her in pure hatred. "How dare you ask me that," she spat. "You throw us in here, tell us next to nothing, and then expect us to chase after you again? You *abandoned* us, Genevieve!"

"You should have turned around."

"We didn't! We tried to finish the mission!"

"As did I. As I continue to do." Genevieve snorted derisively. "You are not a child. This is what our task is. This. We make sacrifices to end the Blight. That is exactly why you followed me here in the first place."

"You're insane." The elf shook her head contemptuously. "If I actually thought what you were doing might end the Blight . . ."

Genevieve cut her off, turning to Duncan. "And you?" she asked him.

He felt caught. What was he supposed to do? In a way, she was right. They were already dead. He would have been executed had it not been for his recruitment into the Grey Wardens. He was living on borrowed time, so what did it matter how he fought the Blight? He could have died just as easily in that cavern or any one of the battles before it . . . at least this way he would have a chance to do something significant.

But the sudden shift startled him. Genevieve had seemed so determined to find her brother and kill him if necessary, as if that were all that mattered. But now she wanted something completely different, based on just a single talk with her brother and this darkspawn friend of his. What had been going on here this entire time? Why would she go along with any of this?

Yet he wanted to trust her. He wanted to prove to her that he could be the kind of Grey Warden she expected him to be.

"I . . ." He stared at her, unable to form a response.

"Don't do it," Maric muttered under his breath.

"Stay out of it!" she snapped.

"No, don't stay out of it!" Fiona slammed her manacles down onto the ground with a loud thud, glaring at Genevieve. "Are we the only sane ones here? You're willing to throw away everything on some gamble! On the word of a darkspawn!"

Genevieve ignored her. "Duncan?" she asked him again.

"I . . . don't know," he admitted.

It felt weak, and his face burned in shame as her expression changed to disappointment. "So be it." She gestured to Utha and the others to go. "We will leave you alone for now, to think on your options." Duncan watched them file through the stone door, and when it closed behind them with a deep *thoom* his heart sank. He somehow felt as if he had missed his opportunity.

The cell felt empty now, with Utha gone. Her manacles and chains lay on the floor beside Kell accusingly, and Duncan tried not to stare at them. The hunter pulled his knees up and rested his head on them, exhausted with grief. Hafter whined and tried to nuzzle his black nose under Kell's arms, offering what support he could to his master.

"What do we do now?" Fiona asked hopelessly.

Nobody responded right away. Eventually Duncan looked at her. "What if you're wrong?" he asked. "What if it's not insane? What if insane is continuing to fight a hopeless battle when we have the chance to do something about it?"

"Is it hopeless?"

"Sure seems that way," he snorted. "You ever met a Grey Warden who's happy about it? How many more Blights are we going to fight before we lose? We could stop that!"

"Or you could make it worse," Maric chimed in.

"Doing nothing is worse!"

Maric sighed in resignation. "Since when has taking a shortcut ever turned out well, Duncan? This is not a plan that is being acted upon rationally. This is your commander grasping at straws, because this way she and her brother get to be heroes."

"I don't think that's it."

"No?" Maric looked incredulous. "Your commander isn't exactly the most stable person, you know."

Kell raised his head from his lap sharply. "It's the Calling," he muttered, barely opening his eyes. "The song is in our heads, and under our skin. It is slowly driving me mad. If Genevieve was farther along than Utha and me . . ."

Maric nodded. "Then it's this Architect who is manipulating them. Waiting for this song you hear—"

"I don't hear it," Duncan insisted.

"My point is that this Bregan fellow must have been well along, himself. Genevieve is exactly the same way. They're at the point where they would need to kill themselves, walking into the Deep Roads. This song is in their head, making them crazy, and what does this darkspawn do? Offers them a chance to make it all better. To give their life meaning."

"What do you think he really wants?"

"Maybe he just wants to get to the Old Gods." Maric paused, considering. "Perhaps this is what starts the Blight the witch warned me about. This Architect being led straight to an Old God."

"Or it starts because we refused to help it," Duncan countered. "That Architect creature isn't like any darkspawn we've seen. Maybe it's not like the other darkspawn at all."

"Does that make it better?" Fiona asked. "These creatures are born of evil, Duncan. You know that. You feel inside you what they have swimming in their veins from birth. Do you really want to trust a creature that's known that and nothing else its entire life?"

"And it has allies," Kell pointed out. "Allies they won't tell us about." He seemed to be coming around to Fiona and Maric's point of view, Duncan saw, though the hunter hardly seemed pleased about it. He shook his head grimly. "Whether this creature is manipulating us or not, we can't take such a risk."

"But Genevieve is right!" Duncan protested. "Our duty is to defeat the Blight!"

Kell's pale eyes bored into him. "Our duty is to defend mankind from the Blight." His voice was low and intense, and as he sat there he seemed to become more and more certain of his words. "There is a difference. We have stood up against the onslaught of the darkspawn time and time again, and that is our task. It is not for us to judge, to gamble with the lives of those in our care."

"But—"

"It is for us to make the hard decisions that must be made. We cannot pretend that this also makes us gods."

Duncan sat back against the stone wall, letting the chill of the stone press against the back of his neck. It felt good. His head swam, and he felt less sure what to think than before. Genevieve had always said the Grey Wardens did whatever needed to be done. If a village needed to be burned to the ground to keep the darkspawn from spreading, then it was burned. Nobody told them different. When a Blight was occurring, their word was paramount.

But this wasn't a Blight, was it? The darkspawn had not yet found their Old God, not yet infected it with the taint and made it rise as an Archdemon. The Grey Wardens' whole purpose had been to come here and prevent that from happening. Genevieve had told him that even the smallest chance of a Blight couldn't be permitted, and yet she had changed her tune. This plan of hers— there *was* a chance it could go awry and start a Blight. If that's what this Architect actually wanted, it could happen, and the Grey Wardens would be facilitating it rather than preventing it.

Genevieve believed the risk was worth it. She believed it fervently, he could see that just by looking at her. And she had wanted him to believe in it, as well. But perhaps she had lost sight of what she had come to do. Perhaps she wanted her life to have some meaning, to justify all the things that she had given up.

Or the things that had been taken from her.

"What do we do next?" he asked into the silence, refusing to look at the others even though he could feel their eyes on him. He stared studiously at his manacles. Part of him wanted to refuse, to spit in their eyes and stand by his commander. He had always thought her larger than life, a superhuman warrior who could do anything. That was why he had followed her to Ferelden, and agreed to go into the Deep Roads. She would defeat this menace single-handedly, prevent the coming Blight and prove herself to the Grey Wardens, and he would be there to support her. He owed it to her, if nothing else.

But then he remembered what she had said in her dream. Duncan had seen a side of her he hadn't even known existed. She was just human, and her dream had been no more grandiose than any of theirs. There was no reason to think that she was without fault. Somehow that left him feeling dejected and empty, like he had lost something incredibly important.

"We get out of here," Kell declared, his voice hushed.

"We need to warn Ferelden," Maric said. "We need to tell them that a Blight may be coming, or something worse."

"And if this Architect is right after all?" Duncan asked.

"Then our warnings will not be needed."

He thought about it, and then slowly nodded. "Okay, then." Rocking back, Duncan brought his knees up between his arms until he could place his boots on the manacles. Fiona seemed about to object, but he ignored her. Pressing hard with the boots, he ignored the painful scraping of the iron on his wrists as he pushed the restraints as far up on his hands as they would go.

With a hiss between clenched teeth, he suddenly jerked his legs and popped his thumbs out of joint. The manacles tore at his skin and left a bloody trail as they slowly slid off his hands. They fell to the ground with a clatter and Duncan collapsed, panting with the effort.

Gritting his teeth, he pressed his hands hard against the ground, pushing his thumbs back into place. The pain was excruciating, and he could feel the tendons in his hands ripping under the flesh. Still, it worked.

He took a moment to get used to the stabbing pain, and then took a deep breath and leaped to his feet. Then he noticed the others staring at him in shock.

"What?" he asked with mock innocence. "You don't really think I haven't broken out of better prisons than this, do you?"

Reaching into his belt, he was pleased to find the lockpick still hidden away inside the leather. He held it up with a grin. "Let's get out of here before they come back."

17

Maker, though the darkness comes upon me,
I shall embrace the light. I shall weather the storm.
I shall endure.
What you have created, no one can tear asunder.

—Canticle of Trials 1:10

The fact that Duncan was able to find their weapons was a stroke of luck.

After some quick healing spells from Fiona, the lad had quietly pulled open the stone door to their cell and poked his head outside to ensure the coast was clear. According to the Grey Wardens' senses, the immediate area around their cell was mostly devoid of the creatures. No guards, no patrols, no locked doors—Duncan opined that even if the darkspawn were now taking prisoners, it clearly wasn't something with which they had much experience.

Maric was inclined to agree. Perhaps their captors couldn't imagine the possibility that they could slip their chains. Or perhaps they couldn't imagine that they might want to. More likely they knew that there was nowhere for them to go but out into a horde of darkspawn.

Duncan had returned with their weapons bundled in his arms not a minute later. They had been stored in another cell next to theirs, along with their packs and the magical brooches that hid the Grey Wardens from darkspawn detection. Presumably all of it had been kept there for the eventuality in which they agreed to

Genevieve's plan. Still, not even having a guard to watch over the weapons seemed foolish.

But perhaps these creatures didn't have guards. The Architect had implied that it didn't have full control over its own fellows. It had needed to swoop in and snatch Maric and the others from the jaws of the darkspawn who were attacking them, rather than ordering the attack to stop. It was an outsider, and thus its supply of minions to do such things as guard prison cells was limited or non-existent. Maric wasn't about to complain.

It felt good to have the dragonbone longsword back in his hands, even covered in the ogre's black ichor as it was. He had to wonder how they had even managed to touch it and bring it back here, but he wasn't about to question that bit of luck, either.

Fiona's staff was there, as was Kell's flail. The only weapons missing were Duncan's twin silverite daggers. The lad dug another weapon out of his pack, however: an obsidian dagger with an odd-looking carved handle. The lad tested the dagger's weight, making several slashes at the air with it. He seemed satisfied, and Maric had to admit it certainly looked deadly enough. The black blade reminded him a little of the Grey Wardens' brooches, though it was far fancier and almost glasslike.

"Well, at least you have a weapon you're familiar with," Maric commented.

"I stole it from the Circle of Magi when we were in the tower," Duncan said lightly. "I'd almost forgotten it was even in my pack."

Fiona had her staff back, and that allowed her the ability to light their way without relying solely on the bright glowstone hanging in their cell.

What followed wasn't luck, but Duncan proving how Genevieve had found him useful for more than his skill with a pair of daggers. The lad slowly led them through the halls of the ruin, occasionally sneaking ahead to scout a proper path but successfully keeping them from encounters with roaming darkspawn. Not that there were many of those—for whatever reason, the ruin seemed to have only a few of the creatures in it, passing through on their way to doing whatever it was that darkspawn did. Maric truly had no idea.

The ruin itself seemed to be some kind of abandoned dwarven fortress, from what Maric could tell. It was crumbling, the walls filled with cracks and gaping holes where the masonry had collapsed, the stones layered with a blackened skin spread by the taint. The entire structure smelled of dust and foulness. Was this in the Deep Roads? Or were they still below it? More important, how long would it be before Genevieve and her new allies discovered that they were gone?

The third time that Duncan came back from one of his brief scouting missions, he was scowling. Maric noticed fresh ichor dripping from his dagger. "It will only be a matter of time now," he groused.

"Did it see you?" Kell asked him.

"Of course not. You think they won't notice anyhow?"

The hunter frowned thoughtfully. "Let's hurry, then."

They picked up the pace, darting into side rooms to hide whenever they sensed darkspawn coming near. Hafter growled deep in his throat as they waited in the darkness, but not loudly enough for the creatures to hear. Kell glared reproachfully at his hound, who at least had the good grace to look apologetic. The brooches still hid the Grey Wardens' presence, apparently. Either that or the darkspawn sensed them simply as others of their kind and didn't care.

After an hour of creeping their way through the dark and deserted hallways, Duncan eventually led them to a wide staircase that led down into darkness. Instead of continuing, however, he stopped and held up his hand behind him. He bit his lip as he stared ahead into the darkness.

"That's a lot of darkspawn," Fiona murmured.

"It sure is."

The Grey Wardens all looked concerned. Even Hafter flattened his ears back as he glared down the stairs, baring his teeth in a quiet growl. "How many are we talking?" Maric asked them.

"A hundred," Kell responded. "Maybe more."

"Is there another way out of here?"

"I was searching for one," Duncan sighed. "There was a larger passage that led out, I think, but it had a lot more darkspawn at the end of it. Thousands, maybe, I don't know. I didn't want to try that way."

"Good idea."

They stood at the top of the stairs, indecisive. This was why Genevieve and the others were unconcerned, after all. Even if they got out of their cell, what then? The only way out of the ruin led into a small army of darkspawn. They couldn't hope to battle their way past.

Duncan crept down the stairs into the shadows, waving at them to remain behind. Kell stared after the lad anxiously, but there was nothing they could do. It was either proceed now or turn back, and behind them lay only trouble. Genevieve would insist on taking them prisoner again, or trying to. And if she succeeded, she and her brother wouldn't make the same mistake twice. The darkspawn emissary might not know much about keeping prisoners, but they had no such shortcoming.

So they waited. Kell sat down on one of the steps, ruffling Hafter's furry head as the hound whined nervously. Fiona peered after Duncan, worry etched onto her face. Maric leaned against the stone wall and found himself staring at her. He watched her dark eyes and the curve of her neck. Odd that he should be fixated on such things as they stood there in that heavy silence, but he couldn't help himself. The thought of their night together kept spinning in his head.

"How will he even see out there?" he finally asked.

"Not well," Fiona said, and for a moment their eyes met. The mage averted her gaze instantly, but not before he saw something there. She was thinking of it, too.

"Fiona . . . ," he said, but his voice trailed off. What was he supposed to say to her? This was hardly the time or the place, but he might not get another chance.

She didn't look at him. "Maric, you don't have to say anything."

"I feel like I do."

She looked like she was about to add something else, but her attention was drawn to Duncan's return. The lad appeared out of the shadows, stealthily creeping back up the stairs in a crouch. He stopped several feet from them, rubbing his chin. "Well," he muttered, "I won't lie to you. It's pretty bad."

Kell nodded slowly. The hunter's eyes were closed, and he looked pained. Patting Hafter's head one last time, he put his hands on his knees and pushed himself to his feet. "Tell us. What did you find?"

"The stairway breaks off at the end, and opens up into a natural cavern. A big one. The darkspawn are all out there. Digging, I think."

"Digging?"

"From what I could hear. I crawled around some, but I couldn't go far. As soon as you step out into the cavern, you're in full view of the darkspawn. There's nowhere to hide, and they won't miss us."

The hunter nodded again. "And? Is there a way out?"

"I couldn't see," Duncan sighed. "It seems like it sloped upward if we turn to the left, but there's no point. We'll never get past that horde. All we'd need is for a single one of them to look up from their digging and we'd be done."

"Then we find another way out," Maric stated firmly.

"No," Kell said. He turned and peered down the dark passage

behind them. "I believe they have already discovered our disappearance and are looking for us now. We are out of time."

"Then we're done." Maric felt frustrated, running a hand through his hair in agitation. "We go back and surrender ourselves, and find another solution. We talk to Genevieve, or her brother. Make them see reason."

Duncan snorted. "You've met Genevieve, right?"

Fiona shook her head. "Maric, I don't think that's going to help."

"So, what? You want to run out there and get ourselves killed?" He strode toward her and took her shoulders in his hands, made her look at him. She seemed dispirited, almost on the verge of tears.

"Maric . . ." She shook her head sadly.

"No! I am not letting you die! And I'm not going to die, either. I came here . . . I think I wanted to die. I think I welcomed it. I felt like I had nothing to live for, but that's changed!" He shook her shoulders emphatically, but it only made her look at him more pityingly.

"Maric, it's too late."

"I refuse to accept that. The Fiona I know, the one who stood up to that bastard who enslaved her, so would she." He set his jaw and stared at her, demanding that she not surrender, as if he could force her by will alone. Instead of wilting under his gaze, she grudgingly straightened and nodded. He saw the determination return to her eyes.

"Have it your way." She scowled.

"Whatever way you have it," Duncan chimed in, "we need to do something soon. The darkspawn are all connected to each other, and word is spreading fast. They're going to be swarming all over us in a minute or two."

"Then we go back and fight," Fiona declared. She pulled herself out of Maric's grasp, blue magical energies beginning to crackle around the head of her staff. "We fight this Architect, and if Genevieve and her brother and Utha want to try and stop us, then we fight them, too."

"No." Kell said the word with enough force that Fiona turned and stared at him with wide eyes. Maric wondered, too. The hunter looked down the stairs toward the cavern with all the darkspawn ahead of them, his face grim determination. His hand tightened on the grip of the flail on his belt until his knuckles turned white. "You need to get warning to the surface. The Grey Wardens need to know that something has changed among the darkspawn. They need to hear it from a witness, someone who can tell them about this Architect and its plans."

Fiona looked confused. "But—"

The hunter reached into his vest and pulled out the bright glow-stone from their cell, its orange radiance filling the hallway instantly. He put it around his neck. "I will draw the darkspawn away. My senses are good enough that I can tell where they are, and evade them at least for a time." He turned and met Fiona's gaze, his pale eyes hard. "Time enough for you."

The elf was alarmed now, and she looked to Maric and Duncan for support. Duncan seemed similarly alarmed, but Maric knew Kell's tone. He had heard Loghain using exactly that voice, when he spoke of something terrible that needed to be done without question. Worse, Maric found he couldn't argue.

"Kell, you can't!" she protested.

"I should have fought harder to turn us around while we had the chance. I should have known better." Kell crouched down in front of Hafter, rubbing the hound's head gravely. Hafter stared back at him with wide, confused eyes. He knew something was amiss. "Take him with you," the hunter said, his voice raw with sudden emotion. "He has survived a long journey and many battles. I would like him to have a chance."

Patting the dog one last time, he stood and gruffly nodded to Duncan. "I am leaving it to you to lead King Maric out. Fiona will help you. I know you can do this."

The lad could only nod, dumbfounded.

Kell turned to Maric and offered his hand. "I am sorry it came to this, Your Majesty. You are a fine warrior, for a lowlander king." The last was offered with a wry grin, as if it were a personal joke.

Maric grinned sadly back at the man and shook his hand. "Maker watch over you, Kell."

The hunter turned and began heading down the stairs without another word. He drew his flail from his belt, the short chain rattling as its spiked head unfurled at his side. Already Maric could hear the stirring of the creatures in the darkness beyond. There was a whisper in the air, a humming that was slowly building all around them. They knew. They knew and they were coming.

Fiona lunged to grab Hafter's collar to restrain him, but the hound was too quick for her. It bounded down toward Kell, letting out an angry *woof*. The hunter turned around, regarding the hound with obvious displeasure. "No," he commanded, pointing back toward Fiona and the others. "Hafter, go with them!"

The hound hung his head low, folding his ears back in confusion. Hafter was an intelligent dog, but he was still a dog. Kell glared down at the animal, growing more furious by the second. "I said go!" he shouted.

"Come here, Hafter!" Fiona urged him.

Mortified that he had done something to offend his master, Hafter prostrated himself at Kell's feet, nuzzling his nose in at the hunter's boots and whining plaintively. Kell angrily grabbed the dog's collar and hauled him up, physically turning him around and shoving him back up the stairs. "Go! Now! You go with them!"

Still Hafter wouldn't go to Fiona, and quickly darted back to Kell, whining in agitation. Kell reeled back, tormented, the large hound whining at his feet like a lost puppy. Without warning, Kell stepped forward and kicked the hound in the side with a loud shout. "Obey me!" he roared.

The kick was hard, and though Hafter had stood up to far worse—he was a warhound built of little more than fur and muscle, after all—still the hound collapsed with a terrified yelp that echoed throughout the passage. Fiona covered her mouth in horror and Maric was speechless. Kell looked toward them, anguished and pleading with his eyes for help. He stared down at the dog trembling in fear at his feet and burst into tears.

"Oh, Hafter, I'm so sorry," he said, his voice cracking with grief. He knelt down and took the dog's head into his arms, patting his fur vigorously. Hafter looked up at him with his large brown eyes and uncertainly wagged his tail. Kell attempted a reassuring smile through his tears. "I'm so sorry, my old friend," he whispered. "Can you ever forgive me?" The hound's ears slowly perked up and his tail thumped against the stairs. There was no need even to ask.

The sounds of the darkspawn were coming closer, and Maric could hear movement in the cavern at the foot of the stairs. Duncan exchanged a worried look with him. They were almost out of time.

Kell stood, his face wet with tears, and Hafter jumped to his feet with him. The man gazed down sadly at his hound and tightened his grip on his flail. "What do you say, my boy?" he asked. "Are you ready for one last battle? Just you and me?" The hound bounded in place, overjoyed that his master was taking him along after all, barking excitedly in anticipation.

The hunter glanced toward the others up the stairs and nodded solemnly. "Give me one minute," he stated firmly. His pale eyes met with Maric's and his meaning was clear: no more, no less.

Without further good-byes, he turned and sped toward the cavern, Hafter bounding after him. Spinning the flail's head, he roared a war cry and burst into the shadows. Hafter joined him with a loud howl. The effect on the darkspawn was instantaneous. Like fire touching water. There was angry hissing and a massive commotion as the creatures moved to attack.

Kell was too fast for them, however. He and Hafter raced to the right, disappearing into darkness and leading the darkspawn off. The last that Maric saw of them was the rapidly dwindling orange glow of the amulet.

"He's gone," Duncan breathed in amazement.

Maric nodded. "Let's not waste the chance he's given us."

They waited an excruciating minute as the sounds of pursuit in the passages behind them increased. Thankfully the chamber ahead grew quieter. Kell had clearly managed to lead them away, at least for the moment. Finally, when Maric could stand it no more, he drew his longsword and began running down the stairs. Fiona and Duncan didn't hesitate, and were right on his heels.

Together they raced out of the dwarven ruins and back into the Deep Roads.

Maric was unsure just how many hours the three of them spent fleeing. Duncan took the lead almost immediately once they got out of the cavern, racing ahead and urging them to greater exertions. The passages sped by almost without notice, blurry shadows lit by Fiona's white staff. Duncan told them to hide when he sensed darkspawn coming too close, and three times they had been forced to attack small groups of passing darkspawn when it became obvious that the shadowy alcoves and crumbled statues just weren't going to be enough to keep them out of sight.

Each time that happened, they were forced to respond to a renewed frenzy of darkspawn activity as the creatures zeroed in on their whereabouts. Each time they were able to narrowly lose their pursuers.

Eventually, the lad stopped them and looked up at the ceiling of the passage they were in. Maric looked up, too, but it didn't look much different than the ceilings they had passed previously, all stone support beams—many of which had crumbled, leading him to wonder just how long it would be before the Deep Roads collapsed entirely. Perhaps that wouldn't be such a bad thing if it happened.

"We're closer to the surface. I think we're going up," Duncan muttered.

Fiona arched a brow at him. "How can you tell?"

"It's a hunch."

They paused for a time, sweat coursing down their faces as they panted in exhaustion. But eventually Duncan urged them onward. Fiona didn't complain, and Maric could only assume that meant they could sense the darkspawn closing in again. So they ran some more. Maric started to wonder if they would eventually end up at Gwaren. He knew these tunnels led out to the eastern city eventually, and that would be amusing only because he'd had the Deep Roads entrance there permanently sealed years ago.

Well, maybe *amusing* wasn't the right word. *Unfortunate* might be more appropriate.

They passed through a long, ruined hall filled with tall pillars and so much masonry fallen from the ceiling that they needed to clamber over the piles. The sounds of deep stalkers were loud there, enough to make Fiona look around in alarm when they got to the top of one of the piles.

"Are they going to come after us?" she asked nervously.

"There are only three of us now, so why not?" Maric had meant it as a joke, but his gasping for breath made that difficult. She eyed him accusingly in response but said nothing.

"If we keep moving, they won't have time to eat us," Duncan admonished them. The lad appeared to have limitless amounts of energy, and he seemed only mildly fatigued, while Fiona and Maric were stumbling along after him and almost ready to fall over. Still, they had managed to survive so far. That could quickly change, so they continued to run.

After an indeterminable amount of time spent trudging through the passages, Maric felt ready to collapse. He wasn't even paying attention to the intersections they were reaching any longer. Duncan had earlier claimed that they weren't going in circles, but Maric had no idea what his method for choosing a direction was. For all he knew, the lad could be leading them back toward the ruin. Perhaps Duncan was simply choosing whatever direction led him away from the darkspawn he sensed? That seemed logical, even if it still might not get them anywhere.

What would Genevieve be doing now, he wondered? Would she be searching for them separately, or did the Architect have more command over the darkspawn than he claimed? He tried to imagine a Grey Warden directing a horde of darkspawn in a systematic search of the caverns, but his mind balked at the image. It was too bizarre. Thankfully, while Genevieve could likely guess their heading, she couldn't know which route they were taking since they didn't know themselves.

Perhaps she wouldn't care. Perhaps she and her brother and Utha would simply proceed with the Architect's plan, chalking up their escape to an unfortunate loss. She claimed they had intended to do it without any help, after all. Somehow Maric found that hard to believe.

They were passing what looked to be the ruined remains of a dwarven outpost when Maric noticed the tarnished statue standing in the middle of it. He halted, staring wide-eyed at it. It was half covered in corruption, but the image of a great dwarven king with his warhammer raised was unmistakable. He walked to the edge of the small cavern the outpost was within, studying the rubble and the collapsed tunnels and the strange debris everywhere. Could it be . . . ?

Fiona stopped ahead, and Duncan turned around as well. "What is it, Maric?" she called back. "What did you find?"

"I've been here." He slowly walked up to the statue, the stones under his boots crunching loudly and echoing in the cavern. He was suddenly aware of just how much his legs ached. Fiona and Duncan edged cautiously into the cavern behind him, looking around as if worrying that subterranean creatures might jump out of the shadows. "This is Endrin Stonehammer," he breathed. "The first of the dwarven kings."

"That's nice," Duncan muttered. "Why are we stopping?"

"The Legion of the Dead brought us here. This was their outpost." He pointed to an area near the statue now covered in debris. "And that is where they buried some of the legionnaires who died fighting the darkspawn when we first encountered them."

"Do you think there's anything left?" Fiona asked.

"There might be. I remember they couldn't take all their supplies along."

Duncan peered at some of the side caves that had collapsed. Something had been through here, something with an eye toward destroying most of what the Legion had left behind. Perhaps the darkspawn? The Legion was one of their most hated enemies, after all, along with the Grey Wardens. Perhaps they came and defaced the area as soon as the dwarves left.

"Anything in there was probably crushed," the lad remarked. "Or spoiled."

"Would it hurt to look?"

Duncan gave Maric an annoyed glance, but Fiona held her hand up. "You know as well as I do that the darkspawn are well behind us. I can't even sense them right now."

"Maybe you're right." Duncan glanced toward the cavern entrance, suddenly troubled. "It's just that I keep expecting Genevieve to appear out of every shadow, all blighted like she is now. I feel like she's right on our heels."

Fiona snorted. "She's only human, Duncan, as she proved quite well."

"Yes, I suppose so." Still, Duncan looked far more sad than frightened, and with a final pensive glance at the entrance, he turned and nodded. "Let's stay here and rest, then. There's only the one entrance to the cavern, and even with all the rubble it's still pretty defensible. This is as good a place as any."

They spent some time searching through the ruins, but other than finding a few stone crates just inside one of the smaller caves, there wasn't as much as Maric had hoped. Cooking utensils, pots and pans, a few worn blankets and some dusty clothing. Thankfully the dwarves had a knack for building sturdy crates that kept the insides protected. Maric was able to find a pair of boots that fit, and Duncan located a grey leather vest that replaced his torn jerkin quite well.

Fiona located a crate with some food supplies that were mostly useless, no doubt left behind for good reason, but at least a few of the stores therein looked edible and they chewed on them in silence. Balls of jerky, though of what meat Maric couldn't really imagine. Perhaps it wasn't meat at all. He seemed to recall that Nalthur, the leader of the Legion, had complained about their lack of decent food. Justifiably, it turned out.

The elf was much more pleased when she located a dusty, cracked basin underneath a pile of rocks. It had a magical dweomer, she exclaimed, and when she ran her hands over it the basin began to fill with water. Maric had seen something similar during his time in Ortan thaig years before, and Fiona explained that it was a simple enough enchantment—one the dwarven Shapers specialized in.

This afforded them the opportunity to wash themselves at least a little, and they took turns at the basin. Maric didn't realize just how filthy he was until he started wiping off some of the dust and dried ichor that had accumulated on him. He ran the water through his hair, watching with alarm as the basin quickly turned a brownish red. Then the water slowly cleared as if by magic.

Or exactly by magic, he corrected himself. *We should get these at the palace.*

He wiped his face once more with the makeshift washcloth, marveling at the feeling of the cool water on his skin. Throwing caution to the wind, he undid the straps on his breastplate and removed the top half of his armor. Then he removed his shirt and proceeded to wash up. The cave was cramped but it allowed a little bit of privacy, and for a brief minute he just enjoyed sitting there in the quiet, listening only to the occasional splashing of the water and feeling human again.

"I wish I'd thought of that," Fiona mused, standing at the entrance to the cave.

He grinned at her. "Where's Duncan?"

"Standing watch at the cavern entrance. He saw me looking over at the cave and rolled his eyes and told me that's exactly where he would be until one of us came to get him." She chuckled, but it trailed off quickly into silence. A shadow crossed behind her eyes and she frowned. "He still isn't hearing the Calling."

"But you are?"

"Yes. And it's getting worse." She walked toward him and knelt down next to him beside the basin, leaning her staff against the wall. She refused to meet Maric's eyes, and he watched as she slowly removed her chain shirt. As soon as her back appeared, he noticed the tell-tale signs of corruption spreading. The stains were small, but noticeable, and he didn't remember seeing anything when they lay together not a night before.

Fiona began to shake suddenly, covering her eyes with her hands and stifling an exhausted sob. "Do you see them?" she asked, her voice anguished.

"Yes."

"Of course you do. How could you not?" She wiped at her eyes, and then shook her head angrily. "It's on my hands, too. I'm going to end up like Kell. Or Utha."

"You're not."

"Don't say such things." Fiona looked at him reproachfully. "Of course I am. There is no coming back from this, is there? Even if we make it to the surface, I'm . . . I'm dead. I don't even feel elven any longer."

He hushed her, and she closed her eyes and took a deep, ragged breath. Dunking his cloth into the basin again, he took it and began to wash her back gently. She jumped, surprised by the cold water, but then quickly acquiesced. For a time he ran the cloth over her skin, including the tainted areas, and she said nothing, continuing to stare ahead. Occasionally she shuddered when his fingers brushed against her. The quiet filled up the small cave, electric and yet somehow still not uncomfortable.

"Maric," she finally asked, "do you think we will really get out of this?"

"Yes, I do."

"Why, exactly? Our chances are not good."

"It's like this—" He smiled. "I've been incredibly lucky most of my life. I barely escaped the night my mother was murdered, and I met Loghain by chance. He saved my life more times than I can count during the rebellion. In fact, he wasn't the only one. I think I'm due for some more luck, now."

"Perhaps you used up all your luck," Fiona said. Her tone was more severe than she probably intended, and she bit her lower lip as soon as she said it. He didn't mind. His grin widened as he wiped the back of her neck with the cold cloth and felt her shiver.

"I think my luck is returning, actually."

The elf finally turned her head and peered at him curiously. Maric continued to wash the dried blood off her skin as she appraised him, the thoughts clearly running about in her head. He didn't ask, and eventually she frowned and spoke her mind. "You know, you don't have to live as you do."

"Oh? How do I live?"

"Like a man who's trapped." Now it was his turn to avoid her piercing eyes. "As a king you have every freedom, Maric. Yet you act as if you were a slave. You act as if this gift the Maker has given you is some kind of burden."

He sighed, taking a long minute to soak the cloth in the basin once again. The ichor bloomed in the water like a dark and deadly flower. "I don't think I'm as free as you think I am."

"Aren't you? What's imprisoning you, exactly?"

"I didn't have a choice about becoming what I am. My country needed me. The way Rowan looked at me and the way Loghain looked at me, they expected me to take my place. To be a strong king. To be a good king. To rebuild Ferelden. And I've done that. But . . . all it feels like is that there's this long, long road ahead of me, with no surprises and no reprieve, and I'm going to keep walking down it until one day I just fall down and die." He chuckled mirthlessly. "I'm sure they'll have a very large funeral, with many Fereldan women weeping over my grave that Maric the Savior is dead."

Fiona's eyes narrowed at him suspiciously. "And you never once wanted to be king? Not even just a little?"

"I wanted to avenge my mother. I wanted to kick the Orlesians out of Ferelden."

"And nothing else?"

"Well . . ."

She turned herself around to face him completely, her skirt rustling loudly on the stone floor. She appeared to be completely oblivious to her bared chest, and firmly took his chin in her hand. "This elven woman you killed. What was her name?"

He felt himself blushing. He didn't really want to talk about this, but the way she stared at him with those dark eyes, it was as if they were boring into his skull. "Katriel," he answered quietly.

"Did you love her?"

"What kind of question is—?"

"Did you *love* her?" she insisted.

"Yes." It was a painful admission. He would have looked away, had she not held his chin tightly. Fiona looked into his eyes and smiled warmly.

"So you punish yourself for what you did, for the rest of your life?" Her eyes teared up as she shook her head, baffled by him. "Maric, you said back on those stairs that you had changed, that you wanted to live. So live! You have every freedom that I never had. Use it! You want to repay this elven woman you wronged so badly? Make sure that nobody ends up like her ever again." Fiona released his chin and blinked away her tears, frowning bashfully for crying in the first place. "There were all these stories about the wonderful Maric the Savior, and I thought for certain it was all just lies. That it was simply a genteel front like my master used to have, smiles on top of the sickness. But Ferelden got lucky and has a good man as its king."

"I'm not such a good man."

She snorted incredulously. "Only a good man would say that." She took the wet cloth from him and studiously began to wipe his face with it. He let her, watching her quietly. Then she paused, looking at him with grave seriousness. "You need to forgive yourself, Maric. Or I'm going to have to punch you in the head, I swear it."

It was almost the same thing that Katriel had said to him in the Fade. The thought sent a pang of regret through him, but still he laughed at Fiona's expression, and it felt good to laugh. She cracked a smile at that. She went to wipe his face again, but he reached up and took her hand, and stopped laughing. "Come with me," he said earnestly. "To Denerim."

"We're not even out of the Deep Roads yet. . . ."

"We could both die, I know that. Come with me anyway."

Her smile was polite, but he could see the refusal even before she said it. "I am a Grey Warden," she sighed. "And an elf. And a mage. And even if that were not enough, I am suffering from the taint. My time is limited."

"I don't care about that."

"I do." He saw that there would be no arguing with her. "And I care about you."

He leaned in and kissed her. She was taken by surprise, just about to speak again, but quieted as she accepted his embrace. He leaned her down to the floor, his kisses growing more passionate, knocking over the dwarven basin so that the cold water ran along the stone and soaked into their clothing.

They barely noticed.

Duncan seemed mostly bemused when he woke them up a while later, clearing his throat loudly just outside the entrance of the cave. When they finally exited, their clothing sopping wet and their armor hastily rearranged, he chuckled at them. "So I guess you're not going to be complaining about each other anymore?"

Fiona's face reddened and he grinned.

He hadn't let them sleep longer, he said, because the darkspawn were closing in. That was when the amusement ended, and they picked up what few supplies they wanted to take with them and headed out quickly. Maric saw the dark circles under Duncan's eyes and felt badly. The lad could have used some sleep, himself, and yet Fiona and he had selfishly used the time up for themselves.

Still, Duncan didn't complain. He also seemed more determined, somehow. Maric wasn't sure he could put his finger on it.

They spent half their time running, the dark corridors speeding past, and while Maric tried to remember the route the Legion of the Dead had taken to reach the outpost, he couldn't piece it together. It wasn't long before he realized he wasn't recognizing the corridors at all.

They kept the punishing pace for several hours, pushing themselves hard. Duncan's apprehensive expression told him that the darkspawn could not be far behind, although Maric couldn't hear the telltale sounds of their approach. The Deep Roads were quiet. Only the sounds of their footsteps echoed, and as the time wore on, Maric noticed that the signs of the taint around them were lessening.

"Are we getting close to the surface?" he asked nobody in particular.

Fiona and Duncan glanced at him, but said nothing.

Another hour passed, the three of them sweating profusely as they trudged. They were definitely moving up a slope; the pain in Maric's legs told him that much. While it slowed them down, they continued on. Up was where they wanted to go, after all.

At the top of the slope, the light from Fiona's staff slowly revealed that the corridor came to a dead end. The roof here had collapsed long ago, leaving the end of the tunnel completely filled with rocks and debris and no way around. They ground to a halt, staring at all the dust with wide eyes.

"Well, so much for that," Duncan grumbled, wiping his forehead. "We'll need to turn back, and quickly, or we'll meet the darkspawn halfway back to the last intersection." He turned around to do just that, but even before he took his first step, Maric held up his hands.

"Wait. Do you smell that?" Maric had become so accustomed to the stench of corruption in the tunnels and the musty smell of the dust that he almost thought his nose had simply stopped working out of self-defense. But as he stood there not ten feet from the massive pile of rocks, he could have sworn he smelled . . .

"Fresh air," Fiona breathed. Her eyes suddenly bright, she approached the rocks and clambered up the slope until she reached near the ceiling. She grinned and looked back at them. "I think this leads outside! I think the surface is past here!"

"Are you sure?" Duncan asked.

"I can't see any light, but there's definitely air coming over the rocks here at the top." She reached up with her hand and pushed it past a number of the larger chunks, frowning in effort. "Yes, I can feel it."

Maric scratched his chin, thinking. "Maybe this led to one of the doorways that sealed the Deep Roads off from the surface? One that's not there anymore."

"It doesn't matter," Duncan sighed. "We'll never be able to dig our way through all this in time to do us any good. The darkspawn will be on us long before then." He glanced back down the passageway into the darkness below. "At least it will be easier going down then coming up."

"No," Fiona stated. She climbed back down the rocks toward them, clutching her staff in her hand firmly. She had a dangerous look that made Maric nervous. "We are getting out of here. Now."

Duncan stared at her, his mouth agape. "You don't mean . . . ?"

She stopped in front of them, frowning severely. "Stand back. Well back."

They did as they were told. Even as Maric and Duncan ran back a ways down the passage, already Fiona was concentrating. Swirls of magical fire were gathering around her hands and working their way up her staff, the flames suddenly growing hotter and more pronounced.

She didn't unleash the energy, however. She held the staff above her head and closed her eyes, her mouth moving in a silent chant. The fire grew. White energy began to course around her body, lighting up the entire tunnel like it was daylight. The staff shook, and it became obvious that the magic was difficult for Fiona to control. She gritted her teeth and clutched the staff tightly, and a halo of flames slowly surrounded her.

"She's mad!" Duncan exclaimed. "She'll bring the roof down upon us."

Maric was not so sure. "Maybe we should move back a bit farther. . . ."

The fireball, when it was unleashed, shook the entire tunnel. There was a massive flash of light and a roar of sound that deafened them, the backlash of force from the blast throwing them both back several feet. Several large chunks of rock fell nearby, followed by a swarm of thick dust and smoke that choked him. He gagged and coughed, thinking for a moment that Duncan might be right, but then he felt something else.

The dust began to move. It swirled as a light breeze moved through the tunnel.

Maric sat up, waving at the dust and coughing some more. Duncan seemed fine, but he couldn't see Fiona through the cloud. He scrambled to his feet and was relieved to find her lying on her back not far away. The mage had been blown back by the fireball, and was now choking and pale but otherwise seemed intact.

The pile of debris was somewhat smaller than before. The walls and ceiling were scorched, and much of the upper portion of the pile had been blown out, somewhere beyond. It was pitch-black, but fresh air was coming in. Lots of it. Nothing had ever smelled so sweet to Maric in his entire life.

"Fiona!" he laughed. "You did it!"

"Wonderful," she groaned weakly. Maric reached down and helped her slowly to her feet. She was trembling. He suspected she had used up her entire store of mana on that blast. Good thing it had actually blown the rocks out and not, say, simply blown them in. Or reflected the fire back at them. Or . . .

He glanced up and saw severe cracks forming on the old masonry along the ceiling, none of which had been in particularly good shape to begin with. More dust and chunks were already falling.

"We need to get out of here," Duncan muttered, limping toward them.

Maric waved him on up the pile. He wasn't as small as Fiona was, but she was exhausted enough that she would need help through. The lad didn't need to be told twice and scrambled up the rocks quickly. The space that had opened up at the top of the pile was not large, and he needed to slowly crawl through, digging his way past obstacles.

Maric and Fiona stood next to each other, watching nervously as rock after rock slowly tumbled down the pile behind Duncan. They could still see his legs; he wasn't through. Meanwhile, more dust and debris shook down from the ceiling. He could see massive cracks forming along the walls, too. This passage was not going to hold itself together.

"My," Fiona remarked, her exhaustion so complete she sounded more bored than frightened. "This could end very poorly."

"You don't say?" Maric grinned at her. Then he turned and shouted up the pile. "Duncan! Time is of the essence!"

He heard a muffled reply from beyond the legs, something that could have been an affirmative or an expletive. Either way, with one final wriggle Duncan's legs finally disappeared. A new shower of smaller rocks was kicked out, scattering down the side of the pile loudly. A moment later, the lad's head appeared out of the hole. "There's a cave beyond!" he exclaimed. "A real cave. And it leads outside."

Maric sent Fiona up next, helping her up until Duncan grabbed hold of her. As soon as she was out of his hands, Maric quickly began removing his armor. If Duncan could barely fit through, he would have even less chance—and wearing his bulky suit of silverite armor, it would no doubt be impossible. The breastplate clattered to the ground, and he worked with frantic haste to rip the rest of it off. Shame to lose such a fine suit of armor, but it had to be done.

As the staff disappeared into the hole, so did his only source of light. The white radiance grew dimmer and dimmer until all he was left were shadows and the slowly growing sounds of crumbling. Something enormously heavy crashed to the ground behind him. Maric found himself rather glad he couldn't see what it was.

A muffled shout came from beyond the pile that sounded like "She's through," and Maric didn't wait. He ran up the pile and threw his sword and his pack on through the gap, then jumped in after them. He didn't get far in before the sound of collapse in the tunnel behind him became deafening, and a rush of dust poured past him.

For a moment he thought he would choke to death in that tiny space. He could see faint light through the dust ahead, and frantically tried to crawl forward as he coughed and gasped. It was almost too much. The weight of the ceiling felt as if it was pressing down on him. He became light-headed and slowed. He heard more collapsing behind him, cracking sounds so alarmingly loud that it sounded like an entire mountain was coming down around his ears. He screamed, and his scream was lost in the thunder of noise.

Then hands grabbed him. He felt himself being hauled through the gap. It was slow, and he tried to kick and wriggle as much as he could, but he was almost too large. Rocks poked painfully through his shirt, and he heard ripping. He felt scraping on his skin, and a sharp pain as his flesh was torn.

And then suddenly he was through. He was being pulled out the other side, and he half rolled and half fell down a rocky slope until he was lying flat and staring up into dust and hazy white light. Duncan and Fiona were coughing, as well; he could hear them but only saw vague shadows through the dust. Maric felt dizzy and nauseated, like the world was spinning around him.

"Let's get him out of here!" Fiona shouted.

Both their hands grabbed him again, attempting to haul him to his feet. This time Maric did his best to help them, trying to get up and mostly doing a poor job of it. He saw his longsword lying on the rocks and snatched it up, and then he was being pulled in another direction.

He stumbled along, all three of them hacking and coughing. He got a definite impression through the dust that the cave was filled with ruins of some kind. He saw the remains of one of the great metal doorways the dwarves used to seal the entrances half blocking the cave passage, but this one was so rusted it was barely even identifiable for what it was.

It occurred to him to wonder that there was even a cave to move through at all. Shouldn't that pile of rocks have come from the tunnel collapsing? Unless someone had piled those rocks there to seal off the Deep Roads. He had to wonder if that was something done from the outside or from within.

A cool breeze struck him in the face before he realized they were out of the cave and in the open air, standing on a rocky slope covered in snow. It was nighttime, with a cloudless sky overhead filled with a million stars and the silvery moon almost full. In that moment, as the three of them stood there, stunned, Maric thought it was the most beautiful sight of his entire life.

Fiona let him go and leaned against the rocks, wiping the sweat off her brow. The snow here was deep, going halfway up their shins. The freezing chill he felt through his boots was wonderful, and he reached down to scoop up some of the snow and smear it on his face. They were all coated in a chalky grey dust that sat on the skin like grit.

Duncan chuckled, and then looked around while he wiped at his face with the back of his hand. Whatever vista was out there was mostly hidden by the rocks around them, but Maric could see a hint of trees in the distance. "Where are we?" the lad said out loud.

"I'm not sure," Maric answered. "We'll need to get higher up to see."

"Wait," Fiona sighed. She pushed herself away from the rocks and put her hands on his shoulder. Maric realized then that his shirt was mostly in tatters, and smeared with blood. He had several deep gashes in his chest, covered in dirt, and they were bleeding profusely.

She closed her eyes, summoning more energy even though she was still pale and weak. He stopped her and shook his head. "No, we can do that later." She didn't argue, which indicated, if nothing else did, just how depleted she was.

They slowly walked up the gentlest nearby slope, Duncan taking the lead and helping them both up. When they reached the top, Maric found that the bright moonlight allowed them to easily see the surrounding snowy countryside. They were in the foothills of the Frostbacks, with trees dotting the rugged hillside as it swept down before them into the flatlands and a thick forest farther out.

"We're in the northwest, I think," he said. He pointed out into the distance. "I think the Circle of Magi's tower is that way. If it was daylight we might even be able to see it from here."

Fiona looked at him, perplexed. "How can you tell?"

"You think I was born in a palace? Remember, I spent half my life hiding in these mountains. I didn't think I paid that much attention, but it seems I did. We're not too far from Lake Calenhad."

Duncan rubbed his arms vigorously, apparently already freezing, and this time without even a fur cloak to keep him warm. He glanced oddly at Maric, who was without his armor and now almost shirtless, and shook his head in amazement. "Let's get going, then," he suggested.

They began marching down the hillside. Fiona did her best to try to reassemble the bloody tatters of Maric's shirt, but it wasn't much help. He didn't mind, as it felt good to feel the breeze and the cold air, but he imagined he would mind it very much before the night was over.

As they walked, however, it became apparent that three figures were approaching them from the bottom of the hill. They emerged from the shadows, at first barely discernible, and initially Maric thought they might be darkspawn. He raised his sword in alarm, and Duncan drew his black dagger, but Fiona pointed excitedly.

"It's mages!" she exclaimed.

And she was correct. They halted their descent as the three mages walked up toward them, their robes now evident as well as their staffs. In fact, the man at the head of the group was none other than First Enchanter Remille himself, smiling amiably and holding up his hand to wave at them.

"The First Enchanter?" Duncan asked, confused.

Maric thought it was strangely convenient as well, but Fiona looked purely relieved. "First Enchanter!" she shouted to him. "Thank the Maker you found us!" She picked up her skirt and began running toward the First Enchanter as the mages drew closer.

Maric held his hand up to restrain her, suddenly alarmed, but she slipped just out of his grasp. "Fiona!" he shouted. Too late, he saw the First Enchanter stop smiling. The man raised his staff above his head, magical energy crackling along its length. The other two mages did the same thing, and suddenly Fiona skidded to a halt, her excitement turning into bewilderment.

Duncan gasped and raced forward. Maric was right behind him, raising his sword and shouting. The mages unleashed a wave of magical energy at them not a moment later, and he felt himself become instantly paralyzed. His sword was frozen in the air, and he couldn't move. Duncan was in midstride in front of him, and Fiona stood, stunned, not three feet away. An aura of power surrounded the three of them, a spell that held them fast.

Remille lowered his staff and smiled again, although this time his expression was far more malicious. He walked over to Fiona, patting her cheek and chuckling as she stared at him in frozen horror. Maric struggled valiantly to try to break free of the spell, wanting nothing more than to cleave the Orlesian mage in two, but he couldn't.

"Well," the man said in amusement, rubbing his pointed beard as he turned from Fiona to Duncan and then to Maric. "The Architect suggested that you might try to come out this way. I didn't think it would be possible, yet here you are."

He gestured to the two mages behind him and they moved forward, producing a sack from which they removed several long chains. Remille grinned at Maric.

"Lucky me." He smiled.

18

The one who repents, who has faith,
Unshaken by the darkness of the world,
She shall know true peace.

—Canticle of Transfigurations 10:1

Duncan bristled angrily as he and the others were led back into the Circle of Magi's tower. They had been chained again, as well as gagged, and Duncan had been bound even more tightly than Maric or Fiona. Evidently the mages had been informed just who was likely responsible for facilitating their earlier escape.

So they were taken back on horseback, Maric and he exchanging looks of dread but otherwise being unable to talk. Fiona looked like she wanted to breathe fire, her fury was so great, and if the looks she shot at the First Enchanter could actually hurt him, he would be in a great deal of trouble. Duncan was inclined to agree. Genevieve and her brother being mad enough to work with the darkspawn in some scheme to end the Blight was one thing, but would the mages do it for the same reason? Even given what little he knew of such men, that seemed highly unlikely.

Remille chatted with his two fellows in Orlesian as they rode, although not a great deal, as they seemed in a hurry. It was enough to tell Duncan a few things, however. For one, all three of the mages were Orlesian. In Ferelden, that was not exactly common. From what he could gather, it also seemed like the tower had been taken over. There was mention of other mages being "brought under control," and even killed.

So the entire Circle was not in agreement on this? Good to know.

It also seemed like there were darkspawn in the tower. Duncan assumed that this was a reference to the Architect, but that still surprised him. The idea of the emissary actually coming to the surface was hard to imagine. What if they meant other darkspawn, as well? What if they meant the tower was full of the creatures? Unthinkable!

There was a large boat waiting for them when they eventually reached an otherwise-deserted strip along the shore of Lake Calenhad, manned by a mage and two templars. Also Orlesian. The three of them were unceremoniously thrown into a shallow hold under the deck, pitch-black except for what little torchlight came through the cracks around the hatch.

At least they were out of the chilly wind, Duncan thought to himself. And there were furs piled on the floor, so it wasn't completely uncomfortable. They had put a shirt on Maric, as well, to keep him from freezing to death. Fiona glared up at the deck above her, and had she not still been gagged he was sure she would have been swearing a blue streak. Eventually, exhausted, he simply fell asleep.

He awoke to light suddenly pouring into the hold. He had no idea how much time had passed. Maric and Fiona were both awake and watching warily as three men came below. One of them, an elderly mage with a cruel look to his eyes, carried a lantern. The other two were scowling templars, heavily armed and holding their swords pointed at their prisoners as if they fully expected them to attack even though they were bound and gagged.

The three of them were marched up onto the deck, where Duncan realized they were in the cavernous dock underneath the tower once again. It was eerily quiet except for the rhythmic lapping of water against the boat. There was a sense of something very wrong in the air.

The old mage removed their gags one by one. Duncan gasped and spat when his was taken. Maric licked his lips, and then sniffed at the air. "Do you smell that?" he asked.

Duncan nodded. There was a faint smell of corruption. They had been all but breathing it for days now, so there was no mistaking it here, of all places.

Without a word, they were marched up the stairs and into the audience chamber where First Enchanter Remille had presented the Grey Wardens with their brooches. It was almost barren now. The gallery was empty, as was the dais with its great white pillars. Only a handful of people stood in the center of the chamber, almost directly underneath the domed window high overhead with its single beam of morning sun shining down through the dust.

The Architect stood there, calm-looking in its brown robe and clasping its hands behind its back. Utha stood beside him, resolute, with her fists clenched. Genevieve and Bregan were there, as well, with their bloodred eyes and blackened skin. First Enchanter Remille was speaking calmly with the darkspawn and didn't turn around when they were led inside, but Genevieve did.

She stared at Duncan accusingly. He wanted to look away, but he felt almost mesmerized by her alien appearance. Bregan looked at him, too, his face twisted into silent fury, and he wondered suddenly what she had told him. Did he know about Guy? Had he known the man? That seemed likely, considering how long Guy had been a Grey Warden.

"Remille!" Fiona shouted across the chamber almost as soon as they entered. "What is the meaning of this? Do you have any idea what you're doing?" The First Enchanter barely glanced her way and continued his quiet talk with the Architect.

Duncan and the others were led well into the room until they were almost in the beam of sunlight. Then a templar kicked at the back of his knees and forced him to collapse. He did the same to Maric and Fiona until all three of them were kneeling, Genevieve and Bregan towering imposingly in front of them in their heavy plate mail armor.

The templars passed a long wrapped bundle over to Bregan, which he took and opened. Duncan saw their weapons inside, Fiona's staff and Maric's longsword in particular. The blue runes on Maric's sword glowed almost angrily, making both Bregan and Genevieve recoil with a sudden hiss. Bregan tossed the bundle aside onto the floor, where it landed with a dull clatter.

The Architect then nodded, agreeing to something, and the First Enchanter finally turned to regard the three of them. He looked triumphant, almost smug in his victory. "Of course I know what I am doing," he answered Fiona with a grin.

"You're allying with the darkspawn?" she spat. "Why?"

"Why, for the good of all mankind!" He spread his hands amicably, but his tone was so false that it was obvious he was lying. Even Genevieve glanced at the man, frowning. "Not to mention that the Architect has access to the most interesting magic. Do you know that the darkspawn possess magic that is quite different from ours? It is driven by the taint, you see, and yet it has a great many uses, even for those of us who are not corrupted."

Maric stared at him incredulously. "But you know what the creature intends?"

"Of course! Don't you?" He shrugged. "I had enough supporters here in the tower to stage my coup. Simply another step in the plan, you see."

The Architect slowly approached, its translucent eyes flicking between Duncan and the others as if studying them curiously. "I apologize for the necessity, but allies were required. I had hoped, in fact, that more Grey Wardens would be lured into the Deep Roads. Even so, the majority of you survived. That is noteworthy."

Duncan absorbed his words for a moment. "*Lured* into the

Deep Roads?" he asked. Genevieve's eyes narrowed curiously at the statement, but the Architect only nodded. It walked forward and removed the onyx brooch attached to Duncan's vest and held it up to the sunlight.

"The brooches hid you from every darkspawn but me," it said admiringly. "I always knew where you were. And they also served to speed up the rate of your corruption."

"My creation"—Remille bowed smugly—"thanks to the Architect's knowledge."

Genevieve turned sharply toward the Architect. "How did you even know we would be coming?" she demanded. "Surely you couldn't have known about my dream."

The emissary glanced back at her as if it found her anger curious, but Remille merely chuckled. "Couldn't he?" he interjected. "You Grey Wardens dream the dreams of darkspawn all the time, do you not? It would be a simple enough matter to find you in the Fade through your brother, simple enough to—"

"I am sorry," the Architect said solemnly, still staring at Genevieve.

Her eyes flashed in anger and she drew the greatsword from her back in one swift motion. The Architect did not move, merely stood there and continued to stare at her. "How dare you!" she roared, but before she could rush at the darkspawn, Bregan put his hand on her shoulder to restrain her.

"Genevieve, he is right."

She spun on her brother, snarling at him in fury. "What do you mean, he is right? We were deceived! We were lured here and sent into the Deep Roads like . . . like . . . I thought that I . . ." She shook her head, unable to find the words.

"He is right that it was necessary," Bregan assured her. "Remember what we are here to do. The Grey Wardens take what allies they can, in order to do what they must."

Utha stepped beside Bregan, nodding solemnly in agreement.

The dwarf stared up at her former commander with bloodred eyes, a look of compassion on her face, and she made a series of quick gestures that Duncan couldn't understand. But she nodded as soon as she finished, as if to emphasize that she utterly believed what she said.

Genevieve seemed less convinced. "If it truly means ending the Blight . . ."

"It does," Bregan stated firmly.

Fiona snorted. "You don't really believe that! How many other things haven't you been told? Why can't you all see you're being manipulated?"

Genevieve turned and glared at the elf coldly, her face stone. It was a look that Duncan was familiar with. "I'm sorry it had to come to this, Fiona. We gave you the chance to take part in something very important, and yet you chose to throw it away. I know it must be very hard for you to trust in anything."

Fiona spat at Genevieve's feet, her face twisted into rage. "And what about Kell?" she demanded. "Was he just some silly elf, too? Someone who didn't know what it meant to be a Grey Warden?"

Genevieve glanced at the pool of spittle before her feet. Utha turned to face Fiona, however, and made several gestures in sudden interest.

"He's dead," the elf declared. "He died heroically. That's the only thing that's asked of Grey Wardens. That's why we drink the blood, not to do *this*."

The dwarf nodded sadly, though she seemed unsurprised. She walked back to stand beside the Architect. It looked down at her with an expression that Duncan could almost have sworn was compassion. "It is unfortunate that one could not be convinced, I agree."

"Enough!" the First Enchanter suddenly exclaimed. "Why are you even continuing to talk to this elf! Obviously she is stubborn! I could have told you that!"

"Perhaps," Genevieve said quietly, still staring at Fiona, "I had hoped . . . no, I suppose you are correct." She sheathed her sword and walked over to Duncan, kneeling down to look him straight in the eyes. He could smell the stench of foulness that clung to her now, like rotted meat. Yet still he couldn't look away. She seemed angry, and yet also hurt, as if she couldn't figure out quite what to say to him. He recalled their confrontation in the dream. She certainly hadn't had any problem then.

But this wasn't the same thing, now, was it?

"Duncan," she began hesitantly, "please reconsider. It was really for you that I had them bring you here. I want you at my side when we go and face the Old God. I *need* you at my side."

He felt mixed emotions. This was his chance to change his mind, then. He could rejoin Genevieve, stand at her side, and maybe even make some good out of what came from this mad plan of hers. He knew a part of her hated him for what he had done, but a part of him hated her, too. She had dragged him into this life he despised. Yet even so, he still found himself wanting her approval.

Then he saw the daggers on her belt. It was the pair of silverite daggers, the ones missing from the pile of their weapons he'd found back in the ruin. His daggers, the ones that she had given to him. The ones that had once belonged to Guy. And suddenly Duncan felt anger. It welled up in him with such force it almost staggered him, like it had been waiting there for so long biding its time, a fury he had nursed and hidden away but never acknowledged.

It wasn't simply that she had taken the daggers. She had taken them away from him, the only weapons in the entire pile that she had confiscated. She had taken them away to punish him for refusing.

"No," he growled at her.

Her eyes went wide with surprise. "No?"

"That's right. No. I won't help you."

She stared at him in disbelief, and then her face hardened into sudden anger. "You won't help me? You *owe* me."

"I owe you? I owe *you*?" Duncan felt his rage only increasing. He shook as he glared at Genevieve. "I think I know why Guy was so relieved when I killed him. It wasn't because he wanted to get away from the Grey Wardens. He was happy to finally get away from *you*."

She jumped up, her hand on her sword hilt. "You dare!"

He looked at her defiantly. "Go ahead. Kill me. Prove what a powerful warrior you are. The fact will remain that I've only been a Grey Warden for six months and I'm a better Grey Warden than you'll *ever* be."

It felt good to say it. It felt freeing. Duncan's heart pounded in his chest, but he knew he was right. He was willing to die being right. Better than dying being wrong. Genevieve glared at him in outrage, her hand tightening on the hilt of her sword.

Bregan stepped forward, putting his hand on her shoulder again. "Leave him. He's made his decision. He is just as foolish as the elf; what did you expect?"

She didn't take her eyes off Duncan. Her lips formed into a snarl, her whole body shaking with rage. "I want to kill him," she gritted between her teeth.

"Then kill him."

For a moment Duncan thought she would. He felt the sweat beading and dribbling down his forehead as he watched her tense. And then she spun on her heel, storming away from her brother. "No," she stated with quiet finality. And he knew that they were done.

Bregan watched Genevieve walk away and wondered if he should just kill the boy now. Both him and the elf, in fact, and spare them any further trouble of trying to convert them. Kell might have been a possibility, and of some use, but these two were little more than spoiled children. The King, however, was quite a different matter.

Noticing his scrutiny, Maric arched a brow at him. "And where do I fit in here, then?" he asked. "Am I just along for the ride?"

"No, you are my prize," the First Enchanter said, stepping closer to the King. Bregan fought to keep from reaching out and crushing the mage's tiny neck. Why the Architect insisted on allying itself with such a treacherous slug, he couldn't say. He supposed that the emissary needed to take what it could, but had Bregan known originally that this man would be part of the plan, he might have considered differently. Well, it was too late now.

"Out of all of this," the mage continued, "you are what pleases me most. When I brought the Grey Wardens to make their request at the palace, I had hoped to snare the famous Loghain, the Hero of River Dane! Ah, to take that arrogant fool before the Emperor . . ." He paused and regarded the King with a wide grin, almost luxuriating in his victory. "But you, the great Maric the Savior, you will please the Emperor more than anything I could possibly have hoped for."

The King spat, suddenly furious. "Is that all this is, then? Some Orlesian trick?"

"Oh, it's much more than that, Your Majesty."

"That's enough," Bregan scolded the First Enchanter. "Why you bother with this is pointless, when you well know that there won't be enough left of Orlais, or any nation, to make such things matter when this is done."

The mage turned toward him, his eyes flashing in annoyance. "We have the enchantments to preserve those who are most important, those who have helped facilitate the Architect's plan, and that will include the Emperor. The Orlesian Empire will live on!"

"What do you mean," King Maric said, his voice low and suspicious. "What does this have to do with stopping the Blight?"

"That is an excellent question." Genevieve strode back toward them, frowning at Bregan. "What does this have to do with the Blight? What are you speaking of?"

Bregan cursed himself for an idiot. He hadn't wanted to tell his sister about this part of the plan, not yet. It had been enough to tell her that the Blights could be ended. That was what a Grey Warden would want to do, and her most of all. She had known that. The true scope of the necessary sacrifice could have been told to her in time.

First Enchanter Remille laughed heartily. "You haven't told her?"

Genevieve didn't look away from Bregan, her expression brittle and suspicious. "It seems that Fiona is correct. I haven't been told a great many things."

He sighed heavily. "This is not how I wanted to tell you."

"Perhaps you should have told me before."

"I told you exactly what you needed to know," he snapped. "That the Blights could be ended! That has not changed!"

"Then what are you speaking of? What would destroy Orlais and every other nation, if not a terrible Blight?"

"I can answer that." The Architect calmly strode into the beam of sunshine that radiated from the window high overhead. Bregan watched it with amazement. The Grey Wardens had thought that the darkspawn could not survive in the sun, that this was why they brought darkness with them when they rose to the surface, why they hid in the Deep Roads in the first place. Yet here this emissary was, unafraid to step into the light. Its very existence challenged all of their assumptions about darkspawn, things that the order had taken as givens for centuries.

"We should speak elsewhere," Bregan growled. "In private."

Genevieve turned toward the Architect, her expression steel. "No. I want to know now."

The darkspawn spread its withered hands and nodded cautiously. "I had wished to speak to you on this, but your brother said you would not understand. I defer to his judgment, for my knowledge of humans and their ways is lacking."

"Then speak to me now," she insisted.

"Ending the Blights is not enough." The Architect put its hands together in front of it, looking almost meditative. "Freed of their compulsions, the darkspawn would tear each other apart. It would be a vast bloodletting. But in time they would regain their numbers, and then the threat of the taint we carry would once again bring us into conflict with your kind."

"And? What is your alternative?"

"You are," it said, watching her with appreciative eyes. "The Grey Wardens possess a resistance that allows them to survive even if their bodies eventually become tainted. You are living proof that a middle path exists, a way for our peoples to exist in harmony."

She frowned in confusion. "But in order for that to . . ." Then her eyes went wide with shock.

"There, she gets it now," the First Enchanter said smugly.

Bregan wanted to kill the mage. Kill him and the Grey Wardens and even the King, too. Kill all the Orlesians in the tower and all the mages they were keeping imprisoned. Let their blood cool on the ground and have the Architect find another way to complete its plan. It would be simpler that way. He felt the blood pumping in his chest, dark and heavy from the taint. It moved through him like sludge. It felt right.

"Genevieve," he said sharply, and his sister turned back toward him. She still seemed stunned, not yet processing the entire implication of the Architect's words. Utha watched him, too, from nearby. She seemed to be considering the matter calmly. Good. She had always been a worthy warrior, one who knew the true depth of the darkspawn threat. "There is a vision here that you must understand. What the Architect speaks of is not simply ending the Blights. It is peace with the darkspawn, real peace. The kind that can last."

She shook her head in disbelief. "Do you have any notion how many would die if they were forced to go through the Joining?

How . . . how can this even be done? We can't possibly force everyone to drink darkspawn blood!"

"It's not the blood," Remille answered her casually. He walked a short distance away, sighing as if all the standing and talking were tiring him. "It's the taint, administered to a body in one dose. Spread the taint quickly enough and it seems we get Grey Wardens, this according to the kind advice of the Architect." He gestured to the darkspawn, who nodded in acknowledgment of the compliment.

"You're mad!" Fiona shouted.

He regarded her with a sly grin. "Oh, no, my dear. This is quite possible. With the power this creature has taught to us, we can easily plant an enchantment within enough cities. Enough to spread the taint quickly and cleanly over all of Thedas." He held out his hand, waving his fingers rhythmically until an orb of blackness formed over it, hovering in the air. Bregan could feel that power reaching out to him, tugging at his blood. Then the orb simply imploded on itself and winked out of existence, leaving the air around it colder. "And what we are left with"—the mage smiled—"is a world of survivors, who will be immune—through our protective enchantments, or by virtue of their blood."

The Architect nodded, pleased. "And what darkspawn remain, now freed from the call of the Old Gods. Enough to gather, and teach. And begin anew."

"We can all begin anew," Bregan added. "A chance at real peace."

He noticed Utha nodding slowly in agreement, but Genevieve only stared at him suspiciously. She walked up to Bregan, peering into his eyes as if she could find the truth there and nowhere else. "Why do you want peace?" she demanded.

"Shouldn't we all want peace?"

"I know you." Her tone was accusing and he didn't like it. He refused to back down, and instead glared back at her. "To think you might have wanted to destroy the Old Gods, for the sake of having served the order for so long, that I could believe. Even if you hated everything about being a Grey Warden, that I could see you wanting. But peace?" She shook her head in dismay. "No, not that."

The Architect stepped toward them, holding up a hand. "Do not grow angry. Let us speak on this further, if you have concerns."

"Shut up," Genevieve snapped at it. Then she looked back at Bregan. "I want to hear what my brother has to say."

He felt the rage building up in him again. Strange that now it seemed like it was all he had left. His fear had been burned away by the taint that ran through him, but it had done nothing to take away the rage and the hatred. They sat in his heart like a poison blacker than anything the darkspawn could have given him.

"Let them die," he swore fervently. "Let them all die. I couldn't care less how many of them suffer. Let them have a taste of what we've had to endure on their behalf."

"You mean what you've had to endure."

He snorted derisively. "Poor sister. She couldn't become a Grey Warden, so she had to beg me to become one so they would take her. She couldn't have Guy, so she had me take him into the order to be with her. And it still wasn't enough. None of it was." He snarled at her, feeling the press of his sharp fangs against his lips. "How many have you poisoned to get what you want, Genevieve?"

She reeled away from the ferocity of his words, but still she didn't retreat. Her eyes welled up with angry, bloodred tears. "And now you've poisoned me in return, is that it?" she asked him, her voice thick with anguish. "Is this your revenge, finally?"

Bregan spat at her feet. "You were already poisoned, the moment you drank that blood! Now do something worthwhile with it! So people will die; they *always* die. They aren't worth saving!" He pointed accusingly at King Maric. "How many years did we spend begging for scraps from their tables, because they decided the Blight was no longer a threat? How quickly they forget the number of times the order has saved them! They're cowardly and stupid—" He held a gauntleted fist up before Genevieve, squeezing his fingers so tightly the metal groaned. "—so let's give them exactly the saving they deserve."

"That's not why I became a Grey Warden!"

He walked up closer to her now, until his face was only inches from hers. "Did you become a great hero, sister? Did anyone care about all your sacrifices? You could kill the Old Gods yourself and still nobody would cheer your name."

Genevieve struggled, torn between fury and torment, but he refused to let her go. He stared her down. They had come this far, allowed the corruption within themselves to turn their bodies into abominations; why should they turn back now? He knew his sister. She would give him what he wanted. She owed him. Ever since he gave up his entire life to allow her to join this pathetic order, to become the great hero she always desired to be, she owed him.

A new commotion just outside the great chamber suddenly drew their attention. The First Enchanter turned toward the entrance, annoyance etched into his face, as distant shouts of alarm rang through the tower's halls. Gesturing to the templars still standing guard behind King Maric and the other prisoners to follow, the mage strode imperiously toward the noise.

Before he even reached the entrance, a younger mage ran in. This was an apprentice, most likely, little past his majority. He skidded to a halt, almost running into the First Enchanter, and then gasped for air so that his excited babble was barely intelligible.

"Slow down, boy!" Remille snapped. "Have our other prisoners escaped? Are we to have mages crawling through the tower soon?"

"No!" The younger mage shook his head, doubling over and putting his hands on his knees as he tried to catch his breath. "Boats! Boats coming!"

The First Enchanter paused, shooting a dubious glance toward the Architect before turning back to regard the panting boy. "In the lake? What manner of boats are these? How many? Speak!" he demanded.

"Three!" the boy gasped. "Big boats! Flying the royal banner!"

Bregan spun about and glared at Maric, who grinned insolently back at him in response. "Don't look at me," the King said with a shrug. "I wish I could summon a bunch of boats at will. That would be handy."

Remille spat. "It's Teyrn Loghain." He said the name with cool derision, then snapped his fingers at the two templars. "Go, seal the entrance under the tower." As those men ran off, he turned back to the young mage. "I want mages on the upper deck. If they attempt to land on the island, burn down their ships."

"But they'll be out of range!"

"Then burn whoever steps off their ships!" he exploded. "Burn the entire island if you have to! Just go! Do it!" With a furious wave he sent the young mage scrambling back into the hall. Already more shouting could be heard outside, and the sound of booted feet racing back and forth.

"If it is Loghain," Maric said, his smile widening, "then you're in trouble."

"With his precious king our hostage? I think not," Bregan sneered.

"Then you don't know Loghain."

The First Enchanter stormed back toward them, swearing angrily. His snarls echoed throughout the massive chamber. The Architect walked calmly over to Bregan, Utha in step beside it. "This is an unfortunate complication," it stated.

Bregan nodded. "There have been *nothing* but complications."

"It may yet be resolved. It must, lest we lose our only opportunity."

"It will," he assured the darkspawn, then looked questioningly at his sister. "Provided Genevieve gets over her cold feet and helps us."

She stood there, indecision written over her features. She backed away slowly from the Architect, glancing warily toward the approaching First Enchanter. She seemed like a cornered cat, he thought. Or a dog. A very stubborn dog.

"What you are planning is wrong," she whispered, barely loud enough to be heard.

"Since when has that ever stopped you before?" Bregan snapped.

Genevieve glared at him hatefully, but said nothing. For a long minute their eyes locked silently. There was a single moment when Bregan thought she was about to break down, to finally accede to his demand. At that moment, however, the dark-skinned rogue chained next to the King spoke up.

"You can still stop this, Genevieve!" he shouted angrily. "You can still do something!"

Bregan snarled and spun around, slapping the lad so hard across his face that he flew back and struck his head against the floor. His chains rattled loudly, and he groaned in pain. Bregan turned back to Genevieve, scowling, and saw it in her eyes: The moment had passed. Her decision had been made.

She drew her greatsword, the metal reflecting the sunlight off its smooth surface as she brandished it toward him. Her look was steady, hateful. "I'm not going to allow you to do this, Bregan," she stated. "Taking part in this was a mistake."

He drew his own sword, a growl emerging from deep in his throat. It surprised him how much he wanted to kill his sister. She was just like the rest of the human waste out there, wasn't she? It had always been coming to this. All the years of jealousy and pride, all those years of resentful glances despite all that he had done for her. He should never have agreed to the Architect's plan to recruit her. He should have killed her in the Deep Roads when he'd had the chance.

"Let's rectify that, then," he said icily.

A blast of black fire struck Genevieve in the chest. She screamed, a peal of terror that turned into torment as she fell back onto the floor. Bregan turned and realized that it was the Architect that had cast the spell, its pale hand still held out before it and wreathed in black flames.

Genevieve clutched at a pool of shadow that spread across her torso. It grew, and appeared to be *eating* her. Bregan watched in dull horror as her screams turned into shrieks. She spasmed wildly, dropping her sword and struggling as the Architect's spell slowly enveloped her. It washed over her arms and her legs, and then finally swallowed her head. Her screaming ended abruptly. The shadow-covered body flailed about twice more, and then the blackness simply collapsed, leaving nothing more than a pool of liquid on the floor.

She was gone. The liquid slowly oozed across the stone, hissing and sizzling wherever the sunlight touched it.

Bregan spun angrily on the Architect. "What did you do?"

The darkspawn studied him curiously, as if his response was unexpected. "It was clear she had changed her mind. I did what was necessary, to preserve our task."

"I don't care about your task! That was my sister!"

"Who you were about to slay, Warden."

"No! No, I wasn't going to do that!" Bregan felt the hate building up inside him again, but instead of fueling him it made him feel sickened. The corruption crawled through every inch of him now, like maggots. He wanted to cut it out, burn it out, whatever he had to do to get rid of it. "You're lying!"

The Architect blinked its large pale eyes at him. Utha put up her fists and crouched down, glaring at Bregan, but the darkspawn restrained her with a withered hand. "I am not lying," it said. "Were you not aware of your argument? Did you not hear her decision?" It steepled its fingers together under its chin. "Perhaps it was a mistake to attempt to bring more Grey Wardens down to us. I assumed they would be more amenable, given that their leader had already changed his mind."

"A mistake?" Bregan scoffed. Then he shook his head incredulously at the creature. "You don't understand us, do you? Not even remotely. We're like insects in a jar that you study, and poke, and cut their wings off if it suits your purposes."

"You know my aim, Warden. I have been forthright with you."

"You're a monster!"

The Architect stared at him blankly. "We are not so different, now."

It was right. Bregan was a monster now, too.

He launched himself at the creature before it could cast one of its spells, slashing hard with his sword at its head. The emissary reacted more quickly than he could have anticipated, however, pulling back at the last second. Bregan's sword sliced across the darkspawn's chest, cutting deep and fast.

The creature stumbled back, a look of shock on its face as it clutched at its wound. Black ichor spurted out between its fingers. Bregan didn't intend to allow it a moment to recoup, leaping up into the air with the intention of stabbing his sword down into the Architect's head.

Something slammed into him before he landed, however, knocking him down to the ground. It took Bregan a moment to realize it was the dwarven woman, Utha. She had tackled him in midair and now was slamming her fists into his face. They were like stone hammers coming down on him, pain exploding as she busted his nose and cracked his jaw.

Fighting through the flurry of blows, he reached up and grabbed her throat with his gauntleted hand and squeezed. She gritted her teeth, pressing her thumbs into his eyes as the two of them struggled for control. He was blinded, the agony burning through his skull, but finally he felt her strength lessen for just a moment. Taking advantage, he roared and slammed the dwarf's head down at the ground beside him. It struck the ground with a loud crack, and he threw her aside and off of him.

As he did so, a dark blast of magic struck him. It was the same black energy that had assaulted Genevieve. He screamed as he felt it begin to eat away at him, chewing away at his chest as the darkspawn sent more and more of the magic streaming toward him.

His vision blurred, and for a moment he couldn't see where the Architect was. He clenched his teeth and willed himself to stop screaming despite the excruciating pain firing through his body. Then, through a dark haze, he saw the vague shape of the emissary. Shouting, he raised his sword and raced toward it. He ran against the stream of magic, feeling it lance into his chest and spread inside him like ice, and when he reached the Architect he brought his blade down and chopped off the creature's hand.

It shrieked, ichor pumping from the stump, but its spell was broken. Bregan slumped to the ground, most of the breastplate covering his chest having been eaten away and his flesh bloody and still sizzling from the dark magic. The Architect fell, too, grasping at its arm and attempting to stanch the flow of ichor from its wound. Its robes were black with its blood.

Bregan forced himself to his feet with agonizing slowness. The pain in his chest was torture. It was as if someone had carved a chunk out of it, leaving nothing but a vacant hole. He lifted his sword, trying to keep it from shaking, and advanced on the Architect. The creature bared its fangs in a defiant hiss. Bregan raised his sword above his head—

—and suddenly lightning struck them both. The flash of light was blinding, and the boom of thunder threw him off his feet. The agony that raced through him forced him to convulse on the floor, electric currents still arcing their way across his body. The Architect reeled in agony as well, not ten feet away, the jolts of electricity leaping from point to point.

"This is convenient." It took a moment for Bregan to realize that this was the First Enchanter speaking. He looked up, quivering from the pain, and saw the mage approach them calmly. His hand still smoked from the spell he had unleashed.

The Architect looked at the man in horror. "What . . . have you done?" it gasped.

Remille snorted. "Did you really think that I would simply go along with your plan, you foolish creature? Originally I was planning on making our enchantments faulty, at least the ones in Orlais, but this makes things much, much easier."

"But . . . the Blight!" the Architect protested.

"What do I care of the Blight? When you first approached me in the Fade, I thought I would play along. Nod my head yes, and tell you everything you wanted to hear. And you gave me your secrets, didn't you?" He held his hand up, black energy crackling between his fingers. "You gave me that and the King of Ferelden both."

"No! You cannot do this, human!"

"I can, and I shall."

Bregan had known the mage for an opportunist and still had blindly allowed himself to be deceived, just as the Architect had been deceived. Only he had no such excuse as the darkspawn had. He knew full well what such men were capable of, and yet he had chosen to ignore it. Because he hadn't cared.

What an utter fool I have been, he cursed himself.

"I wouldn't count on that," came another voice.

Through the haze of pain, Bregan turned his head and saw King Maric and the two other Grey Wardens, now freed from their chains. The King was brandishing his runed blade at the First Enchanter, while the elven mage was already lifting up her white staff and summoning a spell. Out in the halls beyond the great chamber, a terrible crashing sound sent quivers throughout the entire structure. The shouts of men went up in the far distance.

"I don't suppose you'll stand down quietly?" the King asked gravely.

The First Enchanter turned toward him and sneered. "No."

19

Blessed are the righteous, the lights in the shadow.
In their blood the Maker's will is written.

—Canticle of Benedictions 4:11

Duncan watched Genevieve die.

After being struck by Bregan, Fiona had quietly helped Duncan back to his knees just in time to see Genevieve struck by the emissary's spell. He had listened to her agonized shrieks, watched her spasm and writhe like an insect being consumed by black fire. It twisted him up inside to see it. Despite everything she had done, he had still managed to reach her in the end. When he had shouted to her, she had looked at him, and in that moment he had seen the woman he knew before this madness had eaten her up.

Then, as the fight began between Bregan and the Architect, Duncan noticed that the First Enchanter was merely standing to the side, waiting. He knew then that he couldn't dwell on his grief. They had watched helplessly until now, chained and unarmed, but this was the moment to act.

Stretching out with his leg, he was suddenly glad that First Enchanter Remille was so engrossed with the combat. He strained hard until his boot caught the edge of the wrapped bundle that Bregan had so quickly tossed aside, the one with their weapons. Maric and Fiona watched him with wide eyes, nodding as they realized what he was doing. With effort he dragged the bundle closer, close enough that he could reach it.

Maric's dragonbone blade was the key. It was enchanted, and he was willing to bet it could cut through the manacles. Duncan stared at the First Enchanter, willing him silently not to turn around as he pressed his restraints down hard on the sword. It was an awkward position, and once his hands slipped and the blade cut sharply into his arm, but then he tried again. He clenched his teeth, shaking with the effort, until finally the manacles snapped. The edge sliced open the side of one hand, but he pulled away quickly before he lost it entirely.

Ignoring the pain, Duncan moved fast. He reached into his belt and found his lockpick. It took only seconds for him to undo the lock on his chains and slip out of them.

"Hurry!" Maric whispered urgently.

Fiona gasped as the chamber filled with a bright flash of light. The peal of thunder that followed hit Duncan with enough force to knock him over, and briefly he wondered if the First Enchanter had noticed him after all. He jumped back to his feet and saw that, no, the mage had turned on Bregan and the Architect.

"What? Are *all* mages such evil bastards?" he wondered out loud.

"*I'm* a mage!" Fiona snorted.

Good point. Duncan worked quickly to undo their restraints. As soon as they were free, Maric jumped to his feet and snatched up the bundle off the floor. He handed Fiona's staff to her and passed the black-bladed dagger to Duncan. The moment Duncan touched it, he felt a strange pulsing deep within the metal. It was cold and strangely . . . off. Yet it had never felt like this before. What could be happening to it?

"I can, and I shall," came the First Enchanter's pronouncement. Duncan saw the mage lording over the terribly wounded Bregan and the Architect. Frankly, they both deserved to die, but at the moment there was one madman mage to deal with.

Fortunately Maric felt the same way. "I wouldn't count on that!"

First Enchanter Remille turned around, scowling as he saw his prisoners freed. Black energy swirled around his fingers. He was surrounded by an aura of power that chilled the air.

"You needed to announce our attack?" Fiona whispered, annoyed.

"Sorry," Maric sighed. Behind them, Duncan could hear a great crashing sound outside the chamber. It almost felt as if the entire tower was being torn apart; he could feel the vibrations in the floor. Men were shouting to each other in the far distance, and he heard the sounds of battle. Was this Teyrn Loghain, then? Had he broken into the tower by somehow coming through the walls?

"I don't suppose you'll stand down quietly?" Maric asked gravely, raising his sword at the mage and trying to ignore the commotion behind him.

"No," Remille snarled.

"I didn't think so."

Maric rushed at the mage, swinging his longsword around him so quickly that the magical runes left a trail of bluish light in the air. Remille snorted with derision and held up a hand. White energy formed and circled around him and he cast a spell, the same spell that Duncan recognized from the night they arrived out of the Deep Roads.

As the First Enchanter launched the spell at Maric, it suddenly hit an invisible wall directly in front of him, its energies dissipating harmlessly. The mage shot a withering look at Fiona, who had just finished casting a counterspell and now watched him warily.

"I see," Remille snapped.

Maric slashed at the man, slicing through the material of his Circle robes, but the mage jumped aside too quickly for the strike to be lethal. He waved an arm at Maric, a surge of power sending the King hurtling away to crash into the rows of empty benches in the gallery. Then he turned his attention more fully to Fiona.

She brandished her staff, the tip of it forming a ball of flame that was slowly growing as she concentrated. "What a pathetic waste," she growled. "It is men like you that ruin our reputation!"

He snorted. "The mundanes fear us, as they should." Holding up his hand, a surge of black energy surged out of him and lanced toward Fiona. It was the same power that had slain Genevieve, Duncan saw. Fiona responded by shooting a bolt of flame from her staff. The two energies struck each other, creating a whirling inferno of shadow and flame in the center of the room, each struggling to push through the other. It became a duel between the two mages, each of them concentrating to pour more power into the magic racing forth from them.

Duncan gripped his black dagger tightly and crept around the First Enchanter in a wide arc. He didn't want to be noticed, and clearly rushing at the man as Maric did was not going to do anything useful. Glancing toward where he had seen Maric land, he saw the man slowly regaining his feet—not dead, then. Perhaps the King was almost as lucky as he claimed.

The contest between Remille and Fiona continued, and Duncan saw that Fiona was slowly losing. Her jet of flames was diminishing, and she was struggling. Sweat poured down her brow. The First Enchanter was pressing his advantage, his face twisted into a scowl from the effort.

Perhaps breaking his concentration wouldn't be such a bad idea, Duncan thought. He had managed to flank the mage without gaining the man's notice, so he brandished his dagger and swiftly darted toward the man, his boots not making a sound. One slash to the neck, that was all he needed. Or the armpit. With an unarmored opponent, there were so many choices. . . .

Before he could get close enough, however, Remille noticed his approach. The mage's eyes had turned pitch-black. Inky liquid spilled from them like tears. "Thought I'd lost track of you, little guttersnipe?"

"I was hoping!" Duncan raced as fast as he could, intending to stab the man before he could manage another spell. He leaped into the air, his dagger poised for the strike, but it was too late.

Remille raised his other hand and a jet of dark shadow poured forth from it. It struck Duncan in the chest and propelled him backwards. He crashed to the ground well away from the mage, screaming in pain as the shadows spread over him like a blanket. It felt like a million ants crawling over his skin, each one biting and tearing away a piece of flesh. He flailed and swatted at the blackness with his free hand, but it was insubstantial. Like a ghost, his hand simply passed through it even though he could feel it consuming him.

Desperate, he stabbed at the shadow with his dagger. Better to carve off his own flesh than be eaten whole by this magic. To his surprise, he didn't stab himself. The moment the blade so much as touched the shadows, they recoiled from it. He began pressing the blade with frenzied haste against his body wherever the darkness touched him, and each time it retreated.

Within moments he had escaped, backing against a wall and breathing rapidly. Terror raced through him as he stared at the inky black pool that lay just a foot from him, now sizzling. *That could have been me*, he thought. He was covered in sweat. The leather armor on his legs was torn up, the skin beneath it covered in slick blood, but he was whole.

The dagger almost pulsated now. He stared at it as realization slowly dawned on him. He had stolen this from the First Enchanter's quarters, something the man had hidden away, but not from thieves, surely. How many thieves could there be loose in the Circle of Magi's tower? He'd hidden it from the prying eyes of the templars and the other mages. It was made of the same magic that the Architect had taught him!

This was why Duncan hadn't been affected by his brooch like the others had. His skin had never corrupted, he'd never heard the Calling, all because the dagger's enchantment had protected him.

He shakily got to his feet. The First Enchanter was pressing the attack now, his shadow magic almost reaching Fiona. The stream of her flames had been forced back until it was now only a few feet from her, and she was beginning to falter. Suddenly she fell back. "Maric!" she cried out.

Maric appeared, as if summoned from nowhere. He leaped into view, hurtling his longsword with both hands at the First Enchanter. The blade spun end over end, bright runes flashing, making a low and ominous *whup-whup-whup* sound as it flew. Remille's eyes went wide in surprise and he was forced to dodge to the side. The sword missed him and clattered to the ground, but his spell was interrupted.

Fiona collapsed and Maric raced over, catching her before she hit the ground. She looked pale and drained. Maric turned his head, searching. "Duncan!" he called.

"On it!" Duncan replied.

He tried to ignore how shaky his legs were and the pain that was flaring throughout his body. With dagger in hand, he charged at the First Enchanter once again. *So much for stealth*, he thought.

The mage was on the ground, looking a bit drained himself. He noticed Duncan coming and his annoyance grew. "Come for another taste, insect?" he snapped, getting quickly to his feet.

"Looks like your fancy shadows don't work as well as you think they do."

Remille twirled his hands, summoning another black sphere in front of him. It grew rapidly, spreading a dark aura around the mage as he gathered the needed power. Duncan held the dagger out in front of him as he ran, hoping against hope that this worked. If it didn't, he was a dead man.

The mage unleashed the sphere. It flew at Duncan, making a shrieking sound as it sailed through the air, and when it reached him he closed his eyes and swiped at it with the dagger.

The shrieking turned into a burst of sound that resembled a

wail, and he felt a wave of coldness wash over his skin. It was like being dunked into a freezing pool of water, but he didn't slow and he wasn't hurt. When he opened his eyes, he saw the First Enchanter's stunned expression—followed by a flash of recognition as he saw the dagger and realized what it was.

Too late, however. Duncan reached him and with a cry he shoved the dagger into the mage's chest. The man tried to pull away from him, but Duncan grabbed his shoulder and pulled him close, thrusting the dagger even more deeply.

"How's that for an insect?" he whispered into the mage's ear.

Remille's face was filled with wide-eyed shock, and when he opened his mouth, bright red blood gushed out and spilled down his chin and the front of his robes. The blood was streaked with black, Duncan noticed. He stumbled back and this time Duncan let him go, the dagger remaining in his chest.

The mage stared down at the hilt as if not quite comprehending what it was doing there. He pawed at it, then spasmed again as another spurt of blood came out of his mouth. He stumbled once, and then spun around—

—only to face Bregan before him. The ghoulish Grey Warden was limping weakly, covered in wounds seeping black ichor and clutching his chest. He glared at Remille in contempt, raising his sword up in his other hand.

"No!" the mage sputtered in protest, more blood streaming from his mouth.

Bregan snarled, and with one swing he beheaded the First Enchanter.

Duncan watched numbly as the head fell to the floor and rolled a short ways. The body fountained red blood from the neck, but only for a moment before it slumped quietly to the ground. Bregan stood there, staring down at the corpse. He dropped his sword onto the floor, where it landed with a loud clatter.

The sounds of many men rushing into the room made Duncan

turn around. Fereldan soldiers streamed into the chamber, dozens of them in heavy armor with the king's golden banner on their shields. A number of them were bloodied, and they spread out instantly as if expecting a fight from those within. At their head was Teyrn Loghain. The man made for an imposing figure in his dark plate armor, his blade covered in red blood, and he held up his hand to halt the advancing soldiers as his cool blue eyes took in what had occurred.

For a moment nothing happened. The chamber was silent as Maric slowly helped Fiona back to her feet. Loghain spotted the King, and his eyes widened in surprise to see him there. Then he scowled and strode purposefully over to the man.

"I see you're not dead." Duncan couldn't be sure from the man's tone if he was pleased or disappointed. Mostly he sounded annoyed.

"Good to see you, too, Loghain," Maric chuckled tiredly. "How in the Maker's name did you get here? How did you know?"

Loghain frowned. "Know you were here? I didn't know that. What I knew was that the Orlesians would betray you, and I was right." He shot a disgusted glance at the beheaded First Enchanter nearby, his eyes moving warily up to Bregan, who still stood over the body. Bregan made no move to go. "I have been watching for the fool to make his move, and he did. His Orlesian supporters took over the tower two days ago."

"And that's why you're here?" Maric asked him.

"I have most of your army searching for you. The rest are here." The Teyrn shook his head at the King. "It truly figures that you would wind up here, in the middle of things, and yet still unharmed. I expected to learn you were halfway to Orlais, in a box."

He turned to the soldiers behind him and gestured toward Bregan. "Secure the chamber. Make sure that . . . creature does not leave." The soldiers did as they were ordered, spreading out. Several rushed past Duncan to surround Bregan, though he did nothing to oppose them, merely remaining where he was.

As the soldiers moved, however, Duncan scanned the rest of the chamber and paused. "Where is the Architect?" he asked aloud. "And Utha? Where did they go?"

"Gone," Bregan rasped.

"Find them!" Loghain barked. "Nobody leaves the tower!"

One of the lieutenants present nodded and waved to a number of the soldiers, and they ran out of the room in a hurry. Duncan could hear a large amount of yelling out in the halls. The sounds of battle, it seemed, were mostly gone. Had they won? If the Architect was really gone, did that mean this was over? Strange how it was difficult to tell. All the old stories claimed that victories came with blaring trumpets. Wasn't this a victory?

Maric helped Fiona walk toward Bregan, Loghain following behind and studying the former Grey Warden with a dubious eye. The soldiers surrounding Bregan had their spears poised, ready to strike, most of the men looking frightened and no doubt certain they were in the presence of some horrifying darkspawn. Bregan ignored the spears and looked up at Maric and Fiona, his expression almost calm.

"Why didn't you try to escape during the fight?" Maric asked him.

Bregan studied him with those bloodred eyes. "And where would I go, King Maric? Shall I return to the Deep Roads with the Architect?"

Fiona stared at him suspiciously. "So you're really done with that?"

"I was blind." He lowered his head sadly. "I think I know why the Wardens created the Calling, now. Better that than to let the taint fill you up, until all that's left is hatred and bitterness and regret, until you start to think that's all there ever was."

Maric glanced at Fiona, and then licked his lips nervously as he looked back at Bregan once more. "And? What now? Will you help us search for the Architect? He will need to be found."

Bregan closed his eyes. "With your permission, I would like to do what I should have done when I began my Calling. I would like to die with what dignity I have left. I would like to join my sister in the Beyond and . . . apologize."

Loghain looked as if he was about to angrily protest, but Maric held up a hand to forestall him. The King glanced at Fiona, looking for her approval, and she nodded. With a wave of his arm to the soldiers, he gave them the command.

The soldiers carried it out, stabbing Bregan with their many spears.

He did not stop them, and did not cry out. He twitched once, ichor spilling out of him and pooling on the floor in the sunshine, and then he slowly slumped over. The soldiers pulled their spears free and his body fell to the ground, lifeless.

Maric turned and held Fiona, hugging her tightly in his arms as she buried his face into his shoulder. Duncan stared at the corpse on the ground.

He wasn't certain if it was right to feel sorry for the man. Or for Genevieve. Or for Utha. But he did. Despite all they had done, he still felt grief like some gaping hole that had opened up inside his heart.

Perhaps that was what victory felt like.

EPILOGUE

"Your Majesty, Duncan and Fiona of the Grey Wardens have arrived."

Maric looked up from his throne and nodded at the chamberlain, who was wearing his night robes and carrying a lantern and looking more than a little confused as to why he was up in the middle of the night announcing guests in the throne room.

"I know," he said. "Show them in immediately, and then leave us alone." The man bowed and quickly withdrew. Normally Maric imagined that the chamberlain would have reported the unusual activity to Loghain, but he had ordered the man not to in the most forceful manner possible. Considering that Loghain was also conveniently in Gwaren for at least another month, it would be difficult for the man to disobey.

Convincing Loghain to depart without arousing his suspicions had been a challenge. After leaving the mage's tower, the man had been completely unwilling to let Maric out of his sight for even a second, not that he didn't have plenty of justification. Maric had snuck out on him, after all. He had snuck out on the kingdom, and on his son.

During the entire ride back to Denerim, the man had been tight-lipped and furious and had not spoken to Maric at all. Then, after days of silence, when they arrived at the city gates, Loghain had turned to him and made one terse statement: "There will be no Blight, Maric." It was as much a promise as it was a condemnation.

No, he had not forgotten the witch's words, had he? He probably never would.

It had been many months since Fiona and Duncan had left. They had been recalled to Weisshaupt Fortress in the distant Anderfels to explain the incident with the Architect to whatever powers that be existed within the Grey Wardens. Maric had been reluctant to see Fiona go. With the flurry of activity following his return to Denerim, they'd had precious little time even to see each other.

So she had left him with only the briefest of farewells. He thought then that it might be the last time he ever saw her. With the state of her corruption, it seemed almost certain that the Grey Wardens would send her on her Calling. She would be dead and it would be doubtful if he would even be told. So she had said good-bye, and that was that. The fact that Duncan had sent word that Fiona was returning with him had been surprising.

The doors to the chamber opened; the chamberlain ushered Fiona and Duncan in before withdrawing with another bow and shutting the doors behind him. Both of them looked different. Duncan had grown a short beard, and it looked good on him. He was no longer in his dark leathers, but now wore a suit of heavy armor and a tunic with the Grey Wardens' griffon emblazoned on it.

Fiona, meanwhile, was wearing a long red cloak that covered her entire body. Her black hair was slightly longer, and her pale skin looked reddened, as if she had been spending a great deal of time in the sun.

"Come in," he called to them. "I can barely see you in this light."

They walked forward, both of them solemn, until they stood before the throne. He got up and strode down to meet them personally, shaking Duncan's hand and then turning to Fiona. He hesitated. Those dark elven eyes of hers were looking at him cautiously, even guardedly. Their entire manner was strangely reticent.

"I suppose you have bad news for me, then," he said with a sigh.

"Not . . . exactly," Fiona murmured.

Duncan looked around at the dark throne room. There were just a couple of torches lit, leaving most of it in shadow. "Strange time to ask us to come, Your Majesty. I must admit, I've never felt more a thief than creeping through these dark halls in the middle of the night."

"I'd rather Loghain not hear about you coming. He's still not convinced the Grey Wardens weren't in league with Remille, and I'm not sure he'll forgive me for telling your order it could return to Ferelden for good. I think you can expect he'll be watching your every movement like a hawk when you do."

Duncan nodded. "There's only going to be a handful of us, at least until we recruit some new members." He smiled almost bashfully. "I'm to be second-in-command. It feels a bit strange, actually."

Maric arched a brow at Fiona. "Oh? They made you Commander?"

Again the dubious look. "No," she said. Then she turned and put a hand on Duncan's shoulder. "Could you . . . ?" He nodded as if this was expected, and with a brief bow to Maric he turned and walked out of the chamber.

So that left Fiona and him alone. Now he wasn't sure what to think. She gestured to the steps that led up to the throne and they sat down on them. For a moment they were simply silent, and the only sound was the crackling of the torches nearby. She looked beautiful in the firelight. The sunburn had left her with freckles, he noticed, but he didn't see any sign of the taint on her neck or her hands. Had it not spread?

"How are you?" she finally asked him. The way she looked at him with concern told him the question was more than an inquiry after his health.

"Ah," he nodded slowly. "I'm . . . better. Cailan was as upset as you can imagine. He still can't believe that I'm not just going to disappear again; Mother Ailis has to coax him off of my legs every time I see him. He's like me in a lot of ways. I can't believe I didn't see that before."

"And how is it being king?"

"I've thrown myself back into it since I left. Loghain isn't sure whether to be impressed or infuriated, I think. He'd taken over so many of my responsibilities, not that I'd left him any choice. I've invited the new Empress of Orlais to meet with me next month; that had him ranting and raving about here in a fit. Still, I think it . . ." He paused, watching Fiona's eyes tear up as she looked at him affectionately. "You don't want to hear this," he said. "It's boring. I'm boring you."

"No, I'm glad you're doing so well. The way you talk about these things, you sound excited about them. You should hear yourself." She smiled at him and wiped away the tears, even though more came.

"Well, I guess I like boring things." He grinned at her. "But I'd rather hear about you. The taint . . . when you left, you said . . ."

"It's gone," she said flatly. "The mages at Weisshaupt weren't sure if it was because the First Enchanter's brooch sped things up artificially, or . . . at any rate, all the corruption vanished. They don't think it's going to come back, either. There was test after test, but they think I may be the first Grey Warden that never has to endure the Calling again."

"That's good, isn't it?"

"Oh, yes." She nodded. "They're keeping the brooches, in case they can figure out how they worked, but in the meantime they want to keep an eye on me." She hesitated only a moment before adding, "I'm being recalled to Weisshaupt. For good."

Ah. This was it, then. For all that he had feared her reason for returning might be to tell him she was beginning her Calling, a small part of him had hoped for something more. Their time together in the Deep Roads had been brief, but it had meant a great deal to him. It still did. "And you're going?"

"The order isn't leaving me much choice. Plus, they need someone to head the search for the Architect, and to make sure its plan didn't go any further than Remille. Who knows what other allies it didn't mention?"

"Oh," he said, crestfallen.

Fiona smiled warmly at him, reaching out and smoothing the hair out of his eyes. She seemed almost sad again, and doubtful. "Maric, I have something to tell you."

"Something else?"

"When I heard that Duncan was returning to Ferelden, I asked to come with him. I needed to do this in person." She sighed heavily, as if gathering her nerve, and then stood. He stood, as well, growing more nervous by the second. She turned toward the doors and called out more loudly: "Duncan, you can come back in."

The doors opened and Duncan quietly walked back inside. This time, however, he was carrying a small package wrapped in a cloth in his arms. As he drew closer, Maric realized that what he was carrying wasn't a package. It was an infant.

"Congratulations, Your Majesty," Duncan said with a grin. "It's a boy." He carefully handed the child to Maric, who took it numbly. He stared down at this tiny baby, shock more than anything else running through his mind. The child had a wisp of blond hair and rosy pink cheeks, and was sleeping soundly. It was definitely his, however. The boy even looked a bit like Cailan. Maric also noticed that the boy's ears were quite round.

"He's human," he exclaimed out loud. Really there should have been something better to say, but that was all he could think of at the moment.

Fiona nodded. "That's why we stay together in the alienages, mostly. The children of humans and elves are human. If we inter-bred, we would die out."

"I hadn't thought of it." He shook his head, still stunned.

She reached out to relieve him of the child, and he allowed her to. The boy stirred only slightly, scowling in his sleep and wiping his tiny hands across his face. She smiled sadly down at him and shushed him quietly, rocking him in her arms. "The chances of a Grey Warden conceiving are not very large," she said quietly. "Yet here he is. Amazing, isn't it?"

Maric sat down on the steps before his legs simply gave out on him. He ran his hands through his hair, trying to organize his bewildered thoughts. Then he let out a long, ragged breath. "Andraste's grace, but Loghain isn't going to like this."

"It needn't be like that," she said. Fiona handed the child off to Duncan and then sat next to Maric, her expression grim. "I didn't bring him here to provide you with another heir, Maric. You al-ready have an heir. Nor did I come to give you an illegitimate child by an elf. You don't need that, either. I want him to have a life, a good life. The kind of life I didn't have."

He turned and stared at her, suddenly realizing what she was saying. "You don't mean . . ."

"I can't raise him," she said simply. She took a deep, ragged breath and let it out, and he realized this was not easy for her. In fact, it was tearing her up inside. This was why she had come.

"You could come here," he offered. "You could leave the War-dens."

Fiona nodded, but it seemed like she didn't really believe it. "Even if I could," her tone was harsh, "what would I do? Be your mistress? The elven mage? Or would I live at the Circle of Magi's tower? Or maybe I would live in the city somewhere, and you would send me money from time to time and hope nobody would find out?"

"I didn't mean it like that," he protested.

She relented, sighing. "I know. I'm sorry. Outside of the Grey Wardens, I'm no one. I'm either a mage with no freedom, or an elf with no skills." She turned to him and smirked in grim amusement. "Perhaps I could become a washerwoman? Hide from the templars in the alienage, using my magic to stoke the fires? I bet I'd be good at it."

"Maybe not, then. What do . . . what happens normally when a Grey Warden has a child? It must happen, surely."

"It does. We give the child up. I told them I already had a place in mind."

"There isn't another way?"

"I wish . . ." Fiona shook her head firmly. "No, what I want is for him to be human. I want him to be fully human and not in line for your throne, not competing with your other son and tied to this royal blood that has brought you nothing but grief. I want him to have a fresh start." She looked at him hopefully. "You can do that, can't you?"

"I can have him raised away from the court," Maric said, considering. "But people are bound to wonder who his mother is. Loghain will want to know. The child will almost certainly want to know. . . . What will we tell him?"

"Tell him nothing. Let him think his mother human, and dead." She reached over to where Duncan gently cooed and rocked the baby, patting his head with a melancholy smile. "It will be easier, for him and for you."

"What about for you?"

She made no response, simply continued to stroke the child's forehead. He noticed that her eyes glistened brightly, however. No, there wasn't any way this would be easier for her.

"I'll watch him," Duncan vowed. "I can do that without arousing suspicion, make sure he's doing well. Keep him safe. I can even bring you news, from time to time."

Maric looked up at him, surprised. "You would do that?"

"For you, Your Majesty, without hesitation."

It was almost too much to take in. First Fiona had returned and wasn't dying, and now he had a son, and he was losing them both. Yet he understood what she was saying. If he recognized the boy and raised him in the palace, he would be subject to the constant politics and struggles. He would be seen as competition for Cailan. Better to have him raised somewhere quietly, out of sight and allowed his own destiny. But to have the boy believe he was never wanted, to have him never know his true mother? Was being of elven blood truly so terrible?

The ache in his heart threatened to make it explode. Maric knew nothing of being elven, and if Fiona wanted her son to be free of the struggles she endured, he wouldn't deny her that. Let the boy have his chance to be free of both their legacies.

He looked in Fiona's eyes and slowly nodded. "If that's what you want. Yes, I can do that."

"Thank you, Maric."

"And what about you?" he asked her. "Will I see you again?"

He could tell by her expression that the answer was no. Yet she nodded anyway. "If the Maker wills it," she breathed. Then she leaned in and kissed him, and he kissed her back. It felt sweet, and sad, and right. He had this moment, the two of them sitting in the warm firelight as Duncan tactfully wandered with the child to the other side of the room. Even though the parting had the air of finality, somehow Maric still couldn't bring himself to feel sad. This didn't feel like an ending.

It felt like a beginning.

DRAGON AGE™: THE STOLEN THRONE

BY DAVID GAIDER

The thrilling prequel to Dragon Age: Origins, the hit role-playing video game from award-winning developer BioWare!

When his mother, the beloved Rebel Queen, is betrayed and brutally murdered before his eyes, young Maric becomes the leader of a rebel army, fighting for the freedom of his cruelly repressed nation.

In a land controlled by fear, and struggling to command a formidable army, Maric's only allies are the outlaw Loghain and Rowan, the beautiful warrior maiden promised to him since birth. Surrounded by spies and traitors, Maric must find a way to not only survive but achieve Ferelden's freedom and the return of his line to the stolen throne.

DRAGON AGE™: ASUNDER

BY DAVID GAIDER

Return to the dark fantasy world created for the award-winning, triple platinum game, Dragon Age: Origins in this third tie-in novel!

A mystical killer stalks the halls of the White Spire, the heart of templar power in the mighty Orlesian Empire. To prove his innocence, Adrian reluctantly embarks on a journey into the western wastelands that will not only reveal much more than he bargained for but change the fate of his fellow mages forever.

www.titanbooks.com